PENGUIN

THE VALLEY
AND SELECTED CASES

SIR ARTHUR CONAN DOYLE was born in Edinburgh in 1859 and died in 1930. Into these years he crowded a variety of activity and creative work that earned him an international reputation and inspired the French to give him the epithet of 'the good giant'. He was educated at Stonyhurst and later studied medicine at Edinburgh University, where he became the surgeon's clerk to Professor Joseph Bell whose diagnostic methods provided the model for the science of deduction perfected by Sherlock Holmes.

He set up as a doctor at Southsea and it was while waiting for patients that he began to write. His growing success as an author enabled him to give up his practice and to turn his attention to other subjects. He was a passionate advocate of many causes, ranging from divorce law reform and a Channel Tunnel to the issuing of steel helmets to soldiers and inflatable life jackets to sailors. He also campaigned to prove the innocence of individuals, and was instrumental in the introduction of the Court of Criminal Appeal. He was a volunteer physician in the Boer War and later in life became a convert to spiritualism.

As well as his Sherlock Holmes stories, Conan Doyle wrote a number of other works, including historical romances, such as *The Exploits of Brigadier Gerard* (1896) and *Rodney Stone* (1896). In the science fiction tale *The Lost World* (1912), he created another famous character, Professor Challenger, who appears in several later stories.

Sherlock Holmes first appeared in *A Study in Scarlet* in 1887. The Holmes stories soon attracted such a following that Conan Doyle felt the character overshadowed his other work. In 'The Final Problem' (1893) Conan Doyle killed him off, but was obliged by public demand to restore the detective to life. Despite his ambivalence towards Holmes, he remains the character for which Conan Doyle is best known.

CHARLES PALLISER has taught literature and creative writing in universities in the UK and the USA. He has written for the theatre, radio and television. He has published four novels: *The Quincunx*, *The Sensationist*, *Betrayals* and *The Unburied*. He lives in London.

ED GLINERT was born in Dalston, London, and read Classical Hebrew at Manchester University. He recently edited *The Diary of a Nobody* by George and Weedon Grossmith, and has also annotated the collections of Sherlock Holmes stories *The Adventures of Sherlock Holmes* and *The Memoirs of Sherlock Holmes*, *A Study in Scarlet* and *The Sign of Four* for Penguin Classics. He is the author of *A Literary Guide to London* (Penguin, 2000) and is currently working on a new guide to London for Penguin.

ARTHUR CONAN DOYLE

The Valley of Fear and Selected Cases

Introduction by CHARLES PALLISER
Notes by ED GLINERT

PENGUIN BOOKS

PENGUIN BOOKS

Published by the Penguin Group
Penguin Books Ltd, 80 Strand, London WC2R 0RL, England
Penguin Putnam Inc., 375 Hudson Street, New York, New York 10014, USA
Penguin Books Australia Ltd, 250 Camberwell Road, Camberwell, Victoria 3124, Australia
Penguin Books Canada Ltd, 10 Alcorn Avenue, Toronto, Ontario, Canada M4V 3B2
Penguin Books India (P) Ltd, 11 Community Centre, Panchsheel Park, New Delhi – 110 017, India
Penguin Books (NZ) Ltd, Cnr Rosedale and Airborne Roads, Albany, Auckland, New Zealand
Penguin Books (South Africa) (Pty) Ltd, 24 Sturdee Avenue, Rosebank 2196, South Africa

Penguin Books Ltd, Registered Offices: 80 Strand, London WC2R 0RL, England

www.penguin.com

The Valley of Fear first published 1915; *The Return of Sherlock Holmes* first published 1905;
and *His Last Bow* first published 1917
This collection published in Penguin Classics 2001

4

Introduction copyright © Charles Palliser 2001
Notes copyright © Ed Glinert, 2001
All rights reserved

The moral rights of the authors of Introduction
and Notes have been asserted

Set in 10/12.5 pt Monotype Baskerville
Typeset by Rowland Phototypesetting Ltd, Bury St Edmunds, Suffolk
Printed in Great Britain by Clays Ltd, St Ives plc

CONTENTS

INTRODUCTION

WARNING: *In discussing these stories it has sometimes been unavoidable that crucial elements of the plot have been given away. Readers encountering these stories for the first time might therefore prefer to read this Introduction afterwards.*

One of the intriguing questions raised by the Sherlock Holmes stories is the nature of their instant and enduring appeal. Holmes and Watson have been recreated both in straight adaptations and in various parodic forms in innumerable theatrical, cinematic and novelistic versions. And these have ranged across the spectrum from the most popular level to the highly literary works of writers like Borges and Eco. Holmes has become an instantly recognizable figure of myth.

The stories appeal to the reader's vicarious enjoyment of an idealized safety which is then shown to be menaced by danger. Before a threat can be evoked, a sense of what is being risked must first be conveyed. For that reason, American horror movies are conventionally set in a small town of comfortable suburban houses, loving parents and happy teenagers. The Sherlock Holmes stories evoke an equivalent: comfortable bachelor quarters in the West End of London, the capital from which Britain ruled, generally fairly peacefully, a quarter of the world's population. In 1895 the Indian Mutiny is nearly forty years in the past and the Boer War still in the future. 'The Adventure of the Bruce-Partington Plans' begins:

In the third week of November, in the year 1895, a dense yellow fog settled down upon London. From the Monday to the Thursday I doubt whether it was ever possible from our windows in Baker Street to see the loom of the opposite houses. The first day Holmes had spent in cross-indexing his huge book of references. The second and third had been patiently occupied upon a subject which he had recently made his hobby – the music of the Middle Ages.

What kind of world is evoked here? There is the slightly enigmatic 'our windows' which raises very obliquely the mysterious nature of the relationship between the two men. There are hints in the tone in which Watson writes about his friend: 'The first day Holmes had spent in cross-indexing his huge book of references.' That is a striking image of the great detective's compulsion to analyse and organize the world along rational lines. The slight note of irony becomes more obvious in the word 'patiently' and perhaps 'hobby'. Watson presents his friend as a brilliant but easily bored child, resentful that the bad weather is keeping him indoors.

The starting-point, then, is a bachelor ménage which is free from responsibility and which, in the image of Holmes pasting up his scrapbook and pursuing his hobby, suggests two schoolboys 'chumming' together at their public school. The security of this cosy *garçonnerie* is menaced by the vast and sinister metropolis of London. In this passage the city is literally impossible to peer into because of the fog. Out of that threatening presence some danger erupts in all of the stories which threatens the Baker Street world and its assumptions. Suggestively, it is not usually from the rookeries of the poor, the penny-a-night lodging-houses of the East End, or the opium dens of Limehouse that the challenge comes but from the respectable town houses and suburbs. The danger is most often within the milieu – even the family circle – of the client. It often arises from a marriage – particularly that of a respectable Englishman to a foreign woman. (Holmes's client in 'The Dancing Men' is from an ancient Norfolk landed family and has married an American woman with a mysterious past. A similar situation exists in 'The Abbey Grange'.) And this sense that the danger is within must have been all the more unsettling for the original middle-class readers.

When the safety of Baker Street values is challenged Holmes and Watson typically, after a quick look in Bradshaw (a compendium of railway timetables) and a command by Holmes that Watson should bring his revolver, summon a cab and go out to engage with the enemy. And the final scene often takes place back in the Baker Street apartment. That sets up a pattern in which the safety represented by Baker Street modulates into the danger of the outside world, and is eventually re-established. At a more abstract level the pattern can be seen as rationality challenged by mystery and ultimately vindicated.

The nature of the threat is more complicated than might first appear. The issue of physical danger is the least interesting aspect, although it plays a role in that Holmes's clients – and he himself – are sometimes in danger. (And his clients – or other innocent persons – are occasionally killed, as happens in 'The Dancing Men'.) It is the more intangible kinds of danger which are important.

A large part of the appeal of the stories is attributable to nostalgia. This is not just nostalgia for our own childhood, when many of us first read them, but also a historical regret for the innocent world of their original publication which believed in science and progress. What we have in the safety of Baker Street is an image of controlling rationality which has created the world of civilization and government: the world of science and telegrams and Bradshaw and gentlemen's clubs. But reading the stories now we cannot lay aside the knowledge of what science – or rather its misuse – led to: the horrors of the First World War, the evil efficiency of the Holocaust and the atomic bomb. Knowing how science and technology were subsequently misapplied we read back into the stories things that are not explicitly there – the Gatling gun, the tank, the mortar-shell – or whose full implications are not perceived (like the plans for the submarine, the point of the story under discussion, which we cannot help putting in the context of the First World War's U-boat conflict). We also know details of the sufferings of the poor and of the victims of imperialism, of which we merely hear in passing in these stories. (There is, for example, the chilling reference in 'The Speckled Band'* to the fact that while living in India the villainous Roylott beat his butler to death.)

---

* Stories not in this collection are identified with an asterisk at first mention.

So we read the stories with an ironic nostalgia which must be far from the attitude of the original readers. Conan Doyle wrote the final story in this collection after the First World War (in which his son was killed) had begun and 'His Last Bow', in which Holmes steps in like the legendary Sir Francis Drake to save the country in its hour of need, cannot now be read in anything like the spirit of 1917. The story ends on a note that recalls Rupert Brooke's famous poem from his *1914* sequence, 'Peace', where he thanks God for sending the war and represents soldiers going off to fight as 'swimmers into cleanness leaping'. Holmes tells Watson: 'There's an east wind coming . . . It will be cold and bitter . . . But it's God's own wind none the less, and a cleaner, better, stronger land will lie in the sunshine when the storm has cleared.'

The Baker Street apartment, therefore, is inescapably read now in the spirit of the final line of Larkin's poem, 'MCMXIV', which is a kind of riposte to the Brooke poem about the naivety of the volunteers for the First World War: 'Never such innocence again'. So the stories have acquired – like all historical texts but with added poignancy – an extra level of complexity.

Theatricality and Narration

The passage from the opening of 'The Adventure of the Bruce-Partington Plans' continues:

But when, for the fourth time, after pushing back our chairs from breakfast we saw the greasy, heavy brown swirl still drifting past us and condensing in oily drops upon the window-panes, my comrade's impatient and active nature could endure this drab existence no longer. He paced restlessly about our sitting-room in a fever of suppressed energy, biting his nails, tapping the furniture, and chafing against inaction.

'Nothing of interest in the paper, Watson?' he said.

The vividly evoked scene suggests that Conan Doyle's art is essentially dramatic. He has a playwright's strengths. Situations – as here – are presented by means of visual detail. The action is typically conveyed in a series of brisk scenes. The dialogue – especially the banter between Holmes and Watson – is often brilliant.

It is easy to underestimate the importance of the theatrical in Victorian culture because, at least until Pinero, Granville-Barker and Shaw at the very end of the era, there is no dramatic heritage from the period that is still in the theatrical repertoire. But the dramatic mode was the dominant one and spilled into other genres. Wilkie Collins, who illustrates this link in his own work, wrote that 'the Novel and the Play are twin-sisters in the family of Fiction' in that they are 'drama narrated' and 'drama acted' respectively.[1] Popular melodrama, now largely forgotten, was an important part of cultural experience and was matched, in middle-class homes, by the passion for domestic theatricals and for 'charades'. In this game the players create a mysterious tableau intended to convey, in riddling or punning form, a certain meaning. The 'enigmatic tableau' is also found in genre paintings where the situation is explained – though often cryptically – by the title; and in illustrations to novels, which often involve a visual enigma that is explained by the text.

The Holmes stories contain many striking visual and dramatic tableaux. In 'The Empty House', for example, there is the scene when Holmes and Watson look up at the silhouette of the waxed bust of Holmes in his Baker Street window. Such moments frequently encapsulate the enigma which lies at the heart of a story.

Furthermore, the resolution of the stories is often extremely theatrical. 'Black Peter' reaches its denouement when Holmes lures the murderer to Baker Street with an advertisement for a harpooner. When he suggests to the bungling official detective on the case that the murderer is not the obvious suspect, the latter asks: 'As to this terrible person of yours, where is he?' In a brilliantly theatrical moment, Holmes replies, 'I rather fancy that he is on the stair.' And sure enough the murderer enters to be unmasked and persuaded to confess. And the climax of 'The Dancing Men' is similarly theatrical, with the arrival on the scene of the murderer who has been enticed by a note written in his own secret cipher by Holmes himself.

There are numerous theatrical moments of revelation. These often occur when someone suddenly appears from hiding (the woman concealed behind the bed of the old professor in 'The Golden Pince Nez'* or Douglas in his seventeenth-century hiding place in *The Valley of Fear*) or when Holmes whips off a disguise (the moment when he returns from 'death' at the Reichenbach Falls in 'The Empty House' or reveals himself to be disguised as a French labourer in 'The Disappearance of Lady Frances Carfax').

One of the consequences of the essentially theatrical nature of the stories is that the inner life of the characters is of little importance. In a sense it does not exist on the page any more than it can exist on the stage unless it is visually dramatized. There is a revealing illustration of this in 'Black Peter' which concerns the innocent young Neligan, who has the misfortune to blunder into a murder scene and become a suspect. When he is watched by Holmes and Watson revisiting the scene under suspicious circumstances, Watson records how he indicates something 'with an angry gesture of his clenched hand'. That is an unlikely and very theatrical gesture of the kind which characters in the stories have to perform if their inner lives are to be represented.

The stories owe a large part of their success to the use of a 'dramatizing narrator'. That is to say, Watson merely describes what is happening without trying to explain it, because he did not himself understand at that point. (He does, of course, know the full circumstances at the time of writing.) That introduces a gap between dramatizing (Watson's incomprehension at the time) and explaining (his position when he writes). And that opposition is built into the structure of the stories: Holmes acts out the solution to the mystery while Watson recounts baldly what he sees. Afterwards, Holmes explains the underlying significance of what Watson and the reader have viewed. The fact that Conan Doyle is so good at dramatizing incomprehension in Watson's narration is illustrated by his lack of success when he attempts the opposite ploy. In the interpolated narrative in *The Valley of Fear* he tries to tease the reader by using a narrator who, knowing more than he reveals, is reticent or teasingly ambiguous. The effect is much less engaging. Conan Doyle creates other problems for himself in that work by departing in various ways from his usual technique, as will be suggested below.

The clearest example of the split between Watson as uncomprehending narrator and Holmes as performer occurs in 'A Scandal in Bohemia'*. Watson is required by Holmes to take part in a scene to frighten Irene Adler into revealing where she has hidden the photograph with which she is threatening the King of Bohemia. Watson does not understand what is happening and fails to realize that the street is filled with people taking part in a charade, people whom Holmes has hired as if they were so many actors.

Watson, as uncomprehending narrator, is particularly good at conveying striking but baffling or misleading images. There is an interesting parallel with the first great detective novel, *The Moonstone* by Wilkie Collins, to which Conan Doyle owed so much. The heroine, Rachel Verinder, wakes in the middle of the night to watch in horror as the man she loves, Franklin Blake, steals a valuable diamond belonging to her. In its use of a visual, indeed highly theatrical, scene embodying an enigma, that could be the starting point for a Sherlock Holmes story. But what Wilkie Collins does with it is quite unlike Conan Doyle's practice, for much of the novel's interest centres on the issue of how an honourable man could do such a thing and on the moral dilemma that Rachel finds herself in when her attempts to shield the guilty man throw suspicion on others who are innocent. Since Conan Doyle lacks almost entirely Wilkie Collins's interest in psychology, the solution to a mystery rarely depends on insight into human nature. Neither is he much interested in moral issues of the kind that Wilkie Collins explores, but he picks up and concentrates on the earlier writer's fascination with misleading and baffling the reader.

There is an occasional exception which serves to remind us how rarely these stories reveal an interest in character. In 'Black Peter' the foolish detective, Hopkins, outlines a scenario of the murder which is clearly wrong. Holmes exposes its absurdity and one of the reasons he adduces involves the psychological dimension: the suspect could not have committed the murder, he insists, because he is not the right mental type. Holmes asks: 'Do you imagine that this anaemic youth was capable of so frightful an assault? Is he the man who hob-nobbed in rum and water with Black Peter in the dead of night?'

Yet this interest in the external – the visual and theatrical – rather than the internal – the moral and psychological – is surely an important part of the reason for the appeal of the stories to later writers and film-makers. The Sherlock Holmes character and his adventures are both richly detailed and concrete in their setting and, at the same time, an invitingly blank canvas.[2]

Boredom, Danger, and the Outsider

When, in the opening pages of 'The Adventure of the Bruce-Partington Plans', Holmes learns that there is no interesting crime reported in the paper despite the fog, he berates the lack of initiative of London's criminals: 'The thief or the murderer could roam London on such a day as the tiger does the jungle, unseen until he pounces, and then evident only to his victim.' The imaginative relish with which he evokes this image makes it unsurprising that he concludes, 'It is fortunate for this community that I am not a criminal.' His abilities and cast of mind place him outside society and thereby make him a force that can be unleashed in support of the law or against it. (In fact, Holmes turns burglar and breaks into the house of a suspect in this very story, as he does again in 'Charles Augustus Milverton'.) This potential in Holmes was exploited by Conan Doyle's brother-in-law, E. W. Hornung, whose character, Raffles, is a Late Victorian dandy who earns his living by burgling his wealthy associates. In a clear allusion to Holmes, he has a dim-witted assistant, Bunny.[3] Holmes's status as an outsider and his ambiguity, or 'reversibility', in relation to criminality are an important part of what makes him a mythical figure.

It is boredom that makes Holmes dangerous in that it raises the possibility of his devoting his gifts to the opposite side. So a paradox of the safety represented by Baker Street is that it bores Holmes. In short, one might say that an aspect of his ambivalence is that the most dangerous thing for Holmes is safety. (In 'The Yellow Face'* Watson writes of his friend: 'Save for the occasional use of cocaine, he had no vices, and he only turned to the drug as a protest against the monotony of existence when cases were scanty and the papers uninteresting.') At the end of 'The Red-Headed League'* Holmes talks of how the case 'saved me from ennui' and says, 'My life is spent in one long effort to escape from the commonplaces of existence. These little problems help me to do so.' But despite his use of the word, the boredom that he experiences is nothing like Baudelaire's 'monstrous Ennui dreaming of gibbets while smoking a hookah'.[4] In Poe (who was translated by Baudelaire), the lassitude of his detective, Dupin, reflects a philosophical, even spiritual, distaste for humanity. In the case of Holmes one is tempted to suggest – licensed by Watson's ironic tone – that it is more like the boredom of a clever child who has done the schoolwork given him too quickly and now looks round for mischief. Holmes's boredom arises not from self-disgust or contempt for the world, but from a simple lack of inner life, so that he needs stimulation from outside.

But what Holmes does share with Poe's detective is that he is an artist and, if not the *poète maudit* whose gift is also a curse, then certainly an outsider. In denouncing the feebleness of London's criminals, Holmes is a frustrated artist lamenting the deficiencies of the materials he has to work with and his lack of an opportunity to practise his art. In that case, to what kind of artist can he be compared? A writer does not need to wait for permission to write. (In fact, Watson is the writer and it is as if all the space for a writer has been taken up by him. Holmes evinces suspicion towards Watson's writing on many grounds and it is perhaps not surprising to learn in 'His Last Bow' that the literary fruit of his retirement, 'the magnum opus of my latter years', is a manual on bee-keeping.) A musician can play without having to wait for an opportunity – as Holmes plays his violin without being asked. But in that capacity he is an amateur. In his professional capacity Holmes is an artist of the kind who requires that he be asked to practise his art.

That is precisely what happens next in 'The Adventure of the Bruce-Partington Plans', when his brother Mycroft sends a message from the busy world of politics and diplomacy to announce his arrival. Holmes exclaims: 'His Pall Mall lodgings, the Diogenes Club, Whitehall – that is his cycle. Once, and only once, he has been here.' The contrast between the worldly brother who is known in all the political salons and departments of state and the elusive Sherlock is made starkly clear. (Mycroft himself is far from being convivial and his club – named after the ascetic and eccentric Greek Cynic – bans conversation between members! But while both brothers are solitaries, the crucial difference is that Mycroft is inside and Holmes outside the Establishment.)

Watson says in 'A Scandal in Bohemia' that Holmes 'loathed every form of society with his whole Bohemian soul'. Society returns the compliment, and it is hard to imagine the moody, eccentric Holmes as the darling of the salons or even a guest at the more exclusive clubs. He would be excluded by his lack of small talk and his dangerous sense of humour. (When in 'The Disappearance of Lady Frances Carfax' Holmes telegraphs to ask for a description of a man's ear, Watson takes it as an 'ill-timed jest' and writes that 'Holmes's ideas of humour are strange and occasionally offensive'. He hides the stolen jewel in the pocket of the Prime Minister's emissary, Lord Cantlemere, in 'The Adventure of the Mazarin Stone'*, for example. And there is also his passion for throwing off a disguise in the most alarming way.) Holmes is a shunned recluse like Philoctetes, an image of the artist who is both needed and feared by society. (In the myth Philoctetes has the bow and arrows of Heracles without which the Greeks cannot capture Troy, but he also has a horrible-smelling wound which leads him to be avoided by his fellows.)

Braving the stench, Mycroft comes to ask his brother to investigate a mystery which has serious consequences for the security of the nation. (This is one of a number of stories whose premise is that the nation is in danger and that only Holmes can save it.) Mycroft, the embodiment of the political Establishment (whom his brother now calls 'the most indispensable man in the country'), comes to Sherlock precisely because his outsider status means that he can circumvent not merely official channels but even the law itself.

Even more important, Holmes is able to think the unthinkable. This is at the heart of the mysterious gift which makes him unique. One can approach it by contrasting him with his brother, whose function in the state Sherlock now outlines. Mycroft's role is to deal with ideas in a highly processed form: he receives them as 'conclusions'. In short, his approach is entirely theoretical and he is uninterested in actually going into the field to look at the data from first principles.

(In 'The Greek Interpreter'*, incidentally, it is revealed that Mycroft is even more gifted at observation than Sherlock, but he is too lazy to exercise his talent.) Sherlock, on the other hand, is fascinated by that which is unprocessed and prior to any hypothesis. That is why he always wants to examine the scene of the crime for himself; impatiently, and often contemptuously, rejecting the hypotheses of the police, which are invariably based on an obvious and over-simplified interpretation of the evidence.

Many of the cases involve an enigma or 'riddle' which a client or a police detective brings to Holmes. In many cases this involves a striking visual image, often of a highly theatrical nature, which has either been wrongly interpreted or has proved resistant to interpretation. What we have is a kind of charade or an enigmatic tableau. For example, in 'The Man with the Twisted Lip'* Holmes recounts to Watson how the missing man's wife saw her husband at an upper window of what turns out to be a sinister opium den: 'The window was open, and she distinctly saw his face, which she describes as being terribly agitated. He waved his hands frantically to her, and then vanished from the window so suddenly that it seemed to her that he had been plucked back by some irresistible force from behind.' The tableau is eventually reinterpreted by Holmes. In 'The Copper Beeches'* a young governess tells Holmes how, at the insistence of her employer, she is dressed in a certain dress, has her long hair cut off and is posed in a well-lit room with her back to the window at a certain hour and then made to laugh. This baffling tableau is finally elucidated by Holmes.

The Riddle and Forbidden Knowledge

Sherlock Holmes became and has remained a mythical hero, which means that in some way he embodies the fears of his and our society. A mythical hero allows such fears expression and then lays them to rest. In doing so he or she occupies dangerous marginal territory, breaking a sacred taboo and thereby acquiring forbidden knowledge. By possessing it, he or she mediates between two worlds but becomes a despised scapegoat or a feared outsider.

The Oedipus story, which for Freud is the founding myth of civilization, is also the first detective fiction. Oedipus, confronted with the riddle of the sphinx, solves it and becomes king of Thebes. But finding the answer to the second riddle, which is represented by the plague which has fallen on the city, destroys him. For in relation to the double crime which has brought the curse upon his kingdom, he is both detective and offender. So the danger to Thebes turns out to be caused by Oedipus himself and by investigating its origins he brings it down upon himself and becomes the city's scapegoat. Having killed his father and slept with his mother, he has broken the greatest taboos of his society. Oedipus is both king and outcast, denouncer and denounced. Many novels have exploited this idea of a mysterious offence which turns out in some sense to have been perpetrated by the central figure who investigates it. Emma in Jane Austen's novel, Pip in *Great Expectations* and the central figure in Scott Turow's *Presumed Innocent* all have to accept more or less responsibility for what they begin by thinking is the fault of another or of society in the abstract.

The recluse whom Mycroft seeks out for help with his riddle about the disappearance of the Bruce-Partington plans for a new submarine has many of the characteristics of Philoctetes and Oedipus. He is an outsider who inhabits the dangerous margin between criminality and the law, and his apparent lack of interest in sex makes him a mysterious and unusual figure. Above all, he has the dangerous knowledge that his society needs.

What precisely makes Holmes dangerous – to himself as well as to others – is not easy to perceive. And yet something important must be at stake for Holmes to have acquired his mythical status. It is true that when Holmes takes on a case, particularly in rivalry with the police or at the behest of the highest authorities, there is the danger of failing at the cost of his reputation and self-esteem. Holmes is occasionally outwitted but only once compromised. He is made a fool of in *A Study in Scarlet* * when the old woman who, coming to collect a piece of evidence, should have been entrapped by Holmes actually manages to escape. This is because she is in fact an athletic young man in disguise, but Holmes wins in the end.

The one time he is completely outwitted, and thereby compromised, it is by a woman. This occurs in 'A Scandal in Bohemia', interestingly the first Sherlock Holmes short story, when he is defeated by the actress Irene Adler. Since he is also misled by a woman in 'The Yellow Face', one might be tempted to suggest on this evidence that Holmes can only be defeated by a woman or by a man disguised as one, and that he is a Samson figure conquered by his tenderness towards the female sex. The objection to this is that Watson takes pains at the opening of the story to make it clear that Holmes did not love Irene Adler. Watson writes of logic not love as inspiring Holmes and of his abhorrence of emotion. (To assume that Watson cannot be trusted to have recorded the truth raises fascinating but dizzying possibilities.)

Sex is clearly not a dangerous issue in the stories and that is confirmed by the way in which Conan Doyle observes the constraints of the period that limited what could be written about the topic. For example, he can only hint at the idea that Barker and Mrs Douglas might have an adulterous relationship in *The Valley of Fear*. (That turns out to be Watson's misreading of a scene when he catches them together in the garden sharing some secret joy.) And the compromising letters that are bought and sold by the blackmailer Charles Augustus Milverton, in the story of that name, are stated by Holmes to be 'imprudent, Watson, nothing worse'.

Genuine criminality or evil also features very little. The crimes that Holmes investigates are very rarely ones that could have struck real fear in the hearts of readers since they are too far-fetched in their motives and means of execution to be realistic. (This is surprising since Conan Doyle took an active interest in actual crimes.)

Moreover, there is very little sense of evil. Although Holmes refers to Moriarty as the most wicked man in London and talks in several of the stories of the appalling deeds he is responsible for, no conviction of his wickedness is generated by this character. In his interview with Holmes in 'The Final Problem'* Moriarty is quietly and politely menacing, but the encounter conveys no impression of real malevolence. In the portrayal of evil Conan Doyle's theatricality works to his disadvantage, for the characters whose wickedness is displayed become unconvincing caricatures. This is evident in the American narrative in *The Valley of Fear* where the Freemen are melodramatically and uninterestingly villainous. (See below where that novella is discussed more fully.) Conan Doyle's most convincing villains are those middle- or upper-class characters who attempt to hide their unpleasantness. The quietly menacing abductor of the Greek interpreter in the story of that name is an example. One of Conan Doyle's most repellent portraits is the soft-spoken eponymous blackmailer in 'Charles Augustus Milverton'.

Just as Holmes is rarely confronted by real evil in the stories, so he is virtually never placed in moral danger. He is incorruptible in every way – sexually, financially and politically. But that is not difficult since he has no sexual impulses, no financial worries and no political ambitions. Although later detective writers have taken full advantage of the genre's potential for moral complexity – Chandler's Philip Marlowe or Hammett's Sam Spade, for example, are confronted with painful choices – Holmes is untroubled by doubts about the morality of his conduct or guilt at some action of his. (The exception is that he feels some responsibility for failing to act quickly enough on several occasions. For example, he blames himself for arriving too late to save the life of Hilton Cubitt in 'The Dancing Men'.) Watson rarely feels such emotions either but at least in 'A Scandal in Bohemia' he is ashamed of himself for conspiring to outwit Irene. And Holmes's final exchange with the King of Bohemia uniquely suggests that he feels something like regret at the part he has played. When Holmes does accept responsibility it is without any sense of guilt. At the end of 'The Speckled Band' he concedes that he indirectly caused the death of the murderer, Roylott, by unintentionally causing the instrument of murder to turn against its handler, but he says that it will not weigh heavily on his conscience.

The plots frequently conspire to allow Holmes to evade responsibility for punishing someone who is legally, but not morally, guilty. It frequently turns out that a crime has been committed from honourable, or at least pardonable, motives. The most striking example of this occurs at the end of 'The Abbey Grange' where Holmes hears an account of the circumstances of the death of a drunken and brutal husband. He announces: 'I am willing to admit that you acted under the most extreme provocation to which any man could be subjected.

I am not sure that in defence of your own life your action will not be pronounced legitimate.' Holmes then tests the moral worth of the guilty individual and when he passes triumphantly stages a quick trial: 'Watson, you are a British jury, and I never met a man who was more eminently fitted to represent one. I am the judge.' Watson pronounces the 'prisoner' not guilty and Holmes allows him to go unapprehended. This anticipates the theme, in subsequent detective fiction and particularly in American writing, of the private justice of the central character taking precedence over the corrupt justice of his society. And not only does Holmes do nothing to prevent the murder of the blackmailer in 'Charles Augustus Milverton' but he later explains to Lestrade, who asks him to help find the killer, why he will not do so: 'I think there are certain crimes which . . . justify private revenge.' And he adds: 'My sympathies are with the criminals rather than with the victim.'

In cases where Holmes is unable to exculpate someone who is legally guilty but morally pardonable, the plot performs that function. For example, Jefferson Hope, the murderer in *A Study in Scarlet*, turns out to have, if not a good reason for the murders he has committed, then at least an understandable one. By the time Holmes captures him he is in danger of dying from an aortic aneurism and does in fact die before justice can exact its penalty. (In this, Conan Doyle's first Sherlock Holmes fiction, nothing is said to imply that Holmes and Watson feel any sympathy for the murderer.)

The Valley of Fear ends with Holmes uncovering a situation similar to that in 'The Abbey Grange' but on this occasion leaving it to the courts to arrive at the right decision. In the inserted narrative in that novella, Conan Doyle seems almost deliberately to avoid moral complexity. The man known as McMurdo is not faced with a serious moral dilemma, though he might easily have been. The moment when the single decent member of the villainous Freemen, Morris, confides in McMurdo and in doing so exposes them both to danger, creates a potentially agonizing situation. McMurdo might suspect that he is being tested and debate whether to denounce Morris in order to protect himself. One has only to think of the treatment of the double agent in the works of Dostoevsky, Conrad, Greene or Le Carré to see the opportunities that Conan Doyle chooses to pass up.

One of the very few moments of moral danger and complexity in the canon occurs in 'The Adventure of the Dying Detective' when Holmes insults Watson's medical abilities. He asks for a doctor to treat his condition 'in whom I have confidence' rather than his friend of whom he says 'you are only a general practitioner with very limited experience and mediocre qualifications'. Watson records 'I was bitterly hurt'. Since the only area of expertise where Watson can hope to match his friend is his medical skill, the reader experiences this as a moment of real pain.

The Valley of Fear

Because the inserted American narrative is so unlike the Baker Street stories, this novella illustrates in negative form many of the points already made about the appeal of Sherlock Holmes.

The weakness of the framed narrative in the novella is in contrast to the 'set-up', for the investigation by Holmes which is described in the 'outer frame' is vintage Baker Street detection: the coded letter which Holmes cracks without being supplied with the key; the theatrical entrance of the police to announce the murder of the very man named in the letter which Holmes has just deciphered; and then the solving of the mystery of the murder at Birlstone Manor House by a dazzling flash of Holmesian insight.

The relation between the narrative that makes up the frame and the account that it encloses is ingeniously symmetrical in the contrast between Watson as narrator in the framing story and Douglas/McMurdo as narrator in the framed narrative. Watson is, as always, a naïve but uncomprehending reporter of what he sees. Douglas/McMurdo, in contrast, understands much more than he describes. And that notion of a reversal is relevant at the level of the characters. As Douglas is not what he seems (a victim) in the framing narrative, so McMurdo is not what he seems (a villain) in the framed story.

In its use of the framing narrative, *The Valley of Fear* employs the same structure as another of Conan Doyle's longer works, *A Study in Scarlet*. In both novellas there is the investigation of a mystery, the

INTRODUCTION

solution which Holmes reaches by a particularly brilliant piece of ingenuity, and then an inserted narrative explaining the origins of the mystery which Holmes has elucidated. In both cases the 'back-story' is set in America and involves a particular group – in *The Valley of Fear* the Freemen and in *A Study in Scarlet*, Mormons. It is striking that in both works Conan Doyle reverses the usual topos in which the West represents the future and an escape from the past. In his vision, it is out of the USA that there comes the avenging past which one cannot escape by fleeing to Europe.

Perhaps to the detriment of *The Valley*, Conan Doyle inverts the structure of the Baker Street stories in which society is set in opposition to criminality with Holmes as a figure ambiguously straddling that divide. In the eponymous Valley in which the narrative is set, it is society, represented by the Freemen, that is criminal and the law-abiding person is the outsider. The Freemen are a strange mixture of trade-unionists, Freemasons and gangsters. (In that respect they resemble the Mormons in *A Study in Scarlet*.) They might be seen as a nightmarish parable for the liberal that Conan Doyle was: a beneficent friendly society intended to protect the weak has been transformed into a corrupt gang ruling and intimidating society.

The fact that the Freemen are so improbable reveals the whole American scenario to be a kind of fantasy quite unlike the realism of the British settings. That weakens the inserted narrative, but the central problem lies in the narrational mode. Because the narrator dissembles his true position (to the extent that even using the third person is an act of deception) and therefore can reveal virtually nothing of his thoughts, there is no moral dialectic.

That absence of introspection does not matter in the Baker Street stories since Watson is not faced by morally complex issues. But it makes McMurdo a relatively uninteresting narrator. That is illustrated by the passage where he describes the apparent murder of a man he has been ordered to kill and then reveals that the house which he destroyed with explosives was empty because the intended victim and his family had been warned. Later the reader realizes by whom the victim had been warned. The result is that an incident filled with the potential for agonizing dilemmas and decisions is actually presented in muted terms.

It has been suggested that in the Sherlock Holmes stories the issue of physical danger is much less interesting than the possibility of intellectual and social jeopardy. Some suspense arises in the novella from the fact that McMurdo is in physical danger, but there is no threat represented either by an insoluble mystery or a breach of the social order. The 'first-time reader' who does not guess that McMurdo is not what he appears, will assume that he is in no kind of peril among the brutal and lawless Freemen except the merely physical. The disabused reader will see that the physical danger arises from the threat of being unmasked. There is nothing of the almost philosophical danger that lurks in the Baker Street stories – the breakdown of logic or understanding.

Whereas in those stories the reader, presented with Watson's all-revealing and yet unrevealing account, tries, with Holmes himself, to penetrate to the truth, in *The Valley* there is no hidden truth (other than the truth about the narrator). The Freemen reveal themselves from the first in melodramatic terms and there is nothing more to be learned about them.

Conan Doyle presents, in the framed narrative of *The Valley*, a flatly accurate truth presented by a disingenuous narrator who conceals his moral relation to the world he describes. The narrator's reticence paradoxically foregrounds the issue of morality and weakens the novella. That weakness shows by contrast how brilliantly Conan Doyle deploys elsewhere his honest narrator recounting what appears to be the truth but turns out to be only a part, or a distortion, of it. For what has been called above the 'dramatizing' or 'theatrical' mode of narration does not concern itself with the inner life.

The Artist and the Writer

Their lack of interest in the inner life – the whole area of psychology and moral choice – is part of the appeal of the stories and is what makes them so easy to parody and pastiche. It is a function of their essential theatricality, which characterizes their central figure. The theatricality of his mode of investigation makes it clear that Holmes is an actor. Above all at the scene of the crime it is clear that not merely does he need to be the centre of attention, but that he delights in displaying his detective role by means of his distinctive costume, his props (the magnifying glass), and 'business'.

His love of dressing up clinches the point. When in 'A Scandal in Bohemia' he disguises himself as a 'simple-minded Nonconformist clergyman' Watson talks of him as a 'fine actor'. (This is said of Holmes on a number of occasions.) In that story he not only acts a part, but stage-manages a whole scene in order to trick Irene Adler into revealing the hiding place of her incriminating photograph. Organizing charades of this kind is something he does on a number of occasions. In 'The Empty House' he prepares a trap for Colonel Moran with police officers in disguise waiting in the street to arrest him when he shoots at the bust of Holmes arranged in the window. In fact, because Moran chooses to make his attack from the same empty house from which his quarry is observing the scene, Holmes finds himself caught up in the drama, which is happening beside him rather than in the street. There are other occasions on which the performances which Holmes arranges become more real than he had predicted. He dangerously blurs the distinction between acting and reality in 'The Dying Detective' when he starves himself for several days in order to appear to be dying. In defence of that conduct, he offers the dubious and sometimes dangerous proposition, subsequently formalized in the method school of acting, that 'The best way of successfully acting a part is to be it.'

In contrast to Holmes's gift for disguise and improvisation, which has potentially dangerous consequences, is Watson's inability to act a role. Holmes tells him at the end of 'The Dying Detective' that he had to hurt his feelings by insulting his professional competence because he knew that Watson would not be able to pretend, in the presence of the villain, that he believed Holmes really was dying as his plot required. The inability to act a role takes the form, in Watson's narration, of a capacity for recording the facts without understanding and without guile. This contrast between Watson as non-comprehending but truthful recorder and Holmes as non-explaining and deceptive actor allows the stories to be read as a discussion of the difference between the forms of the drama and the novel. The theatrical is external, visual and therefore inherently ambiguous. The novel's domain is the internal and its aim, at least in the case of the Victorian novel, is to offer an unambiguous and complex truth. Watson's narration, then, interestingly juggles with these two conflicting forms.

Seeing Holmes as a brilliant actor and theatrical director highlights the significance of the few occasions when he is taken in. One of them is in 'The Man with the Twisted Lip', which begins with Holmes encountered in disguise by Watson in an opium den as if to signal the importance of switched identities. At the denouement it turns out that Holmes has been deceived – though only temporarily – by a man who was once an actor and has been able to disguise himself as a hideously deformed beggar. The incident in *A Study in Scarlet* when Holmes is taken in by what appears to be an old woman has been cited. His worst defeat is by Irene Adler in 'A Scandal in Bohemia'. After he has carried out, disguised as a clergyman, the elaborate charade which he believes will deliver him the photograph he is seeking, he is greeted by name as he returns home by a 'slim youth'. The youth turns out to be Irene in disguise and it is revealed that she saw through Holmes's impersonation because she is herself an actress. It is not as a woman but as an actress that she outwits Holmes. It is as if the only way to suspend Holmes's innate scepticism is to enter the play in which he is himself engaged, by adopting a role.

Reason Under Threat

If the theatricality of the stories largely restricts their scope to external rather than psychological or moral issues, it must be there that the 'danger' lies which Holmes, as a mythical hero, negotiates. It is striking how often, in the cases that Holmes takes on, his clients (or the police or other authorities) come to him in a state of desperation which is not simply because of their failure to perceive the solution to the riddle that confronts them. Their desperation often arises from the fact that they cannot understand even the nature of the problem. That is to say that they cannot make sense of the facts before them. The danger that is raised, then, is the fear that rationality is not enough, that the world of railway trains and telegrams is an illusion. In taking on the case, Holmes tackles the dangerous possibility that the world is too strange to be understood. What the riddle frequently represents is the fear that the domain of human beings and events is not susceptible to rational analysis. By his procedure, Holmes paradoxically confirms and disconfirms rationality with precisely the ambivalence that one expects of a mythical figure.

The failure on the part of Holmes's clients even to make sense of the problems they bring him is, broadly, owing to two distinct causes. Either the facts are so bizarre as not to yield to rational analysis, or there appears to be a logical impossibility in the circumstances as they present themselves. The latter category is the more intellectually disturbing. In its purest form this threat is encountered in 'The Man with the Twisted Lip' when the riddle is: How can a man disappear without trace in an instant? A few moments after the missing man is seen at the window by his wife in the street below, the room is empty except for a deformed cripple. In 'The Bruce-Partington Plans' the obvious assumption to make is that the body of the young man in whose possession some of the stolen plans are found, fell or was pushed from a carriage of the underground train. But the problem with that is that there is no blood and no ticket is found on him. In *The Valley of Fear* the police accept that the corpse of the murdered man is that of Douglas since the statements of the witnesses and all the evidence – including the distinctive tattoo – confirm that. The logical problem is posed by the fact that Douglas's wedding ring has apparently been removed from between two other rings, the outer of which has been replaced, when there seems to be no motive for such an action. In 'The Golden Pince Nez'* the logical problem is centred on the mystery of how the murderer of the professor's assistant left the house.

Holmes's status as a Philoctetes suggests that the peculiar gift that he possesses is something which places him outside society. And, indeed, the reasoning process that Holmes applies is more than brilliant. It has a ruthlessness that is chilling. In 'The Adventure of the Bruce-Partington Plans' he says: 'when all other contingencies fail, whatever remains, however improbable, must be the truth'. Following that rule often means leaving the human element out of the equation. But Holmes finds that disturbingly easy. In a moment of rare introspective insight, he uses a grotesque image: 'I am a brain, Watson. The rest of me is a mere appendix.' ('The Adventure of the Mazarin Stone')

The paradox is that rationality in its purest form, freed from social assumptions and constraints, is a kind of madness. Chesterton expressed it well when he wrote that 'The madman is not the man who has lost his reason. The madman is the man who has lost everything except his reason.' The insight which allows Holmes to solve a conundrum is often absurd, which is why the employment of the uncomprehending Watson as narrator usefully allows it to be withheld from the reader until the moment when it is proved right. Conan Doyle frequently allows Watson to describe Holmes's words and actions as if he were insane. And there are many occasions on which the reactions of his clients or the police make it clear that they suspect that the great detective is mad. When Holmes tells the detectives investigating the assumed murder of Douglas in *The Valley of Fear* that their best way forward is to take the day off, their faith in his sanity is clearly strained.

It is certainly the case that Holmes's failure to take account of the human element sometimes goes beyond mere eccentricity. There is an example of just such a failure of imagination and humanity in 'The Empty House'. Watson believes that Holmes died two years before at the Reichenbach Falls. Then the old bookseller who has appeared in his lodgings suddenly throws off his disguise and reveals himself to be Sherlock Holmes. Watson faints and the great detective is astonished at the effect his resurrection has had on his old friend: 'I owe you a thousand apologies. I had no idea that you would be so affected.' That admission is astonishing and suggests how far Holmes is an intelligence almost detached from the human context. Holmes is not just possessed of the freshness of vision which is not yet eroded by convention, the quality of the boy in 'The Emperor's New Clothes'. He is more like a partly autistic child who fails to comprehend problems and misunderstandings created by such inescapable human elements as emotion and unexamined assumptions.

Holmes's 'inhuman' intelligence has the capacity to examine the raw data without turning it into a hypothesis. One is reminded of the ability of some autistic children to draw exactly what they see in the most striking manner. Their perception is not 'contaminated' by other kinds of understanding. In a somewhat similar way, Holmes is particularly gifted in his ability to understand visual information before it is distorted by being processed into language.

So it is in a sudden insight that draws on a mixture of inhuman logic and intuition that Holmes perceives the solution to the logical conundrum that baffles others in the logical blind alleys cited above. In 'The Man with the Twisted Lip' Holmes realizes that the answer to the puzzle is that the cripple *is* the man who has disappeared. In 'The Bruce-Partington Plans' Holmes suddenly sees that it was not from the *inside* of the carriage that the body fell but from its roof. In *The Valley of Fear* he understands the reversal of roles between murderer and victim. And in 'The Golden Pince Nez' he realizes that the reason why he cannot understand how the killer left the house is that he or she never did so; he finds her hiding in a secret chamber behind the bed of the old professor. In every case Holmes inverts an obvious assumption which is apparently self-evidently the truth.

In the second type of conundrum, Holmes deals with circumstances that are so bizarre as not to yield to rationality by inventing a concealed plot. In 'The Copper Beeches' the baffling tableau described by the young governess who is required to pose in the window every evening is easily elucidated by Holmes in what he calls the 'obvious' expla-nation: the governess is being made to impersonate the daughter who is imprisoned in the house. Her father is trying to reassure her suitor that she is well and happy. In 'The Red-Headed League' Holmes is told the story of a man invited to take a well-paid job simply because he has red hair. Lesser minds would fail to see beyond this extraordin-ary fact. Holmes, however, says that 'the more bizarre a thing is the less mysterious it proves to be. It is your commonplace, featureless crimes which are really puzzling.' Instead of being diverted by the detail of the red hair, he sees that any distinctive quality in the man might have been chosen and guesses that this is a trick intended to get him away from his business premises during the day. In 'The Six Napoleons' Holmes similarly sees beyond the superficial bizarreness of the criminal's action in smashing plaster busts of the emperor.

In these brilliant leaps Holmes is using his imagination and, in a sense, becoming an inventor of fiction. One of the clearest examples of this is the end of 'The Empty House' – a story which begins with the mysterious murder of the young aristocrat, Adair, but then turns into an account of the return of Holmes and his entrapment of Moriarty's accomplice, Colonel Moran, who is the murderer of Adair. Almost as an afterthought, Watson asks Holmes at the end of the adventure about the still unexplained murder and his friend works out the solution from a few clues like a brilliant novelist inventing a story.

That is one important part of the paradox of Holmes: he has both a chillingly non-human rationality and a novelistic imagination. As a mythic hero he negotiates the dangerous territory between these two domains, functioning as both scientist and magician. The end of the nineteenth century was a period when experimental science was making extraordinary advances that transformed lives. Of course, our own age has seen even more astonishing technological advances, but the difference is that we have come to take them for granted in a way that was not true of the earlier period. Such inventions and discoveries as the telephone, electric lighting, X-rays, sound recording and moving photography must have seemed magical. That paradox – science as magic – is part of the potency of the Holmes myth. For all the advantages they produced, science and technology seemed alarmingly alien in their exercise of a rigorous rationality remote from the human sphere. Holmes both endorses this view and yet reassures the reader that the scientific project requires an element of the merely human, even the non-rational. It's as if the stories are saying that Holmes's ability to perceive the truth beneath the puzzling appearance looks like magic but it is explicable in terms of science and logic, and yet it really is magic after all.

There is a revealing moment in 'The Red-Headed League' when Watson touches on this ambivalence. He writes of Holmes that when he was stimulated by a case, 'the lust of the chase would suddenly come upon him'. And then, Watson goes on, 'his brilliant reasoning power would rise to the level of intuition'. In that last phrase the paradox is – perhaps without either Watson's or Conan Doyle's intending it – encapsulated. The domain of human beings and events is both susceptible to rational understanding alone, and capable of being understood only by the intuition or imagination.

And yet the appeal of Sherlock Holmes works on a much less abstract level as well. When the world's first 'consulting detective' rushes to his Bradshaw to establish that some remote village where an unknown horror has been perpetrated can be reached overnight, orders a cab for the station, and tells Watson to bring his service revolver, then 'the lust of the chase' comes upon all of us.

NOTES

1. 'Letter of Dedication' to *Basil* (1852).
2. For some of the parodies and 'recontextualisations', see Marvin Kaye, ed., *The Game Is Afoot: Parodies, Pastiches, and Ponderings of Sherlock Holmes* (1994).
3. The Raffles stories were first collected in *The Amateur Cracksman* (1899).
4. The phrase is from 'Au Lecteur', the poetic preface to *Les Fleurs du Mal*, published in 1857. The translation is my own.

FURTHER READING

Donald A. Redmond, *Sherlock Holmes: A Study in Sources* (1982). An exercise in insane scholarship which tries to find the origins of every name in the canon. It contains much fascinating information.

Umberto Eco and Thomas A. Sebeok (eds.), *The Sign of Three: Dupin, Holmes, Peirce* (1983). A witty and fascinating but demanding work of semiotics and logic which looks at the stories in the light of the late nineteenth-century American philosopher Peirce's distinction between deduction, induction and abduction (a form of hypothesis or guesswork).

Owen Dudley Edwards, *The Quest for Sherlock Holmes* (1983). An interesting account of the early life of Conan Doyle and its relation to his detective fiction.

Marvin Kaye (ed.), *The Game Is Afoot: Parodies, Pastiches, and Ponderings of Sherlock Holmes* (1994). Includes a number of parodies and pastiches as well as material on various aspects of Sherlock Holmes.

Charles R. Putney, Joseph A. Cutshall King and Sally Sugarman (eds.), *Sherlock Holmes: Victorian Sleuth to Modern Hero* (1996). A collection of mainly academic essays on a wide range of topics, including 'Sherlock Holmes: The Mythic Hero in Criminous Literature' by David Skene-Melvin. It has essays taking feminist, medical and psychoanalytical approaches.

Joseph A. Kestner, *Sherlock's Men: Masculinity, Conan Doyle and Cultural History* (1997). An interesting and jargon-free account of the way the stories illustrate how ideas of masculinity were evolving over the forty years during which the stories were written. The author ranges widely over the social and cultural history of the period. William S. Baring-Gould (ed.), *The Annotated Sherlock Holmes*, 2 vols. (1968). Indispensable.

CHRONOLOGY

A chronology of Arthur Conan Doyle's life and work is likely to be skeletal. As a highly professional writer, a medical specialist, a public campaigner against injustice, a would-be politician, as well as a sportsman, spiritualist, and well-meaning amateur in fields ranging from skiing to weaponry, he threw himself with generous energy into a variety of lives, any one of which would have satisfied most people. A brief account of his activities can, at best, only suggest the range of an extraordinary life.

1859   Arthur Conan Doyle born at 11 Picardy Place, Edinburgh, on 22 May, second of ten children of Charles Doyle, a civil servant, and Mary Doyle, née Foley. (This year also saw the publication of Darwin's *The Origin of Species*.)

1868–70   Spends two years at Hodder Preparatory School, Lancashire.

1870–75   Spends five years in secondary education at Stonyhurst, the leading Jesuit school, in Lancashire.

1875–6   Attends Jesuit college at Feldkirch, Austria.

1876   Enters Edinburgh University to study medicine. Taught by Joseph Bell, a surgeon at the Edinburgh Infirmary, on whom he later bases some of Sherlock Holmes's powers of detection.

1878   Begins first job, assisting a Dr Richardson in Sheffield. Stays with relatives in Maida Vale, London, his first visit to the capital. Writes novel, *The Narrative of John Smith*, which is lost in the post and never recovered. Works as assistant in doctor's practice in Ruyton-of-the-eleven-towns, Shropshire, and then in Birmingham.

1879   Publication of first story, 'The Mystery of Sasassa Valley', in the Edinburgh weekly *Chambers's Journal* (September).

1880   Serves as ship's doctor on Greenland whaler the *Hope*.

1881   Serves as ship's doctor on West African cargo steamer the *Mayumba*. Graduates from Edinburgh as Bachelor of Medicine.

1882–90   Establishes solo general medical practice in Southsea, a suburb of Portsmouth, after a brief and unsuccessful partnership with Dr George Turnavine Budd in Plymouth (1882).

1884   Publication in the *Cornhill* magazine of 'J. Habakuk Jephson's Statement', widely taken as a true explanation of the mystery of the *Marie Celeste*.

1885   Marries Louise Hawkins. Obtains a doctorate from Edinburgh for dissertation on syphilis.

1886   Writes *A Study in Scarlet*, the first Sherlock Holmes story, which is rejected by the *Cornhill* magazine and the publishers Arrowsmith but is accepted by Ward Lock who hold it over for a year before publishing.

1887   *A Study in Scarlet* is published in *Beeton's Christmas Annual*.

1889   Birth of first child, Mary Louise. *Micah Clarke*, Conan Doyle's first historical novel, is published. At a meeting arranged by the magazine publishers Lippincott, Conan Doyle is commissioned to write what becomes *The Sign of Four*, the second Sherlock Holmes story.

1890   Publication of *The Firm of Girdlestone*. *The Sign of Four* published in *Lippincott's* magazine. Leaves for Austria to study ophthalmology in Vienna.

1891   Opens short-lived oculist practice in Marylebone, London, half a mile east of Baker Street. First six Holmes short stories published in the *Strand* magazine. Abandons medical career and moves to Norwood, south-east London, to take up writing full time. Publication of *The White Company*.

1892 Birth of Kingsley Conan Doyle. *The Adventures of Sherlock Holmes* collection of short stories published.

1893 Louise diagnosed with tuberculosis. More Sherlock Holmes short stories published in the *Strand* and later collected as *The Memoirs of Sherlock Holmes*. In one of these, 'The Final Problem', Conan Doyle apparently kills off Holmes at the Reichenbach Falls. His father, Charles Doyle, dies in the same year. *The Refugees* published.

1894 Makes a very successful US lecture tour with his brother Innes. Publication of *Round the Red Lamp*, a collection of medical stories.

1896 Publication of *The Exploits of Brigadier Gerard* and *Rodney Stone*. *The Field Bazaar*, a Conan Doyle Holmes pastiche and the first new Holmes work since the detective's 'death', is published in an Edinburgh University student magazine. Moves to Hindhead, Surrey.

1897 Publication of *Uncle Bernac*. Meets and falls in love with Jean Leckie.

1898 Publication of *The Tragedy of the Korosko* and *Songs of Action*.

1900 Serves as a volunteer doctor in South Africa during the Boer War and produces an account of the struggle in *The Great Boer War*. Stands (unsuccessfully) as Liberal Unionist candidate for Edinburgh constituency.

1901 *The Hound of the Baskervilles*, set before Holmes's 'official' death in 'The Final Problem', begins publication in the *Strand*.

1902 Receives knighthood. *The Hound of the Baskervilles* published in book form.

1903 Publication of *The Adventures of Gerard*. Holmes properly resurrected in 'The Empty House', published in the *Strand*.

1905 *The Return of Sherlock Holmes*, the latest collection of Holmes short stories that began with 'The Empty House', published in book form.

1906 Stands (unsuccessfully) as Unionist candidate for Hawick on the Scottish Borders. Publication of *Sir Nigel*. Death of Louise Conan Doyle.

1907   Marries Jean Leckie. Publication of *Through the Magic Door*.
1908   Publication of *Round the Fire Stories*. Moves to Crow-
          borough, Sussex. A new Holmes short story, 'The Singular
          Experience of Mr John Scott Eccles', later renamed 'The
          Adventure of Wisteria Lodge', published in the *Strand*.
1909   Joins with journalist E. D. Morel (model for Ned Malone
          in *The Lost World*) to campaign against brutality of the
          Belgian Congo regime, and writes *The Crime of the Congo*.
          Birth of son Denis.
1910   Birth of Adrian. Holmes play, *The Speckled Band*, opens at
          the Adelphi, London. Holmes short story 'The Devil's
          Foot' published in the *Strand*.
1911   Holmes short stories 'The Red Circle' and 'The Dis-
          appearance of Lady Frances Carfax' published in the
          Strand. Conan Doyle is converted to Irish Home Rule by
          Sir Roger Casement.
1912   *The Lost World*, now the most famous of Doyle's non-
          Holmes stories, begins serialization in the *Strand* and is
          published in book form in October. Birth of Jean.
1913   Publication of *The Poison Belt*. Holmes short story 'The
          Dying Detective' published in the *Strand*.
1914   Conan Doyle forms volunteer force on outbreak of the
          First World War. Holmes story *The Valley of Fear* begins
          serialization in the *Strand*.
1915   Publication of *The Valley of Fear* in book form.
1916   Conan Doyle makes first of several visits to the front line
          areas and produces an account of the British campaign in
          France. Joins unsuccessful movement to reprieve Irish
          patriot Sir Roger Casement from execution for treason
          following the Easter Rising in Dublin (Lord John Roxton
          in *The Lost World* is partly based on Casement).
1917   'His Last Bow', subtitled 'The War Service of Sherlock
          Holmes', published in the *Strand*. The recent Holmes short
          stories collected as *His Last Bow* and published in book
          form.
1918   Death of eldest son Kingsley from pneumonia after being

wounded at the Somme. Conan Doyle publishes his first book on spiritualism, *The New Revelation*; begins new career as an ardent global campaigner for spiritualism.

1919   Death of younger brother Innes from pneumonia.

1921–7   New Holmes short stories published in the *Strand*.

1921   Death of Conan Doyle's mother, Mary Foley.

1924   Autobiography, *Memories and Adventures*, published.

1926   Publication of third Professor Challenger story, *The Land of Mist* (narrative with a spiritualist theme).

1927   Recent short stories collected in book form as *The Case-Book of Sherlock Holmes*, the last volume of Holmes stories published.

1929   Appearance of the final Professor Challenger story, 'When the World Screamed', in *The Maracot Deep and Other Stories*.

1930   Arthur Conan Doyle dies on 7 July at home in Crowborough.

The Valley of Fear

CONTENTS

PART ONE

The Tragedy of Birlstone

I

The Warning

'I am inclined to think –' said I.[1]

'I should do so,' Sherlock Holmes remarked, impatiently.

I believe that I am one of the most long-suffering of mortals, but I admit that I was annoyed at the sardonic interruption.

'Really, Holmes,' said I, severely, 'you are a little trying at times.'

He was too much absorbed with his own thoughts to give any immediate answer to my remonstrance. He leaned upon his hand, with his untasted breakfast before him, and he stared at the slip of paper which he had just drawn from its envelope. Then he took the envelope itself, held it up to the light, and very carefully studied both the exterior and the flap.

'It is Porlock's writing,'[2] said he, thoughtfully. 'I can hardly doubt that it is Porlock's writing, though I have only seen it twice before. The Greek "e" with the peculiar top flourish is distinctive. But if it is from Porlock, then it must be something of the very first importance.'

He was speaking to himself rather than to me, but my vexation disappeared in the interest which the words awakened.

'Who, then, is Porlock?' I asked.

'Porlock, Watson, is a *nom de plume*,[3] a mere identification mark, but behind it lies a shifty and evasive personality. In a former letter he frankly informed me that the name was not his own, and defied me ever to trace him among the teeming millions of this great city. Porlock is important, not for himself, but for the great man with whom he is in touch. Picture to yourself the pilot-fish with the shark, the jackal with the lion – anything that is insignificant in companionship with what is formidable. Not only formidable, Watson, but sinister – in the highest degree sinister. That is where he comes within my purview. You have heard me speak of Professor Moriarty?[4]

'The famous scientific criminal, as famous among crooks as –'

'My blushes, Watson,' Holmes murmured, in a deprecating voice.

'I was about to say "as he is unknown to the public".'

'A touch – a distinct touch!'[5] cried Holmes. 'You are developing a certain unexpected vein of pawky humour, Watson, against which I must learn to guard myself. But in calling Moriarty a criminal you are uttering libel[6] in the eyes of the law, and there lies the glory and the wonder of it. The greatest schemer of all time, the organizer of every devilry, the controlling brain of the underworld – a brain which might have made or marred the destiny of nations. That's the man. But so aloof is he from general suspicion – so immune from criticism – so admirable in his management and self-effacement, that for those very words that you have uttered he could hale you to a court and emerge with your year's pension as a solatium[7] for his wounded character. Is he not the celebrated author of *The Dynamics of an Asteroid*[8] – a book which ascends to such rarefied heights of pure mathematics that it is said that there was no man in the scientific press capable of criticizing it? Is this a man to traduce? Foul-mouthed doctor and slandered professor – such would be your respective rôles. That's genius, Watson. But if I am spared by lesser men our day will surely come.'

'May I be there to see!' I exclaimed, devoutly. 'But you were speaking of this man Porlock.'

'Ah, yes – the so-called Porlock is a link in the chain some little way from its great attachment. Porlock is not quite a sound link, between ourselves. He is the only flaw in that chain so far as I have been able to test it.'

'But no chain is stronger than its weakest link.'

'Exactly, my dear Watson. Hence the extreme importance of Porlock. Led on by some rudimentary aspirations towards right, and encouraged by the judicious stimulation of an occasional ten-pound note sent to him by devious methods, he has once or twice given me advance information which has been of value – that highest value which anticipates and prevents rather than avenges crime. I cannot doubt that if we had the cipher we should find that this communication is of the nature that I indicate.'

Again Holmes flattened out the paper upon his unused plate. I rose and, leaning over him, stared down at the curious inscription, which ran as follows:

534 C2 13 127 36 31 4 17 21 41
DOUGLAS 109 293 5 37 BIRLSTONE[9]
26 BIRLSTONE 9 127 171

'What do you make of it, Holmes?'

'It is obviously an attempt to convey secret information.'

'But what is the use of a cipher message without the cipher?'

'In this instance, none at all.'

'Why do you say "in this instance"?'

'Because there are many ciphers which I would read as easily as I do the apocrypha[10] of the agony column. Such crude devices amuse the intelligence without fatiguing it. But this is different. It is clearly a reference to the words in a page of some book. Until I am told which page and which book I am powerless.'

'But why "Douglas" and "Birlstone"?'

'Clearly because those are words which were not contained in the page in question.'

'Then why has he not indicated the book?'

'Your native shrewdness, my dear Watson, that innate cunning which is the delight of your friends, would surely prevent you from enclosing cipher and message in the same envelope. Should it miscarry you are undone. As it is, both have to go wrong before any harm comes from it. Our second post is now overdue, and I shall be surprised if it does not bring us either a further letter of explanation or, as is more probable, the very volume to which these figures refer.'

Holmes's calculation was fulfilled within a very few minutes by the appearance of Billy, the page, with the very letter which we were expecting.

'The same writing,' remarked Holmes, as he opened the envelope, 'and actually signed,' he added, in an exultant voice, as he unfolded the epistle. 'Come, we are getting on, Watson.'

His brow clouded, however, as he glanced over the contents.

'Dear me, this is very disappointing! I fear, Watson, that all our expectations come to nothing. I trust that the man Porlock will come to no harm.

' "Dear Mr Holmes," he says, "I will go no further in this matter. It is too dangerous. He suspects me. I can see that he suspects me. He came to me quite unexpectedly after I had actually addressed this envelope with the intention of sending you the key to the cipher. I was able to cover it up. If he had seen it, it would have gone hard with me. But I read suspicion in his eyes. Please burn the cipher message, which can now be of no use to you. – Fred Porlock." '

Holmes sat for some little time twisting this letter between his fingers, and frowning, as he stared into the fire.

'After all,' he said at last, 'there may be nothing in it. It may be only his guilty conscience. Knowing himself to be a traitor, he may have read the accusation in the other's eyes.'

'The other being, I presume, Professor Moriarty?'

'No less. When any of that party talk about "he", you know whom they mean. There is one predominant "he" for all of them.'

'But what can he do?'

'Hum! That's a large question. When you have one of the first brains of Europe up against you and all the powers of darkness at his back, there are infinite possibilities. Anyhow, friend Porlock is evidently scared out of his senses. Kindly compare the writing in the note with that upon its envelope, which was done, he tells us, before this ill-omened visit. The one is clear and firm; the other hardly legible.'

'Why did he write at all? Why did he not simply drop it?'

'Because he feared I would make some inquiry after him in that case, and possibly bring trouble on him.'

'No doubt,' said I. 'Of course' – I had picked up the original cipher message and was bending my brows over it – 'it's pretty maddening to think that an important secret may lie here on this slip of paper, and that it is beyond human power to penetrate it.'

Sherlock Holmes had pushed away his untasted breakfast and lit the unsavoury pipe which was the companion of his deepest meditations.

'I wonder!' said he, leaning back and staring at the ceiling. 'Perhaps there are points which have escaped your Machiavellian[11] intellect. Let us consider the problem in the light of pure reason. This man's reference is to a book. That is our point of departure.'

'A somewhat vague one.'

'Let us see, then, if we can narrow it down. As I focus my mind upon it, it seems rather less impenetrable. What indications have we as to this book?'

'None.'

'Well, well, it is surely not quite so bad as that. The cipher message begins with a large 534, does it not? We may take it as a working hypothesis that 534 is the particular page to which the cipher refers. So our book has already become a *large* book, which is surely something gained. What other indications have we as to the nature of this large book? The next sign is C2. What do you make of that, Watson?'

'Chapter the second, no doubt.'

'Hardly that, Watson. You will, I am sure, agree with me that if the page be given, the number of the chapter is immaterial. Also that if page 534 only finds us in the second chapter, the length of the first one must have been really intolerable.'

'Column!' I cried.

'Brilliant, Watson. You are scintillating this morning. If it is not column, then I am very much deceived. So now, you see, we begin to visualize a large book, printed in double columns, which are each of a considerable length, since one of the words is numbered in the document as the two hundred and ninety-third. Have we reached the limits of what reason can supply?'

'I fear that we have.'

'Surely you do yourself an injustice. One more coruscation, my dear Watson. Yet another brain-wave. Had the volume been an unusual one he would have sent it to me. Instead of that he had intended, before his plans were nipped, to send me the clue in this envelope. He says so in his note. This would seem to indicate that the book is one which he thought that I would have no difficulty in finding for myself. He had it, and he imagined that I would have it too. In short, Watson, it is a very common book.'

'What you say certainly sounds plausible.'

'So we have contracted our field of search to a large book, printed in double columns and in common use.'

'The Bible,' I cried, triumphantly.

'Good, Watson, good! But not, if I may say so, quite good enough. Even if I accepted the compliment for myself, I could hardly name any volume which would be less likely to lie at the elbow of one of Moriarty's associates. Besides, the editions of Holy Writ are so numerous that he could hardly suppose that two copies would have the same pagination. This is clearly a book which is standardized. He knows for certain that his page 534 will exactly agree with my page 534.'

'But very few books would correspond with that.'

'Exactly. Therein lies our salvation. Our search is narrowed down to standardized books which anyone may be supposed to possess.'

'*Bradshaw!*'[12]

'There are difficulties, Watson. The vocabulary of *Bradshaw* is nervous and terse, but limited. The selection of words would hardly lend itself to the sending of general messages. We will eliminate *Bradshaw*. The dictionary is, I fear, inadmissible[13] for the same reason. What, then, is left?'

'An almanack.'

'Excellent, Watson! I am very much mistaken if you have not touched the spot. An almanack! Let us consider the claims of *Whitaker's Almanack*.[14] It is in common use. It has the requisite number of pages. It is in double columns. Though reserved in its earlier vocabulary, it becomes, if I remember right, quite garrulous towards the end.' He picked up the volume from his desk. 'Here is page 534, column two, a substantial block of print dealing, I perceive, with the trade and resources of British India. Jot down the words, Watson. Number thirteen is "Mahratta".[15] Not, I fear, a very auspicious beginning. Number one hundred and twenty-seven is "Government", which at least makes sense, though somewhat irrelevant to ourselves and

Professor Moriarty. Now let us try again. What does the Mahratta Government do? Alas! the next word is "pigs'-bristles". We are undone,[16] my good Watson! It is finished.'

He had spoken in jesting vein, but the twitching of his bushy eyebrows bespoke his disappointment and irritation. I sat helpless and unhappy, staring into the fire. A long silence was broken by a sudden exclamation from Holmes, who dashed at a cupboard, from which he emerged with a second yellow-covered volume in his hand.

'We pay the price, Watson, for being too up-to-date,' he cried. 'We are before our time, and suffer the usual penalties. Being the seventh of January,[17] we have very properly laid in the new almanack. It is more than likely that Porlock took his message from the old one. No doubt he would have told us so had his letter of explanation been written. Now let us see what page 534 has in store for us. Number thirteen is "There", which is much more promising. Number one hundred and twenty-seven is "is" – "There is" ' – Holmes's eyes were gleaming with excitement, and his thin, nervous fingers twitched as he counted the words – ' "danger". Ha! ha! Capital! Put that down, Watson. "There is danger – may – come – very – soon – one". Then we have the name "Douglas" – "rich – country – now – at – Birlstone – House – Birlstone – confidence – is – pressing". There, Watson! what do you think of pure reason and its fruits? If the greengrocer had such a thing as a laurelwreath I should send Billy round for it.'

I was staring at the strange message which I had scrawled, as he deciphered it, upon a sheet of foolscap on my knee.

'What a queer, scrambling way of expressing his meaning!' said I.

'On the contrary, he has done quite remarkably well,' said Holmes. 'When you search a single column for words with which to express your meaning, you can hardly expect to get everything you want. You are bound to leave something to the intelligence of your correspondent. The purport is perfectly clear. Some devilry is intended against one Douglas, whoever he may be, residing as stated, a rich country gentleman. He is sure – "confidence" was as near as he could get to "confident" – that it is pressing. There is our result, and a very workmanlike little bit of analysis it was.'

Holmes had the impersonal joy of the true artist in his better work, even as he mourned darkly when it fell below the high level to which he aspired. He was still chuckling over his success when Billy swung open the door and Inspector MacDonald of Scotland Yard was ushered into the room.

Those were the early days at the end of the 'eighties, when Alec MacDonald was far from having attained the national fame which he has now achieved. He was a young but trusted member of the detective force, who had distinguished himself in several cases which had been entrusted to him. His tall, bony figure gave promise of exceptional physical strength, while his great cranium and deep-set, lustrous eyes spoke no less clearly of the keen intelligence which twinkled out from behind his bushy eyebrows. He was a silent, precise man, with a dour nature and a hard Aberdonian accent. Twice already in his career had Holmes helped him to attain success, his own sole reward being the intellectual joy of the problem. For this reason the affection and respect of the Scotchman for his amateur colleague were profound, and he showed them by the frankness with which he consulted Holmes in every difficulty. Mediocrity knows nothing higher than itself, but talent instantly recognizes genius, and MacDonald had talent enough for his profession to enable him to perceive that there was no humiliation in seeking the assistance of one who already stood alone in Europe, both in his gifts and in his experience. Holmes was not prone to friendship, but he was tolerant of the big Scotchman, and smiled at the sight of him.

'You are an early bird, Mr Mac,' said he. 'I wish you luck with your worm. I fear this means that there is some mischief afoot.'

'If you said "hope" instead of "fear" it would be nearer the truth, I'm thinking, Mr Holmes,' the inspector answered, with a knowing grin. 'Well, maybe a wee nip would keep out the raw morning chill. No, I won't smoke, I thank you. I'll have to be pushing on my way, for the early hours of a case are the precious ones, as no man knows better than your own self. But – but –'

The inspector had stopped suddenly, and was staring with a look of absolute amazement at a paper upon the table. It was the sheet upon which I had scrawled the enigmatic message.

'Douglas!' he stammered. 'Birlstone! What's this, Mr Holmes?

Man, it's witchcraft! Where in the name of all that is wonderful did you get those names?'

'It is a cipher that Dr Watson and I have had occasion to solve. But why – what's amiss with the names?'

The inspector looked from one to the other of us in dazed astonishment.

'Just this,' said he, 'that Mr Douglas, of Birlstone Manor House, was horribly murdered this morning.'

2

Mr Sherlock Holmes Discourses

It was one of those dramatic moments for which my friend existed. It would be an over-statement to say that he was shocked or even excited by the amazing announcement. Without having a tinge of cruelty in his singular composition, he was undoubtedly callous from long over-stimulation. Yet, if his emotions were dulled, his intellectual perceptions were exceedingly active. There was no trace then of the horror which I had myself felt at this curt declaration, but his face showed rather the quiet and interested composure of the chemist who sees the crystals falling into position from his over-saturated solution.

'Remarkable!' said he; 'remarkable!'

'You don't seem surprised.'

'Interested, Mr Mac, but hardly surprised. Why should I be surprised? I receive an anonymous communication from a quarter which I know to be important, warning me that danger threatens a certain person. Within an hour I learn that this danger has actually materialized, and that the person is dead. I am interested, but, as you observe, I am not surprised.'

In a few short sentences he explained to the inspector the facts about the letter and the cipher. MacDonald sat with his chin on his hands, and his great sandy eyebrows bunched into a yellow tangle.

'I was going down to Birlstone this morning,' said he. 'I had come to ask you if you cared to come with me – you and your friend here. But from what you say we might perhaps be doing better work in London.'

'I rather think not,' said Holmes.

'Hang it all, Mr Holmes!' cried the inspector. 'The papers will be full of the Birlstone Mystery in a day or two, but where's the mystery if there is a man in London who prophesied the crime before ever it occurred? We have only to lay our hands on that man and the rest will follow.'

'No doubt, Mr Mac. But how did you propose to lay your hands on the so-called Porlock?'

MacDonald turned over the letter which Holmes had handed him.

'Posted in Camberwell[1] – that doesn't help us much. Name, you say, is assumed. Not much to go on, certainly. Didn't you say that you have sent him money?'

'Twice.'

'And how?'

'In notes to Camberwell post-office.'

'Did you never trouble to see who called for them?'

'No.'

The inspector looked surprised and a little shocked.

'Why not?'

'Because I always keep faith. I had promised when he first wrote that I would not try to trace him.'

'You think there is someone behind him?'

'I *know* there is.'

'This Professor that I have heard you mention?'

'Exactly.'

Inspector MacDonald smiled, and his eyelid quivered as he glanced towards me.

'I won't conceal from you, Mr Holmes, that we think in the C.I.D.[2] that you have a wee bit of a bee in your bonnet over this Professor. I made some inquiries myself about the matter. He seems to be a very respectable, learned, and talented sort of man.'

'I'm glad you've got as far as to recognize the talent.'

'Man, you can't but recognize it. After I heard your view, I made it my business to see him. I had a chat with him on eclipses – how the talk got that way I canna think – but he had out a reflector lantern and a globe and made it all clear in a minute. He lent me a book, but I don't mind saying that it was a bit above my head, though I had a good Aberdeen upbringing. He'd have made a grand meenister, with his thin face and grey hair and solemn-like way of talking. When he put his hand on my shoulder as we were parting, it was like a father's blessing before you go out into the cold, cruel world.'

Holmes chuckled and rubbed his hands.

'Great!' he cried; 'great! Tell me, friend MacDonald; this pleasing and touching interview was, I suppose, in the Professor's study?'

'That's so.'

'A fine room, is it not?'

'Very fine – very handsome indeed, Mr Holmes.'

'You sat in front of his writing-desk?'

'Just so.'

'Sun in your eyes and his face in the shadow?'

'Well, it was evening, but I mind that the lamp was turned on my face.'

'It would be. Did you happen to observe a picture over the Professor's head?'

'I don't miss much, Mr Holmes. Maybe I learned that from you. Yes, I saw the picture – a young woman with her head on her hands, keeking at you sideways.'

'That painting was by Jean Baptiste Greuze.'[3]

The inspector endeavoured to look interested.

'Jean Baptiste Greuze,' Holmes continued, joining his fingertips and leaning well back in his chair, 'was a French artist who flourished between the years 1750 and 1800. I allude, of course, to his working career. Modern criticism has more than endorsed the high opinion formed of him by his contemporaries.'

The inspector's eyes grew abstracted.

'Hadn't we better –' he said.

'We are doing so,' Holmes interrupted. 'All that I am saying has a very direct and vital bearing upon what you have called the Birlstone

Mystery. In fact, it may in a sense be called the very centre of it.'

McDonald smiled feebly, and looked appealingly to me.

'Your thoughts move a bit too quick for me, Mr Holmes. You leave out a link or two, and I can't get over the gap. What in the whole wide world can be the connection between this dead painting man and the affair at Birlstone?'

'All knowledge comes useful to the detective,'[4] remarked Holmes. 'Even the trivial fact that in the year 1865 a picture by Greuze, entitled "La Jeune Fille à l'agneau", fetched not less than four thousand pounds – at the Portalis sale[5] – may start a train of reflection in your mind.'

It was clear that it did. The inspector looked honestly interested.

'I may remind you,' Holmes continued, 'that the Professor's salary can be ascertained in several trustworthy books of reference. It is seven hundred a year.'

'Then how could he buy –'

'Quite so. How could he?'

'Aye, that's remarkable,' said the inspector, thoughtfully. 'Talk away, Mr Holmes. I'm just loving it. It's fine.'

Holmes smiled. He was always warmed by genuine admiration – the characteristic of the real artist.

'What about Birlstone?' he asked.

'We've time yet,' said the inspector, glancing at his watch. 'I've a cab at the door, and it won't take us twenty minutes to Victoria. But about this picture – I thought you told me once, Mr Holmes, that you had never met Professor Moriarty.'

'No, I never have.'

'Then how do you know about his rooms?'

'Ah, that's another matter. I have been three times in his rooms, twice waiting for him under different pretexts and leaving before he came. Once – well, I can hardly tell about the once to an official detective. It was on the last occasion that I took the liberty of running over his papers, with the most unexpected results.'

'You found something compromising?'

'Absolutely nothing. That was what amazed me. However, you have now seen the point of the picture. It shows him to be a very wealthy man. How did he acquire wealth? He is unmarried. His younger brother is a station-master in the West of England. His chair is worth seven hundred a year. And he owns a Greuze.'

'Well?'

'Surely the inference is plain.'

'You mean that he has a great income, and that he must earn it in an illegal fashion?'

'Exactly. Of course, I have other reasons for thinking so – dozens of exiguous threads which lead vaguely up towards the centre of the web where the poisonous motionless creature is lurking. I only mention the Greuze because it brings the matter within the range of your own observation.'

'Well, Mr Holmes, I admit that what you say is interesting. It's more than interesting – it's just wonderful. But let us have it a little clearer if you can. Is it forgery, coining, burglary? Where does the money come from?'

'Have you ever read of Jonathan Wild?'[6]

'Well, the name has a familiar sound. Someone in a novel, was he not? I don't take much stock of detectives in novels – chaps that do things and never let you see how they do them. That's just inspiration, not business.'

'Jonathan Wild wasn't a detective, and he wasn't in a novel.[7] He was a master criminal, and he lived last century – 1750 or thereabouts.'

'Then he's no use to me. I'm a practical man.'

'Mr Mac, the most practical thing that ever you did in your life would be to shut yourself up for three months and read twelve hours a day at the annals of crime. Everything comes in circles, even Professor Moriarty. Jonathan Wild was the hidden force of the London criminals, to whom he sold his brains and his organization on a fifteen per cent commission. The old wheel turns and the same spoke comes up. It's all been done before and will be again. I'll tell you one or two things about Moriarty which may interest you.'

'You'll interest me right enough.'

'I happen to know who is the first link in his chain – a chain with this Napoleon-gone-wrong at one end and a hundred broken fighting men, pickpockets, blackmailers, and card-sharpers at the other, with every sort of crime in between. His chief of staff is Colonel Sebastian Moran,[8] as aloof and guarded and inaccessible to the law as himself. What do you think he pays him?'

'I'd like to hear.'

'Six thousand a year. That's paying for brains, you see – the American business principle. I learned that detail quite by chance. It's more than the Prime Minister[9] gets. That gives you an idea of Moriarty's gains and of the scale on which he works. Another point. I made it my business to hunt down some of Moriarty's cheques lately – just common innocent cheques that he pays his household bills with. They were drawn on six different banks. Does that make any impression on your mind?'

'Queer, certainly. But what do you gather from it?'

'That he wanted no gossip about this wealth. No single man should know what he had. I have no doubt that he has twenty banking accounts – the bulk of his fortune abroad in the Deutsche Bank or the Crédit Lyonnais as likely as not. Some time when you have a year or two to spare I commend to you the study of Professor Moriarty.'

Inspector MacDonald had grown steadily more impressed as the conversation proceeded. He had lost himself in his interest. Now his practical Scotch intelligence brought him back with a snap to the matter in hand.

'He can keep, anyhow,' said he. 'You've got us sidetracked with your interesting anecdotes, Mr Holmes. What really counts is your remark that there is some connection between the Professor and the crime. That you get from the warning received through the man Porlock. Can we for our present practical needs get any farther than that?'

'We may form some conception as to the motives of the crime. It is, as I gather from your original remarks, an inexplicable, or at least an unexplained, murder. Now, presuming that the source of the crime is as we suspect it to be, there might be two different motives. In the first place, I may tell you that Moriarty rules with a rod of iron over his people. His discipline is tremendous. There is only one punishment in his code. It is death. Now, we might suppose that this murdered man – this Douglas, whose approaching fate was known by one of the arch-criminal's subordinates – had in some way betrayed the chief. His punishment followed and would be known to all, if only to put the fear of death into them.'

'Well, that is one suggestion, Mr Holmes.'

'The other is that it has been engineered by Moriarty in the ordinary course of business. Was there any robbery?'

'I have not heard.'

'If so it would, of course, be against the first hypothesis and in favour of the second. Moriarty may have been engaged to engineer it on a promise of part spoils, or he may have been paid so much down to manage it. Either is possible. But, whichever it may be, or if it is some third combination, it is down at Birlstone that we must seek the solution. I know our man too well to suppose that he has left anything up here which may lead us to him.'

'Then to Birlstone we must go!' cried MacDonald, jumping from his chair. 'My word! it's later than I thought. I can give you gentlemen five minutes for preparation, and that is all.'

'And ample for us both,' said Holmes, as he sprang up and hastened to change from his dressing-gown to his coat. 'While we are on our way, Mr Mac, I will ask you to be good enough to tell me all about it.'

'All about it' proved to be disappointingly little, and yet there was enough to assure us that the case before us might well be worthy of the expert's closest attention. He brightened and rubbed his thin hands together as he listened to the meagre but remarkable details. A long series of sterile weeks lay behind us, and here, at last, there was a fitting object for those remarkable powers which, like all special gifts, become irksome to their owner when they are not in use. That razor brain blunted and rusted with inaction. Sherlock Holmes's eyes glistened, his pale cheeks took a warmer hue, and his whole eager face shone with an inward light when the call for work reached him. Leaning forward in the cab, he listened intently to MacDonald's short sketch of the problem which awaited us in Sussex. The inspector was himself dependent, as he explained to us, upon a scribbled account forwarded to him by the milk train in the early hours of the morning. White Mason, the local officer, was a personal friend, and hence MacDonald had been notified very much more promptly than is usual

at Scotland Yard when provincials need their assistance. It is very cold
scent upon which the Metropolitan expert is generally asked to run.

'Dear Inspector MacDonald,' said the letter which he read to us,
'official requisition for your services is in separate envelope. This is for
your private eye. Wire me what train in the morning you can get for
Birlstone, and I will meet it – or have it met if I am too occupied. This
case is a snorter. Don't waste a moment in getting started. If you can
bring Mr Holmes, please do so, for he will find something after his
own heart. You would think the whole thing had been fixed up for
theatrical effect, if there wasn't a dead man in the middle of it. My
word, it *is* a snorter!'

'Your friend seems to be no fool,' remarked Holmes.

'No sir; White Mason is a very live man, if I am any judge.'

'Well, have you anything more?'

'Only that he will give us every detail when we meet.'

'Then how did you get at Mr Douglas and the fact that he had
been horribly murdered?'

'That was in the enclosed official report. It didn't say "horrible".
That's not a recognized official term. It gave the name John Douglas.
It mentioned that his injuries had been in the head, from the discharge
of a shot-gun. It also mentioned the hour of the alarm, which was
close on to midnight last night. It added that the case was undoubtedly
one of murder, but that no arrest had been made, and that the case
was one which presented some very perplexing and extraordinary
features. That's absolutely all we have at present, Mr Holmes.'

'Then, with your permission, we will leave it at that, Mr Mac. The
temptation to form premature theories upon insufficient data is the
bane of our profession. I can only see two things for certain at present:
a great brain in London and a dead man in Sussex. It's the chain
between that we are going to trace.'

3

The Tragedy of Birlstone

And now for a moment I will ask leave to remove my own insignificant personality[1] and to describe events which occurred before we arrived upon the scene by the light of knowledge which came to us afterwards. Only in this way can I make the reader appreciate the people concerned and the strange setting in which their fate was cast.

The village of Birlstone is a small and very ancient cluster of half-timbered cottages on the northern border of the county of Sussex. For centuries it had remained unchanged, but within the last few years its picturesque appearance and situation have attracted a number of well-to-do residents, whose villas peep out from the woods around. These woods are locally supposed to be the extreme fringe of the great Weald forest,[2] which thins away until it reaches the northern chalk downs. A number of small shops have come into being to meet the wants of the increased population, so that there seems some prospect that Birlstone may soon grow from an ancient village into a modern town. It is the centre for a considerable area of country, since Tunbridge Wells,[3] the nearest place of importance, is ten or twelve miles[4] to the eastward, over the borders of Kent.

About half a mile from the town, standing in an old park famous for its huge beech trees, is the ancient Manor House of Birlstone. Part of this venerable building dates back to the time of the first Crusade,[5] when Hugo de Capus[6] built a fortalice in the centre of the estate, which had been granted to him by the Red King.[7] This was destroyed by fire in 1543, and some of its smoke-blackened corner-stones were used when, in Jacobean times,[8] a brick country house rose upon the ruins of the feudal castle. The Manor House, with its many gables and its small, diamond-paned windows, was still much as the builder had left it in the early seventeenth century. Of the double moats which had guarded its more warlike predecessor the outer had been allowed to dry up, and served the humble function of a kitchen garden. The inner one was still there, and lay, forty feet in breadth, though now only a few feet in depth, round the whole house. A small stream fed it and continued beyond it, so that the sheet of water, though turbid, was never ditch-like or unhealthy. The groundfloor windows were within a foot of the surface of the water. The only approach to the house was over a drawbridge, the chains and windlass of which had long been rusted and broken. The latest tenants of the Manor House had, however, with characteristic energy, set this right, and the draw-bridge was not only capable of being raised, but actually was raised every evening and lowered every morning. By thus renewing the custom of the old feudal days the Manor House was converted into an island during the night – a fact which had a very direct bearing upon the mystery which was soon to engage the attention of England.

The house had been untenanted for some years, and was threaten-ing to moulder into a picturesque decay when the Douglases took possession of it. This family consisted of only two individuals, John Douglas and his wife. Douglas was a remarkable man both in character and in person; in age he may have been about fifty, with a strong-jawed, rugged face, a grizzling moustache, peculiarly keen grey eyes, and a wiry, vigorous figure which had lost nothing of the strength and activity of youth. He was cheery and genial to all, but somewhat offhand in his manners, giving the impression that he had seen life in social strata on some far lower horizon than the county society of Sussex. Yet, though looked at with some curiosity and reserve by his more cultivated neighbours, he soon acquired a great popularity among the villagers, subscribing handsomely to all local objects, and attending their smok-ing concerts, and other functions, where, having a remarkably rich tenor voice, he was always ready to oblige with an excellent song. He appeared to have plenty of money, which was said to have been gained in the Californian goldfields, and it was clear from his own talk and that of his wife that he had spent a part of his life in America. The good impression which had been produced by his generosity and by his democratic manners was increased by a reputation gained for utter indifference to danger. Though a wretched rider, he turned out at every meet, and took the most amazing falls in his determination to hold his own with the best. When the vicarage caught fire he distinguished himself also by the fearlessness with which he re-entered the building to save property, after the local fire brigade had given it up as impossible. Thus it came about that John Douglas, of the Manor House, had within five years won himself quite a reputation in Birlstone.

His wife, too, was popular with those who had made her acquaintance, though, after the English fashion, the callers upon a stranger who settled in the county without introductions were few and far between. This mattered less to her as she was retiring by disposition and very much absorbed, to all appearance, in her husband and her domestic duties. It was known that she was an English lady who had met Mr Douglas in London, he being at that time a widower. She was a beautiful woman, tall, dark, and slender, some twenty years younger than her husband, a disparity which seemed in no wise to mar the contentment of their family life. It was remarked sometimes, however, by those who knew them best that the confidence between the two did not appear to be complete, since the wife was either very reticent about her husband's past life or else, as seemed more likely, was very imperfectly informed about it. It had also been noted and commented upon by a few observant people that there were signs sometimes of some nerve-strain upon the part of Mrs Douglas, and that she would display acute uneasiness if her absent husband should ever be particularly late in his return. On a quiet countryside, where all gossip is welcome, this weakness of the lady of the Manor House did not pass without remark, and it bulked larger upon people's memory when the events arose which gave it a very special significance.

There was yet another individual whose residence under that roof was, it is true, only an intermittent one, but whose presence at the time of the strange happenings which will now be narrated brought his name prominently before the public. This was Cecil James Barker, of Hales Lodge, Hampstead. Cecil Barker's tall, loose-jointed figure was a familiar one in the main street of Birlstone village, for he was a frequent and welcome visitor at the Manor House. He was the more noticed as being the only friend of the past unknown life of Mr Douglas who was ever seen in his new English surroundings. Barker was himself an undoubted Englishman, but by his remarks it was clear that he had first known Douglas in America, and had there lived on intimate terms with him. He appeared to be a man of considerable wealth, and was reputed to be a bachelor. In age he was rather younger than Douglas, forty-five at the most, a tall, straight, broad-chested fellow, with a clean-shaven, prize-fighter face, thick, strong, black eyebrows, and a pair of masterful black eyes which might, even without the aid of his very capable hands, clear a way for him through a hostile crowd. He neither rode nor shot, but spent his days in wandering round the old village with his pipe in his mouth, or in driving with his host, or in his absence with his hostess, over the beautiful countryside. 'An easy-going, free-handed gentleman,' said Ames, the butler. 'But, my word, I had rather not be the man that crossed him.' He was cordial and intimate with Douglas, and he was no less friendly with his wife, a friendship which more than once seemed to cause some irritation to the husband, so that even the servants were able to perceive his annoyance. Such was the third person who was one of the family when the catastrophe occurred. As to the other denizens of the old building, it will suffice out of a large household to mention the prim, respectable, and capable Ames and Mrs Allen, a buxom and cheerful person, who relieved the lady of some of her household cares. The other six servants in the house bear no relation to the events of the night of January 6th.

It was at eleven forty-five that the first alarm reached the small local police-station in the charge of Sergeant Wilson, of the Sussex Constabulary. Mr Cecil Barker, much excited, had rushed up to the door and pealed furiously upon the bell. A terrible tragedy had occurred at the Manor House, and Mr John Douglas had been murdered. That was the breathless burden of his message. He had hurried back to the house, followed within a few minutes by the police-sergeant, who arrived at the scene of the crime a little past twelve o'clock, after taking prompt steps to warn the county authorities that something serious was afoot.

On reaching the Manor House the sergeant had found the draw-bridge down, the windows lighted up, and the whole household in a state of wild confusion and alarm. The white-faced servants were huddling together in the hall, with the frightened butler wringing his hands in the doorway. Only Cecil Barker seemed to be master of himself and his emotions. He had opened the door which was nearest to the entrance, and had beckoned to the sergeant to follow him. At that moment there arrived Dr Wood, a brisk and capable general practitioner from the village. The three men entered the fatal room together, while the horror-stricken butler followed at their heels, closing the door behind him to shut out the terrible scene from the maid-servants.

The dead man lay upon his back, sprawling with outstretched limbs in the centre of the room. He was clad only in a pink dressing-gown, which covered his night clothes. There were carpet slippers upon his bare feet. The doctor knelt beside him, and held down the hand-lamp which had stood on the table. One glance at the victim was enough to show the healer that his presence could be dispensed with. The man had been horribly injured. Lying across his chest was a curious weapon, a shot-gun with the barrel sawn off a foot in front of the triggers. It was clear that this had been fired at close range, and that he had received the whole charge in the face, blowing his head almost to pieces. The triggers had been wired together, so as to make the simultaneous discharge more destructive.

The country policeman was unnerved and troubled by the tremendous responsibility which had come so suddenly upon him.

'We will touch nothing until my superiors arrive,' he said, in a hushed voice, staring in horror at the dreadful head.

'Nothing has been touched up to now,' said Cecil Barker. 'I'll answer for that. You see it all exactly as I found it.'

'When was that?' The sergeant had drawn out his notebook.

'It was just half-past eleven. I had not begun to undress, and I was sitting by the fire in my bedroom, when I heard the report. It was not very loud – it seemed to be muffled. I rushed down. I don't suppose it was thirty seconds before I was in the room.'

'Was the door open?'

'Yes, it was open. Poor Douglas was lying as you see him. His bedroom candle was burning on the table. It was I who lit the lamp some minutes afterwards.'

'Did you see no one?'

'No. I heard Mrs Douglas coming down the stair behind me, and I rushed out to prevent her from seeing this dreadful sight. Mrs Allen, the housekeeper, came and took her away. Ames had arrived, and we ran back into the room once more.'

'But surely I have heard that the drawbridge is kept up all night.'

'Yes, it was up until I lowered it.'

'Then how could any murderer have got away? It is out of the question. Mr Douglas must have shot himself.'

'That was our first idea. But see.' Barker drew aside the curtain, and showed that the long, diamond-paned window was open to its full extent. 'And look at this!' He held the lamp down and illuminated a smudge of blood like the mark of a boot-sole upon the wooden sill. 'Someone has stood there in getting out.'

'You mean that someone waded across the moat?'

'Exactly.'

'Then, if you were in the room within half a minute of the crime, he must have been in the water at that very moment.'

'I have not a doubt of it. I wish to Heaven that I had rushed to the window. But the curtain screened it, as you can see, and so it never occurred to me. Then I heard the step of Mrs Douglas, and I could not let her enter the room. It would have been too horrible.'

'Horrible enough!' said the doctor, looking at the shattered head and the terrible marks which surrounded it. 'I've never seen such injuries since the Birlstone railway smash.'

'But, I say,' remarked the police-sergeant, whose slow, bucolic common sense was still pondering over the open window. 'It's all very well your saying that a man escaped by wading this moat, but what I ask you is – how did he ever get into the house at all if the bridge was up?'

'Ah, that's the question,' said Barker.

'At what o'clock was it raised?'

'It was nearly six o'clock,' said Ames, the butler.

'I've heard,' said the sergeant, 'that it was usually raised at sunset. That would be nearer half-past four than six at this time of year.'

'Mrs Douglas had visitors to tea,' said Ames. 'I couldn't raise it until they went. Then I wound it up myself.'

'Then it comes to this,' said the sergeant. 'If anyone came from outside – *if* they did – they must have got in across the bridge before six and been in hiding ever since, until Mr Douglas came into the room after eleven.'

'That is so. Mr Douglas went round the house every night the last thing before he turned in to see that the lights were right. That brought him in here. The man was waiting, and shot him. Then he got away through the window and left his gun behind him. That's how I read it – for nothing else will fit the facts.'

The sergeant picked up a card which lay beside the dead man upon the floor. The initials V.V., and under them the number 341, were rudely scrawled in ink upon it.

'What's this?' he asked, holding it up.

Barker looked at it with curiosity.

'I never noticed it before,' he said. 'The murderer must have left it behind him.'

' "V.V. 341." I can make no sense of that.'

The sergeant kept turning it over in his big fingers.

'What's V.V.? Somebody's initials, maybe. What have you got there, Dr Wood?'

It was a good-sized hammer which had been lying upon the rug in front of the fireplace – a substantial, workmanlike hammer. Cecil Barker pointed to a box of brass-headed nails upon the mantelpiece.

'Mr Douglas was altering the pictures yesterday,' he said. 'I saw him myself standing upon that chair and fixing the big picture above it. That accounts for the hammer.'

'We'd best put it back on the rug where we found it,' said the sergeant, scratching his puzzled head in his perplexity. 'It will want the best brains in the force to get to the bottom of this thing. It will be a London job before it is finished.' He raised the hand-lamp and walked slowly round the room. 'Halloa!' he cried, excitedly, drawing the window curtain to one side. 'What o'clock were those curtains drawn?'

'When the lamps were lit,' said the butler. 'It would be shortly after four.'

'Someone has been hiding here, sure enough.' He held down the light, and the marks of muddy boots were very visible in the corner. 'I'm bound to say this bears out your theory, Mr Barker. It looks as if the man got into the house after four, when the curtains were drawn, and before six, when the bridge was raised. He slipped into this room because it was the first that he saw. There was no other place where he could hide, so he popped in behind this curtain. That all seems clear enough. It is likely that his main idea was to burgle the house, but Mr Douglas chanced to come upon him, so he murdered him and escaped.'

'That's how I read it,' said Barker. 'But, I say, aren't we wasting precious time? Couldn't we start out and scour the country before the fellow gets away?'

The sergeant considered for a moment.

'There are no trains before six in the morning, so he can't get away by rail. If he goes by road with his legs all dripping, it's odds that someone will notice him. Anyhow, I can't leave here myself until I am relieved. But I think none of you should go until we see more clearly how we all stand.'

The doctor had taken the lamp and was narrowly scrutinizing the body.

'What's this mark?' he asked. 'Could this have any connection with the crime?'

The dead man's right arm was thrust out from his dressing-gown and exposed as high as the elbow. About halfway up the forearm was a curious brown design, a triangle inside a circle, standing out in vivid relief upon the lard-coloured skin.

'It's not tattooed,' said the doctor, peering through his glasses. 'I never saw anything like it. The man has been branded at some time, as they brand cattle. What is the meaning of this?'

'I don't profess to know the meaning of it,' said Cecil Barker; 'but I've seen the mark on Douglas any time this last ten years.'

'And so have I,' said the butler. 'Many a time when the master has rolled up his sleeves I have noticed that very mark. I've often wondered what it could be.'

'Then it has nothing to do with the crime, anyhow,' said the sergeant. 'But it's a rum thing all the same. Everything about this case is rum. Well, what is it now?'

The butler had given an exclamation of astonishment, and was pointing at the dead man's outstretched hand.

'They've taken his wedding-ring!' he gasped.

'What!'

'Yes, indeed! Master always wore his plain gold wedding-ring on the little finger of his left hand. That ring with the rough nugget on it was above it, and the twisted snake-ring on the third finger. There's the nugget, and there's the snake, but the wedding-ring is gone.'

'He's right,' said Barker.

'Do you tell me,' said the sergeant, 'that the wedding-ring was *below* the other?'

'Always!'

'Then the murderer, or whoever it was, first took off this ring you call the nugget-ring, then the wedding-ring, and afterwards put the nugget-ring back again.'

'That is so.'

The worthy country policeman shook his head.

'Seems to me the sooner we get London on to this case the better,' said he. 'White Mason is a smart man. No local job has ever been too much for White Mason. It won't be long now before he is here to help us. But I expect we'll have to look to London before we are through. Anyhow, I'm not ashamed to say that it is a deal too thick for the likes of me.'

4

Darkness

At three in the morning the chief Sussex detective, obeying the urgent call from Sergeant Wilson, of Birlstone, arrived from headquarters in a light dog-cart behind a breathless trotter. By the five-forty train in the morning he had sent his message to Scotland Yard, and he was at the Birlstone station at twelve o'clock to welcome us. Mr White

Mason was a quiet, comfortable-looking person, in a loose tweed suit, with a clean-shaven, ruddy face, a stoutish body, and powerful bandy legs adorned with gaiters, looking like a small farmer, a retired game-keeper, or anything upon earth except a very favourable specimen of the provincial criminal officer.

'A real downright snorter, Mr MacDonald,' he kept repeating. 'We'll have the pressmen down like flies when they understand it. I'm hoping we will get our work done before they get poking their noses into it and messing up all the trails. There has been nothing like this that I can remember. There are some bits that will come home to you, Mr Holmes, or I am mistaken. And you also, Dr Watson, for the medicos will have a word to say before we finish. Your room is at the Westville Arms. There's no other place, but I hear that it is clean and good. The man will carry your bags. This way, gentlemen, if *you* please.'

He was a very bustling and genial person, this Sussex detective. In ten minutes we had all found our quarters. In ten more we were seated in the parlour of the inn and being treated to a rapid sketch of those events which have been outlined in the previous chapter. MacDonald made an occasional note, while Holmes sat absorbed with the expression of surprised and reverent admiration with which the botan-ist surveys the rare and precious bloom.

'Remarkable!' he said, when the story was unfolded. 'Most remark-able! I can hardly recall any case where the features have been more peculiar.'

'I thought you would say so, Mr Holmes,' said White Mason, in great delight. 'We're well up with the times in Sussex. I've told you now how matters were, up to the time when I took over from Sergeant Wilson between three and four this morning. My word, I made the old mare go! But I need not have been in such a hurry as it turned out, for there was nothing immediate that I could do. Sergeant Wilson had all the facts. I checked them and considered them, and maybe added a few on my own.'

'What were they?' asked Holmes, eagerly.

'Well, I first had the hammer examined. There was Dr Wood there to help me. We found no signs of violence upon it. I was hoping that, if Mr Douglas defended himself with the hammer, he might have left his mark upon the murderer before he dropped it on the mat. But there was no stain.'

'That, of course, proves nothing at all,' remarked Inspector Mac-Donald. 'There has been many a hammer murder and no trace on the hammer.'

'Quite so. It doesn't prove it wasn't used. But there might have been stains, and that would have helped us. As a matter of fact, there were none. Then I examined the gun. They were buck-shot cartridges, and, as Sergeant Wilson pointed out, the triggers were wired together so that if you pulled on the hinder one both barrels were discharged. Whoever fixed that up had made up his mind that he was going to take no chances of missing his man. The sawn gun was not more than two feet long; one could carry it easily under one's coat. There was no complete maker's name, but the printed letters "PEN" were on the fluting between the barrels, and the rest of the name had been cut off by the saw.'

'A big "P" with a flourish above it – "E" and "N" smaller?' asked Holmes.

'Exactly.'

'Pennsylvania Small Arm Company – well-known American firm,' said Holmes.

White Mason gazed at my friend as the little village practitioner looks at the Harley Street specialist who by a word can solve the difficulties that perplex him.

'That is very helpful, Mr Holmes. No doubt you are right. Wonderful – wonderful! Do you carry the names of all the gunmakers in the world in your memory?'

Holmes dismissed the subject with a wave.

'No doubt it is an American shot-gun,' White Mason continued. 'I seem to have read that a sawed-off shot-gun is a weapon used in some parts of America. Apart from the name upon the barrel, the idea had occurred to me. There is some evidence, then, that this man who entered the house and killed its master was an American.'

MacDonald shook his head. 'Man, you are surely travelling over-fast,' said he. 'I have heard no evidence yet that any stranger was ever in the house at all.'

'The open window, the blood on the sill, the queer card, marks of boots in the corner, the gun.'

'Nothing there that could not have been arranged. Mr Douglas was an American, or had lived long in America. So had Mr Barker. You don't need to import an American from outside in order to account for American doings.'

'Ames, the butler –'

'What about him? Is he reliable?'

'Ten years with Sir Charles Chandos – as solid as a rock. He has been with Douglas ever since he took the Manor House five years ago. He has never seen a gun of this sort in the house.'

'The gun was made to conceal. That's why the barrels were sawn. It would fit into any box. How could he swear there was no such gun in the house?'

'Well, anyhow he had never seen one.'

MacDonald shook his obstinate Scotch head. 'I'm not convinced yet that there was ever anyone in the house,' said he. 'I'm asking you to conseedar' – his accent became more Aberdonian as he lost himself in his argument – 'I'm asking you to conseedar what it involves if you suppose that this gun was ever brought into the house and that all these strange things were done by a person from outside. Oh, man, it's just inconceivable! It's clean against common sense. I put it to you, Mr Holmes, judging it by what we have heard.'

'Well, state your case, Mr Mac,' said Holmes, in his most judicial style.

'The man is not a burglar, supposing that he ever existed. The ring business and the card point to premeditated murder for some private reason. Very good. Here is a man who slips into a house with the deliberate intention of committing murder. He knows, if he knows anything, that he will have a deeficulty in making his escape, as the house is surrounded with water. What weapon would he choose? You would say the most silent in the world. Then he could hope, when the deed was done, to slip quickly from the window, to wade the moat, and to get away at his leisure. That's understandable. But is it understandable that he should go out of his way to bring with him the most noisy weapon he could select, knowing well that it will fetch every human being in the house to the spot as quick as they can run, and that it is all odds that he will be seen before he can get across the moat? Is that credible, Mr Holmes?'

'Well, you put your case strongly,' my friend replied, thoughtfully. 'It certainly needs a good deal of justification. May I ask, Mr White Mason, whether you examined the farther side of the moat at once, to see if there were any signs of the man having climbed out from the water?'

'There were no signs, Mr Holmes. But it is a stone ledge, and one could hardly expect them.'

'No tracks or marks?'

'None.'

'Ha! Would there be any objection, Mr White Mason, to our going down to the house at once? There may possibly be some small point which might be suggestive.'

'I was going to propose it, Mr Holmes, but I thought it well to put you in touch with all the facts before we go. I suppose, if anything should strike you – ' White Mason looked doubtfully at the amateur.

'I have worked with Mr Holmes before,' said Inspector Mac-Donald. 'He plays the game.'

'My own idea of the game, at any rate,' said Holmes, with a smile. 'I go into a case to help the ends of justice and the work of the police. If ever I have separated myself from the official force, it is because they have first separated themselves from me. I have no wish ever to score at their expense. At the same time, Mr White Mason, I claim the right to work in my own way and give my results at my own time – complete, rather than in stages.'

'I am sure we are honoured by your presence and to show you all we know,' said White Mason, cordially. 'Come along, Dr Watson, and when the time comes we'll all hope for a place in your book.'

We walked down the quaint village street with a row of pollarded elms on either side of it. Just beyond were two ancient stone pillars, weather-stained and lichen-blotched, bearing upon their summits a shapeless something which had once been the ramping lion of Capus of Birlstone. A short walk along the winding drive, with such sward and oaks around it as one only sees in rural England; then a sudden turn, and the long, low, Jacobean house of dingy, liver-coloured brick lay before us, with an old-fashioned garden of cut yews on either side of it. As we approached it there were the wooden drawbridge and the beautiful broad moat, as still and luminous as quicksilver in the cold winter sunshine. Three centuries had flowed past the old Manor House, centuries of births and homecomings, of country dances and of the meetings of fox-hunters. Strange that now in its old age this dark business should have cast its shadow upon the venerable walls. And yet those strange peaked roofs and quaint overhung gables were a fitting covering to grim and terrible intrigue. As I looked at the deep-set windows and the long sweep of the dull-coloured, water-lapped front I felt that no more fitting scene could be set for such a tragedy.

'That's the window,' said White Mason: 'that one on the immediate right of the drawbridge. It's open just as it was found last night.'

'It looks rather narrow for a man to pass.'

'Well, it wasn't a fat man, anyhow. We don't need your deductions, Mr Holmes, to tell us that. But you or I could squeeze through all right.'

Holmes walked to the edge of the moat and looked across. Then he examined the stone ledge and the grass border beyond it.

'I've had a good look, Mr Holmes,' said White Mason. 'There is nothing there; no sign that anyone has landed. But why should he leave any sign?'

'Exactly. Why should he? Is the water always turbid?'

'Generally about this colour. The stream brings down the clay.'

'How deep is it?'

'About two feet at each side and three in the middle.'

'So we can put aside all idea of the man having been drowned in crossing?'

'No; a child could not be drowned in it.'

We walked across the drawbridge, and were admitted by a quaint, gnarled, dried-up person who was the butler – Ames. The poor old fellow was white and quivering from the shock. The village sergeant, a tall, formal, melancholy man, still held his vigil in the room of fate. The doctor had departed.

'Anything fresh, Sergeant Wilson?' asked White Mason.

'No, sir.'

'Then you can go home. You've had enough. We can send for you if we want you. The butler had better wait outside. Tell him to warn Mr Cecil Barker, Mrs Douglas, and the housekeeper that we may want a word with them presently. Now, gentlemen, perhaps you will allow me to give you the views I have formed first, and then you will be able to arrive at your own.'

He impressed me, this country specialist. He had a solid grip of fact and a cool, clear, common-sense brain, which should take him some way in his profession. Holmes listened to him intently, with no sign of that impatience which the official exponent too often produced.

'Is it suicide or is it murder – that's our first question, gentlemen, is it not? If it were suicide, then we have to believe that this man began by taking off his wedding-ring and concealing it; that he then came down here in his dressing-gown, trampled mud into a corner behind the curtain in order to give the idea someone had waited for him, opened the window, put the blood on the –'

'We can surely dismiss that,' said MacDonald.

'So I think. Suicide is out of the question. Then a murder has been done. What we have to determine is whether it was done by someone outside or inside the house.'

'Well, let's hear the argument.'

'There are considerable difficulties both ways, and yet one or the other it must be. We will suppose first that some person or persons inside the house did the crime. They got this man down here at a time when everything was still, and yet no one was asleep. They then did the deed with the queerest and noisiest weapon in the world, so as to tell everyone what had happened – a weapon that was never seen in the house before. That does not seem a very likely start, does it?'

'No, it does not.'

'Well, then, everyone is agreed that after the alarm was given only a minute at the most had passed before the whole household – not Mr Cecil Barker alone, though he claims to have been the first, but Ames and all of them – were on the spot. Do you tell me that in that time the guilty person managed to make footmarks in the corner, open the window, mark the sill with blood, take the wedding-ring off the dead man's finger, and all the rest of it? It's impossible!'

'You put it very clearly,' said Holmes. 'I am inclined to agree with you.'

'Well, then, we are driven back to the theory that it was done by someone from outside. We are still faced with some big difficulties, but, anyhow, they have ceased to be impossibilities. The man got into the house between four-thirty and six – that is to say, between dusk and the time when the bridge was raised. There had been some visitors, and the door was open, so there was nothing to prevent him. He may have been a common burglar, or he may have had some private grudge against Mr Douglas. Since Mr Douglas has spent most of his life in America, and this shot-gun seems to be an American weapon, it would seem that the private grudge is the more likely theory. He slipped into this room because it was the first he came to, and he hid behind the curtain. There he remained until past eleven at night. At that time Mr Douglas entered the room. It was a short interview, if there were any interview at all, for Mrs Douglas declares that her husband had not left her more than a few minutes when she heard the shot.'

'The candle shows that,' said Holmes.

'Exactly. The candle, which was a new one, is not burned more than half an inch. He must have placed it on the table before he was attacked, otherwise, of course, it would have fallen when he fell. This shows that he was not attacked the instant that he entered the room. When Mr Barker arrived the lamp was lit and the candle put out.'

'That's all clear enough.'

'Well, now, we can reconstruct things on those lines. Mr Douglas enters the room. He puts down the candle. A man appears from behind the curtain. He is armed with this gun. He demands the wedding-ring – Heaven only knows why, but so it must have been. Mr Douglas gave it up. Then either in cold blood or in the course of a struggle – Douglas may have gripped the hammer that was found upon the mat – he shot Douglas in this horrible way. He dropped his gun and also, it would seem, this queer card, "V.V. 341", whatever that may mean, and he made his escape through the window and across the moat at the very moment when Cecil Barker was discovering the crime. How's that, Mr Holmes?'

'Very interesting, but just a little unconvincing.'

'Man, it would be absolute nonsense if it wasn't that anything else is even worse,' cried MacDonald. 'Somebody killed the man, and whoever it was I could clearly prove to you that he should have done it some other way. What does he mean by allowing his retreat to be cut off like that? What does he mean by using a shot-gun when silence was his one chance of escape? Come, Mr Holmes, it's up to you to give us a lead, since you say Mr White Mason's theory is unconvincing.'

Holmes had sat intently observant during this long discussion, missing no word that was said, with his keen eyes darting to right and to left, and his forehead wrinkled with speculation.

'I should like a few more facts before I get so far as a theory, Mr Mac,' said he, kneeling down beside the body. 'Dear me! these injuries are really appalling. Can we have the butler in for a moment? . . . Ames, I understand that you have often seen this very unusual mark, a branded triangle inside a circle, upon Mr Douglas's forearm?'

'Frequently, sir.'

'You never heard any speculation as to what it meant?'

'No, sir.'

'It must have caused great pain when it was inflicted. It is undoubtedly a burn. Now, I observe, Ames, that there is a small piece of plaster at the angle of Mr Douglas's jaw. Did you observe that in life?'

'Yes, sir; he cut himself in shaving yesterday morning.'

'Did you ever know him cut himself in shaving before?'

'Not for a very long time, sir.'

'Suggestive!' said Holmes. 'It may, of course, be a mere coincidence, or it may point to some nervousness which would indicate that he had reason to apprehend danger. Had you noticed anything unusual in his conduct yesterday, Ames?'

'It struck me that he was a little restless and excited, sir.'

'Ha! The attack may not have been entirely unexpected. We do seem to make a little progress, do we not? Perhaps you would rather do the questioning, Mr Mac?'

'No, Mr Holmes; it's in better hands.'

'Well, then, we will pass to this card – "V.V. 341". It is rough cardboard. Have you any of the sort in the house?'

'I don't think so.'

Holmes walked across to the desk and dabbed a little ink from each bottle on to the blotting-paper. 'It has not been printed in this room,' he said; 'this is black ink, and the other purplish. It has been done by a thick pen, and these are fine. No, it has been done elsewhere, I should say. Can you make anything of the inscription, Ames?'

'No, sir, nothing.'

'What do you think, Mr Mac?'

'It gives me the impression of a secret society of some sort. The same with this badge upon the forearm.'

'That's my idea, too,' said White Mason.

'Well, we can adopt it as a working hypothesis, and then see how far our difficulties disappear. An agent from such a society makes his way into the house, waits for Mr Douglas, blows his head nearly off with this weapon, and escapes by wading the moat, after leaving a card beside the dead man which will, when mentioned in the papers, tell other members of the society that vengeance has been done. That all hangs together. But why this gun, of all weapons?'

'Exactly.'

'And why the missing ring?'

'Quite so.'

'And why no arrest? It's past two now. I take it for granted that since dawn every constable within forty miles has been looking out for a wet stranger?'

'That is so, Mr Holmes.'

'Well, unless he has a burrow close by, or a change of clothes ready, they can hardly miss him. And yet they *have* missed him up to now.' Holmes had gone to the window and was examining with his lens the blood-mark upon the sill. 'It is clearly the tread of a shoe. It is remarkably broad – a splay foot, one would say. Curious, because, so far as one can trace any footmark in this mud-stained corner, one would say it was a more shapely sole. However, they are certainly very indistinct. What's this under the side table?'

'Mr Douglas's dumb-bells,' said Ames.

'Dumb-bell – there's only one. Where's the other?'

'I don't know, Mr Holmes. There may have been only one. I have not noticed them for months.'

'One dumb-bell –' Holmes said, seriously, but his remarks were interrupted by a sharp knock at the door. A tall, sunburned, capable-looking, clean-shaven man looked in at us. I had no difficulty in guessing that it was the Cecil Barker of whom I had heard. His masterful eyes travelled quickly with a questioning glance from face to face.

'Sorry to interrupt your consultation,' said he, 'but you should hear the latest.'

'An arrest?'

'No such luck. But they've found his bicycle. The fellow left his bicycle behind him. Come and have a look. It is within a hundred yards of the hall door.'

We found three or four grooms and idlers standing in the drive inspecting a bicycle which had been drawn out from a clump of evergreens in which it had been concealed. It was a well-used Rudge-Whitworth, splashed as from a considerable journey. There was a saddle-bag with spanner and oil-can, but no clue as to the owner.

'It would be a grand help to the police,' said the inspector, 'if these things were numbered and registered. But we must be thankful for what we've got. If we can't find where he went to, at least we are likely to get where he came from. But what in the name of all that is wonderful made the fellow leave it behind? And how in the world has he got away without it? We don't seem to get a gleam of light in the case, Mr Holmes.'

'Don't we?' my friend answered, thoughtfully. 'I wonder!'

5

The People of the Drama

'Have you seen all you want of the study?' asked White Mason as we re-entered the house.

'For the time,' said the inspector; and Holmes nodded.

'Then perhaps you would now like to hear the evidence of some of the people in the house? We could use the dining-room, Ames. Please come yourself first and tell us what you know.'

The butler's account was a simple and a clear one, and he gave a convincing impression of sincerity. He had been engaged five years ago when Mr Douglas first came to Birlstone. He understood that Mr Douglas was a rich gentleman who had made his money in America. He had been a kind and considerate employer – not quite what Ames was used to, perhaps, but one can't have everything. He never saw any signs of apprehension in Mr Douglas – on the contrary, he was the most fearless man he had ever known. He ordered the drawbridge to be pulled up every night because it was the ancient custom of the old house, and he liked to keep the old ways up. Mr Douglas seldom went to London or left the village, but on the day before the crime he had been shopping at Tunbridge Wells. He, Ames, had observed some restlessness and excitement on the part of Mr Douglas upon that day, for he had seemed impatient and irritable, which was unusual with him. He had not gone to bed that night, but was in the pantry at the back of the house, putting away the silver, when he heard the bell ring violently. He heard no shot, but it was hardly possible he should, as the pantry and kitchens were at the very back of the house and there were several closed doors and a long passage between. The housekeeper had come out of her room, attracted by the violent ringing of the bell. They had gone to the front of the house together. As they reached the bottom of the stair he had seen Mrs Douglas coming down it. No, she was not hurrying – it did not seem to him that she was particularly agitated. Just as she reached the bottom of the stair Mr Barker had rushed out of the study. He had stopped Mrs Douglas and begged her to go back.

'For God's sake, go back to your room!' he cried. 'Poor Jack is dead. You can do nothing. For God's sake, go back!'

After some persuasion upon the stairs Mrs Douglas had gone back. She did not scream. She made no outcry whatever. Mrs Allen, the housekeeper, had taken her upstairs and stayed with her in the bedroom. Ames and Mr Barker had then returned to the study, where they had found everything exactly as the police had seen it. The candle was not lit at that time, but the lamp was burning. They had looked out of the window, but the night was very dark and nothing could be seen or heard. They had then rushed out into the hall, where Ames had turned the windlass which had lowered the drawbridge. Mr Barker had then hurried off to get the police.

Such, in its essentials, was the evidence of the butler.

The account of Mrs Allen, the housekeeper, was, so far as it went, a corroboration of that of her fellow-servant. The housekeeper's room was rather nearer to the front of the house than the pantry in which Ames had been working. She was preparing to go to bed when the loud ringing of the bell had attracted her attention. She was a little hard of hearing. Perhaps that was why she had not heard the sound of the shot, but in any case the study was a long way off. She remembered hearing some sound which she imagined to be the slamming of a door. That was a good deal earlier – half an hour at least before the ringing of the bell. When Mr Ames ran to the front she went with him. She saw Mr Barker, very pale and excited, come out of the study. He intercepted Mrs Douglas, who was coming down the stairs. He entreated her to go back, and she answered him, but what she said could not be heard.

'Take her up. Stay with her!' he had said to Mrs Allen.

She had therefore taken her to the bedroom and endeavoured to soothe her. She was greatly excited, trembling all over, but made no other attempt to go downstairs. She just sat in her dressing-gown by her bedroom fire with her head sunk in her hands. Mrs Allen stayed with her most of the night. As to the other servants, they had all gone to bed, and the alarm did not reach them until just before the police arrived. They slept at the extreme back of the house, and could not possibly have heard anything.

So far the housekeeper – who could add nothing on cross-examination save lamentations and expressions of amazement.

Mr Cecil Barker succeeded Mrs Allen as a witness. As to the occurrences of the night before, he had very little to add to what he had already told the police. Personally, he was convinced that the murderer had escaped by the window. The blood-stain was conclusive, in his opinion, upon that point. Besides, as the bridge was up there was no other possible way of escaping. He could not explain what had become of the assassin, or why he had not taken his bicycle, if it were indeed his. He could not possibly have been drowned in the moat, which was at no place more than three feet deep.

In his own mind he had a very definite theory about the murder. Douglas was a reticent man, and there were some chapters in his life of which he never spoke. He had emigrated to America from Ireland when he was a very young man. He had prospered well, and Barker had first met him in California, where they had become partners in a successful mining claim at a place called Benito Canyon. They had done very well, but Douglas had suddenly sold out and started for England. He was a widower at that time. Barker had afterwards realized his money and come to live in London. Thus they had renewed their friendship. Douglas had given him the impression that some danger was hanging over his head, and he had always looked upon his sudden departure from California, and also his renting a house in so quiet a place in England, as being connected with this peril. He imagined that some secret society, some implacable organization, was on Douglas's track which would never rest until it killed him. Some remarks of his had given him this idea, though he had never told him what the society was, nor how he had come to offend it. He could only suppose that the legend upon the placard had some reference to this secret society.

'How long were you with Douglas in California?' asked Inspector MacDonald.

'Five years altogether.'

'He was a bachelor, you say?'

'A widower.'

'Have you ever heard where his first wife came from?'

'No; I remember his saying that she was of Swedish extraction, and I have seen her portrait. She was a very beautiful woman. She died of typhoid the year before I met him.'

'You don't associate his past with any particular part of America?'

'I have heard him talk of Chicago. He knew that city well and had worked there. I have heard him talk of the coal and iron districts. He had travelled a good deal in his time.'

'Was he a politician? Had this secret society to do with politics?'

'No; he cared nothing about politics.'

'You have no reason to think it was criminal?'

'On the contrary, I never met a straighter man in my life.'

'Was there anything curious about his life in California?'

'He liked best to stay and to work at our claim in the mountains. He would never go where other men were if he could help it. That's why I first thought that someone was after him. Then when he left so suddenly for Europe I made sure that it was so. I believe that he had a warning of some sort. Within a week of his leaving half a dozen men were inquiring for him.'

'What sort of men?'

'Well, they were a mighty hard-looking crowd. They came up to the claim and wanted to know where he was. I told them that he was gone to Europe and that I did not know where to find him. They meant him no good – it was easy to see that.'

'Were these men Americans – Californians?'

'Well, I don't know about Californians. They were Americans all right. But they were not miners. I don't know what they were, and was very glad to see their backs.'

'That was six years ago?'

'Nearer seven.'

'And then you were together five years in California, so that this business dates back not less than eleven years at the least?'

'That is so.'

'It must be a very serious feud that would be kept up with such earnestness for as long as that. It would be no light thing that would give rise to it.'

'I think it shadowed his whole life. It was never quite out of his mind.'

'But if a man had a danger hanging over him, and knew what it was, don't you think he would turn to the police for protection?'

'Maybe it was some danger that he could not be protected against. There's one thing you should know. He always went about armed. His revolver was never out of his pocket. But, by bad luck, he was in his dressing-gown and had left it in the bedroom last night. Once the bridge was up I guess he thought he was safe.'

'I should like these dates a little clearer,' said MacDonald. 'It is quite six years since Douglas left California. You followed him next year, did you not?'

'That is so.'

'And he has been married for five years. You must have returned about the time of his marriage.'

'About a month before. I was his best man.'

'Did you know Mrs Douglas before her marriage?'

'No, I did not. I had been away from England for ten years.'

'But you have seen a good deal of her since?'

Barker looked sternly at the detective.

'I have seen a good deal of *him* since,' he answered. 'If I have seen her, it is because you cannot visit a man without knowing his wife. If you imagine there is any connection –'

'I imagine nothing, Mr Barker. I am bound to make every inquiry which can bear upon the case. But I mean no offence.'

'Some inquiries are offensive,' Barker answered, angrily.

'It's only the facts that we want. It is in your interest and everyone's interests that they should be cleared up. Did Mr Douglas entirely approve your friendship with his wife?'

Barker grew paler, and his great strong hands were clasped convulsively together.

'You have no right to ask such questions!' he cried. 'What has this to do with the matter you are investigating?'

'I must repeat the question.'

'Well, I refuse to answer.'

'You can refuse to answer, but you must be aware that your refusal is in itself an answer, for you would not refuse if you had not something to conceal.'

Barker stood for a moment, with his face set grimly and his strong black eyebrows drawn low in intense thought. Then he looked up with a smile.

'Well, I guess you gentlemen are only doing your clear duty, after all, and that I have no right to stand in the way of it. I'd only ask you not to worry Mrs Douglas over this matter, for she has enough upon her just now. I may tell you that poor Douglas had just one fault in the world, and that was his jealousy. He was fond of me – no man could be fonder of a friend. And he was devoted to his wife. He loved me to come here and was for ever sending for me. And yet if his wife and I talked together or there seemed any sympathy between us, a kind of wave of jealousy would pass over him and he would be off the handle and saying the wildest things in a moment. More than once I've sworn off coming for that reason, and then he would write me such penitent, imploring letters that I just had to. But you can take it from me, gentlemen, if it was my last word, that no man ever had a more loving, faithful wife – and I can say, also, no friend could be more loyal than I.'

It was spoken with fervour and feeling, and yet Inspector Mac-Donald could not dismiss the subject.

'You are aware,' said he, 'that the dead man's wedding-ring has been taken from his finger?'

'So it appears,' said Barker.

'What do you mean by "appears"? You know it as a fact.'

The man seemed confused and undecided.

'When I said "appears", I meant that it was conceivable that he had himself taken off the ring.'

'The mere fact that the ring should be absent, whoever may have removed it, would suggest to anyone's mind, would it not, that the marriage and the tragedy were connected?'

Barker shrugged his broad shoulders.

'I can't profess to say what it suggests,' he answered. 'But if you mean to hint that it could reflect in any way upon this lady's honour' – his eyes blazed for an instant, and then with an evident effort he got a grip upon his own emotions – 'well, you are on the wrong track, that's all.'

'I don't know that I've anything else to ask you at present,' said MacDonald, coldly.

'There was one small point,' remarked Sherlock Holmes. 'When you entered the room there was only a candle lighted upon the table, was there not?'

'Yes, that was so.'

'By its light you saw that some terrible incident had occurred?'

'Exactly.'

'You rang at once for help?'

'Yes.'

'And it arrived very speedily?'

'Within a minute or so.'

'And yet when they arrived they found that the candle was out and that the lamp had been lighted. That seems very remarkable.'

Again Barker showed some signs of indecision.

'I don't see that it was remarkable, Mr Holmes,' he answered, after a pause. 'The candle threw a very bad light. My first thought was to get a better one. The lamp was on the table, so I lit it.'

'And blew out the candle?'

'Exactly.'

Holmes asked no further question, and Barker, with a deliberate look from one to the other of us, which had, as it seemed to me, something of defiance in it, turned and left the room.

Inspector MacDonald had sent up a note to the effect that he would wait upon Mrs Douglas in her room, but she had replied that she would meet us in the dining-room. She entered now, a tall and beautiful woman of thirty, reserved and self-possessed to a remarkable degree, very different from the tragic and distracted figure that I had pictured. It is true that her face was pale and drawn, like that of one who has endured a great shock, but her manner was composed, and the finely-moulded hand which she rested upon the edge of the table was as steady as my own. Her sad, appealing eyes travelled from one to the other of us with a curiously inquisitive expression. That questioning gaze transformed itself suddenly into abrupt speech.

'Have you found out anything yet?' she asked.

Was it my imagination that there was an undertone of fear rather than of hope in the question?

'We have taken every possible step, Mrs Douglas,' said the inspector. 'You may rest assured that nothing will be neglected.'

'Spare no money,' she said, in a dead, even tone. 'It is my desire that every possible effort should be made.'

'Perhaps you can tell us something which may throw some light upon the matter.'

'I fear not, but all I know is at your service.'

'We have heard from Mr Cecil Barker that you did not actually see – that you were never in the room where the tragedy occurred?'

'No; he turned me back upon the stairs. He begged me to return to my room.'

'Quite so. You had heard the shot and you had at once come down.'

'I put on my dressing-gown and then came down.'

'How long was it after hearing the shot that you were stopped on the stair by Mr Barker?'

'It may have been a couple of minutes. It is so hard to reckon time at such a moment. He implored me not to go on. He assured me that I could do nothing. Then Mrs Allen, the housekeeper, led me upstairs again. It was all like some dreadful dream.'

'Can you give us any idea how long your husband had been downstairs before you heard the shot?'

'No, I cannot say. He went from his dressing-room and I did not hear him go. He did the round of the house every night, for he was nervous of fire. It is the only thing that I have ever known him nervous of.'

'That is just the point which I want to come to, Mrs Douglas. You have only known your husband in England, have you not?'

'Yes. We have been married five years.'

'Have you heard him speak of anything which occurred in America and which might bring some danger upon him?'

Mrs Douglas thought earnestly before she answered.

'Yes,' she said at last. 'I have always felt that there was a danger hanging over him. He refused to discuss it with me. It was not from want of confidence in me – there was the most complete love and confidence between us – but it was out of his desire to keep all alarm away from me. He thought I should brood over it if I knew all, and so he was silent.'

'How did you know it, then?'

Mrs Douglas's face lit with a quick smile.

'Can a husband ever carry about a secret all his life and a woman who loves him have no suspicion of it? I knew it in many ways. I knew it by his refusal to talk about some episodes in his American life. I knew it by certain precautions he took. I knew it by certain words he let fall. I knew it by the way he looked at unexpected strangers. I was perfectly certain that he had some powerful enemies, that he believed they were on his track and that he was always on his guard against them. I was so sure of it that for years I have been terrified if ever he came home later than was expected.'

'Might I ask,' said Holmes, 'what the words were which attracted your attention?'

' "The Valley of Fear," ' the lady answered. 'That was an expression he has used when I questioned him. "I have been in the Valley of Fear. I am not out of it yet."[1] "Are we never to get out of the Valley of Fear?" I have asked him, when I have seen him more serious than usual. "Sometimes I think that we never shall," he has answered.'

'Surely you asked him what he meant by the Valley of Fear?'

'I did; but his face would become very grave and he would shake his head. "It is bad enough that one of us should have been in its shadow," he said. "Please God it shall never fall upon you." It was some real valley in which he had lived and in which something terrible had occurred to him – of that I am certain – but I can tell you no more.'

'And he never mentioned any names?'

'Yes; he was delirious with fever once when he had his hunting accident three years ago. Then I remember that there was a name that came continually to his lips. He spoke it with anger and a sort of horror. McGinty was the name – Bodymaster[2] McGinty. I asked him, when he recovered, who Bodymaster McGinty was, and whose body he was master of. "Never of mine, thank God!" he answered, with a laugh, and that was all I could get from him. But there is a connection between Bodymaster McGinty and the Valley of Fear.'

'There is one other point,' said Inspector MacDonald. 'You met Mr Douglas in a boarding-house in London, did you not, and became engaged to him there? Was there any romance, anything secret or mysterious, about the wedding?'

'There was romance. There is always romance. There was nothing mysterious.'

'He had no rival?'

'No; I was quite free.'

'You have heard, no doubt, that his wedding-ring has been taken. Does that suggest anything to you? Suppose that some enemy of his old life had tracked him down and committed this crime, what possible reason could he have for taking his wedding-ring?'

For an instant I could have sworn that the faintest shadow of a smile flickered over the woman's lips.

'I really cannot tell,' she answered. 'It is certainly a most extraordinary thing.'

'Well, we will not detain you any longer, and we are sorry to have put you to this trouble at such a time,' said the inspector. 'There are some other points, no doubt, but we can refer to you as they arise.'

She rose, and I was again conscious of that quick, questioning glance with which she had just surveyed us: 'What impression has my evidence made upon you?' The question might as well have been spoken. Then, with a bow, she swept from the room.

'She's a beautiful woman – a very beautiful woman,' said Mac-Donald, thoughtfully, after the door had closed behind her. 'This man Barker has certainly been down here a good deal. He is a man who might be attractive to a woman. He admits that the dead man was jealous, and maybe he knew best himself what cause he had for jealousy. Then there's that wedding-ring. You can't get past that. The man who tears a wedding-ring off a dead man's – What do you say to it, Mr Holmes?'

My friend had sat with his head upon his hands, sunk in the deepest thought. Now he rose and rang the bell.

'Ames,' he said, when the butler entered, 'where is Mr Cecil Barker now?'

'I'll see, sir.'

He came back in a moment to say that Mr Barker was in the garden.

'Can you remember, Ames, what Mr Barker had upon his feet last night when you joined him in the study?'

'Yes, Mr Holmes. He had a pair of bedroom slippers. I brought him his boots when he went for the police.'

'Where are the slippers now?'

'They are still under the chair in the hall.'

'Very good, Ames. It is, of course, important for us to know which tracks may be Mr Barker's and which from outside.'

'Yes, sir. I may say that I noticed that the slippers were stained with blood – so, indeed, were my own.'

'That is natural enough, considering the condition of the room. Very good, Ames. We will ring if we want you.'

A few minutes later we were in the study. Holmes had brought with him the carpet slippers from the hall. As Ames had observed, the soles of both were dark with blood.

'Strange!' murmured Holmes, as he stood in the light of the window and examined them minutely. 'Very strange indeed!'

Stooping with one of his quick, feline pounces he placed the slipper upon the blood-mark on the sill. It exactly corresponded. He smiled in silence at his colleagues.

The inspector was transfigured with excitement. His native accent rattled like a stick upon railings.

'Man!' he cried, 'there's not a doubt of it! Barker has just marked the window himself. It's a good deal broader than any boot-mark. I mind that you said it was a splay foot, and here's the explanation. But what's the game, Mr Holmes – what's the game?'

'Aye, what's the game?' my friend repeated, thoughtfully.

White Mason chuckled and rubbed his fat hands together in his professional satisfaction.

'I said it was a snorter!' he cried. 'And a real snorter it is!'

6

A Dawning Light

The three detectives had many matters of detail into which to inquire, so I returned alone to our modest quarters at the village inn; but before doing so I took a stroll in the curious old-world garden which flanked the house. Rows of very ancient yew trees, cut into strange designs, girded it round. Inside was a beautiful stretch of lawn with an old sundial in the middle, the whole effect so soothing and restful that it was welcome to my somewhat jangled nerves. In that deeply peaceful atmosphere one could forget or remember only as some fantastic nightmare that darkened study with the sprawling, blood-stained figure upon the floor. And yet as I strolled round it and tried to steep my soul in its gentle balm, a strange incident occurred which brought me back to the tragedy and left a sinister impression on my mind.

I have said that a decoration of yew trees circled the garden. At the end which was farthest from the house they thickened into a continuous hedge. On the other side of this hedge, concealed from the eyes of anyone approaching from the direction of the house, there was a stone seat. As I approached the spot I was aware of voices, some remark in the deep tones of a man, answered by a little ripple of feminine laughter. An instant later I had come round the end of the hedge, and my eyes lit upon Mrs Douglas and the man Barker before they were aware of my presence. Her appearance gave me a shock. In the dining-room she had been demure and discreet. Now all pretence of grief had passed away from her. Her eyes shone with the joy of living, and her face still quivered with amusement at some remark of her companion. He sat forward, his hands clasped and his forearms on his knees, with an answering smile upon his bold, handsome face. In an instant – but it was just one instant too late – they resumed their solemn masks as my figure came into view. A hurried word or two passed between them, and then Barker rose and came towards me.

'Excuse me, sir,' said he, 'but am I addressing Dr Watson?'

I bowed with a coldness which showed, I dare say, very plainly the impression which had been produced upon my mind.

'We thought that it was probably you, as your friendship with Mr Sherlock Holmes is so well known. Would you mind coming over and speaking to Mrs Douglas for one instant?'

I followed him with a dour face. Very clearly I could see in my mind's eye that shattered figure upon the floor. Here within a few hours of the tragedy were his wife and his nearest friend laughing together behind a bush in the garden which had been his. I greeted the lady with reserve. I had grieved with her grief in the dining-room. Now I met her appealing gaze with an unresponsive eye.

'I fear you think me callous and hard-hearted?' said she.

I shrugged my shoulders.

'It is no business of mine,' said I.

'Perhaps some day you will do me justice. If you only realized –'

'There is no need why Dr Watson should realize,' said Barker, quickly. 'As he has himself said, it is no possible business of his.'

'Exactly,' said I, 'and so I will beg leave to resume my walk.'

'One moment, Dr Watson,' cried the woman, in a pleading voice. 'There is one question which you can answer with more authority than anyone else in the world, and it may make a very great difference to me. You know Mr Holmes and his relations with the police better than anyone else can do. Supposing that a matter were brought confidentially to his knowledge, is it absolutely necessary that he should pass it on to the detectives?'

'Yes, that's it,' said Barker, eagerly. 'Is he on his own or is he entirely in with them?'

'I really don't know that I should be justified in discussing such a point.'

'I beg – I implore that you will, Dr Watson, I assure you that you will be helping us – helping me greatly if you will guide us on that point.'

There was such a ring of sincerity in the woman's voice that for the instant I forgot all about her levity and was moved only to do her will.

'Mr Holmes is an independent investigator,' I said. 'He is his own master, and would act as his own judgement directed. At the same time he would naturally feel loyalty towards the officials who were working on the same case, and he would not conceal from them anything which would help them in bringing a criminal to justice. Beyond this I can say nothing, and I would refer you to Mr Holmes himself if you want fuller information.'

So saying I raised my hat and went upon my way, leaving them still seated behind that concealing hedge. I looked back as I rounded the far end of it, and saw that they were still talking very earnestly together, and, as they were gazing after me, it was clear that it was our interview that was the subject of their debate.

'I wish none of their confidences,' said Holmes, when I reported to him what had occurred. He had spent the whole afternoon at the Manor House in consultation with his two colleagues, and returned about five with a ravenous appetite for a high tea which I had ordered for him. 'No confidences, Watson, for they are mighty awkward if it comes to an arrest for conspiracy and murder.'

'You think it will come to that?'

He was in his most cheerful and *débonnaire* humour.

'My dear Watson, when I have exterminated that fourth egg I will be ready to put you in touch with the whole situation. I don't say that we have fathomed it – far from it – but when we have traced the missing dumb-bell –'

'The dumb-bell!'

'Dear me, Watson, is it possible that you have not penetrated the fact that the case hangs upon the missing dumb-bell? Well, well, you need not be downcast, for, between ourselves, I don't think that either Inspector Mac or the excellent local practitioner has grasped the overwhelming importance of this incident. One dumb-bell, Watson! Consider an athlete with one dumb-bell. Picture to yourself the unilateral development – the imminent danger of a spinal curvature. Shocking, Watson; shocking!'

He sat with his mouth full of toast and his eyes sparkling with mischief, watching my intellectual entanglement. The mere sight of his excellent appetite was an assurance of success, for I had very clear recollections of days and nights without a thought of food, when his baffled mind had chafed before some problem whilst his thin, eager features became more attenuated with the asceticism of complete mental concentration. Finally he lit his pipe and, sitting in the ingle-nook of the old village inn, he talked slowly and at random about his case, rather as one thinks aloud than as one who makes a considered statement.

'A lie, Watson – a great big, thumping, obtrusive, uncompromising lie – that's what meets us on the threshold. There is our starting point. The whole story told by Barker is a lie. But Barker's story is corroborated by Mrs Douglas. Therefore she is lying also. They are both lying and in a conspiracy. So now we have the clear problem – why are they lying, and what is the truth which they are trying so hard to conceal? Let us try, Watson, you and I, if we can get behind the lie and reconstruct the truth.

'How do I know that they are lying? Because it is a clumsy fabrication which simply *could* not be true. Consider! According to the story given to us the assassin had less than a minute after the murder had been committed to take that ring, which was under another ring, from the dead man's finger, to replace the other ring – a thing which he would surely never have done – and to put that singular card beside his victim. I say that this was obviously impossible. You may argue – but I have too much respect for your judgement, Watson, to think that you will do so – that the ring may have been taken before the man was killed. The fact that the candle had only been lit a short time shows that there had been no lengthy interview. Was Douglas, from what we hear of his fearless character, a man who would be likely to give up his wedding-ring at such short notice, or could we conceive of his giving it up at all? No, no, Watson, the assassin was alone with the dead man for some time with the lamp lit. Of that I have no doubt at all. But the gunshot was apparently the cause of death. Therefore the gunshot must have been fired some time earlier than we are told. But there could be no mistake about such a matter as that. We are in the presence, therefore, of a deliberate conspiracy upon the part of the two people who heard the gunshot – of the man Barker and of the woman Douglas. When on the top of this I am able to show that the bloodmark upon the windowsill was deliberately placed there by

Barker in order to give a false clue to the police, you will admit that the case grows dark against him.

'Now we have to ask ourselves at what hour the murder actually did occur. Up to half-past ten the servants were moving about the house, so it was certainly not before that time. At a quarter to eleven they had all gone to their rooms with the exception of Ames, who was in the pantry. I have been trying some experiments after you left us this afternoon, and I find that no noise which MacDonald can make in the study can penetrate to me in the pantry when the doors are all shut. It is otherwise, however, from the housekeeper's room. It is not so far down the corridor, and from it I could vaguely hear a voice when it was very loudly raised. The sound from a shot-gun is to some extent muffled when the discharge is at very close range, as it undoubtedly was in this instance. It would not be very loud, and yet in the silence of the night it should have easily penetrated to Mrs Allen's room. She is, as she has told us, somewhat deaf, but none the less she mentioned in her evidence that she did hear something like a door slamming half an hour before the alarm was given. Half an hour before the alarm was given would be a quarter to eleven. I have no doubt that what she heard was the report of the gun, and that this was the real instant of the murder. If this is so, we have now to determine what Mr Barker and Mrs Douglas, presuming that they are not the actual murderers, could have been doing from a quarter to eleven, when the sound of the gun-shot brought them down, until a quarter past eleven, when they rang the bell and summoned the servants. What were they doing, and why did they not instantly give the alarm? That is the question which faces us, and when it has been answered we will surely have gone some way to solve our problem.'

'I am convinced myself,' said I, 'that there is an understanding between those two people. She must be a heartless creature to sit laughing at some jest within a few hours of her husband's murder.'

'Exactly. She does not shine as a wife even in her own account of what occurred. I am not a whole-souled admirer of womankind, as you are aware, Watson, but my experience of life has taught me that there are few wives having any regard for their husbands who would let any man's spoken word stand between them and that husband's dead body. Should I ever marry, Watson, I should hope to inspire my wife with some feeling which would prevent her from being walked off by a housekeeper when my corpse was lying within a few yards of her. It was badly stage-managed, for even the rawest of investigators must be struck by the absence of the usual feminine ululation. If there had been nothing else, this incident alone would have suggested a pre-arranged conspiracy to my mind.'

'You think, then, definitely, that Barker and Mrs Douglas are guilty of the murder?'

'There is an appalling directness about your questions, Watson,' said Holmes, shaking his pipe at me. 'They come at me like bullets. If you put it that Mrs Douglas and Barker know the truth about the murder and are conspiring to conceal it, then I can give you a whole-souled answer. I am sure they do. But your more deadly proposition is not so clear. Let us for a moment consider the difficulties which stand in the way.'

'We will suppose that this couple are united by the bonds of a guilty love and that they have determined to get rid of the man who stands between them. It is a large supposition, for discreet inquiry among servants and others has failed to corroborate it in any way. On the contrary, there is a good deal of evidence that the Douglases were very attached to each other.'

'That I am sure cannot be true,' said I, thinking of the beautiful, smiling face in the garden.

'Well, at least they gave that impression. However, we will suppose that they are an extraordinarily astute couple, who deceive everyone upon this point and who conspire to murder the husband. He happens to be a man over whose head some danger hangs –'

'We have only their word for that.'

Holmes looked thoughtful.

'I see, Watson. You are sketching out a theory by which everything they say from the beginning is false. According to your idea, there was never any hidden menace or secret society or Valley of Fear or Boss MacSomebody or anything else. Well, that is a good, sweeping generalization. Let us see what that brings us to. They invent this theory to account for the crime. They then play up to the idea by leaving this bicycle in the park as a proof of the existence of some outsider. The stain on the window-sill conveys the same idea. So does the card upon the body, which might have been prepared in the house. That all fits into your hypothesis, Watson. But now we come on the nasty angular, uncompromising bits which won't slip into their places. Why a cut-off shot-gun of all weapons – and an American one at that? How could they be so sure that the sound of it would not bring someone on to them? It's a mere chance, as it is, that Mrs Allen did not start out to inquire for the slamming door. Why did your guilty couple do all this, Watson?'

'I confess that I can't explain it.'

'Then, again, if a woman and her lover conspire to murder a husband, are they going to advertise their guilt by ostentatiously removing his wedding-ring after his death? Does that strike you as very probable, Watson?'

'No, it does not.'

'And once again, if the thought of leaving a bicycle concealed outside had occurred to you, would it really have seemed worth doing when the dullest detective would naturally say this is an obvious blind, as the bicycle is the first thing which the fugitive needed in order to make his escape?'

'I can conceive of no explanation.'

'And yet there should be no combination of events for which the wit of man cannot conceive an explanation. Simply as a mental exercise, without any assertion that it is true, let me indicate a possible line of thought. It is, I admit, mere imagination, but how often is imagination the mother of truth?

'We will suppose that there *was* a guilty secret, a really shameful secret, in the life of this man Douglas. This leads to his murder by someone who is, we will suppose, an avenger – someone from outside. This avenger, for some reason which I confess I am still at a loss to explain, took the dead man's wedding-ring. The vendetta might conceivably date back to the man's first marriage and the ring be taken for some such reason. Before this avenger got away Barker and the wife had reached the room. The assassin convinced them that any attempt to arrest him would lead to the publication of some hideous scandal. They were converted to this idea and preferred to let him go. For this purpose they probably lowered the bridge, which can be done quite noiselessly, and then raised it again. He made his escape, and for some reason thought that he could do so more safely on foot than on the bicycle. He therefore left his machine where it would not be discovered until he had got safely away. So far we are within the bounds of possibility, are we not?'

'Well, it is possible, no doubt,' said I, with some reserve.

'We have to remember, Watson, that whatever occurred is certainly something very extraordinary. Well now, to continue our suppositious case, the couple – not necessarily a guilty couple – realize after the murderer is gone that they have placed themselves in a position in which it may be difficult for them to prove that they did not themselves either do the deed or connive at it. They rapidly and rather clumsily meet the situation. The mark was put by Barker's bloodstained slipper upon the window-sill to suggest how the fugitive got away. They obviously were the two who must have heard the sound of the gun, so they gave the alarm exactly as they would have done, but a good half-hour after the event.'

'And how do you propose to prove all this?'

'Well, if there were an outsider he may be traced and taken. That would be the most effective of all proofs. But if not – well, the resources of science are far from being exhausted. I think that an evening alone in that study would help me much.'

'An evening alone!'

'I propose to go up there presently. I have arranged it with the estimable Ames, who is by no means wholehearted about Barker. I shall sit in that room and see if its atmosphere brings me inspiration. I'm a believer in the *genius loci*.[1] You smile, friend Watson. Well, we shall see. By the way, you have that big umbrella of yours, have you not?'

'It is here.'

'Well, I'll borrow that, if I may.'

'Certainly, but what a wretched weapon! If there is danger –'

'Nothing serious, my dear Watson, or I should certainly ask for your assistance. But I'll take the umbrella. At present I am only awaiting the return of our colleagues from Tunbridge Wells, where they are at present engaged in trying for a likely owner to the bicycle.'

It was nightfall before Inspector MacDonald and White Mason came back from their expedition, and they arrived exultant, reporting a great advance in our investigation.

'Man, I'll admeet that I had my doubts if there was ever an outsider,' said MacDonald, 'but that's all past now. We've had the bicycle identified, and we have a description of our man, so that's a long step on our journey.'

'It sounds to me like the beginning of the end,' said Holmes; 'I'm sure I congratulate you both with all my heart.'

'Well, I started from the fact that Mr Douglas had seemed disturbed since the day before, when he had been at Tunbridge Wells. It was at Tunbridge Wells, then, that he had become conscious of some danger. It was clear, therefore, that if a man had come over with a bicycle it was from Tunbridge Wells that he might be expected to have come. We took the bicycle over with us and showed it at the hotels. It was identified at once by the manager of the Eagle Commercial as belonging to a man named Hargrave who had taken a room there two days before. This bicycle and a small valise were his whole belongings. He had registered his name as coming from London, but had given no address. The valise was London-made and the contents were British, but the man himself was undoubtedly an American.'

'Well, well,' said Holmes, gleefully, 'you have indeed done some solid work whilst I have been sitting spinning theories with my friend. It's a lesson in being practical, Mr Mac.'

'Aye, it's just that, Mr Holmes,' said the inspector with satisfaction.

'But this may all fit in with your theories,' I remarked.

'That may or may not be. But let us hear the end, Mr Mac. Was there nothing to identify this man?'

'So little that it was evident he had carefully guarded himself against identification. There were no papers or letters and no marking upon the clothes. A cycle-map of the county lay upon his bedroom table. He had left the hotel after breakfast yesterday morning upon his bicycle, and no more was heard of him until our inquiries.'

'That's what puzzles me, Mr Holmes,' said White Mason. 'If the fellow did not want the hue and cry raised over him, one would imagine that he would have returned and remained at the hotel as an inoffensive tourist. As it is, he must know that he will be reported to the police by the hotel manager, and that his disappearance will be connected with the murder.'

'So one would imagine. Still he has been justified of his wisdom up to date at any rate, since he has not been taken. But his description – what of that?'

MacDonald referred to his notebook.

'Here we have it so far as they could give it. They don't seem to have taken any very particular stock of him, but still the porter, the clerk, and the chambermaid are all agreed that this about covers the points. He was a man about five foot nine in height, fifty or so years of age, his hair slightly grizzled, a greyish moustache, a curved nose and a face which all of them described as fierce and forbidding.'

'Well, bar the expression, that might almost be a description of Douglas himself,' said Holmes. 'He is just over fifty, with grizzled hair and moustache and about the same height. Did you get anything else?'

'He was dressed in a heavy grey suit with a reefer jacket, and he wore a short yellow overcoat and a soft cap.'

'What about the shot-gun?'

'It is less than two feet long. It could very well have fitted into his valise. He could have carried it inside his overcoat without difficulty.'

'And how do you consider that all this bears upon the general case?'

'Well, Mr Holmes,' said MacDonald, 'when we have got our man – and you may be sure that I had his description on the wires within five minutes of hearing it – we shall be able to judge. But even as it stands, we have surely gone a long way. We know that an American calling himself Hargrave came to Tunbridge Wells two days ago with bicycle and valise. In the latter was a sawn-off shot-gun, so he came with the deliberate purpose of crime. Yesterday morning he set off for this place upon his bicycle with his gun concealed in his overcoat. No one saw him arrive, so far as we can learn, but he need not pass through the village to reach the park gates, and there are many cyclists upon the road. Presumably he at once concealed his cycle among the laurels, where it was found, and possibly lurked there himself, with his eye on the house waiting for Mr Douglas to come out. The shot-gun is a strange weapon to use inside a house, but he had intended to use it outside, and then it has very obvious advantages, as it would be impossible to miss with it, and the sound of shots is so common in an English sporting neighbourhood that no particular notice would be taken.'

'That is all very clear!' said Holmes.

'Well, Mr Douglas did not appear. What was he to do next? He left his bicycle and approached the house in the twilight. He found the bridge down and no one about. He took his chance, intending, no doubt, to make some excuse if he met anyone. He met no one. He slipped into the first room that he saw and concealed himself behind the curtain. From thence he could see the drawbridge go up and he knew that his only escape was through the moat. He waited until a quarter past eleven, when Mr Douglas, upon his usual nightly round, came into the room. He shot him and escaped, as arranged. He was aware that the bicycle would be described by the hotel people and be a clue against him, so he left it there and made his way by some other means to London or to some safe hiding-place which he had already arranged. How is that, Mr Holmes.'

'Well, Mr Mac, it is very good and very clear so far as it goes. That is your end of the story. My end is that the crime was committed half an hour earlier than reported; that Mrs Douglas and Mr Barker are both in a conspiracy to conceal something; that they aided the murderer's escape – or at least, that they reached the room before he escaped – and that they fabricated evidence of his escape through the window, whereas in all probability they had themselves let him go by lowering the bridge. That's *my* reading of the first half.'

The two detectives shook their heads.

'Well, Mr Holmes, if this is true we only tumble out of one mystery into another,' said the London inspector.

'And in some ways a worse one,' added White Mason. 'The lady has never been in America in her life. What possible connection could she have with an American assassin which would cause her to shelter him?'

'I freely admit the difficulties,' said Holmes. 'I propose to make a little investigation of my own tonight, and it is just possible that it may contribute something to the common cause.'

'Can we help you, Mr Holmes?'

'No, no! Darkness and Dr Watson's umbrella. My wants are simple. And Ames – the faithful Ames – no doubt he will stretch a point for me. All my lines of thought lead me back invariably to the one basic question – why should an athletic man develop his frame upon so unnatural an instrument as a single dumb-bell?'

It was late that night when Holmes returned from his solitary excursion. We slept in a double-bedded room, which was the best that the little country inn could do for us. I was already asleep when I was partly awakened by his entrance.

'Well, Holmes,' I murmured, 'have you found out anything?'

He stood beside me in silence, his candle in his hand. Then the tall lean figure inclined towards me.

'I say, Watson,' he whispered, 'would you be afraid to sleep in the same room as a lunatic, a man with softening of the brain, an idiot whose mind has lost its grip?'

'Not in the least,' I answered in astonishment.

'Ah, that's lucky,' he said, and not another word would he utter that night.

7

The Solution

Next morning, after breakfast, we found Inspector MacDonald and Mr White Mason seated in close consultation in the small parlour of the local police-sergeant. Upon the table in front of them were piled a number of letters and telegrams, which they were carefully sorting and docketing. Three had been placed upon one side.

'Still on the track of the elusive bicyclist?' Holmes asked, cheerfully. 'What is the latest news of the ruffian?'

MacDonald pointed ruefully to his heap of correspondence.

'He is at present reported from Leicester, Nottingham, South-ampton, Derby, East Ham,[1] Richmond, and fourteen other places. In three of them – East Ham, Leicester, and Liverpool – there is a clear case against him and he has actually been arrested. The country seems to be full of fugitives with yellow coats.'

'Dear me!' said Holmes, sympathetically. 'Now, Mr Mac, and you, Mr White Mason, I wish to give you a very earnest piece of advice. When I went into this case with you I bargained, as you will no doubt remember, that I should not present you with half-proved theories, but that I should retain and work out my own ideas until I had satisfied myself that they were correct. For this reason I am not at the present moment telling you all that is in my mind. On the other hand, I said that I would play the game fairly by you, and I do not think it is a fair game to allow you for one unnecessary moment to waste your energies upon a profitless task. Therefore I am here to advise you this morning, and my advice to you is summed up in three words: Abandon the case.'

MacDonald and White Mason stared in amazement at their celebrated colleague.

'You consider it hopeless?' cried the inspector.

'I consider *your* case to be hopeless. I do not consider that it is hopeless to arrive at the truth.'

'But this cyclist. He is not an invention. We have his description, his valise, his bicycle. The fellow must be somewhere. Why should we not get him?'

'Yes, yes; no doubt he is somewhere, and no doubt we shall get him, but I would not have you waste your energies in East Ham or Liverpool. I am sure that we can find some shorter cut to a result.'

'You are holding something back. It's hardly fair of you, Mr Holmes.' The inspector was annoyed.

'You know my methods of work, Mr Mac. But I will hold it back for the shortest time possible. I only wish to verify my details in one way, which can very readily be done, and then I make my bow and return to London, leaving my results entirely at your service. I owe you too much to act otherwise, for in all my experience I cannot recall any more singular and interesting study.'

'This is clean beyond me, Mr Holmes. We saw you when we returned from Tunbridge Wells last night, and you were in general agreement with our results. What has happened since then to give you a completely new idea of the case?'

'Well, since you ask me, I spent as I told you that I would, some hours last night at the Manor House.'

'Well, what happened?'

'Ah! I can only give you a very general answer to that for the moment. By the way, I have been reading a short, but clear and interesting, account of the old building, purchasable at the modest sum of one penny from the local tobacconist.' Here Holmes drew a small tract, embellished with a rude engraving of the ancient Manor House, from his waistcoat pocket. 'It immensely adds to the zest of an investigation, my dear Mr Mac, when one is in conscious sympathy with the historical atmosphere of one's surroundings. Don't look so impatient, for I assure you that even so bald an account as this raises some sort of picture of the past in one's mind. Permit me to give you a sample. "Erected in the fifth year of the reign of James I,[2] and standing upon the site of a much older building, the Manor House of Birlstone presents one of the finest surviving examples of the moated Jacobean residence —"'

'You are making fools of us, Mr Holmes.'

'Tut, tut, Mr Mac! – the first sign of temper I have detected in you. Well, I won't read it verbatim, since you feel so strongly upon the subject. But when I tell you that there is some account of the taking of the place by a Parliamentary colonel in 1644, of the concealment of Charles for several days in the course of the Civil War, and finally of a visit there by the second George,[3] you will admit that there are various associations of interest connected with this ancient house.'

'I don't doubt it, Mr Holmes, but that is no business of ours.'

'Is it not? Is it not? Breadth of view, my dear Mr Mac, is one of the essentials of our profession. The interplay of ideas and the oblique uses of knowledge are often of extraordinary interest. You will excuse these remarks from one who, though a mere connoisseur of crime, is still rather older and perhaps more experienced than yourself.'

'I'm the first to admit that,' said the detective, heartily. 'You get to your point, I admit, but you have such a deuced round-the-corner way of doing it.'

'Well, well, I'll drop past history and get down to present-day facts. I called last night, as I have already said, at the Manor House. I did not see either Mr Barker or Mrs Douglas. I saw no necessity to disturb them, but I was pleased to hear that the lady was not visibly pining and that she had partaken of an excellent dinner. My visit was specially made to the good Mr Ames, with whom I exchanged some amiabilities which culminated in his allowing me, without reference to anyone else, to sit alone for a time in the study.'

'What! With that!' I ejaculated.

'No, no; everything is now in order. You gave permission for that, Mr Mac, as I am informed. The room was in its normal state, and in it I passed an instructive quarter of an hour.'

'What were you doing?'

'Well, not to make a mystery of so simple a matter, I was looking for the missing dumb-bell. It has always bulked rather large in my estimate of the case. I ended by finding it.'

'Where?'

'Ah! There we come to the edge of the unexplored. Let me go a little farther, a very little farther, and I will promise that you shall share everything that I know.'

'Well, we're bound to take you on your own terms,' said the inspector; 'but when it comes to telling us to abandon the case – Why, in the name of goodness, should we abandon the case?'

'For the simple reason, my dear Mr Mac, that you have not got the first idea what it is that you are investigating.'

'We are investigating the murder of Mr John Douglas, of Birlstone Manor.'

'Yes, yes; so you are. But don't trouble to trace the mysterious gentleman upon the bicycle. I assure you that it won't help you.'

'Then what do you suggest that we do?'

'I will tell you exactly what to do, if you will do it.'

'Well, I'm bound to say I've always found you had reason behind all your queer ways. I'll do what you advise.'

'And you, Mr White Mason?'

The country detective looked helplessly from one to the other. Mr Holmes and his methods were new to him.

'Well, if it is good enough for the inspector it is good enough for me,' he said, at last.

'Capital!' said Holmes. 'Well, then, I should recommend a nice, cheery, country walk for both of you. They tell me that the views from Birlstone Ridge over the Weald are very remarkable. No doubt lunch could be got at some suitable hostelry, though my ignorance of the country prevents me from recommending one. In the evening, tired but happy —'

'Man, this is getting past a joke!' cried MacDonald, rising angrily from his chair.

'Well, well, spend the day as you like,' said Holmes, patting him cheerfully on the shoulder. 'Do what you like and go where you will, but meet me here before dusk without fail — without fail, Mr Mac.'

'That sounds more like sanity.'

'All of it was excellent advice, but I don't insist, so long as you are here when I need you. But now, before we part, I want you to write a note to Mr Barker.'

'Well?'

'I'll dictate it, if you like. Ready?

' "Dear sir, — It has struck me that it is our duty to drain the moat, in the hope that we may find some —" '

'It's impossible,' said the inspector; 'I've made inquiry.'

'Tut, tut, my dear sir! Do, please, do what I ask you.'

'Well, go on.'

' " — in the hope that we may find something which may bear upon our investigation. I have made arrangements, and the workmen will be at work early tomorrow morning diverting the stream —" '

'Impossible!'

' " — diverting the stream, so I thought it best to explain matters beforehand." Now sign that, and send it by hand about four o'clock. At that hour we shall meet again in this room. Until then we can each do what we like, for I can assure you that this inquiry has come to a definite pause.'

Evening was drawing in when we reassembled. Holmes was very serious in his manner, myself curious, and the detectives obviously critical and annoyed.

'Well, gentlemen,' said my friend, gravely, 'I am asking you now to put everything to the test with me, and you will judge for yourselves whether the observations which I have made justify the conclusions to which I have come. It is a chill evening, and I do not know how long our expedition may last, so I beg that you will wear your warmest coats. It is of the first importance that we should be in our places before it grows dark, so, with your permission, we will get started at once.'

We passed along the outer bounds of the Manor House park until we came to a place where there was a gap in the rails which fenced it. Through this we slipped, and then, in the gathering gloom, we followed Holmes until we had reached a shrubbery which lies nearly opposite to the main door and the drawbridge. The latter had not been raised. Holmes crouched down behind the screen of laurels, and we all three followed his example.

'Well, what are we to do now?' asked MacDonald, with some gruffness.

'Possess our souls in patience and make as little noise as possible,'[4] Holmes answered.

'What are we here for at all? I really think that you might treat us with more frankness.'

Holmes laughed.

'Watson insists that I am the dramatist in real life,' said he. 'Some touch of the artist wells up within me and calls insistently for a well-staged performance. Surely our profession, Mr Mac, would be a drab and sordid one if we did not sometimes set the scene so as to glorify our results. The blunt accusation, the brutal tap upon the shoulder – what can one make of such a *dénouement*?[5] But the quick inference, the subtle trap, the clever forecast of coming events, the triumphant vindication of bold theories – are these not the pride and the justification of our life's work? At the present moment you thrill with the glamour of the situation and the anticipation of the hunter. Where would be that thrill if I had been as definite as a time-table? I only ask a little patience, Mr Mac, and all will be clear to you.'

'Well, I hope the pride and justification and the rest of it will come before we all get our death of cold,' said the London detective, with comic resignation.

We all had good reason to join in the aspiration, for our vigil was a long and bitter one. Slowly the shadows darkened over the long sombre face of the old house. A cold, damp reek from the moat chilled us to the bones and set our teeth chattering. There was a single lamp over the gateway and a steady globe of light in the fatal study. Everything else was dark and still.

'How long is this to last?' asked the inspector, suddenly. 'And what is it we are watching for?'

'I have no more notion than you how long it is to last,' Holmes answered with some asperity. 'If criminals would always schedule their movements like railway trains it would certainly be more convenient for all of us. As to what it is we – Well, *that's* what we are watching for.'

As he spoke the bright yellow light in the study was obscured by somebody passing to and fro before it. The laurels among which we lay were immediately opposite the window and not more than a hundred feet from it. Presently it was thrown open with a whining of hinges, and we could dimly see the dark outline of a man's head and shoulders looking out into the gloom. For some minutes he peered forth, in a furtive, stealthy fashion, as one who wishes to be assured that he is unobserved. Then he leaned forward, and in the intense silence we were aware of the soft lapping of agitated water. He seemed to be stirring up the moat with something which he held in his hand. Then suddenly he hauled something in as a fisherman lands a fish – some large, round object which obscured the light as it was dragged through the open casement.

'Now!' cried Holmes. 'Now!'

We were all upon our feet, staggering after him with our stiffened limbs, whilst he, with one of those outflames of nervous energy which could make him on occasion both the most active and the strongest man that I have ever known, ran swiftly across the bridge and rang violently at the bell. There was the rasping of bolts from the other side, and the amazed Ames stood in the entrance. Holmes brushed him aside without a word and, followed by all of us, rushed into the room which had been occupied by the man whom we had been watching.

The oil lamp on the table represented the glow which we had seen from outside. It was now in the hand of Cecil Barker, who held it towards us as we entered. Its light shone upon his strong, resolute, clean-shaven face and his menacing eyes.

'What the devil is the meaning of all this?' he cried. 'What are you after, anyhow?'

Holmes took a swift glance round and then pounced upon a sodden bundle tied together with cord which lay where it had been thrust under the writing-table.

'This is what we are after, Mr Barker. This bundle, weighted with a dumb-bell, which you have just raised from the bottom of the moat.'

Barker stared at Holmes with amazement in his face.

'How in thunder came you to know anything about it?' he asked.

'Simply that I put it there.'

'You put it there! You!'

'Perhaps I should have said "replaced it there",' said Holmes. 'You will remember, Inspector MacDonald, that I was somewhat struck by the absence of a dumb-bell. I drew your attention to it, but with the pressure of other events you had hardly the time to give it the consideration which would have enabled you to draw deductions from it. When water is near and a weight is missing it is not a very far-fetched supposition that something has been sunk in the water. The idea was at least worth testing, so with the help of Ames, who admitted me to the room, and the crook of Dr Watson's umbrella, I was able last night to fish up and inspect this bundle. It was of the first importance, however, that we should be able to prove who placed it there. This we accomplished by the very obvious device of announcing that the moat would be dried tomorrow, which had, of course, the effect that whoever had hidden the bundle would most certainly withdraw it the moment that darkness enabled him to do so. We have no fewer than four witnesses as to who it was who took advantage of the opportunity, and so, Mr Barker, I think the word lies now with you.'

Sherlock Holmes put the sopping bundle upon the table beside the lamp and undid the cord which bound it. From within he extracted a dumb-bell, which he tossed down to its fellow in the corner. Next he drew forth a pair of boots. 'American, as you perceive,' he remarked, pointing to the toes. Then he laid upon the table a long, deadly, sheathed knife. Finally he unravelled a bundle of clothing, comprising a complete set of underclothes, socks, a grey tweed suit, and a short yellow overcoat.

'The clothes are commonplace,' remarked Holmes, 'save only the overcoat, which is full of suggestive touches.' He held it tenderly towards the light, whilst his long, thin fingers flickered over it. 'Here, as you perceive, is the inner pocket prolonged into the lining in such a fashion as to give ample space for the truncated fowling-piece. The tailor's tab is on the neck – Neale, Outfitter, Vermissa,[6] U.S.A. I have spent an instructive afternoon in the rector's library, and have enlarged my knowledge by adding the fact that Vermissa is a flourishing little town at the head of one of the best-known coal and iron valleys in the United States. I have some recollection, Mr Barker, that you associated the coal districts with Mr Douglas's first wife, and it would surely not be too far-fetched an inference that the V.V. upon the card by the dead body might stand for Vermissa Valley, or that this very valley, which sends forth emissaries of murder, may be that Valley of Fear of which we have heard. So much is fairly clear. And now, Mr Barker, I seem to be standing rather in the way of your explanation.'

It was a sight to see Cecil Barker's expressive face during this exposition of the great detective. Anger, amazement, consternation, and indecision swept over it in turn. Finally he took refuge in a somewhat acid irony.

'You know such a lot, Mr Holmes, perhaps you had better tell us some more,' he sneered.

'I have no doubt that I could tell you a great deal more, Mr Barker, but it would come with a better grace from you.'

'Oh, you think so, do you? Well, all I can say is that if there's any secret here it is not my secret, and I am not the man to give it away.'

'Well, if you take that line, Mr Barker,' said the inspector, quietly, 'we must just keep you in sight until we have the warrant and can hold you.'

'You can do what you damn well please about that,' said Barker, defiantly.

The proceedings seemed to have come to a definite end so far as he was concerned, for one had only to look at that granite face to realize that no *peine forte et dure*[7] would ever force him to plead against his will. The deadlock was broken, however, by a woman's voice. Mrs Douglas had been standing listening at the half-opened door, and now she entered the room.

'You have done enough for us, Cecil,' said she. 'Whatever comes of it in the future, you have done enough.'

'Enough and more than enough,' remarked Sherlock Holmes, gravely. 'I have every sympathy with you, madam, and I should strongly urge you to have some confidence in the common sense of our jurisdiction and to take the police voluntarily into your complete confidence. It may be that I am myself at fault for not following up the hint which you conveyed to me through my friend, Dr Watson, but at that time I had every reason to believe that you were directly concerned in the crime. Now I am assured that this is not so. At the same time, there is much that is unexplained, and I should strongly recommend that you ask *Mr Douglas* to tell us his own story.'

Mrs Douglas gave a cry of astonishment at Holmes's words. The detectives and I must have echoed it, when we were aware of a man who seemed to have emerged from the wall, and who advanced now from the gloom of the corner in which he had appeared. Mrs Douglas turned, and in an instant her arms were round him. Barker had seized his outstretched hand.

'It's best this way, Jack,' his wife repeated. 'I am sure that it is best.'

'Indeed, yes, Mr Douglas,' said Sherlock Holmes. 'I am sure that you will find it best.'

The man stood blinking at us with the dazed look of one who comes from the dark into the light. It was a remarkable face – bold grey eyes, a strong, short-clipped, grizzled moustache, a square, projecting chin, and a humorous mouth. He took a good look at us

all, and then, to my amazement, he advanced to me and handed me
a bundle of paper.

'I've heard of you,' said he, in a voice which was not quite English
and not quite American, but was altogether mellow and pleasing.
'You are the historian of this bunch. Well, Dr Watson, you've never
had such a story as that pass through your hands before, and I'd lay
my last dollar on that. Tell it your own way, but there are the facts,
and you can't miss the public so long as you have those. I've been
cooped up two days, and I've spent the daylight hours – as much
daylight as I could get in that rat-trap – in putting the thing into words.
You're welcome to them – you and your public. There's the story of
the Valley of Fear.'

'That's the past, Mr Douglas,' said Sherlock Holmes, quietly. 'What
we desire now is to hear your story of the present.'

'You'll have it, sir,' said Douglas. 'Can I smoke as I talk? Well,
thank you, Mr Holmes; you're a smoker yourself, if I remember right,
and you'll guess what it is to be sitting for two days with tobacco in
your pocket and afraid that the smell will give you away.' He leaned
against the mantelpiece and sucked at the cigar which Holmes had
handed him. 'I've heard of you, Mr Holmes; I never guessed that I
would meet you. But before you are through with that' – he nodded
at my papers – 'you will say I've brought you something fresh.'

Inspector MacDonald had been staring at the newcomer with the
greatest amazement.

'Well, this fairly beats me!' he cried at last. 'If you are Mr John
Douglas, of Birlstone Manor, then whose death have we been
investigating for these two days, and where in the world have you
sprung from now? You seemed to me to come out of the floor like a
Jack-in-the-box.'

'Ah, Mr Mac,' said Holmes, shaking a reproving forefinger, 'you
would not read that excellent local compilation which described the
concealment of King Charles. People did not hide in those days
without reliable hiding-places, and the hiding-place that has once
been used may be again. I had persuaded myself that we should find
Mr Douglas under this roof.'

'And how long have you been playing this trick upon us, Mr

Holmes?' said the inspector, angrily. 'How long have you allowed us to waste ourselves upon a search that you knew to be an absurd one?'

'Not one instant, my dear Mr Mac. Only last night did I form my views of the case. As they could not be put to the proof until this evening, I invited you and your colleague to take a holiday for the day. Pray, what more could I do? When I found the suit of clothes in the moat it at once became apparent to me that the body we had found could not have been the body of Mr John Douglas at all, but must be that of the bicyclist from Tunbridge Wells. No other conclusion was possible. Therefore I had to determine where Mr John Douglas himself could be, and the balance of probability was that, with the connivance of his wife and his friend, he was concealed in a house which had such conveniences for a fugitive, and awaiting quieter times, when he could make his final escape.'

'Well, you figured it out about right,' said Mr Douglas, approvingly. 'I thought I'd dodge your British law, for I was not sure how I stood under it, and also I saw my chance to throw these hounds once for all off my track. Mind you, from first to last I have done nothing to be ashamed of, and nothing that I would not do again, but you'll judge that for yourselves when I tell you my story. Never mind warning me, inspector; I'm ready to stand pat upon the truth.

'I'm not going to begin at the beginning. That's all there' – he indicated my bundle of papers – 'and a mighty queer yarn you'll find it. It all comes down to this: that there are some men that have good cause to hate me and would give their last dollar to know that they had got me. So long as I am alive and they are alive, there is no safety in this world for me. They hunted me from Chicago to California; then they chased me out of America; but when I married and settled down in this quiet spot I thought my last years were going to be peaceable. I never explained to my wife how things were. Why should I pull her into it? She would never have a quiet moment again, but would be always imagining trouble. I fancy she knew something, for I may have dropped a word here or a word there – but until yesterday, after you gentlemen had seen her, she never knew the rights of the matter. She told you all she knew, and so did Barker here, for on the night when this thing happened there was mighty little time for explanations. She knows everything now, and I would have been a wiser man if I had told her sooner. But it was a hard question, dear' – he took her hand for an instant in his own – 'and I acted for the best.

'Well, gentlemen, the day before these happenings I was over in Tunbridge Wells and I got a glimpse of a man in the street. It was only a glimpse, but I have a quick eye for these things, and I never doubted who it was. It was the worst enemy I had among them all – one who has been after me like a hungry wolf after a caribou all these years. I knew there was trouble coming, and I came home and made ready for it. I guessed I'd fight through it all right on my own. There was a time when my luck was the talk of the whole United States. I never doubted that it would be with me still.

'I was on my guard all that next day and never went out into the park. It's as well, or he'd have had the drop on me with that buck-shot gun of his before ever I could draw on him. After the bridge was up – my mind was always more restful when that bridge was up in the evenings – I put the thing clear out of my head. I never figured on his getting into the house and waiting for me. But when I made my round in my dressing-gown, as my habit was, I had no sooner entered the study than I scented danger. I guess when a man has had dangers in his life – and I've had more than most in my time – there is a kind of sixth sense that waves the red flag. I saw the signal clear enough, and yet I couldn't tell you why. Next instant I spotted a boot under the window curtain, and then I saw why plain enough.

'I'd just the one candle that was in my hand, but there was a good light from the hall lamp through the open door. I put down the candle and jumped for a hammer that I'd left on the mantel. At the same moment he sprang at me. I saw the glint of a knife and I lashed at him with the hammer. I got him somewhere, for the knife tinkled down on the floor. He dodged round the table as quick as an eel, and a moment later he'd got his gun from under his coat. I heard him cock it, but I had got hold of it before he could fire. I had it by the barrel, and we wrestled for it all ends up for a minute or more. It was death to the man that lost his grip. He never lost his grip, but he got it butt downwards for a moment too long. Maybe it was I that pulled the trigger. Maybe we just jolted it off between us. Anyhow, he got both barrels in the face, and there I was, staring down at all that was left of Ted Baldwin. I'd recognized him in the township and again when he sprang for me, but his own mother wouldn't recognize him as I saw him then. I'm used to rough work, but I fairly turned sick at the the sight of him.

'I was hanging on to the side of the table when Barker came hurrying down. I heard my wife coming, and I ran to the door and stopped her. It was no sight for a woman. I promised I'd come to her soon. I said a word or two to Barker – he took it all in at a glance – and we waited for the rest to come along. But there was no sign of them. Then we understood that they could hear nothing, and that all that had happened was only known to ourselves.

'It was at that instant that the idea came to me. I was fairly dazzled by the brilliancy of it. The man's sleeve had slipped up and there was the branded mark of the Lodge upon his forearm. See here.'

The man whom we knew as Douglas turned up his own coat and cuff to show a brown triangle within a circle exactly like that which we had seen upon the dead man.

'It was the sight of that which started me on to it. I seemed to see it all clear at a glance. There was his height and hair and figure about the same as my own. No one could swear to his face, poor devil! I brought down this suit of clothes, and in a quarter of an hour Barker and I had put my dressing-gown on him and he lay as you found him. We tied all his things into a bundle, and I weighted them with the only weight I could find and slung them through the window. The card he had meant to lay upon my body was lying beside his own. My rings were put on his finger, but when it came to the wedding-ring' – he held out his muscular hand – 'you can see for yourselves that I had struck my limit. I have not moved it since the day I was married, and it would have taken a file to get it off. I don't know, anyhow, that I would have cared to part with it, but if I had wanted to I couldn't. So we just had to leave the detail to take care of itself. On the other hand, I brought a bit of plaster down and put it where I am wearing one myself at this instant. You slipped up there, Mr Holmes, clever as you are, for if you had chanced to take off that plaster you would have found no cut underneath it.

'Well, that was the situation. If I could lie low for a while and then get away where I would be joined by my wife, we would have a chance at last of living at peace for the rest of our lives. These devils would give me no rest so long as I was above-ground but if they saw in the papers that Baldwin had got his man there would be an end of all my troubles. I hadn't much time to make it clear to Barker and to my wife, but they understood enough to be able to help me. I knew all about this hiding-place, so did Ames, but it never entered his head to connect it with the matter. I retired into it, and it was up to Barker to do the rest.

'I guess you can fill in for yourselves what he did. He opened the window and made the mark on the sill to give an idea of how the murderer escaped. It was a tall order, that, but as the bridge was up there was no other way. Then, when everything was fixed, he rang the bell for all he was worth. What happened afterwards you know – and so, gentlemen, you can do what you please, but I've told you the truth and the whole truth, so help me, God! What I ask you now is, how do I stand by the English law?'

There was a silence, which was broken by Sherlock Holmes.

'The English law is, in the main, a just law. You will get no worse than your deserts from it. But I would ask you how did this man know that you lived here, or how to get into your house, or where to hide to get you?'

'I know nothing of this.'

Holmes's face was very white and grave.

'The story is not over yet, I fear,' said he. 'You may find worse dangers than the English law, or even than your enemies from America. I see trouble before you, Mr Douglas. You'll take my advice and still be on your guard.'

And now, my long-suffering readers, I will ask you to come away with me for a time, far from the Sussex Manor House of Birlstone, and far also from the year of grace in which we made our eventful journey which ended with the strange story of the man who had been known as John Douglas. I wish you to journey back some twenty years in time,[8] and westward some thousands of miles in space, that I may lay before you a singular and a terrible narrative – so singular and so terrible that you may find it hard to believe that, even as I tell it, even so did it occur. Do not think that I intrude one story before another is finished. As you read on you will find that this is not so. And when I have detailed those distant events and you have solved this mystery of the past we shall meet once more in those rooms in Baker Street where this, like so many other wonderful happenings, will find its end.

PART TWO

The Scowrers

I

The Man

It was the fourth of February in the year 1875. It had been a severe winter, and the snow lay deep in the gorges of the Gilmerton Mountains.[1] The steam plough had, however, kept the railtrack open, and the evening train which connects the long line of coal-mining and iron-working settlements was slowly groaning its way up the steep gradients which lead from Stagville on the plain to Vermissa,[2] the central township which lies at the head of the Vermissa Valley. From this point the track sweeps downwards to Barton's Crossing, Helmdale, and the purely agricultural county of Merton. It was a single-track railroad, but at every siding, and they were numerous, long lines of trucks piled with coal and with iron ore told of the hidden wealth which had brought a rude population and a bustling life to this most desolate corner of the United States of America.

For desolate it was. Little could the first pioneer who had traversed it have ever imagined that the fairest prairies and the most lush water-pastures were valueless compared with this gloomy land of black crag and tangled forest. Above the dark and often scarcely penetrable woods upon their sides, the high, bare crowns of the mountains, white snow and jagged rock, towered upon either flank, leaving a long, winding, tortuous valley in the centre. Up this the little train was slowly crawling.

The oil lamps had just been lit in the leading passenger-car, a long, bare carriage in which some twenty or thirty people were seated. The greater number of these were workmen returning from their day's toil in the lower portion of the valley. At least a dozen, by their grimed faces and the safety lanterns which they carried, proclaimed themselves as miners. These sat smoking in a group, and conversed in low voices, glancing occasionally at two men on the opposite side of the car, whose uniform and badges showed them to be policemen. Several women of the labouring class, and one or two travellers who might have been small local storekeepers, made up the rest of the company, with the exception of one young man in a corner by himself. It is with this man that we are concerned. Take a good look at him, for he is worth it.

He is a fresh-complexioned, middle-sized young man, not far, one would guess, from his thirtieth year. He has large, shrewd, humorous grey eyes which twinkle inquiringly from time to time as he looks round through his spectacles at the people about him. It is easy to see that he is of a sociable and possibly simple disposition, anxious to be friendly to all men. Anyone could pick him at once as gregarious in his habits and communicative in his nature, with a quick wit and a ready smile. And yet the man who studied him more closely might discern a certain firmness of jaw and grim tightness about the lips which would warn him that there were depths beyond, and that this pleasant, brown-haired young Irishman might conceivably leave his mark for good or evil upon any society to which he was introduced.

Having made one or two tentative remarks to the nearest miner, and received only short gruff replies, the traveller resigned himself to uncongenial silence, staring moodily out of the window at the fading landscape. It was not a cheering prospect. Through the growing gloom there pulsed the red glow of the furnaces on the sides of the hills. Great heaps of slag and dumps of cinders loomed up on each side, with the high shafts of the collieries towering above them. Huddled groups of mean wooden houses, the windows of which were beginning to outline themselves in light, were scattered here and there along the line, and the frequent halting-places were crowded with their swarthy inhabitants. The iron and coal valleys of the Vermissa district were no resorts for the leisured or the cultured. Everywhere there were stern signs of the crudest battle of life, the rude work to be done, and the rude, strong workers who did it.

The young traveller gazed out into this dismal country with a face of mingled repulsion and interest, which showed that the scene was new to him. At intervals he drew from his pocket a bulky letter to which he referred, and on the margins of which he scribbled some notes. Once from the back of his waist he produced something which one would hardly have expected to find in the possession of so mild-mannered a man. It was a navy revolver of the largest size. As he turned it slantwise to the light, the glint upon the rims of the copper shells within the drum showed that it was fully loaded. He quickly restored it to his secret pocket, but not before it had been observed by a working man who had seated himself upon the adjoining bench.

'Halloa, mate!' said he. 'You seem heeled and ready.'

The young man smiled with an air of embarrassment.

'Yes,' said he; 'we need them sometimes in the place I come from.'

'And where may that be?'

'I'm last from Chicago.'

'A stranger in these parts?'

'Yes.'

'You may find you need it here,' said the workman.

'Ah! Is that so?' The young man seemed interested.

'Have you heard nothing of doings hereabouts?'

'Nothing out of the way.'

'Why, I thought the country was full of it. You'll hear quick enough. What made you come here?'

'I heard there was always work for a willing man.'

'Are you one of the Labour Union?'

'Sure.'

'Then you'll get your job, I guess. Have you any friends?'

'Not yet, but I have the means of making them.'

'How's that, then?'

'I am one of the Ancient Order of Freemen.[3] There's no town without a lodge, and where there is a lodge I'll find my friends.'

The remark had a singular effect upon his companion. He glanced round suspiciously at the others in the car. The miners were still whispering among themselves. The two police officers were dozing. He came across, seated himself close to the young traveller, and held out his hand.

'Put it there,' he said.

A hand-grip passed between the two.

'I see you speak the truth. But it's well to make certain.'

He raised his right hand to his right eyebrow.[4] The traveller at once raised his left hand to his left eyebrow.

'Dark nights are unpleasant,'[5] said the workman.

'Yes, for strangers to travel,' the other answered.

'That's good enough. I'm Brother Scanlan, Lodge 341, Vermissa Valley. Glad to see you in these parts.'

'Thank you. I'm Brother John McMurdo, Lodge 29, Chicago. Bodymaster, J. H. Scott. But I am in luck to meet a brother so early.'

'Well, there are plenty of us about. You won't find the Order more flourishing anywhere in the States than right here in Vermissa Valley. But we could do with some lads like you. I can't understand a spry man of the Labour Union finding no work to do in Chicago.'

'I found plenty of work to do,' said McMurdo.

'Then why did you leave?'

McMurdo nodded towards the policemen and smiled.

'I guess those chaps would be glad to know,' he said.

Scanlan groaned sympathetically.

'In trouble?' he asked in a whisper.

'Deep.'

'A penitentiary job?'

'And the rest.'

'Not a killing?'

'It's early days to talk of such things,' said McMurdo, with the air of a man who had been surprised into saying more than he intended. 'I've my own good reason for leaving Chicago, and let that be enough for you. Who are you that you should take it on yourself to ask such things?'

His grey eyes gleamed with sudden and dangerous anger from behind his glasses.

'All right, mate. No offence meant. The boys will think none the worse of you whatever you may have done. Where are you bound for now?'

'To Vermissa.'

'That's the third halt down the line. Where are you staying?'

McMurdo took out an envelope and held it close to the murky oil lamp.

'Here is the address – Jacob Shafter, Sheridan Street.[6] It's a boarding-house that was recommended by a man I knew in Chicago.'

'Well, I don't know it, but Vermissa is out of my beat. I live at Hobson's Patch, and that's here where we are drawing up. But, say, there's one bit of advice I'll give you before we part. If you're in trouble in Vermissa, go straight to the Union House and see Boss McGinty. He is the bodymaster of Vermissa Lodge, and nothing can happen in these parts unless Black Jack McGinty[7] wants it. So long, mate. Maybe we'll meet in Lodge one of these evenings. But mind my words; if you are in trouble go to Boss McGinty.'

Scanlan descended, and McMurdo was left once again to his thoughts. Night had now fallen, and the flames of the frequent furnaces were roaring and leaping in the darkness. Against their lurid background dark figures were bending and straining, twisting, and turning, with the motion of winch or of windlass, to the rhythm of an eternal clank and roar.

'I guess hell must look something like that,' said a voice.

McMurdo turned and saw that one of the policemen had shifted in his seat and was staring out into the fiery waste.

'For that matter,' said the other policeman, 'I allow that hell must *be* something like that. If there are worse devils down yonder than some we could name, it's more than I'd expect. I guess you are new to this part, young man?'

'Well, what if I am?' McMurdo answered, in a surly voice.

'Just this, mister; that I should advise you to be careful in choosing your friends. I don't think I'd begin with Mike Scanlan or his gang if I were you.'

'What in thunder is it to you who are my friends?' roared McMurdo, in a voice which brought every head in the carriage round to witness the altercation. 'Did I ask you for your advice, or did you think me such a sucker that I couldn't move without it? You speak when you are spoken to, and by the Lord you'd have to wait a long time if it was me!'

He thrust out his face, and grinned at the patrolmen like a snarling dog.

The two policemen, heavy, good-natured men, were taken aback by the extraordinary vehemence with which their friendly advances had been rejected.

'No offence, stranger,' said one. 'It was a warning for your own good, seeing that you are, by your own showing, new to the place.'

'I'm new to the place, but I'm not new to you and your kind,' cried McMurdo, in a cold fury. 'I guess you're the same in all places, shoving your advice in when nobody asks for it.'

'Maybe we'll see more of you before very long,' said one of the patrolmen, with a grin. 'You're a real hand-picked one, if I am a judge.'

'I was thinking the same,' remarked the other. 'I guess we may meet again.'

'I'm not afraid of you, and don't you think it,' cried McMurdo. 'My name's Jack McMurdo – see? If you want me you'll find me at Jacob Shafter's, at Sheridan Street, Vermissa, so I'm not hiding from you, am I? Day or night I dare to look the like of you in the face. Don't make any mistake about that.'

There was a murmur of sympathy and admiration from the miners at the dauntless demeanour of the newcomer, while the two policemen shrugged their shoulders and renewed a conversation between themselves. A few minutes later the train ran into the ill-lit depot and there was a general clearing, for Vermissa was far the largest township on the line. McMurdo picked up his leather grip-sack, and was about to start off into the darkness when one of the miners accosted him.

'By gosh,[8] mate, you know how to speak to the cops,' he said, in a voice of awe. 'It was grand to hear you. Let me carry your grip-sack and show you the road. I'm passing Shafter's on the way to my own shack.'

There was a chorus of friendly 'Good nights' from the other miners as they passed from the platform. Before ever he had set foot in it, McMurdo the turbulent had become a character in Vermissa.

The country had been a place of terror, but the township was in its way even more depressing. Down that long valley there was at least a certain gloomy grandeur in the huge fires and the clouds of drifting smoke, while the strength and industry of man found fitting monuments in the hills which he had spilled by the side of his monstrous excavations. But the town showed a dead level of mean ugliness and squalor. The broad street was churned up by the traffic into a horrible rutted paste of muddy snow. The side-walks were narrow and uneven. The numerous gas-lamps served only to show more clearly a long line of wooden houses, each with its veranda facing the street, unkempt and dirty. As they approached the centre of the town, the scene was brightened by a row of well-lit stores, and even more by a cluster of liquor saloons and gaming-houses, in which the miners spent their hard-earned but generous wages.

'That's the Union House,' said the guide, pointing to one saloon which rose almost to the dignity of being an hotel. 'Jack McGinty is the Boss there.'

'What sort of a man is he?' asked McMurdo.

'What! Have you never heard of the Boss?'

'How could I have heard of him when you know that I am a stranger in these parts?'

'Well, I thought his name was known right across the Union. It's been in the papers often enough.'

'What for?'

'Well' – the miner lowered his voice – 'over the affairs.'

'What affairs?'

'Good Lord, mister, you are queer goods, if I may say it without offence. There's only one set of affairs that you'll hear of in these parts, and that's the affairs of the Scowrers.'

'Why, I seem to have read of the Scowrers in Chicago. A gang of murderers, are they not?'

'Hush, on your life!' cried the miner, standing still in his alarm, and gazing in amazement at his companion. 'Man, you won't live long in these parts if you speak in the open street like that. Many a man has had the life beaten out of him for less.'

'Well, I know nothing about them. It's only what I have read.'

'And I'm not saying that you have not read the truth.' The man looked nervously round him as he spoke, peering into the shadows as if he feared to see some lurking danger. 'If killing is murder, then God knows there is murder and to spare. But don't you dare breathe the name of Jack McGinty in connection with it, stranger, for every whisper goes back to him, and he is not one that is likely to let it pass. Now, that's the house you're after – that one standing back from the street. You'll find old Jacob Shafter that runs it as honest a man as lives in this township.'

'I thank you,' said McMurdo, and shaking hands with his new acquaintance he plodded, his grip-sack in his hand, up the path which led to the dwelling-house, at the door of which he gave a resounding knock. It was opened at once by someone very different from what he had expected.

It was a woman, young and singularly beautiful. She was of the Swedish[9] type, blonde and fair-haired, with the piquant contrast of a pair of beautiful dark eyes, with which she surveyed the stranger with surprise and a pleasing embarrassment which brought a wave of colour over her pale face. Framed in the bright light of the open doorway, it seemed to Mc-Murdo that he had never seen a more beautiful picture, the more attractive for its contrast with the sordid and gloomy surroundings. A lovely violet growing upon one of those black slag-heaps of the mines would not have seemed more surprising. So entranced was he that he stood staring without a word, and it was she who broke the silence.

'I thought it was father,' said she, with a pleasing little touch of a Swedish accent. 'Did you come to see him? He is down town. I expect him back every minute.'

McMurdo continued to gaze at her in open admiration until her eyes dropped in confusion before this masterful visitor.

'No, miss,' he said at last; 'I'm in no hurry to see him. But your house was recommended to me for board. I thought it might suit me, and now I know it will.'

'You are quick to make up your mind,' said she, with a smile.
'Anyone but a blind man could do as much,' the other answered.
She laughed at the compliment.

'Come right in, sir,' she said. 'I'm Miss Ettie Shafter, Mr Shafter's daughter. My mother's dead, and I run the house. You can sit down by the stove in the front room until father comes along. Ah, here he is; so you can fix things with him right away.'

A heavy, elderly man came plodding up the path. In a few words McMurdo explained his business. A man of the name of Murphy had given him the address in Chicago. He in turn had had it from someone else. Old Shafter was quite ready. The stranger made no bones about terms, agreed at once to every condition, and was apparently fairly flush of money. For twelve dollars a week, paid in advance, he was to have board and lodging. So it was that McMurdo, the self-confessed fugitive from justice, took up his abode under the roof of the Shafters, the first step which was to lead to so long and dark a train of events, ending in a far distant land.

2

The Bodymaster

McMurdo was a man who made his mark quickly. Wherever he was the folk around soon knew it. Within a week he had become infinitely the most important person at Shafter's. There were ten or a dozen boarders there, but they were honest foremen or commonplace clerks from the stores, of a very different calibre to the young Irishman. Of an evening when they gathered together his joke was always the readiest, his conversation the brightest, and his song the best. He was a born boon companion, with a magnetism which drew good humour from all around him. And yet he showed again and again, as he had shown in the railway-carriage, a capacity for sudden, fierce anger which compelled the respect and even fear of those who met him. For the law, too, and all connected with it, he exhibited a bitter contempt which delighted some and alarmed others of his fellow-boarders.

From the first he made it evident, by his open admiration, that the daughter of the house had won his heart from the instant that he had set eyes upon her beauty and her grace. He was no backward suitor. On the second day he told her that he loved her, and from then onwards he repeated the same story with an absolute disregard of what she might say to discourage him.

'Someone else!' he would cry. 'Well, the worse luck for someone else! Let him look out for himself! Am I to lose my life's chance and all my heart's desire for someone else? You can keep on saying "No", Ettie! The day will come when you will say "Yes", and I'm young enough to wait.'

He was a dangerous suitor, with his glib Irish tongue and his pretty, coaxing ways. There was about him also that glamour of experience and of mystery which attracts a woman's interest and finally her love. He could talk of the sweet valleys of County Monaghan[1] from which he came, of the lovely distant island, the low hills and green meadows of which seemed the more beautiful when imagination viewed them from this place of grime and snow. Then he was versed in the life of the cities of the North, of Detroit and the lumber-camps of Michigan, of Buffalo,[2] and finally of Chicago, where he had worked in a saw-mill. And afterwards came the hint of romance, the feeling that strange things had happened to him in that great city, so strange and so intimate that they might not be spoken of. He spoke wistfully of a sudden leaving, a breaking of old ties, a flight into a strange world ending in this dreary valley, and Ettie listened, her dark eyes gleaming with pity and with sympathy – those two qualities which may turn so rapidly and so naturally to love.

McMurdo had obtained a temporary job as a book-keeper, for he was a well-educated man. This kept him out most of the day, and he had not found occasion yet to report himself to the head of the Lodge of the Ancient Order of Freemen. He was reminded of his omission, however, by a visit one evening from Mike Scanlan, the fellow-member whom he had met in the train. Scanlan, a small, sharp-faced, nervous, black-eyed man, seemed glad to see him once more. After a glass or two of whisky, he broached the object of his visit.

'Say, McMurdo,' said he, 'I remembered your address, so I made bold to call. I'm surprised that you've not reported to the bodymaster. What's amiss that you've not seen Boss McGinty yet?'

'Well, I had to find a job. I have been busy.'

'You must find time for him if you have none for anything else. Good Lord, man, you're mad not to have been down to the Union House and registered your name the first morning after you came here! If you fall foul of him – well, you *mustn't* – that's all!'

McMurdo showed mild surprise.

'I've been a member of Lodge for over two years, Scanlan, but I never heard that duties were so pressing as all that.'

'Maybe not in Chicago!'

'Well, it's the same society here.'

'Is it?' Scanlan looked at him long and fixedly. There was something sinister in his eyes.

'Is it not?'

'You'll tell me that in a month's time. I hear you had a talk with the patrolmen after I left the train.'

'How did you know that?'

'Oh, it got about – things do get about for good and for bad in this district.'

'Well, yes. I told the hounds what I thought of them.'

'By the Lord, you'll be a man after McGinty's heart!'

'What – does he hate the police, too?'

Scanlan burst out laughing.

'You go and see him, my lad,' said he, as he took his leave. 'It's not the police, but you, that he'll hate if you don't! Now, take a friend's advice and go at once!'

It chanced that on the same evening McMurdo had another more pressing interview which urged him in the same direction. It may have been that his attentions to Ettie had been more evident than before, or that they had gradually obtruded themselves into the slow mind of his good Swedish host; but, whatever the cause, the boarding-house keeper beckoned the young man into his private room and started on to the subject without any circumlocution.

'It seems to me, mister,' said he, 'dat you are gettin' set on my Ettie. Ain't dat so, or am I wrong?'

'Yes, that is so,' the young man answered.

'Well, I vant to tell you right now dat it ain't no manner of use. There's someone slipped in afore you.'

'She told me so.'

'Well, you can lay dat she told you truth! But did she tell you who it vas?'

'No; I asked her, but she would not tell.'

'I dare say not, the leetle baggage. Perhaps she did not vish to vrighten you avay.'

'Frighten!' McMurdo was on fire in a moment.

'Ah, yes, my vriend! You need not be ashamed to be vrightened of him. It is Teddy Baldwin.'

'And who the devil is he?'

'He is a Boss of Scowrers.'

'Scowrers! I've heard of them before. It's Scowrers here and Scowrers there, and always in a whisper! What are you all afraid of? Who *are* the Scowrers?'

The boarding-house keeper instinctively sank his voice, as everyone did who talked about the terrible society.

'The Scowrers,' said he, 'are the Ancient Order of Freemen.'

The young man started.

'Why, I am a member of that Order myself.'

'You! I would never have had you in my house if I had known it – not if you vere to pay me a hundred dollar a veek.'

'What's amiss with the Order? It's for charity and good-fellowship. The rules say so.'

'Maybe in some places. Not here!'

'What is it here?'

'It's a murder society, dat's vat it is.'

McMurdo laughed incredulously.

'How do you prove that?' he asked.

'Prove it! Are there not vifty murders to prove it? Vat about Milman and Van Shorst, and the Nicholson vamily, and old Mr Hyam, and little Billy James, and the others? Prove it! Is dere a man or a voman in dis valley dat does not know it?'

'See here!' said McMurdo, earnestly. 'I want you to take back what you've said or else to make it good. One or the other you must do before I quit this room. Put yourself in my place. Here am I, a stranger in the town. I belong to a society that I know only as an innocent one. You'll find it through the length and breadth of the States, but always as an innocent one. Now, when I am counting upon joining it here, you tell me that it is the same as a murder society called the "Scowrers". I guess you owe me either an apology or else an explanation, Mr Shafter.'

'I can but tell you vat the whole world knows, mister. The bosses of the one are the bosses of the other. If you offend the one it is the other dat vill strike you. We have proved it too often.'

'That's just gossip! I want proof!' said McMurdo.

'If you live here long you vill get your proof. But I vorget dat you are yourself one of dem. You vill soon be as bad as the rest. But you vill find other lodgings, mister. I cannot have you here. Is it not bad enough dat one of these people come courting my Ettie, and dat I dare not turn him down, but dat I should have another for my boarder? Yes, indeed, you shall not sleep here after tonight!'

So McMurdo found himself under sentence of banishment both from his comfortable quarters and from the girl whom he loved. He found her alone in the sitting-room that same evening, and he poured his troubles into her ear.

'Sure, your father is after giving me notice,' he said. 'It's little I would care if it was just my room; but indeed, Ettie, though it's only a week that I've known you, you are the very breath of life to me, and I can't live without you.'

'Oh, hush, Mr McMurdo! Don't speak so!' said the girl. 'I have told you, have I not, that you are too late? There is another, and if I have not promised to marry him at once, at least I can promise no one else.'

'Suppose I had been first, Ettie, would I have had a chance?'

The girl sank her face into her hands.

'I wish to Heaven that you *had* been first,' she sobbed.

McMurdo was down on his knees before her in an instant.

'For God's sake, Ettie, let it stand at that!' he cried. 'Will you ruin your life and my own for the sake of this promise? Follow your heart, acushla![3] 'Tis a safer guide than any promise given before you knew what it was that you were saying.'

He had seized Ettie's white hand between his own strong brown ones.

'Say that you will be mine and we will face it out together.'

'Not here?'

'Yes, here.'

'No, no, Jack!' His arms were round her now. 'It could not be here. Could you take me away?'

A struggle passed for a moment over McMurdo's face, but it ended by setting like granite.

'No, here,' he said. 'I'll hold you against the world, Ettie, right here where we are!'

'Why should we not leave together?'

'No, Ettie, I can't leave here.'

'But why?'

'I'd never hold my head up again if I felt that I had been driven out. Besides, what is there to be afraid of? Are we not free folk in a free country? If you love me and I you, who will dare to come between?'

'You don't know, Jack. You've been here too short a time. You don't know this Baldwin. You don't know McGinty and his Scowrers.'

'No, I don't know them, and I don't fear them, and I don't believe in them!' said McMurdo. 'I've lived among rough men, my darling, and instead of fearing them it has always ended that they have feared me – always, Ettie. It's mad on the face of it! If these men, as your father says, have done crime after crime in the valley, and if everyone knows them by name, how comes it that none are brought to justice? You answer me that, Ettie!'

'Because no witness dares to appear against them. He would not live a month if he did. Also because they have always their own men to swear that the accused one was far from the scene of the crime. But surely, Jack, you must have read all this! I had understood that every paper in the States was writing about it.'

'Well, I have read something, it is true, but I had thought it was a story. Maybe these men have some reason in what they do. Maybe they are wronged and have no other way to help themselves.'

'Oh, Jack, don't let me hear you speak so! That is how he speaks – the other one!'

'Baldwin – he speaks like that, does he?'

'And that is why I loathe him so. Oh, Jack, now I can tell you the truth, I loathe him with all my heart; but I fear him also. I fear him for myself, but, above all, I fear him for Father. I know that some great sorrow would come upon us if I dared to say what I really felt. That is why I have put him off with half-promises. It was in real truth our only hope. But if you would fly with me, Jack, we could take Father with us and live for ever far from the power of these wicked men.'

Again there was a struggle upon McMurdo's face, and again it set like granite.

'No harm shall come to you, Ettie – nor to your father either. As to wicked men, I expect you may find that I am as bad as the worst of them before we're through.'

'No, no, Jack! I would trust you anywhere.'

McMurdo laughed bitterly.

'Good Lord, how little you know of me! Your innocent soul, my darling, could not even guess what is passing in mine. But, halloa, who's the visitor?'

The door had opened suddenly and a young fellow came swaggering in with the air of one who is the master. He was a handsome, dashing young man of about the same age and build as McMurdo himself. Under his broad-brimmed black felt hat, which he had not troubled to remove, a handsome face, with fierce, domineering eyes and curved hawkbill of a nose, looked savagely at the pair who sat by the stove.

Ettie had jumped to her feet, full of confusion and alarm.

'I'm glad to see you, Mr Baldwin,' said she. 'You're earlier than I had thought. Come and sit down.'

Baldwin stood with his hands on his hips looking at McMurdo.

'Who is this?' he asked, curtly.

'It's a friend of mine, Mr Baldwin – a new boarder here. Mr McMurdo, can I introduce you to Mr Baldwin?'

The young men nodded in a surly fashion to each other.

'Maybe Miss Ettie has told you how it is with us?' said Baldwin.

'I didn't understand that there was any relation between you.'

'Did you not? Well, you can understand it now. You can take it from me that this young lady is mine, and you'll find it a very fine evening for a walk.'

'Thank you, I am in no humour for a walk.'

'Are you not?' The man's savage eyes were blazing with anger. 'Maybe you are in a humour for a fight, Mr Boarder?'

'That I am,' cried McMurdo, springing to his feet. 'You never said a more welcome word.'

'For God's sake, Jack! Oh, for God's sake!' cried poor, distracted Ettie. 'Oh, Jack, Jack, he will do you a mischief!'

'Oh, it's "Jack", is it!' said Baldwin, with an oath. 'You've come to that already, have you?'

'Oh, Ted, be reasonable – be kind! For my sake, Ted, if ever you loved me, be great-hearted and forgiving!'

'I think, Ettie, that if you were to leave us alone we could get this thing settled,' said McMurdo, quietly. 'Or maybe, Mr Baldwin, you will take a turn down the street with me. It's a fine evening, and there's some open ground beyond the next block.'

'I'll get even with you without needing to dirty my hands,' said his enemy. 'You'll wish you had never set foot in this house before I am through with you.'

'No time like the present,' cried McMurdo.

'I'll choose my own time, mister. You can leave the time to me. See here!' He suddenly rolled up his sleeve and showed upon his forearm a peculiar sign which appeared to have been branded there. It was a circle with a triangle within it. 'D'you know what that means?'

'I neither know nor care!'

'Well, you will know. I'll promise you that. You won't be much older either. Perhaps Miss Ettie can tell you something about it. As to you, Ettie, you'll come back to me on your knees. D'ye hear, girl? On your knees! And then I'll tell you what your punishment may be. You've sowed – and, by the Lord, I'll see that you reap!'[4] He glared at them both in fury. Then he turned upon his heel, and an instant later the outer door had banged behind him.

For a few moments McMurdo and the girl stood in silence. Then she threw her arms around him.

'Oh, Jack, how brave you were! But it is no use – you must fly! Tonight – Jack – tonight! It's your only hope. He will have your life. I read it in his horrible eyes. What chance have you against a dozen of them, with Boss McGinty and all the power of the Lodge behind them?'

McMurdo disengaged her hands, kissed her, and gently pushed her back into a chair.

'There, acushla, there! Don't be disturbed or fear for me. I'm a Freeman myself. I'm after telling your father about it. Maybe I am no better than the others, so don't make a saint of me. Perhaps you hate me, too, now that I've told you as much.'

'Hate you, Jack! While life lasts I could never do that. I've heard that there is no harm in being a Freeman anywhere but here, so why should I think the worse of you for that? But if you are a Freeman, Jack, why should you not go down and make a friend of Boss McGinty? Oh, hasten, Jack, hasten! Get your word in first, or the hounds will be on your trail.'

'I was thinking the same thing,' said McMurdo. 'I'll go right now and fix it. You can tell your father that I'll sleep here tonight and find some other quarters in the morning.'

The bar of McGinty's saloon was crowded as usual, for it was the favourite lounge of all the rougher elements of the town. The man was popular, for he had a rough, jovial disposition which formed a mask, covering a great deal which lay behind it. But, apart from this popularity, the fear in which he was held throughout the township, and, indeed, down the whole thirty miles of the valley and past the mountains upon either side of it, was enough in itself to fill his bar, for none could afford to neglect his goodwill.

Besides those secret powers which it was universally believed that he exercised in so pitiless a fashion, he was a high public official, a municipal councillor, and a commissioner for roads, elected to the office through the votes of the ruffians who in turn expected to receive favours at his hands. Rates and taxes were enormous, the public works were notoriously neglected, the accounts were slurred over by bribed auditors, and the decent citizen was terrorized into paying public blackmail, and holding his tongue lest some worse thing befall him. Thus it was that, year by year, Boss McGinty's diamond pins became more obtrusive, his gold chains more weighty across a more gorgeous vest, and his saloon stretched farther and farther, until it threatened to absorb one whole side of the Market Square.

McMurdo pushed open the swinging door of the saloon and made his way amid the crowd of men within, through an atmosphere which was blurred with tobacco smoke and heavy with the smell of spirits. The place was brilliantly lighted, and the huge, heavily gilt mirrors upon every wall reflected and multiplied the garish illumination. There were several bartenders in their shirt-sleeves hard at work, mixing drinks for the loungers who fringed the broad, heavily metalled counter. At the far end, with his body resting upon the bar, and a cigar stuck at an acute angle from the corner of his mouth, there stood a tall, strong, heavily built man, who could be none other than the famous McGinty himself. He was a black-maned giant, bearded to the cheek-bones, and with a shock of raven hair which fell to his collar. His complexion was as swarthy as that of an Italian, and his eyes were of a strange, dead black, which, combined with a slight squint, gave them a particularly sinister appearance. All else in the man, his noble proportions, his fine features, and his frank bearing, fitted in with that jovial man-to-man manner which he affected. Here, one would say, is a bluff, honest fellow, whose heart would be sound, however rude his outspoken words might seem. It was only when those dead, dark eyes, deep and remorseless, were turned upon a man that he shrank within himself, feeling that he was face to face with an infinite possibility of latent evil, with a strength and courage and cunning behind it which made it a thousand times more deadly.

Having had a good look at his man, McMurdo elbowed his way forward with his usual careless audacity, and pushed himself through the little group of courtiers who were fawning upon the powerful Boss, laughing uproariously at the smallest of his jokes. The young stranger's bold grey eyes looked back fearlessly through their glasses at the deadly black ones which turned sharply upon him.

'Well, young man, I can't call your face to mind.'

'I'm new here, Mr McGinty.'

'You are not so new that you can't give a gentleman his proper title.'

'He's Councillor McGinty, young man,' said a voice from the group.

'I'm sorry, Councillor. I'm strange to the ways of the place. But I was advised to see you.'

'Well, you see me. This is all there is. What d'you think of me?'

'Well, it's early days. If your heart is as big as your body, and your soul as fine as your face, then I'd ask for nothing better,' said McMurdo.

'By gosh, you've got an Irish tongue in your head, anyhow,' cried the saloon-keeper, not quite certain whether to humour this audacious visitor or to stand upon his dignity. 'So you are good enough to pass my appearance?'

'Sure,' said McMurdo.

'And you were told to see me?'

'I was.'

'And who told you?'

'Brother Scanlan, of Lodge 341, Vermissa. I drink your health, Councillor, and to our better acquaintance.' He raised a glass with which he had been served to his lips and elevated his little finger as he drank it.[5]

McGinty, who had been watching him narrowly, raised his thick black eyebrows.

'Oh, it's like that, is it?' said he. 'I'll have to look a bit closer into this, Mister –'

'McMurdo.'

'A bit closer, Mr McMurdo, for we don't take folk on trust in these parts, nor believe all we're told neither. Come in here for a moment, behind the bar.'

There was a small room there lined round with barrels. McGinty carefully closed the door, and then seated himself on one of them, biting thoughtfully on his cigar, and surveying his companion with those disquieting eyes. For a couple of minutes he sat in complete silence.

McMurdo bore the inspection cheerfully, one hand in his coat-pocket, the other twisting his brown moustache. Suddenly McGinty stooped and produced a wicked-looking revolver.

'See here, my joker,' said he; 'if I thought you were playing any game on us, it would be a short shrift for you.'

'This is a strange welcome,' McMurdo answered, with some dignity, 'for the bodymaster of a Lodge of Freemen to give to a strange brother.'

'Aye, but it's just that same that you have to prove,' said McGinty, 'and God help you if you fail. Where were you made?'

'Lodge 29, Chicago.'

'When?'

'June 24th, 1872.'

'What bodymaster?'

'James H. Scott.'

'Who is your district ruler?'

'Bartholomew Wilson.'

'Hum! You seem glib enough in your tests. What are you doing here?'

'Working, the same as you, but a poorer job.'

'You have your back answer quick enough.'

'Yes, I was always quick of speech.'

'Are you quick of action?'

'I have had that name among those who knew me best.'

'Well, we may try you sooner than you think. Have you heard anything of the Lodge in these parts?'

'I've heard that it takes a man to be a brother.'

'True for you, Mr McMurdo. Why did you leave Chicago?'

'I'm hanged if I tell you that.'

McGinty opened his eyes. He was not used to being answered in such fashion, and it amused him.

'Why won't you tell me?'

'Because no brother may tell another a lie.'

'Then the truth is too bad to tell?'

'You can put it that way if you like.'

'See here, mister; you can't expect me, as bodymaster, to pass into the Lodge a man for whose past he can't answer.'

McMurdo looked puzzled. Then he took a worn newspaper-cutting from an inner pocket.

'You wouldn't squeal on a fellow?' said he.

'I'll wipe my hand across your face if you say such words to me,' cried McGinty, hotly.

'You are right, Councillor,' said McMurdo, meekly. 'I should apologize. I spoke without thought. Well, I know that I am safe in your hands. Look at that cutting.'

McGinty glanced his eyes over the account of the shooting of one Jonas Pinto, in the Lake Saloon, Market Street, Chicago, in the New Year week of '74.

'Your work?' he asked, as he handed back the paper.

McMurdo nodded.

'Why did you shoot him?'

'I was helping Uncle Sam to make dollars. Maybe mine were not as good gold as his, but they looked as well and were cheaper to make. This man Pinto helped me to shove the queer –'

'To do what?'

'Well, it means to pass the dollars out into circulation. Then he said he would split. Maybe he did split. I didn't wait to see. I just killed him and lighted out for the coal country.'

'Why the coal country?'

''Cause I'd read in the papers that they weren't too particular in those parts.'

McGinty laughed.

'You were first a coiner and then a murderer, and you came to these parts because you thought you'd be welcome?'

'That's about the size of it,' McMurdo answered.

'Well, I guess you'll go far. Say, can you make those dollars yet?'

McMurdo took half a dozen from his pocket. 'Those never passed the Washington mint,' said he.

'You don't say!' McGinty held them to the light in his enormous hand, which was as hairy as a gorilla's. 'I can see no difference! Gosh, you'll be a mighty useful brother, I'm thinking. We can do with a bad man or two amongst us, friend McMurdo, for there are times when we have to take our own part. We'd soon be against the wall if we didn't shove back at those that were pushing us.'

'Well, I guess I'll do my share of shoving with the rest of the boys.'

'You seem to have a good nerve. You didn't flinch when I put this pistol on you.'

'It was not me that was in danger.'

'Who, then?'

'It was you, Councillor.' McMurdo drew a cocked pistol from the side-pocket of his pea-jacket. 'I was covering you all the time. I guess my shot would have been as quick as yours.'

McGinty flushed an angry red and then burst into a roar of laughter.

'By gosh!' said he. 'Say, we've had no such holy terror come to hand this many a year. I reckon the Lodge will learn to be proud of you. Well, what the deuce do you want? And can't I speak alone with a gentleman for five minutes but you must butt in upon us?'

The bartender stood abashed.

'I'm sorry, Councillor, but it's Mr Ted Baldwin. He says he must see you this very minute.'

The message was unnecessary, for the set, cruel face of the man himself was looking over the servant's shoulder. He pushed the bartender out and closed the door on him.

'So,' said he, with a furious glance at McMurdo, 'you got here first, did you? I've a word to say to you, Councillor, about this man.'

'Then say it here and now, before my face,' cried McMurdo.

'I'll say it at my own time, in my own way.'

'Tut, tut!' said McGinty, getting off his barrel. 'This will never do. We have a new brother here, Baldwin, and it's not for us to greet him in such a fashion. Hold out your hand, man, and make it up.'

'Never!' cried Baldwin, in a fury.

'I've offered to fight him if he thinks I have wronged him,' said McMurdo. 'I'll fight him with fists, or, if that won't satisfy him, I'll fight him any other way he chooses. Now I'll leave it to you, Councillor, to judge between us as a bodymaster should.'

'What is it, then?'

'A young lady. She's free to choose for herself.'

'Is she?' cried Baldwin.

'As between two brothers of the Lodge, I should say that she was,' said the Boss.

'Oh, that's your ruling, is it?'

'Yes, it is, Ted Baldwin,' said McGinty, with a wicked stare. 'Is it you that would dispute it?'

'You would throw over one that has stood by you this five years in favour of a man that you never saw before in your life? You're not bodymaster for life, Jack McGinty, and, by God, when next it comes to a vote –'

The Councillor sprang at him like a tiger. His hand closed round the other's neck and he hurled him back across one of the barrels. In his mad fury he would have squeezed the life out of him if McMurdo had not interfered.

'Easy, Councillor! For Heaven's sake, go easy!' he cried, as he dragged him back.

McGinty released his hold, and Baldwin, cowed and shaken, gasping for breath, and shivering in every limb as one who has looked over the very edge of death, sat up on the barrel over which he had been hurled.

'You've been asking for it this many a day, Ted Baldwin. Now you've got it,' cried McGinty, his huge chest rising and falling. 'Maybe you think if I were voted down from bodymaster you would find yourself in my shoes. It's for the Lodge to say that. But so long as I am the chief, I'll have no man lift his voice against me or my rulings.'

'I have nothing against you,' mumbled Baldwin, feeling his throat.

'Well, then,' cried the other, relapsing in a moment into a bluff joviality, 'we are all good friends again, and there's an end of the matter.'

He took a bottle of champagne down from the shelf and twisted out the cork.

'See now,' he continued, as he filled three high glasses, 'let us drink the quarrelling toast of the Lodge. After that, as you know, there can be no bad blood between us. Now, then, the left hand on the apple of my throat, I say to you, Ted Baldwin, what is the offence, sir?'

'The clouds are heavy,' answered Baldwin.

'But they will for ever brighten.'

'And this I swear.'

The men drank their wine, and the same ceremony was performed between Baldwin and McMurdo.

'There,' cried McGinty, rubbing his hands, 'that's the end of the black blood. You come under Lodge discipline if it goes farther, and that's a heavy hand in these parts, as Brother Baldwin knows, and as you will very soon find out, Brother McMurdo, if you ask for trouble.'

'Faith, I'd be slow to do that,' said McMurdo. He held out his hand to Baldwin. 'I'm quick to quarrel and quick to forgive. It's my hot Irish blood, they tell me. But it's over for me, and I bear no grudge.'

Baldwin had to take the proffered hand, for the baleful eye of the terrible Boss was upon him. But his sullen face showed how little the words of the other had moved him.

McGinty clapped them both on the shoulders.

'Tut! These girls, these girls!' he cried. 'To think that the same petticoats should come between two of my boys. It's the devil's own luck. Well, it's the colleen inside of them that must settle the question, for it's outside the jurisdiction of a bodymaster, and the Lord be praised for that. We have enough on us, without the women as well. You'll have to be affiliated to Lodge 341, Brother McMurdo. We have our own ways and methods, different to Chicago. Saturday night is our meeting, and if you come then we'll make you free for ever of the Vermissa Valley.'

3

Lodge 341, Vermissa

On the day following the evening which had contained so many exciting events McMurdo moved his lodgings from old Jacob Shafter's and took up his quarters at the widow MacNamara's, on the extreme outskirts of the town. Scanlan, his original acquaintance aboard the train, had occasion shortly afterwards to move into Vermissa, and the two lodged together. There was no other boarder, and the hostess was an easy-going old Irish-woman who left them to themselves, so that they had a freedom for speech and action welcome to men who had secrets in common. Shafter had relented to the extent of letting McMurdo come to his meals there when he liked, so that his intercourse with Ettie was by no means broken. On the contrary, it drew closer and more intimate as the weeks went by. In his bedroom at his new abode McMurdo felt it to be safe to take out the coining moulds, and under many a pledge of secrecy a number of the brothers from the Lodge were allowed to come in and see them, each of them carrying away in his pocket some examples of the false money, so cunningly struck that there was never the slightest difficulty or danger in passing it. Why, with such a wonderful art at his command, McMurdo should condescend to work at all was a perpetual mystery to his companions, though he made it clear to anyone who asked him that if he lived without any visible means it would very quickly bring the police on his track.

One policeman was, indeed, after him already, but the incident, as luck would have it, did the adventurer a great deal more good than harm. After the first introduction there were few evenings when he did not find his way to McGinty's saloon, there to make closer acquaintance with 'the boys', which was the jovial title by which the dangerous gang who infested the place were known to each other. His dashing manner and fearlessness of speech made him a favourite with them all, while the rapid and scientific way in which he polished off his antagonist in an 'all in' bar-room scrap earned the respect of that rough community. Another incident, however, raised him even higher in their estimation.

Just at the crowded hour one night the door opened and a man entered with the quiet blue uniform and peaked cap of the Coal and Iron Police. This was a special body raised by the railways and colliery owners to supplement the efforts of the ordinary civil police, who were perfectly helpless in the face of the organized ruffianism which terrorized the district. There was a hush as he entered, and many a curious glance was cast at him, but the relations between policemen and criminals are peculiar in the States, and McGinty himself, standing behind the counter, showed no surprise when the inspector enrolled himself among his customers.

'A straight whisky, for the night is bitter,' said the police-officer. 'I don't think we have met before, Councillor?'

'You'll be the new captain?' said McGinty.

'That's so. We're looking to you, Councillor, and to the other leading citizens, to help us in upholding law and order in this township. Captain Marvin is my name – of the Coal and Iron.'

'We'd do better without you, Captain Marvin,' said McGinty, coldly. 'For we have our own police of the township, and no need for any imported goods. What are you but the paid tool of the men of capital,[1] hired by them to club or to shoot your poorer fellow-citizens?'

'Well, well, we won't argue about that,' said the police-officer, good-humouredly. 'I expect we all do our duty same as we see it, but we can't all see it the same.' He had drunk off his glass and had turned to go, when his eyes fell upon the face of Jack McMurdo, who was scowling at his elbow. 'Halloa! halloa!' he cried, looking him up and down. 'Here's an old acquaintance.'

McMurdo shrank away from him.

'I was never a friend to you nor any other cursed copper in my life,' said he.

'An acquaintance isn't always a friend,' said the police-captain, grinning. 'You're Jack McMurdo of Chicago, right enough, and don't deny it.'

McMurdo shrugged his shoulders.

'I'm not denying it,' said he. 'D'ye think I'm ashamed of my own name?'

'You've got good cause to be, anyhow.'

'What the devil d'you mean by that?' he roared, with his fists clenched.

'No, no, Jack; bluster won't do with me. I was an officer in Chicago before ever I came to this darned coal-bunker, and I know a Chicago crook when I see one.'

McMurdo's face fell.

'Don't tell me that you're Marvin of the Chicago Central!' he cried.

'Just the same old Teddy Marvin at your service. We haven't forgotten the shooting of Jonas Pinto up there.'

'I never shot him.'

'Did you not? That's good impartial evidence, ain't it? Well, his death came in uncommon handy for you, or they would have had you for shoving the queer. Well, we can let that be bygones, for, between you and me – and perhaps I'm going farther than my duty in saying it – they could get no clear case against you, and Chicago's open to you tomorrow.'

'I'm very well where I am.'

'Well, I've given you the office, and you're a sulky dog not to thank me for it.'

'Well, I suppose you mean well, and I do thank you,' said McMurdo, in no very gracious manner.

'It's mum with me so long as I see you living on the straight,' said the captain. 'But, by gum, if you get off on the cross after this it's another story! So good night to you – and good night, Councillor.'

He left the bar-room, but not before he had created a local hero. McMurdo's deeds in far Chicago had been whispered before. He had put off all questions with a smile as one who did not wish to have greatness thrust upon him.[2] But now the thing was officially confirmed. The bar-loafers crowded round him and shook him heartily by the hand. He was free of the community from that time on. He could drink hard and show little trace of it, but that evening, had his mate Scanlan not been at hand to lead him home, the fêted hero would surely have spent his night under the bar.

On a Saturday night McMurdo was introduced to the Lodge. He had thought to pass in without ceremony as being an initiate of Chicago; but there were particular rites in Vermissa³ of which they were proud, and these had to be undergone by every postulant. The assembly met in a large room reserved for such purposes at the Union House. Some sixty members assembled at Vermissa, but that by no means represented the full strength of the organization, for there were several other lodges in the valley, and others across the mountains on either side, who exchanged members when any serious business was afoot, so that a crime might be done by men who were strangers to the locality. Altogether, there were not fewer than five hundred scattered over the coal district.

In the bare assembly room the men were gathered round a long table. At the side was a second one laden with bottles and glasses, on which some members of the company were already turning their eyes. McGinty sat at the head with a flat black velvet cap upon his shock of tangled black hair and a coloured purple stole round his neck, so that he seemed to be a priest presiding over some diabolical ritual. To right and left of him were the higher Lodge officials, the cruel, handsome face of Ted Baldwin among them. Each of these wore some scarf or medallion as emblem of his office. They were, for the most part, men of mature age, but the rest of the company consisted of young fellows from eighteen to twenty-five, the ready and capable agents who carried out the commands of their seniors. Among the older men were many whose features showed the tigerish, lawless souls within, but looking at the rank and file it was difficult to believe that these eager and open-faced young fellows were in very truth a dangerous gang of murderers, whose minds had suffered such complete moral perversion that they took a horrible pride in their proficiency at the business, and looked with the deepest respect at the man who had the reputation for making what they called a 'clean job'. To their contorted natures it had become a spirited and chivalrous thing to volunteer for service against some man who had never injured them, and whom, in many cases, they had never seen in their lives. The crime committed, they quarrelled as to who had actually struck the fatal blow, and amused each other and the company by describing the cries and contortions of the murdered man. At first they had shown some secrecy in their arrangements, but at the time which this narrative describes their proceedings were extraordinarily open, for the repeated failures of the law had proved to them that, on the one hand, no one would dare to witness against them, and, on the other, they had an unlimited number of staunch witnesses upon whom they could call, and a well-filled treasure chest from which they could draw the funds to engage the best legal talent in the State. In ten long years of outrage there had been no single conviction, and the only danger that ever threatened the Scowrers lay in the victim himself, who, however outnumbered and taken by surprise, might, and occasionally did, leave his mark upon his assailants.

McMurdo had been warned that some ordeal lay before him, but no one would tell him in what it consisted. He was led now into an outer room by two solemn brothers. Through the plank partition he could hear the murmur of many voices from the assembly within. Once or twice he caught the sound of his own name, and he knew that they were discussing his candidature. Then there entered an inner guard, with a green and gold sash across his chest.

'The bodymaster orders that he shall be trussed, blinded, and entered,' said he. The three of them then removed his coat, turned up the sleeve of his right arm, and finally passed a rope round above the elbows and made it fast. They next placed a thick black cap right over his head and the upper part of his face, so that he could see nothing. He was then led into the assembly hall.

It was pitch-dark and very oppressive under his hood. He heard the rustle and murmur of the people round him, and then the voice of McGinty sounded, dull and distant, through the covering of his ears.

'John McMurdo,' said the voice, 'are you already a member of the Ancient Order of Freemen?'

He bowed in assent.

'Is your lodge No. 29, Chicago?'

He bowed again.

'Dark nights are unpleasant,' said the voice.

'Yes, for strangers to travel,' he answered.

'The clouds are heavy.'

'Yes; a storm is approaching.'

'Are the brethren satisfied?' asked the bodymaster.

There was a general murmur of assent.

'We know, brother, by your sign and by your counter-sign, that you are indeed one of us,' said McGinty. 'We would have you know, however, that in this county and in other counties of these parts we have certain rites, and also certain duties of our own, which call for good men. Are you ready to be tested?'

'I am.'

'Are you of stout heart?'

'I am.'

'Take a stride forward to prove it.'

As the words were said he felt two hard points in front of his eyes, pressing upon them so that it appeared as if he could not move forward without a danger of losing them. None the less, he nerved himself to step resolutely out, and as he did so the pressure melted away. There was a low murmur of applause.

'He is of stout heart,' said the voice. 'Can you bear pain?'

'As well as another,' he answered.

'Test him!'

It was all he could do to keep himself from screaming out, for an agonizing pain shot through his forearm. He nearly fainted at the sudden shock of it, but he bit his lip and clenched his hands to hide his agony.

'I can take more than that,' said he.

This time there was loud applause. A finer first appearance had never been made in the Lodge. Hands clapped him on the back, and the hood was plucked from his head. He stood blinking and smiling amid the congratulations of the brothers.

'One last word, Brother McMurdo,' said McGinty. 'You have already sworn the oath of secrecy and fidelity, and you are aware that the punishment for any breach of it is instant and inevitable death?'

'I am,' said McMurdo.

'And you accept the rule of the bodymaster for the time being under all circumstances?'

'I do.'

'Then, in the name of Lodge 341, Vermissa, I welcome you to its privileges and debates. You will put the liquor on the table, Brother Scanlan, and we will drink to our worthy brother.'

McMurdo's coat had been brought to him, but before putting it on he examined his right arm, which still smarted heavily. There, on the flesh of the forearm, was a clear-cut circle with a triangle within it, deep and red, as the branding-iron had left it. One or two of his neighbours pulled up their sleeves and showed their own Lodge marks.

'We've all had it,' said one, 'but not all as brave as you over it.'

'Tut! It was nothing,' said he, but it burned and ached all the same.

When the drinks which followed the ceremony of initiation had all been disposed of, the business of the Lodge proceeded. McMurdo, accustomed only to the prosaic performances of Chicago, listened with open ears, and more surprise than he ventured to show, to what followed.

'The first business on the agenda paper,' said McGinty, 'is to read the following letter from Division Master Windle, of Merton County, Lodge 249. He says:

"Dear Sir, – There is a job to be done on Andrew Rae, of Rae and Sturmash, coal-owners near this place. You will remember that your Lodge owes us a return, having had the services of two brethren in the matter of the patrolman last fall. If you will send two good men they will be taken charge of by Treasurer Higgins of this Lodge, whose address you know. He will show them when to act and where. – Yours in freedom. J. W. Windle, D.M.A.O.F."[4] Windle has never refused us when we have had occasion to ask for the loan of a man or two, and it is not for us to refuse him.' McGinty paused and looked round the room with his dull, malevolent eyes. 'Who will volunteer for the job?'

Several young fellows held up their hands. The bodymaster looked at them with an approving smile.

'You'll do, Tiger Cormac. If you handle it as well as you did the last you won't be amiss. And you, Wilson.'

'I've no pistol,' said the volunteer, a mere boy in his teens.

'It's your first, is it not? Well, you have to be blooded some time. It will be a great start for you. As to the pistol, you'll find it waiting for you, or I'm mistaken. If you report yourselves on Monday it will be time enough. You'll get a great welcome when you return.'

'Any reward this time?' asked Cormac, a thick-set, dark-faced, brutal-looking young man, whose ferocity had earned him the nickname of 'Tiger'.

'Never mind the reward. You just do it for the honour of the thing. Maybe when it is done there will be a few odd dollars at the bottom of the box.'

'What has the man done?' asked young Wilson.

'Sure, it's not for the likes of you to ask what the man has done. He has been judged over there. That's no business of ours. All we have to do is to carry it out for them, same as they would for us. Speaking of that, two brothers from the Merton Lodge are coming over to us next week to do some business in this quarter.'

'Who are they?' asked someone.

'Faith, it is wiser not to ask. If you know nothing you can testify nothing, and no trouble can come of it. But they are men who will make a clean job when they are about it.'

'And time, too!' cried Ted Baldwin. 'Folk are getting out of hand in these parts. It was only last week that three of our men were turned off by Foreman Blaker. It's been owing him a long time, and he'll get it full and proper.'

'Get what?' McMurdo whispered to his neighbour.

'The business end of a buck-shot cartridge,' cried the man, with the loud laugh. 'What think you of our ways, brother?'

McMurdo's criminal soul seemed to have already absorbed the spirit of the vile association of which he was now a member.

'I like it well,' said he. ' 'Tis a proper place for a lad of mettle.'

Several of those who sat around heard his words and applauded them.

'What's that?' cried the black-maned bodymaster, from the end of the table.

' 'Tis our new brother, sir, who finds our ways to his taste.'

McMurdo rose to his feet for an instant.

'I would say, Worshipful Master, that if a man should be wanted I should take it as an honour to be chosen to help the Lodge.'

There was great applause at this. It was felt that a new sun was pushing its rim above the horizon. To some of the elders it seemed that the progress was a little too rapid.

'I would move,' said the secretary, Harraway, a vulture-faced old greybeard who sat near the chairman, 'that Brother McMurdo should wait until it is the good pleasure of the Lodge to employ him.'

'Sure, that was what I meant. I'm in your hands,' said McMurdo.

'Your time will come, brother,' said the chairman. 'We have marked you down as a willing man, and we believe that you will do good work in these parts. There is a small matter tonight in which you may take a hand, if it so please you.'

'I will wait for something that is worth while.'

'You can come tonight, anyhow, and it will help you to know what we stand for in this community. I will make the announcement later. Meanwhile' – he glanced at his agenda paper – 'I have one or two more points to bring before the meeting. First of all, I will ask the treasurer as to our bank balance. There is the pension to Jim Carnaway's widow. He was struck down doing the work of the Lodge, and it is for us to see that she is not the loser.'

'Jim was shot last month when they tried to kill Chester Wilcox, of Marley Creek,' McMurdo's neighbour informed him.

'The funds are good at the moment,' said the treasurer, with the bank-book in front of him. 'The firms have been generous of late. Max Linder and Co. paid five hundred to be left alone. Walker Brothers sent in a hundred, but I took it on myself to return it and ask for five. If I do not hear by Wednesday their winding gear may get out of order. We had to burn their breaker last year before they became reasonable. Then the West Section Coaling Company has paid its annual contribution. We have enough in hand to meet any obligations.'

'What about Archie Swindon?' asked a brother.

'He has sold out and left the district. The old devil left a note for us to say that he had rather be a free crossing-sweeper in New York than a large mine-owner under the power of a ring of blackmailers. By gosh, it was as well that he made a break for it before the note reached us! I guess he dare not show his face in this valley again.'

An elderly, clean-shaven man, with a kindly face and a good brow, rose from the end of the table which faced the chairman.

'Mr Treasurer,' he asked, 'may I ask who has bought the property of this man that we have driven out of the district?'

'Yes, Brother Morris. It has been bought by the State and Merton County Railroad Company.'

'And who bought the mines of Todman and of Lee that came into the market in the same way last year?'

'The same company, Brother Morris.'

'And who bought the ironworks of Manson and of Shuman and of Van Deher and of Atwood, which have all been given up of late?'

'They were all bought by the West Gilmerton General Mining Company.'

'I don't see, Brother Morris,' said the chairman, 'that it matters a nickel to us who buys them, since they can't carry them out of the district.'

'With all respect to you, Worshipful Master, I think that it may matter very much to us. This process has been going on now for ten long years. We are gradually driving all the small men out of trade. What is the result? We find in their places great companies like the Railroad or the General Iron, who have their directors in New York or Philadelphia, and care nothing for our threats. We can take it out of their local bosses, but it only means that others will be sent in their stead. And we are making it dangerous for ourselves. The small men could not harm us. They had not the money nor the power. So long as we did not squeeze them too dry, they would stay on under our power. But if these big companies find that we stand between them and their profits, they will spare no pains and no expense to hunt us down and bring us to court.'

There was a hush at these ominous words, and every face darkened as gloomy looks were exchanged. So omnipotent and unchallenged had they been that the very thought that there was possible retribution in the background had been banished from their minds. And yet the idea struck a chill to the most reckless of them.

'It is my advice,' the speaker continued, 'that we bear less heavily upon the small men. On the day that they have all been driven out the power of this society will have been broken.'

Unwelcome truths are not popular. There were angry cries as the speaker resumed his seat. McGinty rose with gloom upon his brow.

'Brother Morris,' said he, 'you were always a croaker. So long as the members of the Lodge stand together there is no power in this United States that can touch them. Sure, have we not tried it often enough in the law courts? I expect the big companies will find it easier to pay than to fight, same as the little companies do. And now, brethren' – McGinty took off his black velvet cap and his stole as he spoke – 'this Lodge has finished its business for the evening save for one small matter which may be mentioned when we are parting. The time has now come for fraternal refreshment and for harmony.'

Strange indeed is human nature. Here were these men to whom murder was familiar, who again and again had struck down the father of the family, some man against whom they had no personal feeling, without one thought of compunction or of compassion for his weeping wife or helpless children, and yet the tender or pathetic in music could move them to tears. McMurdo had a fine tenor voice, and if he had failed to gain the goodwill of the Lodge before, it could no longer have been withheld after he had thrilled them with 'I'm Sitting on the Stile, Mary', and 'On the Banks of Allan Water'. In his very first night the new recruit had made himself one of the most popular of the brethren, marked already for advancement and high office. There were other qualities, however, besides those of good fellowship, to make a worthy Freeman, and of these he was given an example before the evening was over. The whisky bottle had passed round many times, and the men were flushed and ripe for mischief, when their bodymaster rose once more to address them.

'Boys,' said he, 'there's one man in this town that wants trimming up, and it's for you to see that he gets it. I'm speaking of James Stanger, of the *Herald*.[5] You've seen how he's been opening his mouth against us again?'

There was a murmur of assent, with many a muttered oath. McGinty took a slip of paper from his waistcoat pocket.

' "Law and Order!" That's how he heads it. "Reign of Terror in the Coal and Iron District. Twelve years have now elapsed since the first assassinations which proved the existence of a criminal organization in our midst. From that day these outrages have never ceased, until now they have reached a pitch which makes us the opprobrium of the civilized world. Is it for such results as this that our great country welcomes to its bosom the alien who flies from the despotisms of Europe? Is it that they shall themselves become tyrants over the very men who have given them shelter, and that a state of terrorism and lawlessness should be established under the very shadow of the sacred folds of the starry flag of freedom which would raise horror in our minds if we read of it as existing under the most effete monarchy of the East? The men are known. The organization is patent and public. How long are we to endure it? Can we for ever live –" Sure, I've read enough of the slush!' cried the chairman, tossing the paper down upon the table. 'That's what he says of us. The question I'm asking you is, What shall we say to him?'

'Kill him!' cried a dozen fierce voices.

'I protest against that,' said Brother Morris, the man of the good brow and shaven face. 'I tell you, brethren, that our hand is too heavy in this valley, and that there will come a point where, in self-defence, every man will unite to crush us out. James Stanger is an old man. He is respected in the township and the district. His paper stands for all that is solid in the valley. If that man is struck down, there will be a stir through this State that will only end with our destruction.'

'And how would they bring about our destruction, Mister Standback?' cried McGinty. 'Is it by the police? Sure, half of them are in our pay and half of them afraid of us. Or is it by the law courts and the judge? Haven't we tried that before now, and what ever came of it?'

'There is a Judge Lynch that might try the case,' said Brother Morris.

A general shout of anger greeted the suggestion.

'I have but to raise my finger,' cried McGinty, 'and I could put two hundred men into this town that would clear it out from end to end.' Then, suddenly raising his voice and bending his huge black brows into a terrible frown: 'See here, Brother Morris, I have my eye on you, and have had for some time. You've no heart yourself, and you try to take the heart out of others. It will be an ill day for you, Brother Morris, when your own name comes on our agenda paper, and I'm thinking that it's just there that I ought to place it.'

Morris had turned deadly pale and his knees seemed to give way under him as he fell back into his chair. He raised his glass in his trembling hand and drank before he could answer.

'I apologize, Worshipful Master, to you and to every brother in this Lodge if I have said more than I should. I am a faithful member – you all know that – and it is my fear lest evil come to the Lodge which makes me speak in anxious words. But I have greater trust in your judgement than in my own, Worshipful Master, and I promise you that I will not offend again.'

The bodymaster's scowl relaxed as he listened to the humble words.

'Very good, Brother Morris. It's myself that would be sorry if it were needful to give you a lesson. But so long as I am in this chair we shall be a united Lodge in word and in deed. And now, boys,' he continued, looking round at the company, 'I'll say this much – that if Stanger got his full deserts there would be more trouble than we need ask for. These editors hang together, and every journal in the State would be crying out for police and troops. But I guess you can give him a pretty severe warning. Will you fix it, Brother Baldwin?'

'Sure!' said the young man, eagerly.

'How many will you take?'

'Half-a-dozen, and two to guard the door. You'll come, Gower, and you, Mansel, and you, Scanlan, and the two Willabys.'

'I promised the new brother he should go,' said the chairman.

Ted Baldwin looked at McMurdo with eyes which showed that he had not forgotten nor forgiven.

'Well, he can come if he wants,' he said, in a surly voice. 'That's enough. The sooner we get to work the better.'

The company broke up with shouts and yells and snatches of drunken song. The bar was still crowded with revellers, and many of the brethren remained there. The little band who had been told off for duty passed out into the street, proceeding in twos and threes along the sidewalk so as not to provoke attention. It was a bitterly cold night, with a half-moon shining brilliantly in a frosty, star-spangled sky. The men stopped and gathered in a yard which faced a high building. The words 'Vermissa Herald' were printed in gold lettering between the brightly-lit windows. From within came the clanking of the printing-press.

'Here, you,' said Baldwin to McMurdo; 'you can stand below at the door and see that the road is kept open for us. Arthur Willaby can stay with you. You others come with me. Have no fear, boys, for we have a dozen witnesses that we are in the Union bar at this very moment.'

It was nearly midnight, and the street was deserted save for one or two revellers upon their way home. The party crossed the road and, pushing open the door of the newspaper office, Baldwin and his men rushed in and up the stair which faced them. McMurdo and another remained below. From the room above came a shout, a cry for help, and then the sound of trampling feet and of falling chairs. An instant later a grey-haired man rushed out on to the landing. He was seized before he could get farther, and his spectacles came tinkling down to McMurdo's feet. There was a thud and a groan. He was on his face and half-a-dozen sticks were clattering together as they fell upon him. He writhed, and his long, thin limbs quivered under the blows. The others ceased at last, but Baldwin, his cruel face set in an infernal smile, was hacking at the man's head, which he vainly endeavoured to defend with his arms. His white hair was dabbled with patches of blood. Baldwin was still stooping over his victim, putting in a short, vicious blow whenever he could see a part exposed, when McMurdo dashed up the stair and pushed him back.

'You'll kill the man,' said he. 'Drop it!'

Baldwin looked at him in amazement.

'Curse you!' he cried. 'Who are you to interfere – you that are new to the Lodge? Stand back!' He raised his stick, but McMurdo had whipped his pistol out of his hip pocket.

'Stand back yourself!' he cried. 'I'll blow your face in if you lay a hand on me. As to the Lodge, wasn't it the order of the bodymaster that the man was not to be killed, and what are you doing but killing him?'

'It's truth he says,' remarked one of the men.

'By gosh, you'd best hurry yourselves!' cried the man below. 'The windows are all lighting up and you'll have the whole township on your back inside of five minutes.'

There was indeed the sound of shouting in the street, and a little group of compositors and typesetters was forming in the hall below and nerving itself to action. Leaving the limp and motionless body of the editor at the head of the stair, the criminals rushed down and made their way swiftly along the street. Having reached the Union House, some of them mixed with the crowd in McGinty's saloon, whispering across the bar to the Boss that the job had been well carried through. Others, and among them McMurdo, broke away into side-streets, and so by devious paths to their own homes.

4

The Valley of Fear

When McMurdo awoke next morning he had good reason to remember his initiation into the Lodge. His head ached with the effect of the drink, and his arm, where he had been branded, was hot and swollen. Having his own peculiar source of income, he was irregular in his attendance at his work, so he had a late breakfast and remained at home for the morning, writing a long letter to a friend. Afterwards he read the *Daily Herald*. In a special column, put in at the last moment, he read, 'Outrage at the *Herald* Office. Editor seriously injured.' It was a short account of the facts with which he was himself more familiar than the writer could have been. It ended with the statement:

The matter is now in the hands of the police, but it can hardly be hoped that their exertions will be attended by any better results than in the past. Some of the men were recognized, and there is hope that a conviction may be obtained. The source of the outrage was, it need hardly be said, that infamous society which has held this community in bondage for so long a period, and against which the *Herald* has taken so uncompromising a stand. Mr Stanger's many friends will rejoice to hear that, though he has been cruelly and brutally beaten and has sustained severe injuries about the head, there is no immediate danger to his life.

Below, it stated that a guard of Coal and Iron Police, armed with Winchester rifles, had been requisitioned for the defence of the office.

McMurdo had laid down the paper, and was lighting his pipe with a hand which was shaky from the excesses of the previous evening, when there was a knock outside, and his landlady brought to him a note which had just been handed in by a lad. It was unsigned, and ran thus:

I should wish to speak to you, but had rather not do so in your house. You will find me beside the flagstaff upon Miller Hill. If you will come there now I have something which it is important for you to hear and for me to say.

McMurdo read the note twice with the utmost surprise, for he could not imagine what it meant or who was the author of it. Had it been in a feminine hand he might have imagined that it was the beginning of one of those adventures which had been familiar enough in his past life. But it was the writing of a man, and of a well-educated one, too. Finally, after some hesitation, he determined to see the matter through.

Miller Hill is an ill-kept public park in the very centre of the town. In summer it is a favourite resort of the people, but in winter it is desolate enough. From the top of it one has a view not only of the whole grimy, straggling town, but of the winding valley beneath, with its scattered mines and factories blackening the snow on either side of it, and of the wooded and white-capped ranges which flank it. McMurdo strolled up the winding path hedged in with evergreen until he reached the deserted restaurant which forms the centre of summer gaiety. Beside it was a bare flagstaff, and underneath it a man, his hat drawn down and the collar of his overcoat raised up. When he turned his face McMurdo saw that it was Brother Morris, he who had incurred the anger of the bodymaster the night before. The Lodge sign was given and exchanged as they met.

'I wanted to have a word with you, Mr McMurdo,' said the older man, speaking with a hesitation which showed that he was on delicate ground. 'It was kind of you to come.'

'Why did you not put your name to the note?'

'One has to be cautious, mister. One never knows in times like these how a thing may come back to one. One never knows either who to trust or who not to trust.'

'Surely one may trust brothers of the Lodge?'

'No, no; not always,' cried Morris, with vehemence. 'Whatever we say, even what we think, seems to go back to that man, McGinty.'

'Look here,' said McMurdo, sternly; 'it was only last night, as you know well, that I swore good faith to our bodymaster. Would you be asking me to break my oath?'

'If that is the view you take,' said Morris, sadly, 'I can only say that I am sorry I gave you the trouble to come to meet me. Things have come to a bad pass when two free citizens cannot speak their thoughts to each other.'

McMurdo, who had been watching his companion very narrowly, relaxed somewhat in his bearing.

'Sure, I spoke for myself only,' said he. 'I am a newcomer, as you know, and I am strange to it all. It is not for me to open my mouth, Mr Morris, and if you think well to say anything to me I am here to hear it.'

'And to take it back to Boss McGinty,' said Morris bitterly.

'Indeed, then, you do me injustice there,' cried McMurdo. 'For myself I am loyal to the Lodge, and so I tell you straight, but I would be a poor creature if I were to repeat to any other what you might say to me in confidence. It will go no further than me, though I warn you that you may get neither help nor sympathy.'

'I have given up looking for either the one or the other,' said Morris. 'I may be putting my very life in your hands by what I say, but, bad as you are – and it seemed to me last night that you were shaping to be as bad as the worst – still you are new to it, and your conscience cannot yet be as hardened as theirs. That was why I thought to speak with you.'

'Well, what have you to say?'

'If you give me away, may a curse be on you!'

'Sure, I said I would not.'

'I would ask you, then, when you joined the Freemen's Society in Chicago, and swore vows of charity and fidelity, did ever it cross your mind that you might find it would lead you to crime?'

'If you call it crime,' McMurdo answered.

'Call it crime!' cried Morris, his voice vibrating with passion. 'You have seen little of it if you can call it anything else. Was it crime last night when a man, old enough to be your father, was beaten till the blood dripped from his white hairs? Was that crime – or what else would you call it?'

'There are some would say it was war,' said McMurdo. 'A war of two classes with all in, so that each struck as best it could.'

'Well, did you think of such a thing when you joined the Freemen's Society in Chicago?'

'No, I'm bound to say I did not.'

'Nor did I when I joined it at Philadelphia. It was just a benefit club and a meeting-place for one's fellows. Then I heard of this place – curse the hour that the name first fell upon my ears! – and I came to better myself. My God, to better myself! My wife and three children came with me. I started a dry-goods store in Market Square, and I prospered well. The word had gone round that I was a Freeman, and I was forced to join the local Lodge, same as you did last night. I've the badge of shame on my forearm, and something worse branded on my heart. I found that I was under the orders of a black villain, and caught in a meshwork of crime. What could I do? Every word I said to make things better was taken as treason, same as it was last night. I can't get away, for all I have in the world is in my store. If I leave the society, I know well that it means murder to me, and God knows what to my wife and children. Oh, man, it is awful – awful!' He put his hands to his face, and his body shook with convulsive sobs.

McMurdo shrugged his shoulders.

'You were too soft for the job,' said he. 'You are the wrong sort for such work.'

'I had a conscience and a religion, but they made me a criminal among them. I was chosen for a job. If I backed down I knew well what would come to me. Maybe I'm a coward. Maybe it's the thought of my poor little woman and the children that makes me one. Anyhow, I went. I guess it will haunt me for ever. It was a lonely house, twenty miles from here, over the range yonder. I was told off for the door, same as you were last night. They could not trust me with the job. The others went in. When they came out their hands were crimson to the wrists. As we turned away a child was screaming out of the house behind us. It was a boy of five who had seen his father murdered. I nearly fainted with the horror of it, and yet I had to keep a bold and smiling face, for well I knew that if I did not it would be out of my house that they would come next with their bloody hands, and it would be my little Fred that would be screaming for his father. But I was a criminal then – part sharer in a murder, lost for ever in this world, and lost also in the next. I am a good Catholic, but the priest would have no word with me when he heard I was a Scowrer, and I am excommunicated from my faith. That's how it stands with me. And I see you going down the same road, and I ask you what the end is to be? Are you ready to be a cold-blooded murderer also, or can we do anything to stop it?'

'What would you do?' asked McMurdo, abruptly. 'You would not inform?'

'God forbid!' cried Morris. 'Sure, the very thought would cost me my life.'

'That's well,' said McMurdo. 'I'm thinking that you are a weak man, and that you make too much of the matter.'

'Too much! Wait till you have lived here longer. Look down the valley. See the cloud of a hundred chimneys that over-shadows it. I tell you that the cloud of murder hangs thicker and lower than that over the heads of the people. It is the Valley of Fear – the Valley of Death. The terror is in the hearts of the people from the dusk to the dawn. Wait, young man, and you will learn for yourself.'

'Well, I'll let you know what I think when I have seen more,' said McMurdo, carelessly. 'What is very clear is that you are not the man for the place, and that the sooner you sell out – if you only get a dime a dollar for what the business is worth – the better it will be for you.

What you have said is safe with me, but, by gosh! if I thought you were an informer –'

'No, no!' cried Morris, piteously.

'Well, let it rest at that. I'll bear what you have said in mind, and maybe some day I'll come back to it. I expect you meant kindly by speaking to me like this. Now I'll be getting home.'

'One word before you go,' said Morris. 'We may have been seen together. They may want to know what we have spoken about.'

'Ah, that's well thought of.'

'I offer you a clerkship in my store.'

'And I refuse it. That's our business. Well, so long, Brother Morris, and may you find things go better with you in the future.'

That same afternoon, as McMurdo sat smoking, lost in thought, beside the stove of his sitting-room, the door swung open, and its frame-work was filled with the huge figure of Boss McGinty. He passed the sign, and then, seating himself opposite to the young man, he looked at him steadily for some time, a look which was as steadily returned.

'I'm not much of a visitor, Brother McMurdo,' he said, at last. 'I guess I am too busy over the folk that visit me. But I thought I'd stretch a point and drop down to see you in your own house.'

'I'm proud to see you here, Councillor,' McMurdo answered, heartily, bringing his whisky-bottle out of the cupboard. 'It's an honour that I had not expected.'

'How's the arm?' asked the Boss.

McMurdo made a wry face.

'Well, I'm not forgetting it,' he said. 'But it's worth it.'

'Yes, it's worth it,' the other answered, 'to those that are loyal, and go through with it, and are a help to the Lodge. What were you speaking to Brother Morris about on Miller Hill this morning?'

The question came so suddenly that it was well that he had his answer prepared. He burst into a hearty laugh.

'Morris didn't know I could earn a living here at home. He sha'n't know either, for he has got too much conscience for the likes of me. But he's a good-hearted old chap. It was his idea that I was at a loose end, and that he would do me a good turn by offering me a clerkship in a dry-goods store.'

'Oh, that was it?'

'Yes, that was it.'

'And you refused it?'

'Sure. Couldn't I earn ten times as much in my own bedroom with four hours' work?'

'That's so. But I wouldn't get about too much with Morris.'

'Why not?'

'Well, I guess because I tell you not. That's enough for most folk in these parts.'

'It may be enough for most folks, but it ain't enough for me, Councillor,' said McMurdo, boldly. 'If you are a judge of men you'll know that.'

The swarthy giant glared at him, and his hairy paw closed for an instant round the glass as though he would hurl it at the head of his companion. Then he laughed in his loud, boisterous, insincere fashion.

'You're a queer card, for sure,' said he. 'Well, if you want reasons I'll give them. Did Morris say nothing to you against the Lodge?'

'No.'

'Nor against me?'

'No.'

'Well, that's because he daren't trust you. But in his heart he is not a loyal brother. We know that well, so we watch him, and we wait for the time to admonish him. I'm thinking that the time is drawing near. There's no room for scabby sheep in our pen. But if you keep company with a disloyal man, we might think that you were disloyal, too. See?'

'There's no chance of my keeping company with him, for I dislike the man,' McMurdo answered. 'As to being disloyal, if it was any man but you, he would not use the word to me twice.'

'Well, that's enough,' said McGinty, draining off his glass. 'I came down to give you a word in season and you've had it.'

'I'd like to know,' said McMurdo, 'how you ever came to learn that I had spoken with Morris at all.'

McGinty laughed.

'It's my business to know what goes on in this township,' said he. 'I guess you'd best reckon on my hearing all that passes. Well, time's up, and I'll just say –'

But his leave-taking was cut short in a very unexpected fashion. With a sudden crash the door flew open, and three frowning, intent faces glared in at them from under the peaks of police caps. McMurdo sprang to his feet and half drew his revolver, but his arm stopped midway as he became conscious that two Winchester rifles were levelled at his head. A man in uniform advanced into the room, a six-shooter in his hand. It was Captain Marvin, once of Chicago, and now of the Coal and Iron Constabulary. He shook his head with a half smile at McMurdo.

'I thought you'd be getting into trouble, Mr Crooked McMurdo of Chicago,' said he. 'Can't keep out of it, can you? Take your hat and come along with us.'

'I guess you'll pay for this, Captain Marvin,' said McGinty. 'Who are you, I'd like to know, to break into a house in this fashion, and molest honest, law-abiding men?'

'You're standing out in this deal, Councillor McGinty,' said the police captain. 'We are not out after you, but after this man McMurdo. It is for you to help, not to hinder us in our duty.'

'He is a friend of mine, and I'll answer for his conduct,' said the Boss.

'By all accounts, Mr McGinty, you may have to answer for your own conduct some of these days,' the police captain answered. 'This man McMurdo was a crook before ever he came here, and he's a crook still. Cover him, patrolman, while I disarm him.'

'There's my pistol,' said McMurdo, coolly. 'Maybe, Captain Marvin, if you and I were alone and face to face, you would not take me so easily.'

'Where's your warrant?' asked McGinty. 'By gosh! a man might as well live in Russia as in Vermissa while folk like you are running the police. It's a capitalist outrage, and you'll hear more of it, I reckon.'

'You do what you think is your duty the best way you can, Councillor. We'll look after ours.'

'What am I accused of?' asked McMurdo.

'Of being concerned in the beating of old Editor Stanger at the *Herald* office. It wasn't your fault that it isn't a murder charge.'

'Well, if that's all you have against him,' cried McGinty, with a laugh, 'you can save yourself a deal of trouble by dropping it right now. This man was with me in my saloon playing poker up to midnight, and I can bring a dozen to prove it.'

'That's your affair, and I guess you can settle it in court tomorrow. Meanwhile, come on, McMurdo, and come quietly if you don't want a gun-butt across your head. You stand wide, Mr McGinty, for I warn you I will brook no resistance when I am on duty.'

So determined was the appearance of the captain that both McMurdo and his Boss were forced to accept the situation. The latter managed to have a few whispered words with the prisoner before they parted.

'What about –' He jerked his thumb upwards to signify the coining plant.

'All right,' whispered McMurdo, who had devised a safe hiding-place under the floor.

'I'll bid you good-bye,' said the Boss, shaking hands. 'I'll see Reilly, the lawyer, and take the defence upon myself. Take my word for it that they won't be able to hold you.'

'I wouldn't bet on that. Guard the prisoner, you two, and shoot him if he tries any games. I'll search the house before I leave.'

Marvin did so, but apparently found no trace of the concealed plant. When he had descended he and his men escorted McMurdo to the headquarters. Darkness had fallen and a keen blizzard was blowing, so that the streets were nearly deserted, but a few loiterers followed the group and, emboldened by invisibility, shouted imprecations at the prisoner.

'Lynch the cursed Scowrer!' they cried. 'Lynch him!' They laughed and jeered as he was pushed into the police depot. After a short formal examination from the inspector-in-charge, he was handed on to the common cell. Here he found Baldwin and three other criminals of the night before, all arrested that afternoon, and waiting their trial next morning.

But even within this inner fortress of the law the long arm of the Freemen was able to extend. Late at night there came a jailer with a straw bundle for their bedding, out of which he extracted two bottles of whisky, some glasses, and a pack of cards. They spent an hilarious night without an anxious thought as to the ordeal of the morning.

Nor had they cause, as the result was to show. The magistrate could not possibly, on the evidence, have brought in the sentence which would have carried the matter to a higher court. On the one hand, the compositors and pressmen were forced to admit that the light was uncertain, that they were themselves much perturbed, and that it was difficult for them to absolutely swear to the identity of the assailants, although they believed that the accused were among them. Cross-examined by the clever attorney who had been engaged by McGinty, they were even more nebulous in their evidence.

The injured man had already deposed that he was so taken by surprise by the suddenness of the attack that he could state nothing beyond the fact that the first man who struck him wore a moustache. He added that he knew them to be Scowrers, since no one else in the community could possibly have any enmity to him, and he had long been threatened on account of his outspoken editorials. On the other hand, it was clearly shown by the united and unfaltering evidence of six citizens, including that high municipal official Councillor McGinty, that the men had been at a card party at the Union House until an hour very much later than the commission of the outrage. Needless to say that they were discharged with something very near to an apology from the Bench for the inconvenience to which they had been put, together with an implied censure of Captain Marvin and the police for their officious zeal.

The verdict was greeted with loud applause by a Court in which McMurdo saw many familiar faces. Brothers of the Lodge smiled and waved. But there were others who sat with compressed lips and brooding eyes as the men filed out of the dock. One of them, a little dark-bearded, resolute fellow, put the thoughts of himself and comrades into words as the ex-prisoners passed him.

'You damned murderers!' he said. 'We'll fix you yet.'

5

The Darkest Hour

If anything had been needed to give an impetus to Jack McMurdo's popularity among his fellows, it would have been his arrest and acquittal. That a man on the very night of joining the Lodge should have done something which brought him before the magistrate was a new record in the annals of the society. Already he had earned the reputation of a good boon companion, a cheery reveller, and withal a man of high temper, who would not take an insult even from the all-powerful Boss himself. But, in addition to this, he impressed his comrades with the idea that among them all there was not one whose brain was so ready to devise a bloodthirsty scheme, or whose hand would be more capable of carrying it out. 'He'll be the boy for the clean job,' said the oldsters to each other, and waited their time until they could set him to his work. McGinty had instruments enough already, but he recognized that this was a supremely able one. He felt like a man holding a fierce bloodhound in leash. There were curs to do the smaller work, but some day he would slip this creature upon its prey. A few members of the Lodge, Ted Baldwin among them, resented the rapid rise of the stranger, and hated him for it, but they kept clear of him, for he was as ready to fight as to laugh.

But if he gained favour with his fellows, there was another quarter, one which had become even more vital to him, in which he lost it. Ettie Shafter's father would have nothing more to do with him, nor would he allow him to enter the house. Ettie herself was too deeply in love to give him up altogether, and yet her own good sense warned her of what would come from a marriage with a man who was regarded as a criminal. One morning after a sleepless night she determined to see him, possibly for the last time, and make one strong endeavour to draw him from those evil influences which were sucking him down. She went to his house, as he had often begged her to do, and made her way into the room which he used as his sitting-room.

He was seated at a table with his back turned and a letter in front of him. A sudden spirit of girlish mischief came over her – she was still only nineteen. He had not heard her when she pushed open the door. Now she tip-toed forward, and laid her hand lightly upon his bended shoulders.

If she had expected to startle him, she certainly succeeded, but only in turn to be startled herself. With a tiger spring he turned on her, and his right hand was feeling for her throat. At the same instant, with the other hand he crumpled up the paper that lay before him. For a moment he stood glaring. Then astonishment and joy took the place of the ferocity which had convulsed his features – a ferocity which had sent her shrinking back in horror as from something which had never before intruded into her gentle life.

'It's you!' said he, mopping his brow. 'And to think that you should come to me, heart of my hearts, and I should find nothing better to do than to want to strangle you! Come then, darling,' and he had held out his arms. 'Let me make it up to you.'

But she had not recovered from that sudden glimpse of guilty fear which she had read in the man's face. All her woman's instinct told her that it was not the mere fright of a man who is startled. Guilt – that was it – guilt and fear.

'What's come over you, Jack?' she cried. 'Why were you so scared of me? Oh, Jack, if your conscience was at ease, you would not have looked at me like that.'

'Sure, I was thinking of other things, and when you came tripping so lightly on those fairy feet of yours – '

'No, no; it was more than that, Jack.' Then a sudden suspicion seized her. 'Let me see that letter you were writing.'

'Ah, Ettie, I couldn't do that.'

Her suspicions became certainties.

'It's to another woman!' she cried. 'I know it. Why else should you hold it from me? Was it to your wife that you were writing? How am I to know that you are not a married man – you, a stranger, that nobody knows?'

'I am not married, Ettie. See now, I swear it. You're the only one woman on earth to me. By the Cross of Christ, I swear it!'

He was so white with passionate earnestness that she could not but believe him.

'Well, then,' she cried, 'why will you not show me the letter?'

'I'll tell you, acushla,' said he. 'I'm under oath not to show it, and just as I wouldn't break my word to you, so I would keep it to those who hold my promise. It's the business of the Lodge, and even to you it's secret. And if I was scared when a hand fell on me, can't you understand it when it might have been the hand of a detective?'

She felt that he was telling the truth. He gathered her into his arms, and kissed away her fears and doubts.

'Sit here by me, then. It's a queer throne for such a queen, but it's the best your poor lover can find. He'll do better for you some of these days, I'm thinking. Now your mind is easy once again, is it not?'

'How can it ever be at ease, Jack, when I know that you are a criminal among criminals – when I never know the day that I may hear that you are in the dock for murder? McMurdo the Scowrer – that was what one of our boarders called you yesterday. It went through my heart like a knife.'

'Sure, hard words break no bones.'

'But they were true.'

'Well, dear, it's not as bad as you think. We are but poor men that are trying in our own way to get our rights.'

Ettie threw her arms round her lover's neck.

'Give it up, Jack! For my sake – for God's sake, give it up! It was to ask you that I came here today. Oh, Jack, see, I beg it of you on my bended knees. Kneeling here before you, I implore you to give it up.'

He raised her, and soothed her with her head against his breast.

'Sure, my darlin', you don't know what it is you are asking. How could I give it up when it would be to break my oath and to desert my comrades? If you could see how things stand with me, you could never ask it of me. Besides, if I wanted to, how could I do it? You don't suppose that the Lodge would let a man go free with all its secrets?'

'I've thought of that, Jack. I've planned it all. Father has saved some money. He is weary of this place, where the fear of these people darkens our lives. He is ready to go. We would fly together to Philadelphia or New York, where we should be safe from them.'

McMurdo laughed.

'The Lodge has a long arm. Do you think it could not stretch from here to Philadelphia or New York?'

'Well, then, to the West, or to England, or to Sweden, whence father came. Anywhere to get away from this Valley of Fear.'

McMurdo thought of old Brother Morris.

'Sure, it is the second time I have heard the valley so named,' said he. 'The shadow does indeed seem to lie heavy on some of you.'

'It darkens every moment of our lives. Do you suppose that Ted Baldwin has ever forgiven us? If it were not that he fears you, what do you suppose that our chances would be? If you saw the look in those dark, hungry eyes of his when they fall on me!'

'By gosh! I'd teach him better manners if I caught him at it. But see here, little girl. I can't leave here. I can't. Take that from me once and for all. But if you will leave me to find my own way, I will try to prepare a way of getting honourably out of it.'

'There is no honour in such a matter.'

'Well, well, it's just how you look at it. But if you'll give me six months I'll work it so as I can leave without being ashamed to look others in the face.'

The girl laughed with joy.

'Six months!' she cried. 'Is it a promise?'

'Well, it may be seven or eight. But within a year at the farthest we will leave the valley behind us.'

It was the most that Ettie could obtain, and yet it was something. There was this distant light to illuminate the gloom of the immediate future. She returned to her father's house more lighthearted than she had ever been since Jack McMurdo had come into her life.

It might be thought that as a member all the doings of the society would be told to him, but he was soon to discover that the organization was wider and more complex than the simple Lodge. Even Boss McGinty was ignorant as to many things, for there was an official named the county delegate, living at Hobson's Patch, farther down the line, who had power over several different Lodges, which he wielded in a sudden and arbitrary way. Only once did McMurdo see him, a sly little grey-haired rat of a man with a slinking gait and a sidelong glance which was charged with malice. Evans Pott[1] was his name, and even the great Boss of Vermissa felt towards him something of the repulsion and fear which the huge Danton may have felt for the puny but dangerous Robespierre.[2]

One day Scanlan, who was McMurdo's fellow-boarder, received a note from McGinty, enclosing one from Evans Pott, which informed him that he was sending over two good men, Lawler and Andrews,[3] who had instructions to act in the neighbourhood, though it was best for the cause that no particulars as to their objects should be given. Would the bodymaster see to it that suitable arrangements be made for their lodgings and comfort until the time for action should arrive? McGinty added that it was impossible for anyone to remain secret at the Union House, and that, therefore, he would be obliged if McMurdo and Scanlan would put the strangers up for a few days in their boarding-house.

The same evening the two men arrived, each carrying his grip-sack. Lawler was an elderly man, shrewd, silent, and self-contained, clad in an old black frock-coat, which, with his soft felt hat and ragged, grizzled beard, gave him a general resemblance to an itinerant preacher. His companion, Andrews, was little more than a boy, frank-faced and cheerful, with the breezy manner of one who is out for a holiday, and means to enjoy every minute of it. Both of the men were total abstainers, and behaved in all ways as exemplary members of society, with the one single exception that they were assassins who had often proved themselves to be most capable instruments for this Association of murder. Lawler had already carried out fourteen commissions of the kind, and Andrews three.

They were, as McMurdo found, quite ready to converse about their deeds in the past, which they recounted with the half-bashful pride of men who had done good and unselfish service for the community. They were reticent, however, as to the immediate job in hand.

'They chose us because neither I nor the boy here drink,' Lawler explained. 'They can count on us saying no more than we should.

You must not take it amiss but it is the orders of the county delegate that we obey.'

'Sure, we are all in it together,' said Scanlan, McMurdo's mate, as the four sat together at supper.

'That's true enough, and we'll talk till the cows come home of the killing of Charlie Williams, or of Simon Bird, or any other job in the past. But till the work is done we say nothing.'

'There are half a dozen about here that I have a word to say to,' said McMurdo, with an oath. 'I suppose it isn't Jack Knox, of Ironhill, that you are after? I'd go some way to see him get his deserts.'

'No; it's not him yet.'

'Or Herman Strauss?'

'No, nor him either.'

'Well, if you won't tell us, we can't make you, but I'd be glad to know.'

Lawler smiled, and shook his head. He was not to be drawn.

In spite of the reticence of their guests, Scanlan and McMurdo were quite determined to be present at what they called the 'fun'. When, therefore, at an early hour one morning McMurdo heard them creeping down the stairs, he awakened Scanlan, and the two hurried on their clothes. When they were dressed they found that the others had stolen out, leaving the door open behind them. It was not yet dawn, and by the light of the lamps they could see the two men some distance down the street. They followed them warily, treading noiselessly in the deep snow.

The boarding-house was near the edge of the township, and soon they were at the cross-roads which are beyond its boundary. Here three men were waiting, with whom Lawler and Andrews held a short, eager conversation. Then they all moved on together. It was clearly some notable job which needed numbers. At this point there are several trails which led to various mines. The strangers took that which led to the Crow Hill, a huge business which was in strong hands, who had been able, thanks to their energetic and fearless New England manager, Josiah H. Dunn,[4] to keep some order and discipline during the long reign of terror.

Day was breaking now, and a line of workmen were slowly making their way, singly and in groups, along the blackened path.

McMurdo and Scanlan strolled on with the others, keeping in sight of the men whom they followed. A thick mist lay over them, and from the heart of it there came the sudden scream of a steam whistle. It was the ten-minute signal before the cages descended and the day's labour began.

When they reached the open space round the mineshaft there were a hundred miners waiting, stamping their feet and blowing on their fingers, for it was bitterly cold. The strangers stood in a little group under the shadow of the engine-house. Scanlan and McMurdo climbed a heap of slag, from which the whole scene lay before them. They saw the mine engineer, a great bearded Scotsman named Menzines, come out of the engine-house and blow his whistle for the cages to be lowered. At the same instant a tall, loose-framed young man, with a clean-shaven, earnest face, advanced eagerly towards the pit-head. As he came forward his eyes fell upon the group, silent and motionless, under the engine-house. The men had drawn down their hats and turned up their collars to screen their faces. For a moment the presentiment of death laid its cold hand upon the manager's heart. At the next he had shaken it off and saw only his duty towards intrusive strangers.

'Who are you?' he asked, as he advanced. 'What are you loitering there for?'

There was no answer, but the lad Andrews stepped forward and shot him in the stomach. The hundred waiting miners stood as motionless and helpless as if they were paralysed. The manager clapped his two hands to the wound and doubled himself up. Then he staggered away, but another of the assassins fired, and he went down sideways, kicking and clawing among a heap of clinkers. Menzies, the Scotsman, gave a roar of rage at the sight, and rushed with an iron spanner at the murderers, but was met by two balls in the face, which dropped him dead at their very feet. There was a surge forward of some of the miners, and an inarticulate cry of pity and of anger, but a couple of the strangers emptied their six-shooters over the heads of the crowd, and they broke and scattered, some of them rushing wildly back to their homes in Vermissa. When a few of the bravest had rallied, and there was a return to the mine, the murderous gang had vanished in

THE VALLEY OF FEAR

the mists of the morning without a single witness being able to swear to the identity of these men who in front of a hundred spectators had wrought this double crime.

Scanlan and McMurdo made their way back, Scanlan somewhat subdued, for it was the first murder job that he had seen with his own eyes, and it appeared less funny than he had been led to believe. The horrible screams of the dead manager's wife pursued them as they hurried to the town. McMurdo was absorbed and silent, but he showed no sympathy for the weakening of his companion.

'Sure, it is like a war,' he repeated. 'What is it but a war between us and them, and we hit back where we best can?'

There was high revel in the Lodge room at the Union House that night, not only over the killing of the manager and engineer of the Crow Hill mine, which would bring this organization into line with the other blackmailed and terror-stricken companies of the district, but also over a distant triumph which had been wrought by the hands of the Lodge itself. It would appear that when the county delegate had sent over five good men to strike a blow in Vermissa, he had demanded that, in return, three Vermissa men should be secretly selected and sent across to kill William Hales, of Stake Royal, one of the best-known and most popular mine-owners in the Gilmerton district, a man who was believed not to have an enemy in the world, for he was in all ways a pattern employer. He had insisted, however, upon efficiency in the work, and had therefore paid off certain drunken and idle *employés* who were members of the all-powerful society. Coffin notices hung outside his door had not weakened his resolution, and so in a free, civilized country he found himself condemned to death.

The execution had now been duly carried out. Ted Baldwin, who sprawled in the seat of honour beside the bodymaster, had been the chief of the party. His flushed face and glazed, bloodshot eyes told of sleeplessness and drink. He and his two comrades had spent the night before among the mountains. They were unkempt and weather-stained. But no heroes, returning from a forlorn hope, could have had a warmer welcome from their comrades. The story was told and retold amid cries of delight and shouts of laughter. They had waited for their man as he drove home at nightfall, taking their station at the top of a steep hill, where his horse must be at a walk. He was so furred to keep out the cold that he could not lay his hand on his pistol. They had pulled him out and shot him again and again.

None of them knew the man, but there is eternal drama in a killing, and they had shown the Scowrers of Gilmerton that the Vermissa men were to be relied upon. There had been one *contretemps*, for a man and his wife had driven up while they were still emptying their revolvers into the silent body. It had been suggested that they should shoot them both, but they were harmless folk who were not connected with the mines, so they were sternly bidden to drive on and keep silent, lest a worse thing befall them. And so the blood-mottled figure had been left as a warning to all such hard-hearted employers, and the three noble avengers had hurried off into the mountains where unbroken Nature comes down to the very edge of the furnaces and the slag-heaps.

It had been a great day for the Scowrers. The shadow had fallen even darker over the valley. But as the wise general chooses the moment of victory in which to redouble his efforts, so that his foes may have no time to steady themselves after disaster, so Boss McGinty, looking out upon the scene of his operations with brooding and malicious eyes, had devised a new attack upon those who opposed him. That very night, as the half-drunken company broke up, he touched McMurdo on the arm and led him aside into that inner room where they had their first interview.

'See here, my lad,' said he, 'I've got a job that's worthy of you at last. You'll have the doing of it in your own hands.'

'Proud I am to hear it,' McMurdo answered.

'You can take two men with you – Manders and Reilly. They have been warned for service. We'll never be right in this district until Chester Wilcox has been settled, and you'll have the thanks of every Lodge in the coalfields if you can down him.'

'I'll do my best, anyhow. Who is he, and where shall I find him?'

McGinty took his eternal half-chewed, half-smoked cigar from the corner of his mouth, and proceeded to draw a rough diagram on a page torn from his notebook.

'He's the chief foreman of the Iron Dyke Company. He's a hard citizen, an old colour-sergeant of the war, all scars and grizzle. We've had two tries at him, but had no luck, and Jim Carnaway lost his life over it. Now it's for you to take it over. That's the house, all alone at the Iron Dyke cross-road, same as you see here in the map, without another within earshot. It's no good by day. He's armed, and shoots quick and straight, with no questions asked. But at night – well, there he is, with his wife, three children, and a hired help. You can't pick or choose. It's all or none. If you could get a bag of blasting powder at the front door with a slow match to it –'

'What's the man done?'

'Didn't I tell you he shot Jim Carnaway?'

'Why did he shoot him?'

'What in thunder has that to do with you? Carnaway was about his house at night, and he shot him. That's enough for me and you. You've got to set the thing right.'

'There's these two women and the children. Do they go up, too?'

'They have to, else how can we get him?'

'It seems hard on them, for they've done nothing amiss.'

'What sort of talk is this? Do you stand back from it?'

'Easy, Councillor, easy. What have I ever said or done that you should think I would be after standing back from an order of the bodymaster of my own Lodge? If it's right or if it's wrong it's for you to decide.'

'You'll do it, then?'

'Of course I will do it.'

'When?'

'Well, you had best give me a night or two that I may see the house and make my plans. Then –'

'Very good,' said McGinty, shaking him by the hand. 'I leave it with you. It will be a great day when you bring us the news. It's just the last stroke that will bring them all to their knees.'

McMurdo thought long and deeply over the commission which had been so suddenly placed in his hands. The isolated house in which Chester Wilcox lived was about five miles off in an adjacent valley. That very night he started off all alone to prepare for the attempt. It was daylight before he returned from his reconnaissance. Next day he interviewed his two subordinates, Manders and Reilly, reckless youngsters, who were as elated as if it were a deer hunt. Two nights later they met outside the town, all three armed, and one of them carrying a sack stuffed with the powder which was used in the quarries. It was two in the morning before they came to the lonely house. The night was a windy one, with broken clouds drifting swiftly across the face of a three-quarter moon. They had been warned to be on their guard against bloodhounds, so they moved forward cautiously, with their pistols cocked in their hands. But there was no sound save the howling of the wind and no movement but the swaying branches above them. McMurdo listened at the door of the lonely house, but all was still within. Then he leaned the powder bag against it, ripped a hole in it with his knife, and attached the fuse. When it was well alight, he and his two companions took to their heels, and were some distance off, safe and snug in a sheltering ditch, before the shattering roar of the explosion, with the low, deep rumble of the collapsing building, told them that their work was done. No cleaner job had ever been carried out in the blood-stained annals of the society. But, alas that work so well organized and boldly conceived should all have gone for nothing! Warned by the fate of the various victims, and knowing that he was marked down for destruction, Chester Wilcox had moved himself and his family only the day before to some safer and less known quarters, where a guard of police should watch over them. It was an empty house which had been torn down by the gunpowder, and the grim old colour-sergeant of the war was still teaching discipline to the miners of Iron Dyke.

'Leave him to me,' said McMurdo. 'He's my man, and I'll get him sure, if I have to wait a year for him.'

A vote of thanks and confidence was passed in full Lodge, and so for the time the matter ended. When a few weeks later it was reported in the papers that Wilcox had been shot at from an ambuscade, it was an open secret that McMurdo was still at work upon his unfinished job.

Such were the methods of the Society of Freemen, and such were the deeds of the Scowrers by which they spread their rule of fear over the great and rich district which was for so long a period haunted by their terrible presence. Why should these pages be stained by further crimes? Have I not said enough to show the men and their methods? These deeds are written in history, and there are records wherein one may read the details of them. There one may learn of the shooting of Policemen Hunt and Evans[5] because they had ventured to arrest two members of the society – a double outrage planned at the Vermissa Lodge, and carried out in cold blood upon two helpless and disarmed men. There also one may read of the shooting of Mrs Larbey[6] whilst she was nursing her husband, who had been beaten almost to death by orders of Boss McGinty. The killing of the elder Jenkins, shortly followed by that of his brother, the mutilation of James Murdoch, the blowing-up of the Staphouse family, and the murder of the Stendals all followed hard upon each other in the same terrible winter. Darkly the shadow lay upon the Valley of Fear. The spring had come with running brooks and blossoming trees. There was hope for all Nature, bound so long in an iron grip; but nowhere was there any hope for the men and women who lived under the yoke of the terror. Never had the cloud above them been so dark and hopeless as in the early summer of the year '75.

6

Danger

It was the height of the reign of terror. McMurdo, who had already been appointed inner Deacon, with every prospect of some day succeeding McGinty as bodymaster, was now so necessary to the councils of his comrades that nothing was done without his help and advice. The more popular he became, however, with the Freemen, the blacker were the scowls which greeted him as he passed along the streets of Vermissa. In spite of their terror the citizens were taking heart to bind themselves together against their oppressors. Rumours had reached the Lodge of secret gatherings in the *Herald* office and of distribution of firearms among the law-abiding people. But McGinty and his men were undisturbed by such reports. They were numerous, resolute, and well armed. Their opponents were scattered and powerless. It would all end, as it had done in the past, in aimless talk, and possibly in impotent arrests. So said McGinty, McMurdo, and all the bolder spirits.

It was a Saturday evening in May. Saturday was always the Lodge night, and McMurdo was leaving his house to attend it, when Morris, the weaker brother of the Order, came to see him. His brow was creased with care and his kindly face was drawn and haggard.

'Can I speak with you freely, Mr McMurdo?'

'Sure.'

'I can't forget that I spoke my heart to you once, and that you kept it to yourself, even though the Boss himself came to ask you about it.'

'What else could I do if you trusted me? It wasn't that I agreed with what you said.'

'I know that well. But you are the one here I can speak to and be safe. I've a secret here' – he put his hand to his breast – 'and it is just burning the life out of me. I wish it had come to anyone of you but me. If I tell it, it will mean murder, for sure. If I don't, it may bring the end of us all. God help me, but I am near out of my wits over it!'

McMurdo looked at the man earnestly. He was trembling in every limb. He poured some whisky into a glass and handed it to him.

'That's the physic for the likes of you,' said he. 'Now let me hear of it.'

Morris drank, and his white face took a tinge of colour.

'I can tell it you all in one sentence,' said he. 'There's a detective on our trail.'

McMurdo stared at him in astonishment.

'Why, man, you're crazy!' he said. 'Isn't the place full of police and detectives, and what harm did they ever do us?'

'No, no; it's no man of the district. As you say, we know them, and it is little that they can do. But you've heard of Pinkerton's?'[1]

'I've read of some folk of that name.'

'Well, you can take it from me you've no show when they are on your trail. It's not a take-it-or-miss-it Government concern. It's a dead earnest business proposition that's out for results, and keeps out till, by hook or by crook, it gets them. If a Pinkerton man is deep in this business we are all destroyed.'

'We must kill him.'

'Ah, it's the first thought that came to you! So it will be up at the Lodge. Didn't I say to you that it would end in murder?'

'Sure, what is murder? Isn't it common enough in these parts?'

'It is indeed, but it's not for me to point out the man that is to be murdered. I'd never rest easy again. And yet it's our own necks that may be at stake. In God's name what shall I do?' He rocked to and fro in his agony of indecision.

But his words had moved McMurdo deeply. It was easy to see that he shared the other's opinion as to the danger, and the need for meeting it. He gripped Morris's shoulder, and shook him in his earnestness.

'See here, man,' he cried, and he almost screeched the words in his excitement, 'you won't gain anything by sitting keening like an old wife at a wake. Let's have the facts. Who is the fellow? Where is he? How did you hear of him? Why did you come to me?'

'I came to you, for you are the one man that would advise me. I told you that I had a store in the East before I came here. I left good friends behind me, and one of them is in the telegraph service. Here's a letter that I had from him yesterday. It's this part from the top of the page. You can read it for yourself.'

This was what McMurdo read:

How are the Scowrers getting on in your parts? We read plenty of them in the papers. Between you and me I expect to hear news from you before long. Five big corporations and the two railroads have taken the thing up in dead earnest. They mean it, and you can bet they'll get there. They are right deep down into it. Pinkerton has taken hold under their orders, and his best man, Birdy Edwards, is operating. The thing has got to be stopped right now.

'Now read the postscript.'

Of course, what I give you is what I learned in business, so it goes no further. It's a queer cipher that you handle by the yard every day and can get no meaning from.

McMurdo sat in silence for some time with the letter in his restless hands. The mist had lifted for a moment, and there was the abyss before him.

'Does anyone else know of this?' he asked.

'I have told no one else.'

'But this man – your friend – has he any other person that he would be likely to write to?'

'Well, I dare say he knows one or two more.'

'Of the Lodge?'

'It's likely enough.'

'I was asking because it is likely that he may have given some description of this fellow, Birdy Edwards. Then we could get on his trail.'

'Well, it's possible. But I should not think he knew him. He is just telling me the news that came to him by way of business. How would he know this Pinkerton man?'

McMurdo gave a violent start.

'By gosh!' he cried, 'I've got him. What a fool I was not to know it! Lord, but we're in luck! We will fix him before he can do any harm. See here, Morris; will you leave this thing in my hands?'

'Sure, if you will only take it off mine!'

'I'll do that. You can stand right back and let me run it. Even your name need not be mentioned. I'll take it all on myself as if it were to me that this letter has come. Will that content you?'

'It's just what I would ask.'

'Then leave it at that and keep your head shut. Now I'll get down to the Lodge, and we'll soon make old man Pinkerton sorry for himself.'

'You wouldn't kill this man?'

'The less you know, friend Morris, the easier your conscience will be and the better you will sleep. Ask no questions, and let things settle themselves. I have hold of it now.'

Morris shook his head sadly as he left.

'I feel that his blood is on my hands,' he groaned.

'Self-protection is no murder, anyhow,' said McMurdo, smiling grimly. 'It's him or us. I guess this man would destroy us all if we left him long in the valley. Why, Brother Morris, we'll have to elect you bodymaster yet, for you've surely saved the Lodge.'

And yet it was clear from his actions that he thought more seriously of this new intrusion than his words would show. It may have been his guilty conscience; it may have been the reputation of the Pinkerton organization; it may have been the knowledge that great rich corporations had set themselves the task of clearing out the Scowrers; but, whatever his reason, his actions were those of a man who is preparing for the worst. Every paper which could incriminate him was destroyed before he left the house. After that he gave a long sigh of satisfaction, for it seemed to him that he was safe; and yet the danger must still have pressed somewhat upon him, for on his way to the Lodge he stopped at old Shafter's. The house was forbidden him, but when he tapped at the window Ettie came out to him. The dancing Irish devilry had gone from her lover's eyes. She read his danger in his earnest face.

'Something has happened!' she cried. 'Oh Jack, you are in danger!'

'Sure, it is not very bad, my sweetheart. And yet it may be wise that we make a move before it is worse.'

'Make a move!'

'I promised you once that I would go some day. I think the time is coming. I had news tonight – bad news – and I see trouble coming.'

'The police?'

'Well, a Pinkerton. But, sure, you wouldn't know what that is, acushla, nor what it may mean to the likes of me. I'm too deep in this thing, and I may have to get out of it quick. You said you would come with me if I went.'

'Oh, Jack, it would be the saving of you.'

'I'm an honest man in some things, Ettie. I wouldn't hurt a hair of your bonnie head for all that the world can give, nor ever pull you down one inch from the golden throne above the clouds where I always see you. Would you trust me?'

She put her hand in his without a word.

'Well, then, listen to what I say and do as I order you, for indeed it's the only way for us. Things are going to happen in this valley. I feel it in my bones. There may be many of us that will have to look out for ourselves. I'm one, anyhow. If I go, by day or night, it's you that must come with me!'

'I'd come after you, Jack.'

'No, no; you shall come *with* me. If this valley is closed to me and I can never come back, how can I leave you behind, and me perhaps in hiding from the police with never a chance of a message? It's with me you must come. I know a good woman in the place I come from, and it's there I'd leave you till we can get married. Will you come?'

'Yes, Jack, I will come.'

'God bless you for your trust in me. It's a fiend out of hell that I should be if I abused it. Now, mark you, Ettie, it will be just a word to you, and when it reaches you you will drop everything and come right down to the waiting-hall at the depot and stay there till I come for you.'

'Day or night, I'll come at the word, Jack.'

Somewhat eased in mind now that his own preparations for escape had been begun, McMurdo went on to the Lodge. It had already assembled, and only by complicated signs and counter-signs could he pass through the outer guard and inner guard who close-tiled it. A buzz of pleasure and welcome greeted him as he entered. The long room was crowded, and through the haze of tobacco-smoke he saw the tangled black mane of the bodymaster, the cruel, unfriendly features of Baldwin, the vulture face of Harraway, the secretary, and a dozen more who were among the leaders of the Lodge. He rejoiced that they should all be there to take counsel over his news.

'Indeed, it's glad we are to see you, brother!' cried the chairman. 'There's business here that wants a Solomon in judgement[2] to set it right.'

'It's Lander and Egan,' explained his neighbour, as he took his seat. 'They both claim the head-money given by the Lodge for the shooting of old man Crabbe over at Stylestown, and who's to say which fired the bullet?'

McMurdo rose in his place and raised his hand. The expression of his face froze the attention of the audience. There was a dead hush of expectation.

'Worshipful Master,' he said, in a solemn voice, 'I claim urgency.'

'Brother McMurdo claims urgency,' said McGinty. 'It's a claim that by the rules of this Lodge takes precedence. Now, brother, we attend you.'

McMurdo took the letter from his pocket.

'Worshipful Master and brethren,' he said, 'I am the bearer of ill news this day, but it is better that it should be known and discussed than that a blow should fall upon us without warning which would destroy us all. I have information that the most powerful and richest organizations in this State have bound themselves together for our destruction, and that at this very moment there is a Pinkerton detective, one Birdy Edwards, at work in the valley collecting the evidence which may put a rope round the neck of many of us, and send every man in this room into a felon's cell. That is the situation for the discussion of which I have made a claim of urgency.'

There was a dead silence in the room. It was broken by the chairman.

'What is your evidence for this, Brother McMurdo?' he asked.

'It is in this letter which has come into my hands,' said McMurdo. He read the passage aloud. 'It is a matter of honour with me that I can give no further particulars about the letter, nor put it into your hands, but I assure you that there is nothing else in it which can affect the interests of the Lodge. I put the case before you as it has reached me.'

'Let me say, Mr Chairman,' said one of the older brethren, 'that I have heard of Birdy Edwards, and that he has the name of being the best man in the Pinkerton service.'

'Does anyone know him by sight?' asked McGinty.

'Yes,' said McMurdo, 'I do.'

There was a murmur of astonishment through the hall.

'I believe we hold him in the hollow of our hands,' he continued, with an exulting smile upon his face. 'If we act quickly and wisely we can cut this thing short. If I have your confidence and your help it is little that we have to fear.'

'What have we to fear anyhow? What can he know of our affairs?'

'You might say so if all were as staunch as you, Councillor. But this man has all the millions of the capitalists at his back. Do you think there is no weaker brother among all our Lodges that could not be bought? He will get at our secrets – maybe has got them already. There's only one sure cure.'

'That he never leaves the valley,' said Baldwin.

McMurdo nodded.

'Good for you, Brother Baldwin,' he said. 'You and I have had our differences, but you have said the true word tonight.'

'Where is he, then? How shall we know him?'

'Worshipful Master,' said McMurdo, earnestly, 'I would put it to you that this is too vital a thing for us to discuss in open Lodge. God forbid that I should throw a doubt on anyone here, but if so much as a word of gossip got to the ears of this man there would be an end of any chance of our getting him. I would ask the Lodge to choose a trusty committee, Mr Chairman – yourself, if I might suggest it, and Brother Baldwin here, and five more. Then I can talk freely of what I know and of what I would advise should be done.'

The proposition was at once adopted and the committee chosen. Besides the chairman and Baldwin, there were the vulture-faced secretary, Harraway; Tiger Cormac, the brutal young assassin; Carter, the treasurer; and the brothers Willaby, who were fearless and desperate men who would stick at nothing.

The usual revelry of the Lodge was short and subdued, for there was a cloud upon the men's spirits, and many there for the first time began to see the cloud of avenging Law drifting up in that serene sky under which they had dwelled so long. The horrors which they had dealt out to others had been so much a part of their settled lives that the thought of retribution had become a remote one, and so seemed the more startling now that it came so closely upon them. They broke up early and left their leaders to their council.

'Now, McMurdo,' said McGinty, when they were alone. The seven men sat frozen in their seats.

'I said just now that I knew Birdy Edwards,' McMurdo explained. 'I need not tell you that he is not here under that name. He's a brave man, I dare bet, but not a crazy one. He passes under the name of Steve Wilson, and he is lodging at Hobson's Patch.'

'How do you know this?'

'Because I fell into talk with him. I thought little of it at the time,
nor would have given it a second thought but for this letter, but now
I'm sure it's the man. I met him on the cars when I went down the
line on Wednesday – a hard case if ever there was one. He said he
was a pressman. I believed it for the moment. Wanted to know all he
could get about the Scowrers and what he called "the outrages" for
the *New York Press*. Asked me every kind of question so as to get
something for his paper. You bet I was giving nothing away. "I'd pay
for it, and pay well," said he, "if I could get some stuff that would suit
my editor." I said what I thought would please him best, and he
handed me a twenty-dollar bill for my information. "There's ten times
that for you," said he, "if you can find me all that I want."'

'What did you tell him, then?'

'Any stuff I could make up.'

'How do you know he wasn't a newspaper man?'

'I'll tell you. He got out at Hobson's Patch, and so did I. I chanced
into the telegraph bureau, and he was leaving it.

'"See here," said the operator, after he'd gone out, "I guess we
should charge double rates for this." "I guess you should," said I. He
had filled the form with stuff that might have been Chinese for all we
could make of it. "He fires a sheet of this off every day," said the clerk.
"Yes," said I; "it's special news for his paper, and he's scared that the
others should tap it." That was what the operator thought and what
I thought at the time, but I think different now.'

'By gosh, I believe you are right!' said McGinty. 'But what do you
allow that we should do about it?'

'Why not go right down now and fix him?' someone suggested.

'Aye, the sooner the better.'

'I'd start this next minute if I knew where we could find him,' said
McMurdo. 'He's in Hobson's Patch, but I don't know the house. I've
got a plan, though, if you'll only take my advice.'

'Well, what is it?'

'I'll go to the Patch tomorrow morning. I'll find him through the
operator. He can locate him, I guess. Well, then, I'll tell him that I'm
a Freeman myself. I'll offer him all the secrets of the Lodge for a price.
You bet he'll tumble to it. I'll tell him the papers are at my house, and

that it's as much as my life would be worth to let him come while folk were about. He'll see that that's horse sense. Let him come at ten o'clock at night, and he shall see everything. That will fetch him, sure.'

'Well?'

'You can plan the rest for yourselves. Widow MacNamara's is a lonely house. She's as true as steel and as deaf as a post. There's only Scanlan and me in the house. If I get his promise – and I'll let you know if I do – I'd have the whole seven of you come to me by nine o'clock. We'll get him in. If ever he gets out alive – well, he can talk of Birdy Edwards's luck for the rest of his days.'

'There's going to be a vacancy at Pinkerton's or I'm mistaken,' said McGinty. 'Leave it at that, McMurdo. At nine tomorrow we shall be with you. You once get the door shut behind him, and you can leave the rest with us.'

7

The Trapping of Birdy Edwards

As McMurdo had said, the house in which he lived was a lonely one and very well suited for such a crime as they had planned. It was on the extreme fringe of the town, and stood well back from the road. In any other case the conspirators would have simply called out their man, as they had many a time before, and emptied their pistols into his body; but in this instance it was very necessary to find out how much he knew, how he knew it, and what had been passed on to his employers. It was possible that they were already too late and that the work had been done. If that were indeed so, they could at least have their revenge upon the man who had done it. But they were hopeful that nothing of great importance had yet come to the detective's knowledge, as otherwise, they argued, he would not have troubled to write down and forward such trivial information as McMurdo claimed to have given him. However, all this they would learn from his own lips. Once in their power they would find a way to make him speak. It was not the first time they had handled an unwilling witness.

McMurdo went to Hobson's Patch as agreed. The police seemed to take a particular interest in him that morning, and Captain Marvin – he who had claimed the old acquaintance with him at Chicago – actually addressed him as he waited at the depot. McMurdo turned away and refused to speak with him. He was back from his mission in the afternoon, and saw McGinty at the Union House.

'He is coming,' he said.

'Good!' said McGinty. The giant was in his shirtsleeves, with chains and seals gleaming athwart his ample waistcoat and a diamond twinkling through the fringe of his bristling beard. Drink and politics had made the Boss a very rich as well as powerful man. The more terrible, therefore, seemed that glimpse of the prison or the gallows which had risen before him the night before.

'Do you reckon he knows much?' he asked, anxiously.

McMurdo shook his head gloomily.

'He's been here some time – six weeks at the least. I guess he didn't come into these parts to look at the prospect. If he has been working among us all that time with the railroad money at his back, I should expect that he has got results, and that he has passed them on.'

'There's not a weak man in the Lodge,' cried McGinty. 'True as steel, every man of them. And yet, by the Lord, there is that skunk Morris. What about him? If any man gives us away it would be he. I've a mind to send a couple of the boys round before evening to give him a beating up and see what they can get from him.'

'Well, there would be no harm in that,' McMurdo answered. 'I won't deny that I have a liking for Morris and would be sorry to see him come to harm. He has spoken to me once or twice over Lodge matters, and though he may not see them the same as you or I, he never seemed the sort that squeals. But still, it is not for me to stand between him and you.'

'I'll fix the old devil,' said McGinty, with an oath. 'I've had my eye on him this year past.'

'Well, you know best about that,' McMurdo answered. 'But whatever you do must be tomorrow, for we must lie low until the Pinkerton affair is settled up. We can't afford to set the police buzzing today of all days.'

'True for you,' said McGinty. 'And we'll learn from Birdy Edwards himself where he got his news, if we have to cut his heart out first. Did he seem to scent a trap?'

McMurdo laughed.

'I guess I took him on his weak point,' he said. 'If he could get on a good trail of the Scowrers he's ready to follow it home. I took his money' – McMurdo grinned as he produced a wad of dollar notes – 'and as much more when he has seen all my papers.'

'What papers?'

'Well, there are no papers. But I filled him up about constitutions and books of rules and forms of membership. He expects to get right down to the end of everything before he leaves.'

'Faith, he's right there,' said McGinty, grimly. 'Didn't he ask you why you didn't bring him the papers?'

'As if I would carry such things, and me a suspected man, and Captain Marvin after speaking to me this very day at the depot!'

'Aye, I heard of that,' said McGinty. 'I guess the heavy end of this business is coming on to you. We could put him down an old shaft when we've done with him, but however we work it we can't get past the man living at Hobson's Patch and you being there today.'

McMurdo shrugged his shoulders.

'If we handle it right they can never prove the killing,' said he. 'No one can see him come to the house after dark, and I'll lay to it that no one will see him go. Now, see here, Councillor. I'll show you my plan, and I'll ask you to fit the others into it. You will all come in good time. Very well. He comes at ten. He is to tap three times, and me to open the door for him. Then I'll get behind him and shut it. He's our man then.'

'That's all easy and plain.'

'Yes, but the next step wants considering. He's a hard proposition. He's heavily armed. I've fooled him proper, and yet he is likely to be on his guard. Suppose I show him right into a room with seven men in it where he expected to find me alone. There is going to be shooting and somebody is going to be hurt.'

'That's so.'

'And the noise is going to bring every blamed copper in the township on to the top of us.'

'I guess you are right.'

'This is how I should work it. You will all be in the big room – same as you saw when you had a chat with me. I'll open the door for him, show him into the parlour beside the door, and leave him there while I get the papers. That will give me the chance of telling you how things are shaping. Then I will go back to him with some faked papers. As he is reading them I will jump for him and get my grip on his pistol arm. You'll hear me call, and in you will rush. The quicker the better, for he is as strong a man as I, and I may have more than I can manage. But I allow that I can hold him till you come.'

'It's a good plan,' said McGinty. 'The Lodge will owe you a debt for this. I guess when I move out of the chair I can put a name to the man that's coming after me.'

'Sure, Councillor, I am little more than a recruit,' said McMurdo, but his face showed what he thought of the great man's compliment.

When he had returned home he made his own preparations for the grim evening in front of him. First he cleaned, oiled, and loaded his Smith and Wesson revolver. Then he surveyed the room in which the detective was to be trapped. It was a large apartment, with a long deal table in the centre and the big stove at one end. At each of the other sides were windows. There were no shutters to these – only light curtains which drew across. McMurdo examined these attentively. No doubt it must have struck him that the apartment was very exposed for so secret a matter. Yet its distance from the road made it of less consequence. Finally he discussed the matter with his fellow-lodger. Scanlan, though a Scowrer, was an inoffensive little man who was too weak to stand against the opinion of his comrades, but was secretly horrified by the deeds of blood at which he had sometimes been forced to assist. McMurdo told him shortly what was intended.

'And if I were you, Mike Scanlan, I would take a night off and keep clear of it. There will be bloody work here before morning.'

'Well, indeed, then, Mac,' Scanlan answered, 'it's not the will but the nerve that is wanting in me. When I saw Manager Dunn go down at the colliery yonder it was just more than I could stand. I'm not made for it, same as you or McGinty. If the Lodge will think none the worse of me, I'll just do as you advise, and leave you to yourselves for the evening.'

The men came in good time as arranged. They were outwardly respectable citizens, well-clad and cleanly, but a judge of faces would have read little hope for Birdy Edwards in those hard mouths and remorseless eyes. There was not a man in the room whose hands had not been reddened a dozen times before. They were as hardened to human murder as a butcher to sheep. Foremost, of course, both in appearance and in guilt, was the formidable Boss. Harraway, the secretary, was a lean, bitter man, with a long, scraggy neck and nervous, jerky limbs – a man of incorruptible fidelity where the finances of the Order were concerned, and with no notion of justice or honesty to anyone beyond. The treasurer, Carter, was a middle-aged man with an impassive, rather sulky expression and a yellow parchment skin. He was a capable organizer, and the actual details of nearly every outrage had sprung from his plotting brain. The two Willabys were men of action, tall, lithe young fellows with determined faces, while their companion, Tiger Cormac, a heavy, dark youth, was feared even by his own comrades for the ferocity of his disposition. These were the men who assembled that night under the roof of McMurdo for the killing of the Pinkerton detective.

Their host had placed whisky upon the table, and they had hastened to prime themselves for the work before them. Baldwin and Cormac were already half drunk, and the liquor had brought out all their ferocity. Cormac placed his hands on the stove for an instant – it had been lighted, for the spring nights were still cold.

'That will do,' said he, with an oath.

'Aye,' said Baldwin, catching his meaning. 'If he is strapped to that we will have the truth out of him.'

'We'll have the truth out of him, never fear,' said McMurdo. He had nerves of steel, this man, for, though the whole weight of the affair was on him, his manner was as cool and unconcerned as ever. The others marked it and applauded.

'You are the one to handle him,' said the Boss, approvingly. 'Not a warning will he get till your hand is on his throat. It's a pity there are no shutters to your windows.'

McMurdo went from one to the other and drew the curtain tighter.

'Sure, no one can spy upon us now. It's close upon the hour.'

'Maybe he won't come. Maybe he'll get a sniff of danger,' said the secretary.

'He'll come, never fear,' McMurdo answered. 'He is as eager to come as you can be to see him. Hark to that!'

They all sat like wax figures, some with their glasses arrested halfway to their lips. Three loud knocks had sounded at the door.

'Hush!'

McMurdo raised his hand in caution. An exulting glance went round the circle and hands were laid upon hidden weapons.

'Not a sound for your lives!' McMurdo whispered, as he went from the room, closing the door carefully behind him.

With strained ears the murderers waited. They counted the steps of their comrade down the passage. Then they heard him open the outer door. There were a few words as of greeting. Then they were aware of a strange step inside and of an unfamiliar voice. An instant later came the slam of the door and the turning of the key in the lock. Their prey was safe within the trap. Tiger Cormac laughed horribly, and Boss McGinty clapped his great hand across his mouth.

'Be quiet, you fool!' he whispered. 'You'll be the undoing of us yet.'

There was a mutter of conversation from the next room. It seemed interminable. Then the door opened and McMurdo appeared, his finger upon his lip.

He came to the end of the table and looked round at them. A subtle change had come over him. His manner was as of one who has great work to do. His face had set into granite firmness. His eyes shone with a fierce excitement behind his spectacles. He had become a visible leader of men. They stared at him with eager interest, but he said nothing. Still with the same singular gaze, he looked from man to man.

'Well,' cried Boss McGinty at last, 'is he here? Is Birdy Edwards here?'

'Yes,' McMurdo answered slowly. 'Birdy Edwards is here. I am Birdy Edwards!'[1]

There were ten seconds after that brief speech during which the room might have been empty, so profound was the silence. The hissing of a kettle upon the stove rose sharp and strident to the ear. Seven white faces, all turned upwards to this man who dominated them, were set motionless with utter terror. Then, with a sudden shivering of glass, a bristle of glistening rifle-barrels broke through each window, while the curtains were torn from their hangings. At the sight Boss McGinty gave the roar of a wounded bear and plunged for the half-opened door. A levelled revolver met him there, with the stern blue eyes of Captain Marvin of the Coal and Iron Police gleaming behind the sights. The Boss recoiled and fell back into his chair.

'You're safer there, Councillor,' said the man whom they had known as McMurdo. 'And you, Baldwin, if you don't take your hand off your gun you'll cheat the hangman yet. Pull it out, or, by the Lord that made me – There, that will do. There are forty armed men round this house, and you can figure it out for yourselves what chance you have. Take their guns, Marvin!'

There was no possible resistance under the menace of those rifles. The men were disarmed. Sulky, sheepish, and very amazed, they still sat round the table.

'I'd like to say a word to you before we separate,' said the man who had trapped them. 'I guess we may not meet again until you see me on the stand in the court-house. I'll give you something to think over betwixt now and then. You know me now for what I am. At last I can put my cards on the table. I am Birdy Edwards, of Pinkerton's.[2] I was chosen to break up your gang. I had a hard and a dangerous game to play. Not a soul, not one soul, not my nearest and dearest knew that I was playing it, except Captain Marvin here and my employers. But it's over tonight, thank God, and I am the winner!'

The seven pale, rigid faces looked up at him. There was an unappeasable hatred in their eyes. He read the relentless threat.

'Maybe you think that the game is not over yet. Well, I take my chance on that. Anyhow, some of you will take no further hand, and there are sixty more besides yourselves that will see a jail this night. I'll tell you this, that when I was put upon this job I never believed there was such a society as yours. I thought it was paper talk, and that

I would prove it so. They told me it was to do with the Freemen, so I went to Chicago and was made one. Then I was surer than ever that it was just paper talk, for I found no harm in the society, but a deal of good. Still, I had to carry out my job, and I came for the coal valleys. When I reached this place I learned that I was wrong and that it wasn't a dime novel after all. So I stayed to look after it. I never killed a man in Chicago. I never minted a dollar in my life. Those I gave you were as good as any others, but I never spent money better. I knew the way into your good wishes, and so I pretended to you that the law was after me. It all worked just as I thought.

'So I joined your infernal Lodge and I took my share in your councils. Maybe they will say that I was as bad as you. They can say what they like, so long as I get you. But what is the truth? The night I joined you beat up old man Stanger. I could not warn him, for there was no time, but I held your hand, Baldwin, when you would have killed him. If ever I have suggested things, so as to keep my place among you, they were things which I knew that I could prevent. I could not save Dunn and Menzies, for I did not know enough, but I will see that their murderers are hanged. I gave Chester Wilcox warning, so that when I blew his house in he and his folk were in hiding. There was many a crime that I could not stop, but if you look back and think how often your man came home the other road, or was down in town when you went for him, or stayed indoors when you thought that he would come out, you'll see my work.'

'You blasted traitor!' hissed McGinty, through his closed teeth.

'Aye, John McGinty, you may call me that if it eases your smart. You and your like have been the enemy of God and man in these parts. It took a man to get between you and the poor devils of men and women that you held under your grip. There was just one way of doing it, and I did it. You call me a "traitor", but I guess there's many a thousand will call me a "deliverer" that went down into hell to save them. I've had three months of it.[3] I wouldn't have three such months again if they let me loose in the Treasury at Washington for it. I had to stay till I had it all, every man and every secret, right here in this hand. I'd have waited a little longer if it hadn't come to my knowledge that my secret was coming out. A letter had come into the town that would have set you wise to it all. Then I had to act, and act quickly. I've nothing more to say to you, except that when my time comes I'll die the easier when I think of the work I have done in this valley. Now, Marvin, I'll keep you no more. Have them in and get it over.'

There is little more to tell. Scanlan had been given a sealed note to be left at the address of Miss Ettie Shafter – a mission which he had accepted with a wink and a knowing smile. In the early hours of the morning a beautiful woman and a much-muffled man boarded a special train which had been sent by the railroad company, and made a swift, unbroken journey out of the land of danger. It was the last time that ever either Ettie or her lover set foot in the Valley of Fear. Ten days later they were married in Chicago, with old Jacob Shafter as witness of the wedding.

The trial of the Scowrers[4] was held far from the place where their adherents might have terrified the guardians of the law. In vain they struggled. In vain the money of the Lodge – money squeezed by blackmail out of the whole countryside – was spent like water in the attempt to save them. That cold, clear, unimpassioned statement from one who knew every detail of their lives, their organization, and their crimes was unshaken by all the wiles of their defenders. At last, after so many years, they were broken and scattered. The cloud was lifted for ever from the valley. McGinty met his fate upon the scaffold, cringing and whining[5] when the last hour came. Eight of his chief followers shared his fate. Fifty odd had various degrees of imprisonment. The work of Birdy Edwards was complete.

And yet, as he had guessed, the game was not over yet. There was another hand to be played, and yet another and another. Ted Baldwin, for one, had escaped the scaffold; so had the Willabys; so had several other of the fiercest spirits of the gang. For ten years they were out of the world, and then came a day when they were free once more – a day which Edwards, who knew his men, was very sure would be an end of his life of peace. They had sworn an oath on all that they thought holy to have his blood as a vengeance for their comrades. And well they strove to keep their vow. From Chicago he was chased, after two attempts so near to success that it was sure that the third would get him. From Chicago he went, under a changed name, to

California, and it was there that the light went for a time out of his life when Ettie Edwards died. Once again he was nearly killed, and once again, under the name of Douglas, he worked in a lonely canyon, where, with an English partner named Barker, he amassed a fortune. At last there came a warning to him that the bloodhounds were on his track once more, and he cleared – only just in time – for England. And here came the John Douglas who for a second time married a worthy mate and lived for five years as a Sussex country gentleman – a life which ended with the strange happenings of which we have heard.

Epilogue

The police-court proceedings had passed, in which the case of John Douglas was referred to a higher court. So had the Assizes, at which he was acquitted as having acted in self-defence. 'Get him out of England at any cost,' wrote Holmes to the wife. 'There are forces here which may be more dangerous than those he has escaped. There is no safety for your husband in England.'

Two months had gone by, and the case had to some extent passed from our minds. Then one morning there came an enigmatic note slipped into our letter-box. 'Dear me, Mr Holmes! Dear me!' said this singular epistle. There was neither superscription nor signature. I laughed at the quaint message, but Holmes showed an unwonted seriousness.

'Devilry, Watson!' he remarked, and sat long with a clouded brow.

Late that night Mrs Hudson, our landlady, brought up a message that a gentleman wished to see Holmes, and that the matter was of the utmost importance. Close at the heels of his messenger came Mr Cecil Barker, our friend of the moated Manor House. His face was drawn and haggard.

'I've had bad news – terrible news, Mr Holmes,' said he.

'I feared as much,' said Holmes.

'You have not had a cable, have you?'

'I have had a note from someone who has.'

'It's poor Douglas. They tell me his name is Edwards, but he will always be Jack Douglas of Benito Canyon to me. I told you that they started together for South Africa in the *Palmyra* three weeks ago.'

'Exactly.'

'The ship reached Cape Town last night. I received this cable from Mrs Douglas this morning:

'"Jack has been lost overboard in gale off St Helena. No one knows how accident occurred – Ivy Douglas."'

'Ha! It came like that, did it?' said Holmes, thoughtfully. 'Well, I've no doubt it was well stage-managed.'

'You mean that you think there was no accident?'

'None in the world.'

'He was murdered?'[1]

'Surely!'

'So I think also. These infernal Scowrers, this cursed vindictive nest of criminals –'

'No, no, my good sir,' said Holmes. 'There is a master hand here. It is no case of sawed-off shot-guns and clumsy six-shooters. You can tell an old master by the sweep of his brush. I can tell a Moriarty when I see one. This crime is from London, not from America.'

'But for what motive?'

'Because it is done by a man who cannot afford to fail – one whose whole unique position depends upon the fact that all he does must succeed. A great brain and a huge organization have been turned to the extinction of one man. It is crushing the nut with the hammer – an absurd extravagance of energy – but the nut is very effectually crushed all the same.'

'How came this man to have anything to do with it?'

'I can only say that the first word that ever came to us of the business was from one of his lieutenants. These Americans were well advised. Having an English job to do, they took into partnership, as any foreign criminal could do, this great consultant in crime. From that moment their man was doomed. At first he would content himself by using his machinery in order to find their victim. Then he would indicate how the matter might be treated. Finally, when he read in the reports of the failure of this agent, he would step in himself with a master touch. You heard me warn this man at Birlstone Manor House that the coming danger was greater than the past. Was I right?'

Barker beat his head with his clenched fist in his impotent anger.

'Do you tell me that we have to sit down under this? Do you say that no one can ever get level with this king-devil?'

'No, I don't say that,' said Holmes, and his eyes seemed to be looking far into the future. 'I don't say that he can't be beat. But you must give me time – you must give me time!'

We all sat in silence for some minutes, while those fateful eyes still strained to pierce the veil.

The Return of Sherlock Holmes

CONTENTS

THE EMPTY HOUSE

It was in the spring of the year 1894 that all London was interested, and the fashionable world dismayed, by the murder of the Honourable[1] Ronald Adair, under most unusual and inexplicable circumstances. The public has already learned those particulars of the crime which came out in the police investigation; but a good deal was suppressed upon that occasion, since the case for the prosecution was so over-whelmingly strong that it was not necessary to bring forward all the facts. Only now, at the end of nearly ten years,[2] am I allowed to supply those missing links which make up the whole of that remarkable chain. The crime was of interest in itself, but that interest was as nothing to me compared to the inconceivable sequel, which afforded me the greatest shock and surprise of any event in my adventurous life. Even now, after this long interval, I find myself thrilling as I think of it, and feeling once more that sudden flood of joy, amazement and incredulity which utterly submerged my mind. Let me say to that public which has shown some interest in those glimpses which I have occasionally given them of the thoughts and actions of a very remarkable man that they are not to blame me if I have not shared my knowledge with them, for I should have considered it my first duty to have done so had I not been barred by a positive prohibition from his own lips, which was only withdrawn upon the third of last month.

It can be imagined that my close intimacy with Sherlock Holmes had interested me deeply in crime, and that after his disappearance I never failed to read with care the various problems which came before the public, and I even attempted more than once for my own private satisfaction to employ his methods in their solution, though with indifferent success. There was none, however, which appealed to me like this tragedy of Ronald Adair. As I read the evidence at the inquest which led up to a verdict of wilful murder against some person or persons unknown, I realized more clearly than I had ever done the loss which the community had sustained by the death of Sherlock Holmes. There were points about this strange business which would, I was sure, have specially appealed to him, and the efforts of the police would have been supplemented, or more probably anticipated, by the trained observation and the alert mind of the first criminal agent in Europe. All day as I drove upon my round I turned over the case in my mind, and found no explanation which appeared to me to be adequate. At the risk of telling a twice-told tale I will recapitulate the facts as they were known to the public at the conclusion of the inquest.

The Honourable Ronald Adair was the second son of the Earl of Maynooth,[3] at that time Governor of one of the Australian colonies. Adair's mother had returned from Australia to undergo an operation for cataract, and she, her son Ronald and her daughter Hilda were living together at 427 Park Lane.[4] The youth moved in the best society, had, so far as was known, no enemies and no particular vices. He had been engaged to Miss Edith Woodley, of Carstairs, but the engagement had been broken off by mutual consent some months before, and there was no sign that it had left any very profound feeling behind it. For the rest, the man's life moved in a narrow and conventional circle, for his habits were quiet and his nature unemotional. Yet it was upon this easy-going young aristocrat that death came in most strange and unexpected form between the hours of ten and eleven-twenty on the night of March 30th, 1894.

Ronald Adair was fond of cards, playing continually, but never for such stakes as would hurt him. He was a member of the Baldwin,[5] the Cavendish[6] and the Bagatelle[7] Card Clubs. It was shown that after dinner on the day of his death he had played a rubber of whist at the latter club. He had also played there in the afternoon. The evidence of those who had played with him – Mr Murray, Sir John Hardy and Colonel Moran – showed that the game was whist, and there was a fairly equal fall of the cards. Adair might have lost five pounds, but no more. His fortune was a considerable one, and such a loss could not in any way affect him. He had played nearly every day at one club or other, but he was a cautious player, and usually rose a winner. It came out in evidence that in partnership with Colonel Moran he had actually won as much as £420 in a sitting some weeks before from Godfrey Milner and Lord Balmoral. So much for his recent history, as it came out at the inquest.

On the evening of the crime he returned from the club exactly at ten. His mother and sister were out spending the evening with a relation. The servant deposed that she heard him enter the front room on the second floor, generally used as his sitting-room. She had lit a fire there, and as it smoked she had opened the window. No sound was heard from the room until eleven-twenty, the hour of the return of Lady Maynooth and her daughter. Desiring to say good night, she had attempted to enter her son's room. The door was locked on the inside, and no answer could be got to their cries and knocking. Help was obtained and the door forced. The unfortunate young man was found lying near the table. His head had been horribly mutilated by an expanded revolver bullet, but no weapon of any sort was to be found in the room. On the table lay two bank-notes for £10 each and £17 10s. in silver and gold, the money arranged in little piles of varying amount. There were some figures also upon a sheet of paper with the names of some club friends opposite to them, from which it was conjectured that before his death he was endeavouring to make out his losses or winnings at cards.

A minute examination of the circumstances served only to make the case more complex. In the first place, no reason could be given why the young man should have fastened the door upon the inside. There was the possibility that the murderer had done this and had afterwards escaped by the window. The drop was at least twenty feet, however, and a bed of crocuses in full bloom[8] lay beneath. Neither the flowers nor the earth showed any sign of having been disturbed, nor were there any marks upon the narrow strip of grass which separated the house from the road. Apparently, therefore, it was the young man himself who had fastened the door. But how did he come by his death? No one could have climbed up to the window without leaving traces. Suppose a man had fired through the window, it would indeed be a remarkable shot who could with a revolver inflict so deadly a wound. Again, Park Lane is a frequented thoroughfare, and there is a cabstand within a hundred yards of the house. No one had heard a shot. And yet there was the dead man, and there the revolver bullet, which had mushroomed out, as soft-nosed bullets will, and so inflicted a wound which must have caused instantaneous death. Such were the circumstances of the Park Lane Mystery, which were further complicated by entire absence of motive, since, as I have said, young Adair was not known to have any enemy, and no attempt had been made to remove the money or valuables in the room.

All day I turned these facts over in my mind, endeavouring to hit upon some theory which could reconcile them all, and to find that line of least resistance which my poor friend had declared to be the starting-point of every investigation. I confess that I made little progress. In the evening I strolled across the Park, and found myself about six o'clock at the Oxford Street end of Park Lane. A group of loafers upon the pavements, all staring up at a particular window, directed me to the house which I had come to see. A tall, thin man with coloured glasses, whom I strongly suspected of being a plain-clothes detective, was pointing out some theory of his own, while the others crowded round to listen to what he said. I got as near as I could, but his observations seemed to me to be absurd, so I withdrew again in some disgust. As I did so I struck against an elderly deformed man, who had been behind me, and I knocked down several books which he was carrying. I remember that as I picked them up I observed the title of one of them, *The Origin of Tree Worship*,[9] and it struck me that the fellow must be some poor bibliophile who, either as a trade or as a hobby, was a collector of obscure volumes. I endeavoured to apologize for the accident, but it was evident that these books which I had so unfortunately maltreated were very precious objects in the eyes of their owner. With a snarl of contempt he turned upon his heel, and I saw his curved back and white side-whiskers disappear among the throng.

My observations of No. 427 Park Lane did little to clear up the problem in which I was interested. The house was separated from the street by a low wall and railing, the whole not more than five feet high.

It was perfectly easy, therefore, for anyone to get into the garden; but the window was entirely inaccessible, since there was no water-pipe or anything which could help the most active man to climb it. More puzzled than ever, I retraced my steps to Kensington. I had not been in my study five minutes when the maid entered to say that a person desired to see me. To my astonishment, it was none other than my strange old book-collector, his sharp, wizened face peering out from a frame of white hair, and his precious volumes, a dozen of them at least, wedged under his right arm.

'You're surprised to see me, sir,' said he, in a strange, croaking voice.

I acknowledged that I was.

'Well, I've a conscience, sir, and when I chanced to see you go into this house, as I came hobbling after you, I thought to myself, I'll just step in and see that kind gentleman, and tell him that if I was a bit gruff in my manner there was not any harm meant, and that I am much obliged to him for picking up my books.'

'You make too much of a trifle,' said I. 'May I ask how you knew who I was?'

'Well, sir, if it isn't too great a liberty, I am a neighbour of yours, for you'll find my little bookshop at the corner of Church Street,[10] and very happy to see you, I am sure. Maybe you collect yourself, sir; here's *British Birds*,[11] and *Catullus*[12] and *The Holy War*[13] – a bargain every one of them. With five volumes you could just fill that gap on that second shelf. It looks untidy, does it not, sir?'

I moved my head to look at the cabinet behind me. When I turned again Sherlock Holmes was standing smiling at me across my study table. I rose to my feet, stared at him for some seconds in utter amazement, and then it appears that I must have fainted for the first and the last time in my life. Certainly a grey mist swirled before my eyes, and when it cleared I found my collar-ends undone and the tingling aftertaste of brandy upon my lips. Holmes was bending over my chair, his flask in his hand.

'My dear Watson,' said the well-remembered voice, 'I owe you a thousand apologies. I had no idea that you would be so affected.'

I gripped him by the arm.

'Holmes!' I cried. 'Is it really you? Can it indeed be that you are alive? Is it possible that you succeeded in climbing out of that awful abyss?'

'Wait a moment!' said he. 'Are you sure that you are really fit to discuss things? I have given you a serious shock by my unnecessarily dramatic appearance.'

'I am all right; but indeed, Holmes, I can hardly believe my eyes. Good heavens, to think that you – you of all men – should be standing in my study!' Again I gripped him by the sleeve and felt the thin, sinewy arm beneath it. 'Well, you're not a spirit, anyhow,' said I. 'My dear chap, I am overjoyed to see you. Sit down, and tell me how you came alive out of that dreadful chasm.'

He sat opposite to me and lit a cigarette in his old nonchalant manner. He was dressed in the seedy frock-coat of the book merchant, but the rest of that individual lay in a pile of white hair and old books upon the table. Holmes looked even thinner and keener than of old, but there was a dead-white tinge in his aquiline face which told me that his life recently had not been a healthy one.

'I am glad to stretch myself, Watson,' said he. 'It is no joke when a tall man has to take a foot off his stature for several hours on end. Now, my dear fellow, in the matter of these explanations we have, if I may ask for your co-operation, a hard and dangerous night's work in front of us. Perhaps it would be better if I gave you an account of the whole situation when that work is finished.'

'I am full of curiosity. I should much prefer to hear now.'

'You'll come with me tonight?'

'When you like and where you like.'

'This is indeed like the old days. We shall have time for a mouthful of dinner before we need go. Well, then, about that chasm. I had no serious difficulty in getting out of it, for the very simple reason that I never was in it.'

'You never were in it?'

'No, Watson, I never was in it. My note to you was absolutely genuine. I had little doubt that I had come to the end of my career when I perceived the somewhat sinister figure of the late Professor Moriarty standing upon the narrow pathway which led to safety. I read an inexorable purpose in his grey eyes. I exchanged some remarks with him, therefore, and obtained his courteous permission to write the short note which you afterwards received. I left it with my cigarette-box and my stick, and I walked along the pathway, Moriarty still at my heels. When I reached the end I stood at bay. He drew no weapon, but he rushed at me and threw his long arms around me. He knew that his own game was up, and was only anxious to revenge himself upon me. We tottered together upon the brink of the fall. I have some knowledge, however, of *baritsu*,[14] or the Japanese system of wrestling, which has more than once been very useful to me. I slipped through his grip, and he with a horrible scream kicked madly for a few seconds and clawed the air with both his hands. But for all his efforts he could not get his balance, and over he went. With my face over the brink I saw him fall for a long way. Then he struck a rock, bounded off and splashed into the water.'

I listened with amazement to this explanation, which Holmes delivered between the puffs of his cigarette.

'But the tracks!' I cried. 'I saw with my own eyes that two went down the path and none returned.'

'It came about in this way. The instant that the professor had disappeared it struck me what a really extraordinarily lucky chance Fate had placed in my way. I knew that Moriarty was not the only man who had sworn my death. There were at least three others whose desire for vengeance upon me would only be increased by the death of their leader. They were all most dangerous men. One or other would certainly get me. On the other hand, if all the world was convinced that I was dead they would take liberties, these men; they would lay themselves open, and sooner or later I could destroy them. Then it would be time for me to announce that I was still in the land of the living.[15] So rapidly does the brain act that I believe I had thought this all out before Professor Moriarty had reached the bottom of the Reichenbach Fall.

'I stood up and examined the rocky wall behind me. In your picturesque account of the matter, which I read with great interest some months later, you assert that the wall was sheer. This was not literally true. A few small footholds presented themselves, and there was some indication of a ledge. The cliff is so high that to climb it all was an obvious impossibility, and it was equally impossible to make my way along the wet path without leaving some tracks. I might, it is true, have reversed my boots, as I have done on similiar occasions, but the sight of three sets of tracks in one direction would certainly have suggested a deception. On the whole, then, it was best that I should risk the climb. It was not a pleasant business, Watson. The fall roared beneath me. I am not a fanciful person, but I give you my word that I seemed to hear Moriarty's voice screaming at me out of the abyss. A mistake would have been fatal. More than once, as tufts of grass came out in my hand or my foot slipped in the wet notches of the rock, I thought that I was gone. But I struggled upwards, and at last I reached a ledge several feet deep and covered with soft green moss, where I could lie unseen in the most perfect comfort. There I was stretched when you, my dear Watson, and all your following were investigating in the most sympathetic and inefficient manner the circumstances of my death.

'At last, when you had all formed your inevitable and totally erroneous conclusions, you departed for the hotel, and I was left alone. I had imagined that I had reached the end of my adventures, but a very unexpected occurrence showed me that there were surprises still in store for me. A huge rock, falling from above, boomed past me, struck the path and bounded over into the chasm. For an instant I thought that it was an accident; but a moment later, looking up, I saw a man's head against the darkening sky, and another stone struck the very ledge upon which I was stretched, within a foot of my head. Of course, the meaning of this was obvious. Moriarty had not been alone. A confederate – and even that one glance had told me how dangerous a man that confederate was – had kept guard while the professor had attacked me. From a distance, unseen by me, he had been a witness of his friend's death and of my escape. He had waited, and then, making his way round to the top of the cliff, he had endeavoured to succeed where his comrade had failed.

'I did not take long to think about it, Watson. Again I saw that grim face look over the cliff, and I knew that it was the precursor of another stone. I scrambled down on to the path. I don't think I could have done it in cold blood. It was a hundred times more difficult than getting up. But I had no time to think of the danger for another stone sang past me as I hung by my hands from the edge of the ledge. Half-way down I slipped, but by the blessing of God I landed, torn and bleeding, upon the path. I took to my heels, did ten miles over the mountains in the darkness, and a week later I found myself in Florence, with the certainty that no one in the world knew what had become of me.

'I had only one confidant – my brother Mycroft. I owe you many apologies, my dear Watson, but it was all-important that it should be thought I was dead, and it is quite certain that you would not have written so convincing an account of my unhappy end had you not yourself thought that it was true. Several times during the last three years I have taken up my pen to write to you, but always I feared lest your affectionate regard for me should tempt you to some indiscretion which would betray my secret. For that reason I turned away from you this evening when you upset my books, for I was in danger at the time, and any show of surprise and emotion upon your part might have drawn attention to my identity and led to the most deplorable and irreparable results. As to Mycroft, I had to confide in him in order to obtain the money which I needed. The course of events in London did not run so well as I had hoped, for the trial of the Moriarty gang left two of its most dangerous members, my own most vindictive enemies, at liberty. I travelled for two years in Tibet, therefore, and amused myself by visiting Lhasa[16] and spending some days with the head Lama.[17] You may have read of the remarkable explorations of a Norwegian named Sigerson,[18] but I am sure that it never occurred to you that you were receiving news of your friend. I then passed through Persia, looked in at Mecca,[19] and paid a short but interesting visit to the Khalifa at Khartoum,[20] the results of which I have communicated to the Foreign Office. Returning to France, I spent some months in a research into the coal-tar derivatives, which I conducted in a laboratory at Montpellier, in the south of France. Having concluded this to my satisfaction, and learning that only one of my enemies was now left in London, I was about to return, when my movements were hastened by the news of this remarkable Park Lane Mystery, which not only appealed to me by its own merits, but which seemed to offer some most peculiar personal opportunities. I came over at once to London, called in my own person at Baker Street, threw Mrs Hudson into violent hysterics, and found that Mycroft had preserved my rooms and my papers exactly as they had always been. So it was, my dear Watson, that at two o'clock today I found myself in my old armchair in my own old room, and only wishing that I could have seen my old friend Watson in the other chair which he has so often adorned.'

Such was the remarkable narrative to which I listened on that April evening – a narrative which would have been utterly incredible to me had it not been confirmed by the actual sight of the tall, spare figure and the keen, eager face which I had never thought to see again. In some manner he had learned of my own sad bereavement,[21] and his sympathy was shown in his manner rather than in his words. 'Work is the best antidote to sorrow, my dear Watson,' said he, 'and I have a piece of work for us both tonight which, if we can bring it to a successful conclusion, will in itself justify a man's life on this planet.' In vain I begged him to tell me more. 'You will hear and see enough before morning,' he answered. 'We have three years of the past to discuss. Let that suffice until half-past nine, when we start upon the notable adventure of the empty house.'

It was indeed like old times when, at that hour, I found myself seated beside him in a hansom,[22] my revolver in my pocket and the thrill of adventure in my heart. Holmes was cold and stern and silent. As the gleam of the street-lamps flashed upon his austere features, I saw that his brows were drawn down in thought and his thin lips compressed. I knew not what wild beast we were about to hunt down in the dark jungle of criminal London, but I was well assured from the bearing of this master huntsman that the adventure was a most grave one, while the sardonic smile which occasionally broke through his ascetic gloom boded little good for the object of our quest.

I had imagined that we were bound for Baker Street, but Holmes stopped the cab at the corner of Cavendish Square.[23] I observed that as he stepped out he gave a most searching glance to right and left, and at every subsequent street corner he took the utmost pains to assure that he was not followed. Our route was certainly a singular one.[24] Holmes's knowledge of the byways of London was extraordinary, and on this occasion he passed rapidly, and with an assured step, through a network of mews and stables the very existence of which I had never known. We emerged at last into a small road, lined with old, gloomy houses,[25] which led us into Manchester Street, and so to Blandford Street. Here he turned swiftly down a narrow passage, passed through a wooden gate into a deserted yard, and then opened with a key the back door of a house.[26] We entered together, and he closed it behind us.

The place was pitch dark, but it was evident to me that it was an empty house. Our feet creaked and crackled over the bare planking, and my outstretched hand touched a wall from which the paper was hanging in ribbons. Holmes's cold, thin fingers closed round my wrist and led me forward down a long hall, until I dimly saw the murky fanlight over the door. Here Holmes turned suddenly to the right, and we found ourselves in a large, square, empty room, heavily shadowed in the corners, but faintly lit in the centre from the lights of the street beyond. There was no lamp near, and the window was thick with dust, so that we could only just discern each other's figures within. My companion put his hand upon my shoulder, and his lips close to my ear.

'Do you know where we are?' he whispered.

'Surely that is Baker Street,' I answered, staring through the dim window.

'Exactly. We are in Camden House,[27] which stands opposite[28] to our own old quarters.'

'But why are we here?'

'Because it commands so excellent a view of that picturesque pile. Might I trouble you, my dear Watson, to draw a little nearer to the window, taking every precaution not to show yourself, and then to look up at our old rooms – the starting-point of so many of our little adventures? We will see if my three years of absence have entirely taken away my power to surprise you.'

I crept forward and looked across at the familiar window. As my eyes fell upon it I gave a gasp and a cry of amazement. The blind was down, and a strong light was burning in the room. The shadow of a man who was seated in a chair within was thrown in hard, black outline upon the luminous screen of the window. There was no mistaking the poise of the head, the squareness of the shoulders, the sharpness of the features. The face was turned half-round, and the effect was that of one of those silhouettes which our grandparents loved to frame. It was a perfect reproduction of Holmes. So amazed was I that I threw out my hand to make sure that the man himself was standing beside me. He was quivering with silent laughter.

'Well?' said he.

'Good heavens!' I cried. 'It's marvellous.'

'I trust that age doth not wither nor custom stale my infinite variety,'[29] said he, and I recognized in his voice the joy and pride which the artist takes in his own creation. 'It really is rather like me, is it not?'

'I should be prepared to swear that it was you.'

'The credit of the execution is due to Monsieur Oscar Meunier, of Grenoble, who spent some days in doing the moulding. It is a bust in wax. The rest I arranged myself during my visit to Baker Street this afternoon.'

'But why?'

'Because, my dear Watson, I had the strongest possible reason for wishing certain people to think that I was there when I was really elsewhere.'

'And you thought the rooms were watched?'

'I *knew* that they were watched.'

'By whom?'

'By my old enemies, Watson. By the charming society whose leader lies in the Reichenbach Fall. You must remember that they knew, and only they knew, that I was still alive. Sooner or later they believed that I should come back to my rooms. They watched them continuously, and this morning they saw me arrive.'

'How do you know?'

'Because I recognized their sentinel when I glanced out of my window. He is a harmless enough fellow, Parker by name, a garrotter by trade, and a remarkable performer upon the jew's harp.[30] I cared nothing for him. But I cared a great deal for the much more formidable person who was behind him, the bosom friend of Moriarty, the man who dropped the rocks over the cliff, the most cunning and dangerous criminal in London. That is the man who is after me tonight, Watson, and that is the man who is quite unaware that we are after *him*.'

My friend's plans were gradually revealing themselves. From this convenient retreat the watchers were being watched and the trackers tracked. That angular shadow up yonder was the bait, and we were the hunters. In silence we stood together in the darkness and watched the hurrying figures who passed and repassed in front of us. Holmes was silent and motionless; but I could tell that he was keenly alert, and that his eyes were fixed intently upon the stream of passers-by. It was a bleak and boisterous night, and the wind whistled shrilly down the long street. Many people were moving to and fro, most of them muffled in their coats and cravats. Once or twice it seemed to me that I had seen the same figure before, and I especially noticed two men who appeared to be sheltering themselves from the wind in the doorway of a house some distance up the street. I tried to draw my companion's attention to them, but he gave a little ejaculation of impatience, and continued to stare into the street. More than once he fidgeted with his feet and tapped rapidly with his fingers upon the wall. It was evident to me that he was becoming uneasy, and that his plans were not working out altogether as he had hoped. At last, as midnight approached and the street gradually cleared, he paced up and down the room in uncontrollable agitation. I was about to make some remark to him, when I raised my eyes to the lighted window, and again experienced almost as great a surprise as before. I clutched Holmes's arm and pointed upwards.

'The shadow has moved!' I cried.

It was, indeed, no longer the profile, but the back, which was turned towards us.

Three years had certainly not smoothed the asperities of his temper, or his impatience with a less active intelligence than his own.

'Of course it has moved,' said he. 'Am I such a farcical bungler, Watson, that I should erect an obvious dummy and expect that some of the sharpest men in Europe would be deceived by it? We have been in this room two hours, and Mrs Hudson has made some change in that figure eight times, or once every quarter of an hour. She works it from the front so that her shadow may never be seen. Ah!' He drew in his breath with a shrill, excited intake. In the dim light I saw his head thrown forward, his whole attitude rigid with attention. Those two men might still be crouching in the doorway, but I could no longer see them. All was still and dark, save only that brilliant yellow screen in front of us with the black figure outlined upon its centre. Again in the utter silence I heard that thin, sibilant note which spoke of intense suppressed excitement. An instant later he pulled me back into the blackest corner of the room, and I felt his warning hand upon my lips. The fingers which clutched me were quivering. Never had I known my friend more moved, and yet the dark street still stretched lonely and motionless before us.

But suddenly I was aware of that which his keener senses had already distinguished. A low, stealthy sound came to my ears, not from the direction of Baker Street, but from the back of the very house in which we lay concealed. A door opened and shut. An instant later steps crept down the passage – steps which were meant to be silent, but which reverberated harshly through the empty house. Holmes crouched back against the wall, and I did the same, my hand closing upon the handle of my revolver. Peering through the gloom, I saw the vague outline of a man a shade blacker than the blackness of the open door. He stood for an instant, and then he crept forward, crouching, menacing, into the room. He was within three yards of us, this sinister figure, and I had braced myself to meet his spring, before I realized that he had no idea of our presence. He passed close beside us, stole over to the window, and very softly and noiselessly raised it for half a foot. As he sank to the level of this opening the light of the street, no longer dimmed by the dusty glass, fell full upon his face. The man seemed to be beside himself with excitement. His two eyes shone like stars, and his features were working convulsively. He was an elderly man, with a thin projecting nose, a high, bald forehead, and a huge grizzled moustache. An opera-hat was pushed to the back of his head, and an evening dress shirt-front gleamed out through his open overcoat. His face was gaunt and swarthy, scored with deep, savage lines. In his hand he carried what appeared to be a stick, but as he laid it down upon the floor it gave a metallic clang. Then from the pocket of his overcoat he drew a bulky object, and he busied himself in some task which ended with a loud, sharp click, as if a spring or bolt had fallen into its place. Still kneeling upon the floor, he bent forward and threw all his weight and strength upon some lever, with the result that there came a long, whirling, grinding noise, ending once more in a powerful click. He straightened himself then, and I saw that what he held in his hand was a sort of gun, with a curiously misshapen butt. He opened it at the breech, put something in, and snapped the breech-block. Then, crouching down, he rested the end of the barrel upon the ledge of the open window, and I saw his long moustache droop over the stock and his eye gleam as it peered along the sights. I heard a little sigh of satisfaction as he cuddled the butt into his shoulder, and saw that amazing target, the black man on the yellow ground, standing clear at the end of his foresight. For an instant he was rigid and motionless. Then his finger tightened on the trigger. There was a strange, loud whiz and a long, silvery tinkle of broken glass. At that instant Holmes sprang like a tiger on to the marksman's back and hurled him flat upon his face. He was up again in a moment, and with convulsive strength he seized Holmes by the throat; but I struck him on the head with the butt of my revolver, and he dropped again upon the floor. I fell upon him, and as I held him my comrade blew a shrill call upon a whistle. There was the clatter of running feet upon the pavement, and two policemen in uniform, with one plain-clothes detective, rushed through the front entrance and into the room.

'That you, Lestrade?' said Holmes.

'Yes, Mr Holmes. I took the job myself. It's good to see you back in London, sir.'

'I think you want a little unofficial help. Three undetected murders in one year won't do, Lestrade. But you handled the Molesey Mystery with less than your usual – that's to say, you handled it fairly well.'

We had all risen to our feet, our prisoner breathing hard, with a stalwart constable on each side of him. Already a few loiterers had begun to collect in the street. Holmes stepped up to the window, closed it, and dropped the blinds. Lestrade had produced two candles, and the policemen had uncovered their lanterns. I was able at last to have a good look at our prisoner.

It was a tremendously virile and yet sinister face which was turned towards us. With the brow of a philosopher above and the jaw of a sensualist below, the man must have started with great capacities for good or for evil. But one could not look upon his cruel blue eyes, with their drooping, cynical lids, or upon the fierce, aggressive nose and the threatening, deep-lined brow, without reading Nature's plainest danger-signals. He took no heed of any of us, but his eyes were fixed upon Holmes's face with an expression in which hatred and amazement were equally blended. 'You fiend!' he kept on muttering – 'you clever, clever fiend!'

'Ah, Colonel,' said Holmes, arranging his crumpled collar, ' "journeys end in lovers' meetings," as the old play says.[31] I don't think I have had the pleasure of seeing you since you favoured me with those attentions as I lay on the ledge above the Reichenbach Fall.'

The colonel still stared at my friend like a man in a trance. 'You cunning, cunning fiend!' was all that he could say.

'I have not introduced you yet,' said Holmes. 'This, gentlemen, is Colonel Sebastian Moran, once of Her Majesty's Indian Army, and the best heavy game shot that our Eastern Empire has ever produced. I believe I am correct, Colonel, in saying that your bag of tigers still remains unrivalled?'

The fierce old man said nothing, but still glared at my companion; with his savage eyes and bristling moustache, he was wonderfully like a tiger himself.

'I wonder that my very simple stratagem could deceive so old a shikari,'[32] said Holmes. 'It must be very familiar to you. Have you not tethered a young kid under a tree, lain above it with your rifle, and waited for the bait to bring up your tiger? This empty house is my tree, and you are my tiger. You have possibly had other guns in reserve in case there should be several tigers, or in the unlikely supposition of your own aim failing you. These,' he pointed around, 'are my other guns. The parallel is exact.'

Colonel Moran sprang forward with a snarl of rage, but the constables dragged him back. The fury upon his face was terrible to look at.

'I confess that you had one small surprise for me,' said Holmes. 'I did not anticipate that you would yourself make use of this empty house and this convenient front window. I had imagined you as operating from the street, where my friend Lestrade and his merry men were awaiting you. With that exception, all has gone as I expected.'

Colonel Moran turned to the official detective.

'You may or may not have just cause for arresting me,' said he, 'but at least there can be no reason why I should submit to the gibes of this person. If I am in the hands of the law, let things be done in a legal way.'

'Well, that's reasonable enough,' said Lestrade. 'Nothing further you have to say, Mr Holmes, before we go?'

Holmes had picked up the powerful air-gun[33] from the floor and was examining its mechanism.

'An admirable and unique weapon,' said he, 'noiseless and of tremendous power. I knew Von Herder, the blind German mechanic,[34] who constructed it to the order of the late Professor Moriarty. For years I have been aware of its existence, though I have never before had an opportunity of handling it. I commend it very specially to your attention, Lestrade, and also the bullets which fit it.'

'You can trust us to look after that, Mr Holmes,' said Lestrade, as the whole party moved towards the door. 'Anything further to say?'

'Only to ask what charge you intend to prefer?'

'What charge, sir? Why, of course, the attempted murder of Mr Sherlock Holmes.'

'Not so, Lestrade. I do not propose to appear in the matter at all. To you, and to you only, belongs the credit of the remarkable arrest which you have effected. Yes, Lestrade, I congratulate you! With your usual happy mixture of cunning and audacity you have got him.'

'Got him! Got whom, Mr Holmes?'

'The man whom the whole Force has been seeking in vain – Colonel Sebastian Moran, who shot the Honourable Ronald Adair with an expanding bullet from an air-gun through the open window of the second-floor front of No. 427 Park Lane, upon the 30th of last month. That's the charge, Lestrade. And now, Watson, if you can endure the draught from a broken window, I think that half an hour in my study over a cigar may afford you some profitable amusement.'

Our old chambers had been left unchanged, through the supervision of Mycroft Holmes and the immediate care of Mrs Hudson. As I entered I saw, it is true, an unwonted tidiness, but the old landmarks were all in their places. There were the chemical corner and the acid-stained deal-topped table. There upon a shelf was the row of formidable scrapbooks and books of reference which many of our fellow citizens would have been so glad to burn. The diagrams, the violin-case, and the pipe-rack – even the Persian slipper which contained the tobacco – all met my eye as I glanced round me. There were two occupants of the room – one Mrs Hudson, who beamed upon us both as we entered; the other, the strange dummy which had played so important a part in the evening's adventures. It was a wax-coloured model of my friend, so admirably done that it was a perfect facsimile. It stood on a small pedestal table with an old dressing-gown of Holmes's so draped round it that the illusion from the street was absolutely perfect.

'I hope you preserved all precautions, Mrs Hudson?' said Holmes.

'I went to it on my knees, sir, just as you told me.'

'Excellent. You carried the thing out very well. Did you observe where the bullet went?'

'Yes, sir. I'm afraid it has spoilt your beautiful bust, for it passed right through the head and flattened itself on the wall. I picked it up from the carpet. Here it is!'

Holmes held it out to me. 'A soft revolver bullet, as you perceive, Watson. There's genius in that – for who would expect to find such a thing fired from an air-gun? All right, Mrs Hudson, I am much obliged for your assistance. And now, Watson, let me see you in your old seat once more, for there are several points which I should like to discuss with you.'

He had thrown off the seedy frock-coat, and now he was the Holmes of old, in the mouse-coloured dressing-gown which he took from his effigy.

'The old shikari's nerves have not lost their steadiness nor his eyes their keenness,' said he, with a laugh, as he inspected the shattered forehead of his bust.

'Plumb in the middle of the back of the head and smack through the brain. He was the best shot in India, and I expect that there are few better in London. Have you heard the name?'

'No, I have not.'

'Well, well, such is fame! But then, if I remember aright, you had not heard the name of Professor James Moriarty, who had one of the great brains of the century. Just give me down my index of biographies from the shelf.'

He turned over the pages lazily, leaning back in his chair and blowing great clouds of smoke from his cigar.

'My collection of M's is a fine one,' said he. 'Moriarty himself is enough to make any letter illustrious, and here is Morgan the poisoner, and Merridew of abominable memory, and Mathews, who knocked out my left canine in the waiting-room at Charing Cross, and, finally, here is our friend of tonight.'

He handed over the book, and I read: '*Moran, Sebastian, Colonel.* Unemployed. Formerly 1st Bengalore Pioneers.[35] Born London, 1840. Son of Sir Augustus Moran, C.B., once British Minister to Persia. Educated Eton and Oxford. Served in Jowaki[36] Campaign, Afghan Campaign,[37] Charasiab[38] (dispatches), Sherpur,[39] and Cabull[40] Author of *Heavy Game of the Western Himalayas*, 1881; *Three Months in the Jungle*, 1884. Address: Conduit Street.[41] Clubs: The Anglo-Indian,[42] the Tankerville,[43] the Bagatelle Card Club.[44]

On the margin was written in Holmes's precise hand: 'The second most dangerous man in London.'

'This is astonishing,' said I, as I handed back the volume. 'The man's career is that of an honourable soldier.'

'It is true,' Holmes answered. 'Up to a certain point he did well. He was always a man of iron nerve, and the story is still told in India how he crawled down a drain after a wounded man-eating tiger.[45] There are some trees, Watson, which grow to a certain height and then suddenly develop some unsightly eccentricity. You will see it often in humans. I have a theory that the individual represents in his development the whole procession of his ancestors, and that such a sudden turn to good or evil stands for some strong influence which came into the line of his pedigree. The person becomes, as it were, the epitome of the history of his own family.'

'It is surely rather fanciful.'

'Well, I don't insist upon it. Whatever the cause, Colonel Moran began to go wrong. Without any open scandal, he still made India too hot to hold him. He retired, came to London, and again acquired an evil name. It was at this time that he was sought out by Professor Moriarty, to whom for a time he was chief of the staff. Moriarty supplied him liberally with money, and used him only in one or two very high-class jobs which no ordinary criminal could have undertaken. You may have some recollection of the death of Mrs Stewart, of Lauder,[46] in 1887. Not? Well, I am sure Moran was at the bottom of it; but nothing could be proved. So cleverly was the colonel concealed that even when the Moriarty gang was broken up we could not incriminate him. You remember at that date, when I called upon you in your rooms, how I put up the shutters for fear of air-guns? No doubt you thought me fanciful. I knew exactly what I was doing, for I knew of the existence of this remarkable gun, and I knew also that one of the best shots in the world would be behind it. When we were in Switzerland he followed us with Moriarty, and it was undoubtedly he who gave me that evil five minutes on the Reichenbach ledge.

'You may think that I read the papers with some attention during my sojourn in France, on the lookout for any chance of laying him by the heels. So long as he was free in London my life would really not have been worth living. Night and day the shadow would have been over me, and sooner or later his chance must have come. What could I do? I could not shoot him at sight, or I should myself be in the dock. There was no use appealing to a magistrate. They cannot interfere on the strength of what would appear to them to be a wild suspicion. So I could do nothing. But I watched the criminal news, knowing that sooner or later I should get him. Then came the death of this Ronald Adair. My chance had come at last! Knowing what I did, was it not certain that Colonel Moran had done it? He had played cards with the lad; he had followed him home from the club; he had shot him through the open window. There was not a doubt of it. The bullets alone are enough to put his head in a noose. I came over at once. I was seen by the sentinel, who would, I knew, direct the colonel's attention to my presence. He could not fail to connect my sudden return with his crime, and to be terribly alarmed. I was sure that he would make an attempt to get me out of the way *at once*, and would bring round his murderous weapon for that purpose. I left him an excellent mark in the window, and, having warned the police that they might be needed – by the way, Watson, you spotted their presence in that doorway with unerring accuracy – I took up what seemed to me to be a judicious post for observation, never dreaming that he would choose the same spot for his attack. Now, my dear Watson, does anything remain for me to explain?'

'Yes,' said I. 'You have not made it clear what was Colonel Moran's motive in murdering the Honourable Ronald Adair.'

'Ah! my dear Watson, there we come into those realms of conjecture where the most logical mind may be at fault. Each may form his own hypothesis upon the present evidence, and yours is as likely to be correct as mine.'

'You have formed one, then?'

'I think that it is not difficult to explain the facts. It came out in evidence that Colonel Moran and young Adair had between them won a considerable amount of money. Now, Moran undoubtedly played foul – of that I have long been aware. I believe that on the day of the murder, Adair had discovered that Moran was cheating. Very likely he had spoken to him privately, and had threatened to expose him unless he voluntarily resigned his membership of the club and promised not to play cards again. It is unlikely that a youngster like Adair would at once make a hideous scandal by exposing a well-known man so much older than himself. Probably he acted as I suggest. The exclusion from his clubs would mean ruin to Moran, who lived by his ill-gotten card gains. He therefore murdered Adair, who at the time was endeavouring to work out how much money he should himself return, since he could not profit by his partner's foul play. He locked the door, lest the ladies should surprise him and insist upon knowing what he was doing with these names and coins. Will it pass?'

'I have no doubt that you have hit upon the truth.'

'It will be verified or disproved at the trial. Meanwhile, come what may, Colonel Moran will trouble us no more,[47] the famous air-gun of Von Herder will embellish the Scotland Yard Museum, and once again Mr Sherlock Holmes is free to devote his life to examining those interesting little problems which the complex life of London so plentifully presents.'

THE DANCING¹ MEN

Holmes had been seated for some hours in silence, with his long, thin back curved over a chemical vessel in which he was brewing a particularly malodorous product. His head was sunk upon his breast, and he looked from my point of view like a strange, lank bird, with dull grey plumage and a black top-knot.

'So, Watson,' said he suddenly, 'you do not propose to invest in South African securities?'[2]

I gave a start of astonishment. Accustomed as I was to Holmes's curious faculties, this sudden intrusion into my most intimate thoughts[3] was utterly inexplicable.

'How on earth do you know that?' I asked.

He wheeled round upon his stool, with a steaming test-tube in his hand and a gleam of amusement in his deep-set eyes.

'Now, Watson, confess yourself utterly taken aback,' said he.

'I am.'

'I ought to make you sign a paper to that effect.'

'Why?'

'Because in five minutes you will say that it is all so absurdly simple.'

'I am sure that I shall say nothing of the kind.'

'You see, my dear Watson' – he propped his test-tube in the rack and began to lecture with the air of a professor addressing his class – 'it is not really difficult to construct a series of inferences, each dependent upon its predecessor and each simple in itself. If, after doing so, one simply knocks out all the central inferences and presents one's audience with the starting-point and the conclusion, one may produce a startling, though possibly a meretricious, effect. Now, it was not really difficult, by an inspection of the groove between your left forefinger and thumb, to feel sure that you did *not* propose to invest your small capital in the goldfields.'

'I see no connection.'

'Very likely not; but I can quickly show you a close connection. Here are the missing links of the very simple chain: 1. You had chalk between your left finger and thumb when you returned from the club last night. 2. You put chalk there when you play billiards to steady the cue. 3. You never play billiards except with Thurston.⁴ 4. You told me four weeks ago that Thurston had an option on some South African property which would expire in a month, and which he desired you to share with him. 5. Your cheque-book is locked in my drawer, and you have not asked for the key. 6. You do not propose to invest your money in this manner.'

'How absurdly simple!' I cried.

'Quite so!' said he, a little nettled. 'Every problem becomes very childish when once it is explained to you. Here is an unexplained one. See what you can make of that, friend Watson.' He tossed a sheet of paper upon the table, and turned once more to his chemical analysis.

I looked with amazement at the absurd hieroglyphics upon the paper.

'Why, Holmes, it is a child's drawing!' I cried.

'Oh, that's your idea!'

'What else should it be?'

'That is what Mr Hilton Cubitt, of Ridling Thorpe Manor, Norfolk,⁵ is very anxious to know. This little conundrum came by the first post, and he was to follow by the next train. There's a ring at the bell, Watson. I should not be very much surprised if this were he.'

A heavy step was heard upon the stairs, and an instant later there entered a tall, ruddy, clean-shaven gentleman, whose clear eyes and florid cheeks told of a life led far from the fogs of Baker Street. He seemed to bring a whiff of his strong, fresh, bracing, east-coast air with him as he entered. Having shaken hands with each of us, he was about to sit down, when his eye rested upon the paper with the curious markings, which I had just examined and left upon the table.

'Well, Mr Holmes, what do you make of these?' he cried. 'They told me that you were fond of queer mysteries, and I don't think you can find a queerer one than that. I sent the paper on ahead so that you might have time to study it before I came.'

'It is certainly rather a curious production,' said Holmes. 'At first sight it would appear to be some childish prank. It consists of a number of absurd little figures dancing across the paper upon which they are drawn. Why should you attribute any importance to so grotesque an object?'

'I never should, Mr Holmes. But my wife does. It is frightening her to death. She says nothing, but I can see terror in her eyes. That's why I want to sift the matter to the bottom.'

Holmes held up the paper so that the sunlight shone full upon it. It was a page torn from a notebook. The markings were done in pencil, and ran in this way:

Holmes examined it for some time, and then, folding it carefully up, he placed it in his pocket-book.

'This promises to be a most interesting and unusual case,' said he. 'You gave me a few particulars in your letter, Mr Hilton Cubitt, but I should be very much obliged if you would kindly go over it all again for the benefit of my friend, Dr Watson.'

'I'm not much of a story-teller,' said our visitor, nervously clasping and unclasping his great, strong hands. 'You'll just ask me anything that I don't make clear. I'll begin at the time of my marriage last year; but I want to say first of all that, though I'm not a rich man, my people have been at Ridling Thorpe for a matter of five centuries, and there is no better-known family in the county of Norfolk. Last year I came up to London for the Jubilee,[6] and I stopped at a boarding-house in Russell Square,[7] because Parker, the vicar of our parish, was staying in it. There was an American young lady there – Patrick was the name – Elsie Patrick. In some way we became friends, until before my month was up I was as much in love as a man could be. We were quietly married at a registry office, and we returned to Norfolk a wedded couple. You'll think it very mad, Mr Holmes, that a man of a good family should marry a wife in this fashion, knowing nothing of her past or of her people; but if you saw her and knew her it would help you to understand.

'She was very straight about it, was Elsie. I can't say that she did not give me every chance of getting out of it if I wished to do so. "I have had some very disagreeable associations in my life," said she; "I wish to forget all about them. I would rather never allude to the past, for it is very painful to me. If you take me, Hilton, you will take a woman who has nothing that she need be personally ashamed of; but you will have to be content with my word for it, and to allow me to be silent as to all that passed up to the time when I became yours. If these conditions are too hard, then go back to Norfolk and leave me to the lonely life in which you found me." It was only the day before our wedding that she said those very words to me. I told her that I was content to take her on her own terms, and I have been as good as my word.

'Well, we have been married now for a year, and very happy we have been. But about a month ago, at the end of June, I saw for the first time signs of trouble. One day my wife received a letter from America. I saw the American stamp. She turned deadly white, read the letter, and threw it into the fire. She made no allusion to it afterwards and I made none, for a promise is a promise; but she has never known an easy hour from that moment. There is always a look of fear upon her face – a look as if she were waiting and expecting. She would do better to trust me. She would find that I was her best friend. But until she speaks I can say nothing. Mind you, she is a truthful woman, Mr Holmes, and whatever trouble there may have been in her past life, it has been no fault of hers. I am only a simple Norfolk squire, but there is not a man in England who ranks his family honour more highly than I do. She knows it well, and she knew it well before she married me. She would never bring any stain upon it – of that I am sure.

'Well, now I come to the queer part of my story. About a week ago – it was the Tuesday of last week – I found on one of the window-sills a number of absurd little dancing figures, like these upon the paper.

They were scrawled with chalk. I thought that it was the stable-boy who had drawn them, but the lad swore he knew nothing about it. Anyhow, they had come there during the night. I had them washed out, and I only mentioned the matter to my wife afterwards. To my surprise she took it very seriously, and begged me if any more came to let her see them. None did come for a week, and then yesterday morning I found this paper lying on the sundial in the garden. I showed it to Elsie, and down she dropped in a dead faint. Since then she has looked like a woman in a dream, half dazed, and with terror always lurking in her eyes. It was then that I wrote and sent the paper to you, Mr Holmes. It was not a thing that I could take to the police, for they would have laughed at me, but you will tell me what to do. I am not a rich man; but if there is any danger threatening my little woman, I would spend my last copper to shield her.'

He was a fine creature, this man of the old English soil, simple, straight and gentle, with his great, earnest, blue eyes and broad, comely face. His love for his wife and his trust in her shone in his features. Holmes had listened to his story with the utmost attention, and now he sat for some time in silent thought.

'Don't you think, Mr Cubitt,' said he at last, 'that your best plan would be to make a direct appeal to your wife, and to ask her to share her secret with you?'

Hilton Cubitt shook his massive head.

'A promise is a promise, Mr Holmes. If Elsie wished to tell me, she would. If not, it is not for me to force her confidence. But I am justified in taking my own line – and I will.'

'Then I will help you with all my heart. In the first place, have you heard of any strangers being seen in your neighbourhood?'

'No.'

'I presume that it is a very quiet place. Any fresh face would cause comment?'

'In the immediate neighbourhood, yes. But we have several small watering-places not very far away. And the farmers take in lodgers.'

'These hieroglyphics have evidently a meaning. If it is a purely arbitrary one, it may be impossible for us to solve it. If, on the other hand, it is systematic, I have no doubt that we shall get to the bottom of it. But this particular sample is so short that I can do nothing, and the facts which you have brought me are so indefinite that we have no basis for an investigation. I would suggest that you return to Norfolk, that you keep a keen lookout, and that you take an exact copy of any fresh dancing men which may appear. It is a thousand pities that we have not a reproduction of those which were done in chalk upon the window-sill. Make a discreet inquiry, also, as to any strangers in the neighbourhood. When you have collected some fresh evidence, come to me again. That is the best advice which I can give you, Mr Hilton Cubitt. If there are any pressing fresh developments, I shall be always ready to run down and see you in your Norfolk home.'

The interview left Sherlock Holmes very thoughtful, and several times in the next few days I saw him take his slip of paper from his notebook and look long and earnestly at the curious figures inscribed upon it. He made no allusion to the affair, however, until one afternoon a fortnight or so later. I was going out, when he called me back.

'You had better stay here, Watson.'

'Why?'

'Because I had a wire from Hilton Cubitt this morning – you remember Hilton Cubitt, of the dancing men? He was to reach Liverpool Street at one-twenty. He may be here at any moment. I gather from his wire that there have been some new incidents of importance.'

We had not long to wait, for our Norfolk squire came straight from the station as fast as a hansom could bring him. He was looking worried and depressed, with tired eyes and a lined forehead.

'It's getting on my nerves, this business, Mr Holmes,' said he, as he sank, like a wearied man, into an armchair. 'It's bad enough to feel that you are surrounded by unseen, unknown folk who have some kind of design upon you; but when, in addition to that, you know that it is just killing your wife by inches, then it becomes as much as flesh and blood can endure. She's wearing away under it – just wearing away before my eyes.'

'Has she said anything yet?'

'No, Mr Holmes, she has not. And yet there have been times when the poor girl has wanted to speak, and yet could not quite bring herself to take the plunge. I have tried to help her; but I dare say I did it clumsily, and scared her off from it. She has spoken about my old family, and our reputation in the county, and our pride in our unsullied honour, and I always felt it was leading to the point; but somehow it turned off before we got there.'

'But you have found out something for yourself?'

'A good deal, Mr Holmes. I have several fresh dancing men pictures for you to examine, and, what is more important, I have seen the fellow.'

'What – the man who draws them?'

'Yes, I saw him at his work. But I will tell you everything in order. When I got back after my visit to you, the very first thing I saw next morning was a fresh crop of dancing men. They had been drawn in chalk upon the black wooden door of the tool-house, which stands beside the lawn in full view of the front windows. I took an exact copy, and here it is.' He unfolded a paper and laid it upon the table. Here is a copy of the hieroglyphics:

'Excellent!' said Holmes. 'Excellent! Pray continue.'

When I had taken the copy I rubbed out the marks; but two mornings later a fresh inscription had appeared. I have a copy of it here':

Holmes rubbed his hands and chuckled with delight.

'Our material is rapidly accumulating,' said he.

'Three days later a message was left scrawled upon paper, and placed under a pebble upon the sundial. Here it is. The characters are, as you see, exactly the same as the last one. After that I determined to lie in wait; so I got out my revolver and I sat up in my study, which overlooks the lawn and garden. About two in the morning I was seated by the window, all being dark save for the moonlight outside, when I heard steps behind me, and there was my wife in her dressing-gown. She implored me to come to bed. I told her frankly that I wished to see who it was who played such absurd tricks upon us. She answered that it was some senseless practical joke, and that I should not take any notice of it.

'"If it really annoys you, Hilton, we might go and travel, you and I, and so avoid this nuisance."

'"What, be driven out of our own house by a practical joker?" said I. "Why, we should have the whole county laughing at us!"

'"Well, come to bed," said she, "and we can discuss it in the morning."

'Suddenly, as she spoke, I saw her white face grow whiter yet in the moonlight, and her hand tightened upon my shoulder. Something was moving in the shadow of the tool-house. I saw a dark, creeping figure which crawled round the corner and squatted in front of the door. Seizing my pistol I was rushing out, when my wife threw her arms round me and held me with convulsive strength. I tried to throw her off, but she clung to me most desperately. At last I got clear, but by the time I had opened the door and reached the house the creature was gone. He had left a trace of his presence, however, for there on the door was the very same arrangement of dancing men which had already twice appeared, and which I have copied on that paper. There was no other sign of the fellow anywhere, though I ran all over the grounds. And yet the amazing thing is that he must have been there all the time, for when I examined the door again in the morning he had scrawled some more of his pictures under the line which I had already seen.'

'Have you that fresh drawing?'

'Yes; it is very short, but I made a copy of it, and here it is.'

Again he produced a paper. The new dance was in this form:

'Tell me,' said Holmes — and I could see by his eyes that he was much excited — 'was this a mere addition to the first, or did it appear to be entirely separate?'

'It was on a different panel of the door.'

'Excellent! This is far the most important of all for our purpose. It fills me with hopes. Now, Mr Hilton Cubitt, please continue your most interesting statement.'

'I have nothing more to say, Mr Holmes, except that I was angry with my wife that night for having held me back when I might have caught the skulking rascal. She said that she feared that I might come to harm. For an instant it had crossed my mind that perhaps what she really feared was that *he* might come to harm, for I could not doubt that she knew who this man was and what he meant by these strange signals. But there is a tone in my wife's voice, Mr Holmes, and a look in her eyes which forbid doubt, and I am sure that it was indeed my own safety that was in her mind. There's the whole case, and now I want your advice as to what I ought to do. My own inclination is to put half a dozen of my farm lads in the shrubbery, and when this fellow comes again to give him such a hiding that he will leave us in peace for the future.'

'I fear it is too deep a case for such simple remedies,' said Holmes. 'How long can you stop in London?'

'I must go back today. I would not leave my wife alone at night for anything. She is very nervous and begged me to come back.'

'I dare say you are right. But if you could have stopped I might possibly have been able to return with you in a day or two. Meanwhile, you will leave me these papers, and I think that it is very likely that I shall be able to pay you a visit shortly and to throw some light upon your case.'

Sherlock Holmes preserved his calm professional manner until our visitor had left us, although it was easy for me, who knew him so well, to see that he was profoundly excited. The moment that Hilton Cubitt's broad back had disappeared through the door my comrade rushed to the table, laid out all the slips of paper containing dancing men in front of him, and threw himself into an intricate and elaborate calculation.

For two hours I watched him as he covered sheet after sheet of paper with figures and letters, so completely absorbed in his task that he had evidently forgotten my presence. Sometimes he was making progress, and whistled and sang at his work; sometimes he was puzzled and would sit for a long spell with a furrowed brow and a vacant eye. Finally he sprang from his chair with a cry of satisfaction, and walked up and down the room rubbing his hands together. Then he wrote a long telegram upon a cable form. 'If my answer to this is as I hope, you will have a very pretty case to add to your collection, Watson,' said he. 'I expect that we shall be able to go down to Norfolk tomorrow, and to take our friend some very definite news as to the secret of his annoyance.'

I confess that I was filled with curiosity, but I was aware that Holmes liked to make his disclosures at his own time and in his own way; so I waited until it should suit him to take me into his confidence.

But there was a delay in that answering telegram, and two days of impatience followed, during which Holmes pricked up his ears at every ring of the bell. On the evening of the second there came a letter from Hilton Cubitt. All was quiet with him, save that a long inscription had appeared that morning upon the pedestal of the sundial. He enclosed a copy of it, which is here reproduced:

Holmes bent over this grotesque frieze for some minutes and then suddenly sprang to his feet with an exclamation of surprise and dismay. His face was haggard with anxiety.

'We have let this affair go far enough,' said he. 'Is there a train to North Walsham[8] tonight?'

I turned up the time-table. The last had just gone.

'Then we shall breakfast early and take the very first in the morning,' said Holmes. 'Our presence is most urgently needed. Ah, here is our expected cablegram. One moment, Mrs Hudson – there may be an answer. No, that is quite as I expected. This message makes it even more essential that we should not lose an hour in letting Hilton Cubitt know how matters stand, for it is a singular and dangerous web in which our simple Norfolk squire is entangled.'

So, indeed, it proved, and as I come to the dark conclusion of a story which had seemed to me to be only childish and bizarre, I experience once again the dismay and horror with which I was filled. Would that I had some brighter ending to communicate to my readers; but these are the chronicles of facts, and I must follow to their dark crisis the strange chain of events which for some days made Ridling Thorpe Manor a household word through the length and breadth of England.

We had hardly alighted at North Walsham, and mentioned the name of our destination, when the station-master hurried towards us. 'I suppose that you are the detectives from London?' said he.

A look of annoyance passed over Holmes's face.

'What makes you think such a thing?'

'Because Inspector Martin from Norwich has just passed through. But maybe you are the surgeons. She's not dead – or wasn't by last accounts. You may be in time to save her yet – though it be for the gallows.'

Holmes's brow was dark with anxiety.

'We are going to Ridling Thorpe Manor,' said he, 'but we have heard nothing of what has passed there.'

'It's a terrible business,' said the station-master. 'They are shot, both Mr Hilton Cubitt and his wife. She shot him and then herself – so the servants say. He's dead, and her life is despaired of. Dear, dear! one of the oldest families in the county of Norfolk, and one of the most honoured.'

Without a word Holmes hurried to a carriage, and during the long, seven-miles drive he never opened his mouth. Seldom have I seen him so utterly despondent. He had been uneasy during all our journey from town, and I had observed that he had turned over the morning papers with anxious attention; but now this sudden realization of his worst fears left him in a blank melancholy. He leaned back in his seat, lost in gloomy speculation. Yet there was much around us to interest us, for we were passing through as singular a countryside as any in England, where a few scattered cottages represented the population of today, while on every hand enormous square-towered churches[9] bristled up from the flat, green landscape and told of the glory and prosperity of old East Anglia. At last the violet rim of the German Ocean[10] appeared over the green edge of the Norfolk coast, and the driver pointed with his whip to two old brick-and-timber gables which projected from a grove of trees. 'That's Ridling Thorpe Manor,' said he.

As we drove up to the porticoed front door I observed in front of it, beside the tennis lawn, the black tool-house and the pedestalled sundial with which we had such strange associations. A dapper little man, with a quick, alert manner and a waxed moustache, had just descended from a high dog-cart. He introduced himself as Inspector Martin, of the Norfolk Constabulary, and he was considerably astonished when he heard the name of my companion.

'Why, Mr Holmes, the crime was only committed at three this morning! How could you hear of it in London and get to the spot as soon as I?'

'I anticipated it. I came in the hope of preventing it.'

'Then you must have important evidence of which we are ignorant, for they were said to be a most united couple.'

'I have only the evidence of the dancing men,' said Holmes. 'I will explain the matter to you later. Meanwhile, since it is too late to prevent this tragedy, I am very anxious that I should use the knowledge which I possess in order to ensure that justice be done. Will you associate me in your investigation, or will you prefer that I should act independently?'

'I should be proud to feel that we were acting together, Mr Holmes,' said the inspector earnestly.

'In that case I should be glad to hear the evidence and to examine the premises without an instant of unnecessary delay.'

Inspector Martin had the good sense to allow my friend to do things in his own fashion, and contented himself with carefully noting the results. The local surgeon, an old, white-haired man, had just come down from Mrs Hilton Cubitt's room, and he reported that her injuries were serious, but not necessarily fatal. The bullet had passed through the front of her brain,[11] and it would probably be some time before she could regain consciousness. On the question of whether she had been shot or had shot herself he would not venture to express any decided opinion. Certainly the bullet had been discharged at very close quarters. There was only the one pistol found in the room, two barrels of which had been emptied. Mr Hilton Cubitt had been shot through the heart. It was equally conceivable that he had shot her and then himself, or that she had been the criminal, for the revolver lay upon the floor midway between them.

'Has he been moved?' asked Holmes.

'We have moved nothing except the lady. We could not leave her lying wounded upon the floor.'

'How long have you been here, doctor?'

'Since four o'clock.'

'Anyone else?'

'Yes, the constable here.'

'And you have touched nothing?'

'Nothing.'

'You have acted with great discretion. Who sent for you?'

'The housemaid, Saunders.'

'Was it she who gave the alarm?'

'She and Mrs King, the cook.'

'Where are they now?'

'In the kitchen, I believe.'

'Then I think we had better hear their story at once.'

The old hall, oak-panelled and high windowed, had been turned into a court of investigation. Holmes sat in a great, old-fashioned chair, his inexorable eyes gleaming out of his haggard face. I could read in them a set purpose to devote his life to this quest until the client whom he had failed to save should at last be avenged. The trim Inspector Martin, the old grey-headed country doctor, myself and a stolid village policeman made up the rest of that strange company.

The two women told their story clearly enough. They had been aroused from their sleep by the sound of an explosion, which had been followed a minute later by a second one. They slept in adjoining rooms, and Mrs King had rushed in to Saunders. Together they had descended the stairs. The door of the study was open and a candle was burning upon the table. Their master lay upon his face in the centre of the room. He was quite dead. Near the window his wife was crouching, her head leaning against the wall. She was horribly wounded, and the side of her face was red with blood. She breathed heavily, but was incapable of saying anything. The passage, as well as the room, was full of smoke and the smell of powder. The window was certainly shut and fastened upon the inside. Both women were positive upon the point. They had at once sent for the doctor and for the constable. Then, with the aid of the groom and the stable-boy, they had conveyed their injured mistress to her room. Both she and her husband had occupied the bed. She was clad in her dress – he in his dressing-gown, over his night-clothes. Nothing had been moved in the study. So far as they knew, there had never been any quarrel between husband and wife. They had always looked upon them as a very united couple.

These were the main points of the servants' evidence. In answer to Inspector Martin they were clear that every door was fastened upon the inside and that no one could have escaped from the house. In answer to Holmes, they both remembered that they were conscious of the smell of powder from the moment that they ran out of their rooms upon the top floor. 'I commend that fact very carefully to your attention,' said Holmes to his professional colleague. 'And now I think that we are in a position to undertake a thorough examination of the room.'

The study proved to be a small chamber, lined on three sides with books, and with a writing-table facing an ordinary window, which looked out upon the garden. Our first attention was given to the body of the unfortunate squire, whose huge frame lay stretched across the room. His disordered dress showed that he had been hastily aroused from sleep. The bullet had been fired at him from the front, and had remained in his body after penetrating the heart. His death had certainly been instantaneous and painless. There was no powder-marking either upon his dressing-gown or on his hands. According to the country surgeon, the lady had stains upon her face, but none upon her hand.

'The absence of the latter means nothing, though its presence may

mean everything,' said Holmes. 'Unless the powder from a badly
fitting cartridge happens to spurt backwards, one may fire many shots
without leaving a sign. I would suggest that Mr Cubitt's body may
now be removed. I suppose, doctor, you have not recovered the bullet
which wounded the lady?'

'A serious operation will be necessary before that can be done. But
there are still four cartridges in the revolver. Two have been fired and
two wounds inflicted, so that each bullet can be accounted for.'

'So it would seem,' said Holmes. 'Perhaps you can account also
for the bullet which has so obviously struck the edge of the
window?'

He had turned suddenly, and his long, thin finger was pointing to
a hole which had been drilled right through the lower window-sash
about an inch above the bottom.

'By George!' cried the inspector. 'How ever did you see that?'

'Because I looked for it.'

'Wonderful!' said the country doctor. 'You are certainly right, sir.
Then a third shot has been fired, and therefore a third person must
have been present. But who could that have been, and how could he
have got away?'

'That is the problem which we are now about to solve,' said
Sherlock Holmes. 'You remember, Inspector Martin, when the servants said that on leaving their room they were at once conscious of a
smell of powder. I remarked that the point was an extremely important
one?'

'Yes, sir; but I confess I did not quite follow you.'

'It suggested that at the time of the firing the window as well as the
door of the room had been open. Otherwise the fumes of powder
could not have been blown so rapidly through the house. A draught
in the room was necessary for that. Both door and window were only
open for a short time, however.'

'How do you prove that?'

'Because the candle has not guttered.'

'Capital!' cried the inspector. 'Capital!'

'Feeling sure that the window had been open at the time of the
tragedy, I conceived that there might have been a third person in the

affair, who stood outside this opening and fired through it. Any shot directed at this person might hit the sash. I looked, and there, sure enough, was the bullet mark!'

'But how came the window to be shut and fastened?'

'The woman's first instinct would be to shut and fasten the window. But, halloa! what is this?'

It was a lady's hand-bag which stood upon the study table – a trim little hand-bag of crocodile-skin and silver. Holmes opened it and turned the contents out. There were twenty fifty-pound notes of the Bank of England, held together by an india-rubber band – nothing else.

'This must be preserved, for it will figure in the trial,' said Holmes, as he handed the bag with its contents to the inspector. 'It is now necessary that we should try to throw some light upon this third bullet, which has clearly, from the splintering of the wood, been fired from inside the room. I should like to see Mrs King, the cook, again . . . You said, Mrs King, that you were awakened by a *loud* explosion. When you said that, did you mean that it seemed to you to be louder than the second one?'

'Well, sir, it wakened me from my sleep, and so it is hard to judge. But it did seem very loud.'

'You don't think that it might have been two shots fired almost at the same instant?'

'I am sure I couldn't say, sir.'

'I believe that it was undoubtedly so. I rather think, Inspector Martin, that we have now exhausted all that this room can teach us. If you will kindly step round with me we shall see what fresh evidence the garden has to offer.'

A flower-bed extended up to the study window, and we all broke into an exclamation as we approached it. The flowers were trampled down, and the soft soil was imprinted all over with footmarks. Large, masculine feet they were, with peculiarly long, sharp toes. Holmes hunted about among the grass and leaves like a retriever after a wounded bird. Then, with a cry of satisfaction, he bent forward and picked up a little brazen cylinder.

'I thought so,' said he; 'the revolver had an ejector, and here is the third cartridge. I really think, Inspector Martin, that our case is almost complete.'

The country inspector's face had shown his intense amazement at the rapid and masterful progress of Holmes's investigations. At first he had shown some disposition to assert his own position; but now he was overcome with admiration, and ready to follow without question wherever Holmes led.

'Whom do you suspect?' he asked.

'I'll go into that later. There are several points in this problem which I have not been able to explain to you yet. Now that I have got so far I had best proceed on my own lines, and then clear the whole matter up once and for all.'

'Just as you wish, Mr Holmes, so long as we get our man.'

'I have no desire to make mysteries, but it is impossible at the moment of action to enter into long and complex explanations. I have the threads of this affair all in my hand. Even if this lady should never recover consciousness we can still reconstruct the events of last night and ensure that justice be done. First of all I wish to know whether there is any inn in this neighbourhood known as Elrige's?'

The servants were cross-questioned, but none of them had heard of such a place. The stable-boy threw a light upon the matter by remembering that a farmer of that name lived some miles off in the direction of East Ruston.[12]

'Is it a lonely farm?'

'Very lonely, sir.'

'Perhaps they have not heard yet of all that happened here during the night?'

'Maybe not, sir.'

Holmes thought for a little, and then a curious smile played over his face.

'Saddle a horse, my lad,' said he. 'I shall wish you to take a note to Elrige's Farm.'

He took from his pocket the various slips of the dancing men. With these in front of him he worked for some time at the study table. Finally he handed a note to the boy, with directions to put it into the hands of the person to whom it was addressed, and especially to answer no questions of any sort which might be put to him. I saw the outside of the note, addressed in straggling, irregular characters, very unlike Holmes's usual precise hand. It was consigned to Mr Abe Slaney, Elrige's Farm, East Ruston, Norfolk.

'I think, Inspector,' Holmes remarked, 'that you would do well to telegraph for an escort, as, if my calculations prove to be correct, you may have a particularly dangerous prisoner to convey to the county gaol. The boy who takes this note could no doubt forward your telegram. If there is an afternoon train to town, Watson, I think we should do well to take it, as I have a chemical analysis of some interest to finish, and this investigation draws rapidly to a close.'

When the youth had been dispatched with the note, Sherlock Holmes gave his instructions to the servants. If any visitor were to call asking for Mrs Hilton Cubitt no information should be given as to her condition, but he was to be shown at once into the drawing-room. He impressed these points upon them with the utmost earnestness. Finally he led the way into the drawing-room, with the remark that the business was now out of our hands, and that we must while away the time as best we might until we could see what was in store for us. The doctor had departed to his patients, and only the inspector and myself remained.

'I think I can help you to pass an hour in an interesting and profitable manner,' said Holmes, drawing his chair up to the table and spreading out in front of him the various papers upon which were recorded the antics of the dancing men. 'As to you, friend Watson, I owe you every atonement for having allowed your natural curiosity to remain so long unsatisfied. To you, Inspector, the whole incident may appeal as a remarkable professional study. I must tell you first of all the interesting circumstances connected with the previous consultations which Mr Hilton Cubitt has had with me in Baker Street.' He then shortly recapitulated the facts which have already been recorded.

'I have here in front of me these singular productions, at which one might smile had they not proved themselves to be the forerunners of so terrible a tragedy. I am fairly familiar with all forms of secret writings,[13] and am myself the author of a trifling monograph upon the subject, in which I analyse one hundred and sixty separate ciphers;

but I confess that this is entirely new to me. The object of those who invented the system has apparently been to conceal that these characters convey a message, and to give the idea that they are the mere random sketches of children.

'Having once recognized, however, that the symbols stood for letters, and having applied the rules which guide us in all forms of secret writings, the solution was easy enough. The first message submitted to me was so short that it was impossible for me to do more than guess with some confidence which symbol stood for E. As you are aware, E is the most common letter in the English alphabet[14] and it predominates to so marked an extent that even in a short sentence one would expect to find it most often. Out of fifteen symbols in the first message four were the same, so it was reasonable to set this down as E. It is true that in some cases the figure was bearing a flag, and in some cases not, but it was probable from the way in which the flags were distributed that they were used to break the sentence up into words. I accepted this as an hypothesis, and noted that E was represented by

'But now came the real difficulty of the inquiry. The order of the English letters after E is by no means well-marked, and any preponderance which may be shown in an average of a printed sheet may be reversed in a single short sentence. Speaking roughly, T, A, O, I, N, S, H, R, D and L are the numerical order in which letters occur;[15] but T, A, O and I are very nearly abreast of each other, and it would be an endless task to try each combination until a meaning was arrived at. I, therefore, waited for fresh material. In my second interview with Mr Hilton Cubitt he was able to give me two other short sentences and one message, which appeared – since there was no flag – to be a single word. Here are the symbols:

Now, in the single word I have already got the two E's coming second and fourth in a word of five letters. It might be "sever", or "lever", or "never". There can be no question that the latter as a reply to an appeal is far the most probable, and the circumstances pointed to its being a reply written by the lady. Accepting it as correct we are now able to say that the symbols stand respectively for N, V and R.

'Even now I was in considerable difficulty, but a happy thought put me in possession of several other letters. It occurred to me that if these appeals came, as I expected, from someone who had been intimate with the lady in her life, a combination which contained two E's with three letters between might very well stand for the name "ELSIE". On examination I found that such a combination formed the termination of the message which was three times repeated. It was certainly some appeal to "Elsie". In this way I had got my L, S and I. But what appeal could it be? There were only four letters in the word which preceded "Elsie", and it ended in E. Surely the word must be "COME". I tried all other four letters ending in E, but could find none to fit the case. So now I was in possession of C, O and M, and I was in a position to attack the first message once more, dividing it into words and putting dots for each symbol which was still unknown. So treated it worked out in this fashion.

. M . ERE .. E SL . NE.

'Now, the first letter can only be A, which is a most useful discovery, since it occurs no fewer than three times in this short sentence, and the H is also apparent in the second word. Now it becomes:

AM HERE A . E SLANE.

Or, filling in the obvious vacancies in the name:

AM HERE ABE SLANEY

I had so many letters now that I could proceed with considerable confidence to the second message, which worked out in this fashion:

A . ELRI . ES

Here I could only make sense by putting T and G for the missing letters, and supposing that the name was that of some house or inn at which the writer was staying.'

Inspector Martin and I had listened with the utmost interest to the full and clear account of how my friend had produced results which had led to so complete a command over our difficulties.

'What did you do then, sir?' asked the inspector.

'I had every reason to suppose that this Abe Slaney was an American, since Abe is an American contraction, and since a letter from America had been the starting-point of all the trouble. I had also every cause to think that there was some criminal secret in the matter. The lady's allusions to her past and her refusal to take her husband into her confidence both pointed in that direction. I therefore cabled to my friend, Wilson Hargreave, of the New York Police Bureau, who has more than once made use of my knowledge of London crime. I asked him whether the name of Abe Slaney was known to him. Here is his reply: "The most dangerous crook in Chicago." On the very evening upon which I had his answer Hilton Cubitt sent me the last message from Slaney. Working with known letters it took this form:

ELSIE . RE . ARE TO MEET THY GO.

The addition of a P and a D completed a message which showed me that the rascal was proceeding from persuasion to threats, and my knowledge of the crooks of Chicago prepared me to find that he might very rapidly put his words into action. I at once came to Norfolk with my friend and colleague, Dr Watson, but, unhappily, only in time to find that the worst had already occurred.'

'It is a privilege to be associated with you in the handling of a case,' said the inspector warmly. 'You will excuse me, however, if I speak frankly to you. You are only answerable to yourself, but I have to answer to my superiors. If this Abe Slaney, living at Elrige's, is indeed the murderer, and if he has made his escape while I am seated here, I should certainly get into serious trouble.'

'You need not be uneasy. He will not try to escape.'

'How do you know?'

'To fly would be a confession of guilt.'

'Then let us go to arrest him.'

'I expect him here every instant.'

'But why should he come?'

'Because I have written and asked him.'

'But this is incredible, Mr Holmes! Why should he come because you have asked him? Would not such a request rather rouse his suspicions and cause him to fly?'

'I think I have known how to frame the letter,' said Sherlock Holmes. 'In fact, if I am not very much mistaken, here is the gentleman himself coming up the drive.'

A man was striding up the path which led to the door. He was a tall, handsome, swarthy fellow, clad in a suit of grey flannel, with a Panama hat, a bristling black beard and a great, aggressive, hooked nose, and flourishing a cane as he walked. He swaggered up the path as if the place belonged to him, and we heard his loud, confident peal at the bell.

'I think, gentlemen,' said Holmes quietly, 'that we had best take up our position behind the door. Every precaution is necessary when dealing with such a fellow. You will need your handcuffs, Inspector. You can leave the talking to me.'

We waited in silence for a minute – one of those minutes which one can never forget. Then the door opened, and the man stepped in. In an instant Holmes clapped a pistol to his head, and Martin slipped the handcuffs over his wrists. It was all done so swiftly and deftly that the fellow was helpless before he knew that he was attacked. He glared from one to the other of us with a pair of blazing black eyes. Then he burst into a bitter laugh.

'Well, gentlemen, you have the drop on me this time. I seem to have knocked up against something hard. But I came here in answer to a letter from Mrs Hilton Cubitt. Don't tell me that she is in this? Don't tell me that she helped to set a trap for me?'

'Mrs Hilton Cubitt was seriously injured, and is at death's door.'

The man gave a hoarse cry of grief which rang through the house.

'You're crazy!' he cried fiercely. 'It was he that was hurt, not she. Who would have hurt little Elsie? I may have threatened her, God forgive me, but I would not have touched a hair of her pretty head. Take it back – you! Say that she is not hurt!'

'She was found badly wounded by the side of her dead husband.'

He sank with a deep groan on to the settee, and buried his face in his manacled hands. For five minutes he was silent. Then he raised his face once more, and spoke with the cold composure of despair.

'I have nothing to hide from you, gentlemen,' said he. 'If I shot the man he had his shot at me, and there's no murder in that. But if you think I could have hurt that woman, then you don't know either me or her. I tell you there was never a man in this world loved a woman more than I loved her. I had a right to her. She was pledged to me years ago. Who was this Englishman that he should come between us? I tell you that I had the first right to her, and that I was only claiming my own.'

'She broke away from your influence when she found the man that you are,' said Holmes sternly. 'She fled from America to avoid you, and she married an honourable gentleman in England. You dogged her and followed her, and made her life a misery to her in order to induce her to abandon the husband whom she loved and respected in order to fly with you, whom she feared and hated. You have ended by bringing about the death of a noble man and driving his wife to suicide. That is your record in this business, Mr Abe Slaney, and you will answer for it to the law.'

'If Elsie dies I care nothing what becomes of me,' said the American. He opened one of his hands and looked at a note crumpled up in his palm. 'See here, mister,' he cried, with a gleam of suspicion in his eyes, 'you're not trying to scare me over this, are you? If the lady is hurt as bad as you say, who was it that wrote this note?' He tossed it forward on to the table.

'I wrote it to bring you here.'

'You wrote it? There was no one on earth outside the Joint who knew the secret of the dancing men. How came you to write it?'

'What one man can invent another can discover,'[16] said Holmes. 'There is a cab coming to convey you to Norwich, Mr Slaney. But,

207

meanwhile, you have time to make some small reparation for the injury you have wrought. Are you aware that Mrs Hilton Cubitt has herself lain under grave suspicion of the murder of her husband, and that it was only my presence here and the knowledge which I happened to possess which has saved her from the accusation? The least that you owe her is to make it clear to the whole world that she was in no way directly or indirectly responsible for his tragic end.'

'I ask nothing better,' said the American. 'I guess the very best case I can make for myself is the absolute naked truth.'

'It is my duty to warn you that it will be used against you,' cried the inspector, with the magnificent fair-play of the British criminal law.

Slaney shrugged his shoulders.

'I'll chance that,' said he. 'First of all, I want you gentlemen to understand that I have known this lady since she was a child. There were seven of us in a gang in Chicago, and Elsie's father was the boss of the Joint. He was a clever man, was old Patrick. It was he who invented that writing, which would pass as a child's scrawl unless you just happened to have the key to it. Well, Elsie learned some of our ways; but she couldn't stand the business, and she had a bit of honest money of her own, so she gave us all the slip and got away to London. She had been engaged to me, and she would have married me, I believe, if I had taken over another profession; but she would have nothing to do with anything on the cross. It was only after her marriage to this Englishman that I was able to find out where she was. I wrote to her, but got no answer. After that I came over, and, as letters were of no use, I put my messages where she could read them.

'Well, I have been here a month now. I lived in that farm, where I had a room down below, and could get in and out every night, and no one the wiser. I tried all I could to coax Elsie away. I knew that she read the messages, for once she wrote an answer under one of them. Then my temper got the better of me, and I began to threaten her. She sent me a letter then, imploring me to go away, and saying that it would break her heart if any scandal should come upon her husband. She said that she would come down when her husband was asleep at three in the morning, and speak with me through the end window, if

I would go away afterwards and leave her in peace. She came down and brought money with her, trying to bribe me to go. This made me mad, and I caught her arm and tried to pull her through the window. At that moment in rushed the husband with his revolver in his hand. Elsie had sunk down upon the floor, and we were face to face. I was heeled also, and I held up my gun to scare him off and let me get away. He fired and missed me. I pulled off almost at the same instant, and down he dropped. I made away across the garden, and as I went I heard the window shut behind me. That's God truth, gentlemen, every word of it, and I heard no more about it until that lad came riding up with a note which made me walk in here, like a jay, and give myself into your hands.'

A cab had driven up whilst the American had been talking. Two uniformed policemen sat inside. Inspector Martin rose and touched his prisoner on the shoulder.

'It is time for us to go.'

'Can I see her first?'

'No, she is not conscious. Mr Sherlock Holmes, I only hope that if ever again I have an important case I shall have the good fortune to have you by my side.'

We stood at the window and watched the cab drive away. As I turned back my eye caught the pellet of paper which the prisoner had tossed upon the table. It was the note with which Holmes had decoyed him.

'See if you can read it, Watson,' said he, with a smile.

It contained no word, but this little line of dancing men:

'If you use the code which I have explained,' said Holmes, 'you will find that it simply means "Come here at once." I was convinced that it was an invitation which he would not refuse, since he could never imagine that it could come from anyone but the lady. And so, my dear Watson, we have ended by turning the dancing men to good when they have so often been the agents of evil, and I think that I have fulfilled my promise of giving you something unusual for your notebook. Three forty is our train, and I fancy we should be back in Baker Street for dinner.'

Only one word of epilogue.

The American, Abe Slaney, was condemned to death at the winter assizes at Norwich; but his penalty was changed to penal servitude in consideration of mitigating circumstances, and the certainty that Hilton Cubitt had fired the first shot.

Of Mrs Hilton Cubitt I only know that I have heard she recovered entirely, and that she still remains a widow, devoting her whole life to the care of the poor and to the administration of her husband's estate.

BLACK PETER

I have never known my friend to be in better form, both mental and physical, than in the year '95. His increasing fame had brought with it an immense practice, and I should be guilty of an indiscretion if I were even to hint at the identity of some of the illustrious clients who crossed our humble threshold in Baker Street. Holmes, however, like all great artists, lived for his art's sake, and, save in the case of the Duke of Holdernesse,[1] I have seldom known him claim any large reward for his inestimable services. So unworldly was he – or so capricious – that he frequently refused his help to the powerful and wealthy where the problem made no appeal to his sympathies, while he would devote weeks of most intense application to the affairs of some humble client whose case presented those strange and dramatic qualities which appealed to his imagination and challenged his ingenuity.

In this memorable year '95 a curious and incongruous succession of cases had engaged his attention, ranging from his famous investigation of the sudden death of Cardinal Tosca – an inquiry which was carried out by him at the express desire of his Holiness the Pope[2] – down to his arrest of Wilson, the notorious canary-trainer, which removed a plague-spot from the East End of London. Close on the heels of these two famous cases came the tragedy of Woodman's Lee, and the very obscure circumstances which surrounded the death of Captain Peter Carey. No record of the doings of Mr Sherlock Holmes would be complete which did not include some account of this very unusual affair.

During the first week of July my friend had been absent so often and so long from our lodgings that I knew he had something on hand. The fact that several rough-looking men called during that time and inquired for Captain Basil made me understand that Holmes was working somewhere under one of the numerous disguises and names with which he concealed his own formidable identity. He had at least five small refuges in different parts of London in which he was able to change his personality. He said nothing of his business to me, and it was not my habit to force a confidence. The first positive sign which he gave me of the direction which his investigation was taking was an extraordinary one. He had gone out before breakfast, and I had sat down to mine, when he strode into the room, his hat upon his head, and a huge barb-headed spear tucked like an umbrella under his arm.

'Good gracious, Holmes!' I cried. 'You don't mean to say that you have been walking about London with that thing?'

'I drove to the butcher's and back.'

'The butcher's?'

'And I return with an excellent appetite. There can be no question, my dear Watson, of the value of exercise before breakfast. But I am prepared to bet that you will not guess the form that my exercise has taken.'

'I will not attempt it.'

He chuckled as he poured out the coffee.

'If you could have looked into Allardyce's back shop you would have seen a dead pig swung from a hook in the ceiling, and a gentleman in his shirt-sleeves furiously stabbing at it with this weapon. I was that energetic person, and I have satisfied myself that by no exertion of my strength can I transfix the pig with a single blow. Perhaps you would care to try?'

'Not for worlds. But why were you doing this?'

'Because it seemed to me to have an indirect bearing upon the mystery of Woodman's Lee. Ah, Hopkins, I got your wire last night, and I have been expecting you. Come and join us.'

Our visitor was an exceedingly alert man, thirty years of age, dressed in a quiet tweed suit, but retaining the erect bearing of one who was accustomed to official uniform. I recognized him at once as Stanley Hopkins, a young police inspector for whose future Holmes had high hopes, while he in turn professed the admiration and respect of a pupil for the scientific methods of the famous amateur. Hopkins's brow was clouded and he sat down with an air of deep dejection.

'No, thank you, sir. I breakfasted before I came round. I spent the night in town, for I came up yesterday to report.'

'And what had you to report?'

'Failure, sir – absolute failure.'

'You have made no progress?'

'None.'

'Dear me! I must have a look at the matter.'

'I wish to heavens that you would, Mr Holmes. It's my first big chance, and I am at my wits' end. For goodness' sake come down and lend me a hand.'

'Well, well, it happens that I have already read all the available evidence, including the report of the inquest, with some care. By the way, what do you make of that tobacco-pouch found on the scene of the crime? Is there no clue there?'

Hopkins looked surprised.

'It was the man's own pouch, sir. His initials were inside it. And it was of sealskin – and he was an old sealer.'

'But he had no pipe.'

'No, sir, we could find no pipe: indeed, he smoked very little. And yet he might have kept some tobacco for his friends.'

'No doubt. I only mention it because if I had been handling the case I should have been inclined to make that the starting point of my investigation. However, my friend Dr Watson knows nothing of this matter, and I should be none the worse for hearing the sequence of events once more. Just give us some short sketch of the essentials.'

Stanley Hopkins drew a slip of paper from his pocket.

'I have a few dates here which will give you the career of the dead man, Captain Peter Carey. He was born in '45 – fifty years of age. He was a most daring and successful seal and whale fisher.[3] In 1883 he commanded the steam sealer *Sea Unicorn*, of Dundee. He had then had several successful voyages in succession, and in the following year, 1884, he retired. After that he travelled for some years, and finally he bought a small place called Woodman's Lee, near Forest Row, in

Sussex.[4] There he has lived for six years, and there he died just a week ago today.

'There were some most singular points about the man. In ordinary life he was a strict Puritan – a silent, gloomy fellow. His household consisted of his wife, his daughter, aged twenty, and two female servants. These last were continually changing, for it was never a very cheery situation, and sometimes it became past all bearing. The man was an intermittent drunkard, and when he had the fit on him he was a perfect fiend. He has been known to drive his wife and his daughter out of doors in the middle of the night, and flog them through the park until the whole village outside the gates was aroused by their screams.

'He was summoned once for a savage assault upon the old vicar, who had called upon him to remonstrate with him upon his conduct. In short, Mr Holmes, you would go far before you found a more dangerous man than Peter Carey, and I have heard that he bore the same character when he commanded his ship. He was known in the trade as Black Peter, and the name was given him, not only on account of his swarthy features and the colour of his huge beard, but for the humours which were the terror of all around him. I need not say that he was loathed and avoided by every one of his neighbours, and that I have not heard one single word of sorrow about his terrible end.

'You must have read in the account of the inquest about the man's cabin, Mr Holmes; but perhaps your friend here has not heard of it. He had built himself a wooden outhouse – he always called it "the cabin" – a few hundred yards from his house, and it was here that he slept every night. It was a little, single-roomed hut, sixteen feet by ten. He kept the key in his pocket, made his own bed, cleaned it himself, and allowed no other foot to cross the threshold. There are small windows on each side, which were covered by curtains, and never opened. One of these windows was turned towards the high-road, and when the light burned in it at night the folk used to point it out to each other, and wonder what Black Peter was doing in there. That's the window, Mr Holmes, which gave us one of the few bits of positive evidence that came out at the inquest.

'You remember that a stonemason, named Slater, walking from

Forest Row about one o'clock in the morning – two days before the murder – stopped as he passed the grounds and looked at the square of light still shining among the trees. He swears that the shadow of a man's head turned sideways was clearly visible on the blind, and that this shadow was certainly not that of Peter Carey, whom he knew well. It was that of a bearded man, but the beard was short, and bristled forwards in a way very different from that of the captain. So he says, but he had been two hours in the public-house, and it is some distance from the road to the window. Besides, this refers to the Monday, and the crime was done upon the Wednesday.

'On the Tuesday Peter Carey was in one of his blackest moods, flushed with drink and as savage as a dangerous wild beast. He roamed about the house, and the women ran for it when they heard him coming. Late in the evening he went down to his own hut. About two o'clock the following morning his daughter, who slept with her window open, heard a most fearful yell from that direction, but it was no unusual thing for him to bawl and shout when he was in drink, so no notice was taken. On rising at seven one of the maids noticed that the door of the hut was open, but so great was the terror which the man caused that it was midday before anyone would venture down to see what had become of him. Peeping into the open door, they saw a sight which sent them flying with white faces into the village. Within an hour I was on the spot, and had taken over the case.

'Well, I have fairly steady nerves, as you know, Mr Holmes, but I give you my word that I got a shake when I put my head into that little house. It was droning like a harmonium with the flies and bluebottles, and the floor and walls were like a slaughterhouse. He had called it a cabin, and a cabin it was, sure enough, for you would have thought that you were in a ship. There was a bunk at one end, a sea-chest, maps and charts, a picture of the *Sea Unicorn*, a line of log-books on a shelf, all exactly as one would expect to find it in a captain's room. And there in the middle of it was the man himself, his face twisted like a lost soul in torment, and his great brindled beard stuck upwards in his agony. Right through his broad breast a steel harpoon had been driven, and it had sunk deep into the wood of the wall behind him. He was pinned like a beetle on a card. Of course, he was quite dead, and had been so from the instant that he uttered that last yell of agony.

'I know your methods, sir, and I applied them. Before I permitted anything to be moved I examined most carefully the ground outside, and also the floor of the room. There were no footmarks.'

'Meaning that you saw none?'

'I assure you, sir, that there were none.'

'My good Hopkins, I have investigated many crimes, but I have never yet seen one which was committed by a flying creature. As long as the criminal remains upon two legs so long must there be some indentation, some abrasion, some trifling displacement which can be detected by the scientific searcher. It is incredible that this blood-bespattered room contained no trace which could have aided us. I understand, however, from the inquest that there were some objects which you failed to overlook?'

The young inspector winced at my companion's ironical comments.

'I was a fool not to call you in at the time, Mr Holmes. However, that's past praying for now. Yes, there were several objects in the room which called for special attention. One was the harpoon with which the deed was committed. It had been snatched down from a rack on the wall. Two others remained there, and there was a vacant place for the third. On the stock was engraved "SS *Sea Unicorn*, Dundee". This seemed to establish that the crime had been done in a moment of fury, and that the murderer had seized the first weapon which came in his way. The fact that the crime was committed at two in the morning, and yet Peter Carey was fully dressed, suggested that he had an appointment with the murderer, which is borne out by the fact that a bottle of rum and two dirty glasses stood upon the table.'

'Yes,' said Holmes; 'I think that both inferences are permissible. Was there any other spirit but rum in the room?'

'Yes; there was a tantalus⁵ containing brandy and whisky on the sea-chest. It is of no importance to us, however, since the decanters were full and it had therefore not been used.'

'For all that its presence has some significance,' said Holmes. 'However, let us hear some more about the objects which do seem to you to bear upon the case.'

'There was this tobacco-pouch upon the table.'

'What part of the table?'

'It lay in the middle. It was of coarse sealskin – the straight-haired skin, with a leather thong to bind it. Inside was "PC" on the flap. There was half an ounce of strong ship's tobacco in it.'

'Excellent! What more?'

Stanley Hopkins drew from his pocket a drab-covered note-book. The outside was rough and worn, the leaves were discoloured. On the first page were written the initials 'J. H. N.', and the date '1883'. Holmes laid it on the table and examined it in his minute way, while Hopkins and I gazed over each shoulder. On the second page were printed the letters 'C. P. R.', and then came several sheets of numbers. Another heading was Argentine, another Costa Rica, and another San Paulo, each with pages of signs and figures after it.

'What do you make of these?' asked Holmes.

'They appear to be lists of Stock Exchange securities. I thought that "J. H. N." were the initials of a broker, and that "C. P. R." may have been his client.'

'Try Canadian Pacific Railway,' said Holmes.

Stanley Hopkins swore between his teeth, and struck his thigh with his clenched hand.

'What a fool I have been!' he cried. 'Of course it is as you say. Then "J. H. N." are the only initials we have to solve. I have already examined the old Stock Exchange lists, and I can find no one in 1883 either in the House or among the outside brokers whose initials correspond with these. Yet I feel that the clue is the most important one that I hold. You will admit, Mr Holmes, that there is a possibility that these initials are those of the second person who was present – in other words, of the murderer. I would also urge that the introduction into the case of a document relating to large masses of valuable securities gives us for the first time some indication of a motive for the crime.'

Sherlock Holmes's face showed that he was thoroughly taken aback by this new development.

'I must admit both your points,' said he. 'I confess that the notebook, which did not appear at the inquest, modifies any views which I may have formed. I had come to a theory of the crime in which I can find no place for this. Have you endeavoured to trace any of the securities here mentioned?'

'Inquiries are now being made at the offices, but I fear that the complete register of the stock-holders of these South American concerns is in South America, and that some weeks must elapse before we can trace the shares.'

Holmes had been examining the cover of the notebook with his magnifying lens.

'Surely there is some discoloration here,' said he.

'Yes, sir, it is a blood-stain. I told you that I picked the book off the floor.'

'Was the blood-stain above or below?'

'On the side next to the boards.'

'Which proves, of course, that the book was dropped after the crime was committed.'

'Exactly, Mr Holmes. I appreciated that point, and I conjectured that it was dropped by the murderer on his hurried flight. It lay near the door.'

'I suppose that none of these securities have been found among the property of the dead man?'

'No, sir.'

'Have you any reason to suspect robbery?'

'No, sir. Nothing seemed to have been touched.'

'Dear me, it is certainly a very interesting case. Then there was a knife, was there not?'

'A sheath-knife, still in its sheath. It lay at the feet of the dead man. Mrs Carey has identified it as being her husband's property.'

Holmes was lost in thought for some time.

'Well,' said he at last, 'I suppose I shall have to come out and have a look at it.'

Stanley Hopkins gave a cry of joy.

'Thank you, sir. That will indeed be a weight off my mind.'

Holmes shook his finger at the inspector.

'It would have been an easier task a week ago,' said he. 'But even now my visit may not be entirely fruitless. Watson, if you can spare the time, I should be very glad of your company. If you will call a four-wheeler, Hopkins, we shall be ready to start for Forest Row in a quarter of an hour.'

Alighting at the small wayside station, we drove for some miles through the remains of widespread woods, which were once part of that great forest which for so long held the Saxon invaders at bay – the impenetrable 'weald', for sixty years the bulwark of Britain. Vast sections of it have been cleared, for this is the seat of the first ironworks of the country, and the trees have been felled to smelt the ore. Now the richer fields of the North have absorbed the trade, and nothing save these ravaged groves and great scars in the earth show the work of the past. Here in a clearing upon the green slope of a hill stood a long, low stone house, approached by a curving drive running through the fields. Nearer the road, and surrounded on three sides by bushes, was a small outhouse, one window and the door facing in our direction. It was the scene of the murder.

Stanley Hopkins led us first to the house, where he introduced us to a haggard, grey-haired woman, the widow of the murdered man, whose gaunt and deep-lined face, with the furtive look of terror in the depths of her red-rimmed eyes, told of the years of hardship and ill-usage which she had endured. With her was her daughter, a pale, fair-haired girl, whose eyes blazed defiantly at us as she told us that she was glad that her father was dead, and that she blessed the hand which had struck him down. It was a terrible household that Black Peter Carey had made for himself, and it was with a sense of relief that we found ourselves in the sunlight again and making our way along the path which had been worn across the fields by the feet of the dead man.

The outhouse was the simplest of dwellings, wooden-walled, single-roofed, one window beside the door, and one on the farther side. Stanley Hopkins drew the key from his pocket, and had stooped to the lock, when he paused with a look of attention and surprise upon his face.

'Someone has been tampering with it,' he said.

There could be no doubt of the fact. The woodwork was cut, and the scratches showed white through the paint, as if they had been that instant done. Holmes had been examining the window.

'Someone has tried to force this also. Whoever it was has failed to make his way in. He must have been a very poor burglar.'

'This is a most extraordinary thing,' said the inspector; 'I could swear that these marks were not here yesterday evening.'

'Some curious person from the village, perhaps,' I suggested.

'Very unlikely. Few of them would dare to set foot in the grounds, far less try to force their way into the cabin. What do you think of it, Mr Holmes?'

'I think that fortune is very kind to us.'

'You mean that the person will come again?'

'It is very probable. He came expecting to find the door open. He tried to get in with the blade of a very small penknife. He could not manage it. What would he do?'

'Come again next night with a more useful tool.'

'So I should say. It will be our fault if we are not there to receive him. Meanwhile, let me see the inside of the cabin.'

The traces of the tragedy had been removed, but the furniture of the little room still stood as it had been on the night of the crime. For two hours, with the most intense concentration, Holmes examined every object in turn, but his face showed that his quest was not a successful one. Once only he paused in his patient investigation.

'Have you taken anything off this shelf, Hopkins?'

'No; I have moved nothing.'

'Something has been taken. There is less dust in this corner of the shelf than elsewhere. It may have been a book lying on its side. It may have been a box. Well, well, I can do nothing more. Let us walk in these beautiful woods, Watson, and give a few hours to the birds and the flowers. We shall meet you here later, Hopkins, and see if we can come to closer quarters with the gentleman who has paid this visit in the night.'

It was past eleven o'clock when we formed our little ambuscade. Hopkins was for leaving the door of the hut open, but Holmes was of the opinion that this would rouse the suspicions of the stranger. The lock was a perfectly simple one, and only a strong blade was needed to push it back. Holmes also suggested that we should wait, not inside the hut, but outside it among the bushes which grew round the farther window. In this way we should be able to watch our man if he struck a light, and see what his object was in this stealthy nocturnal visit.

It was a long and melancholy vigil, and yet it brought with it something of the thrill which the hunter feels when he lies beside the water-pool and waits for the coming of the thirsty beast of prey. What savage creature was it which might steal upon us out of the darkness? Was it a fierce tiger of crime, which could only be taken fighting hard with flashing fang and claw, or would it prove to be some skulking jackal, dangerous only to the weak and unguarded? In absolute silence we crouched amongst the bushes, waiting for whatever might come. At first the steps of a few belated villagers, or the sound of voices from the village, lightened our vigil; but one by one these interruptions died away, and an absolute stillness fell upon us; save for the chimes of the distant church, which told us of the progress of the night, and for the rustle and whisper of a fine rain falling amid the foliage which roofed us in.

Half-past two had chimed, and it was the darkest hour which precedes the dawn, when we all started as a low but sharp click came from the direction of the gate. Someone had entered the drive. Again there was a long silence, and I had begun to fear that it was a false alarm, when a stealthy step was heard upon the other side of the hut, and a moment later a metallic scraping and clicking. The man was trying to force the lock! This time his skill was greater or his tool was better, for there was a sudden snap and the creak of the hinges. Then a match was struck, and next instant the steady light from a candle filled the interior of the hut. Through the gauze curtain our eyes were all riveted upon the scene within.

The nocturnal visitor was a young man, frail and thin, with a black moustache which intensified the deadly pallor of his face. He could not have been much above twenty years of age. I have never seen any human being who appeared to be in such a pitiable fright, for his teeth were visibly chattering, and he was shaking in every limb. He was dressed like a gentleman, in Norfolk jacket and knickerbockers, with a cloth cap upon his head. We watched him staring round with frightened eyes. Then he laid the candle-end upon the table and disappeared from our view into one of the corners. He returned with a large book, one of the log-books which formed a line upon the shelves. Leaning on the table, he rapidly turned over the leaves of this volume until he came to the entry which he sought. Then, with an angry gesture of his clenched hand, he closed the book, replaced it in the corner, and put out the light. He had hardly turned to leave the hut when Hopkins's hand was on the fellow's collar, and I heard his loud gasp of terror as he understood that he was taken. The candle was relit, and there was our wretched captive shivering and cowering in the grasp of the detective. He sank down upon the sea-chest, and looked helplessly from one of us to the other.

'Now, my fine fellow,' said Stanley Hopkins, 'who are you, and what do you want here?'

The man pulled himself together and faced us with an effort at self-composure.

'You are detectives, I suppose?' said he. 'You imagine I am connected with the death of Captain Peter Carey. I assure you that I am innocent.'

'We'll see about that,' said Hopkins. 'First of all, what is your name?'

'It is John Hopley Neligan.'

I saw Holmes and Hopkins exchange a quick glance.

'What are you doing here?'

'Can I speak confidentially?'

'No, certainly not.'

'Why should I tell you?'

'If you have no answer it may go badly with you at the trial.'

The young man winced.

'Well, I will tell you,' he said. 'Why should I not? And yet I hate to think of this old scandal gaining a new lease of life. Did you ever hear of Dawson & Neligan?'

I could see from Hopkins's face that he never had; but Holmes was keenly interested.

'You mean the West Country bankers,' said he. 'They failed for a million, ruined half the county families of Cornwall, and Neligan disappeared.'

'Exactly. Neligan was my father.'

At last we were getting something positive, and yet it seemed a long gap between an absconding banker and Captain Peter Carey pinned against the wall with one of his own harpoons. We all listened intently to the young man's words.

'It was my father who was really concerned. Dawson had retired. I was only ten years of age at the time, but I was old enough to feel the shame and horror of it all. It has always been said that my father stole all the securities and fled. It is not true. It was his belief that if he were given time in which to realize them all would be well, and every creditor paid in full. He started in his little yacht for Norway just before the warrant was issued for his arrest. I can remember that last night when he bade farewell to my mother. He left us a list of the securities he was taking, and he swore that he would come back with his honour cleared, and that none who had trusted him would suffer. Well, no word was ever heard from him again. Both the yacht and he vanished utterly. We believed, my mother and I, that he and it, with the securities that he had taken with him, were at the bottom of the sea. We had a faithful friend, however, who is a business man, and it was he who discovered some time ago that some of the securities which my father had with him have reappeared on the London market. You can imagine our amazement. I spent months in trying to trace them, and at last, after many doublings and difficulties, I discovered that the original seller had been Captain Peter Carey, the owner of this hut.

'Naturally I made some inquiries about the man. I found that he had been in command of a whaler which was due to return from the Arctic seas at the very time when my father was crossing to Norway. The autumn of that year was a stormy one and there was a long succession of southerly gales. My father's yacht may well have been blown to the north, and there met by Captain Peter Carey's ship. If that were so, what had become of my father? In any case, if I could prove from Peter Carey's evidence how these securities came in the market, it would be a proof that my father had not sold them, and that he had no view to personal profit when he took them.

'I came down to Sussex with the intention of seeing the captain, but it was at this moment that his terrible death occurred. I read at the inquest a description of his cabin, in which it stated that the old log-books of his vessel were preserved in it. It struck me that if I could see what occurred in the month of August, 1883, on board the *Sea Unicorn*, I might settle the mystery of my father's fate. I tried last night to get at these log-books, but was unable to open the door. Tonight I tried again, and succeeded; but I find that the pages which deal with that month have been torn from the book. It was at that moment I found myself a prisoner in your hands.'

'Is that all?' asked Hopkins.

'Yes, that is all.' His eyes shifted as he said it.

'You have nothing else to tell us?'

He hesitated.

'No; there is nothing.'

'You have not been here before last night?'

'No.'

'Then how do you account for *that*?' cried Hopkins, as he held up the damning notebook, with the initials of our prisoner on the first leaf, and the blood-stain on the cover.

The wretched man collapsed. He sank his face in his hands and trembled all over.

'Where did you get it?' he groaned. 'I did not know. I thought I had lost it at the hotel.'

'That is enough,' said Hopkins sternly. 'Whatever else you have to say you must say in court. You will walk down with me now to the police-station. Well, Mr Holmes, I am very much obliged to you and to your friend for coming down to help me. As it turns out your presence was unnecessary, and I would have brought the case to this successful issue without you; but none the less I am very grateful. Rooms have been reserved for you at the Brambletye Hotel, so we can all walk down to the village together.'

'Well, Watson, what do you think of it?' asked Holmes as we travelled back next morning.

'I can see that you are not satisfied.'

'Oh, yes, my dear Watson, I am perfectly satisfied. At the same time Stanley Hopkins's methods do not commend themselves to me.

I am disappointed in Stanley Hopkins. I had hoped for better things from him. One should always look for a possible alternative and provide against it. It is the first rule of criminal investigation.'

'What, then, is the alternative?'

'The line of investigation which I have myself been pursuing. It may give nothing. I cannot tell. But at least I shall follow it to the end.'

Several letters were waiting for Holmes at Baker Street. He snatched one of them up, opened it, and burst out into a triumphant chuckle of laughter.

'Excellent, Watson. The alternative develops. Have you telegraph forms? Just write a couple of messages for me: "Sumner, Shipping Agent, Ratcliff Highway.[6] Send three men on, to arrive ten tomorrow morning. – Basil." That's my name in those parts. The other is "Inspector Stanley Hopkins, 46 Lord Street,[7] Brixton. Come breakfast tomorrow at nine-thirty. Important. Wire if unable to come. – Sherlock Holmes." There, Watson, this infernal case had haunted me for ten days. I hereby banish it completely from my presence. Tomorrow I trust that we shall hear the last of it for ever.'

Sharp at the hour named Inspector Stanley Hopkins appeared, and we sat down together to the excellent breakfast which Mrs Hudson had prepared. The young detective was in high spirits at his success.

'You really think that your solution must be correct?' asked Holmes.

'I could not imagine a more complete case.'

'It did not seem to me conclusive.'

'You astonish me, Mr Holmes. What more could one ask for?'

'Does your explanation cover every point?'

'Undoubtedly. I find that young Neligan arrived at the Brambletye Hotel on the very day of the crime. He came on the pretence of playing golf. His room was on the ground floor, and he could get out when he liked. That very night he went down to Woodman's Lee, saw Peter Carey at the hut, quarrelled with him, and killed him with the harpoon. Then, horrified by what he had done, he fled out of the hut, dropping the notebook which he had brought with him in order to question Peter Carey about these different securities. You may have observed that some of them were marked with ticks, and the others – the great majority – were not. Those which are ticked have been traced on the London market; but the others presumably were still in the possession of Carey, and young Neligan, according to his own account, was anxious to recover them in order to do the right thing by his father's creditors. After his flight he did not dare to approach the hut again for some time; but at last he forced himself to do so in order to obtain the information which he needed. Surely that is all simple and obvious?'

Holmes smiled and shook his head.

'It seems to me to have only one drawback, Hopkins, and that is that it is intrinsically impossible. Have you tried to drive a harpoon through a body? No? Tut, tut, my dear sir, you must really pay attention to these details. My friend Watson could tell you that I spent a whole morning in that exercise. It is no easy matter, and requires a strong and practised arm. But this blow was delivered with such violence that the head of the weapon sank deep into the wall. Do you imagine that this anaemic youth was capable of so frightful an assault? Is he the man who hob-nobbed in rum and water with Black Peter in the dead of the night? Was it his profile that was seen on the blind two nights before? No, no, Hopkins; it is another and a more formidable person for whom we must seek.'

The detective's face had grown longer and longer during Holmes's speech. His hopes and his ambitions were all crumbling about him. But he would not abandon his position without a struggle.

'You can't deny that Neligan was present that night, Mr Holmes. The book will prove that. I fancy that I have evidence enough to satisfy a jury, even if you are able to pick a hole in it. Besides, Mr Holmes, I have laid my hand upon *my* man. As to this terrible person of yours, where is he?'

'I rather fancy that he is on the stair,' said Holmes serenely. 'I think, Watson, that you would do well to put that revolver where you can reach it.' He rose, and laid a written paper upon a side-table. 'Now we are ready,' said he.

There had been some talking in gruff voices outside, and now Mrs Hudson opened the door to say that there were three men inquiring for Captain Basil.

'Show them in one by one,' said Holmes.

The first who entered was a little ribston-pippin[8] of a man, with ruddy cheeks and fluffy white side-whiskers. Holmes had drawn a letter from his pocket.

'What name?' he asked.

'James Lancaster.'

'I am sorry, Lancaster, but the berth is full. Here is half a sovereign for your trouble. Just step into this room and wait there for a few minutes.'

The second man was a long, dried-up creature, with lank hair and sallow cheeks. His name was Hugh Pattins. He also received his dismissal, his half-sovereign, and the order to wait.

The third applicant was a man of remarkable appearance. A fierce, bulldog face was framed in a tangle of hair and beard, and two bold dark eyes gleamed behind the cover of thick, tufted, overhung eyebrows. He saluted and stood sailor-fashion, turning his cap round in his hands.

'Your name?' asked Holmes.

'Patrick Cairns.'[9]

'Harpooner?'

'Yes, sir. Twenty-six voyages.'

'Dundee, I suppose?'

'Yes, sir.'

'And ready to start with an exploring ship?'

'Yes, sir.'

'What wages?'

'Eight pounds a month.'

'Could you start at once?'

'As soon as I get my kit.'

'Have you your papers?'

'Yes, sir.' He took a sheaf of worn and greasy forms from his pocket. Holmes glanced over them and returned them.

'You are just the man I want,' said he. 'Here's the agreement on the side-table. If you sign it the whole matter will be settled.'

The seaman lurched across the room and took up the pen.

'Shall I sign here?' he asked, stooping over the table.

Holmes leaned over his shoulder and passed both hands over his neck.

'This will do,' said he.

I heard a click of steel and a bellow like an enraged bull. The next instant Holmes and the seaman were rolling on the ground together. He was a man of such gigantic strength that, even with the handcuffs which Holmes had so deftly fastened upon his wrist, he would have quickly overpowered my friend had Hopkins and I not rushed to his rescue. Only when I pressed the cold muzzle of the revolver to his temple did he at last understand that resistance was vain. We lashed his ankles with cord and rose breathless from the struggle.

'I must really apologize, Hopkins,' said Sherlock Holmes; 'I fear that the scrambled eggs are cold. However, you will enjoy the rest of your breakfast all the better, will you not, for the thought that you have brought your case to a triumphant conclusion?'

Stanley Hopkins was speechless with amazement.

'I don't know what to say, Mr Holmes,' he blurted out at last, with a very red face. 'It seems to me that I have been making a fool of myself from the beginning. I understand now, what I should never have forgotten, that I am the pupil and you are the master. Even now I see what you have done, but I don't know how you did it, or what it signifies.'

'Well, well,' said Holmes good-humouredly. 'We all learn by experience, and your lesson this time is that you should never lose sight of the alternative. You were so absorbed in young Neligan that you could not spare a thought to Patrick Cairns, the true murderer of Peter Carey.'

The hoarse voice of the seaman broke in on our conversation.

'See here, mister,' said he, 'I make no complaint of being manhandled in this fashion, but I would have you call things by their right names. You say I murdered Peter Carey; I say I *killed* Peter Carey, and there's all the difference. Maybe you don't believe what I say. Maybe you think I am just slinging you a yarn.'

'Not at all,' said Holmes. 'Let us hear what you have to say.'

'It's soon told, and, by the Lord, every word of it is truth. I knew Black Peter, and when he pulled out his knife I whipped a harpoon through him sharp, for I knew that it was him or me. That's how he died. You can call it murder. Anyhow, I'd as soon die with a rope round my neck as with Black Peter's knife in my heart.'

'How came you there?' asked Holmes.

'I'll tell it you from the beginning. Just sit me up a little so I can speak easy. It was in '83 that it happened – August of that year. Peter Carey was master of the *Sea Unicorn*, and I was spare harpooner. We were coming out of the ice-pack on our way home, with head winds and a week's southerly gale, when we picked up a little craft that had been blown north. There was one man on her – a landsman. The crew had thought she would founder, and had made for the Norwegian coast in the dinghy. I guess they were all drowned. Well, we took him on board, this man, and he and the skipper had some long talks in the cabin. All the baggage we took off with him was one tin box. So far as I know the man's name was never mentioned, and on the second night he disappeared as if he had never been. It was given out that he had either thrown himself overboard or fallen overboard in the heavy weather that we were having. Only one man knew what had happened to him, and that was me, for with my own eyes I saw the skipper tip up his heels and put him over the rail in the middle watch of a dark night, two days before we sighted the Shetland lights.[10]

'Well, I kept my knowledge to myself and waited to see what would come of it. When we got back to Scotland it was easily hushed up, and nobody asked any questions. A stranger died by an accident, and it was nobody's business to inquire. Shortly after Peter Carey gave up the sea, and it was long years before I could find where he was. I guessed that he had done the deed for the sake of what was in that tin box, and that he could afford now to pay me well for keeping my mouth shut.

'I found out where he was through a sailor man that had met him in London, and down I went to squeeze him. The first night he was reasonable enough, and was ready to give me what would make me free of the sea for life. We were to fix it all two nights later. When I came I found him three-parts drunk and in a vile temper. We sat down and we drank and we yarned about old times, but the more he drank the less I liked the look on his face. I spotted that harpoon upon the wall, and I thought I might need it before I was through. Then at last he broke out at me spitting and cursing, with murder in his eyes and a great clasp-knife in his hand. He had not time to get it from the sheath before I had the harpoon through him. Heavens! what a yell he gave; and his face gets between me and my sleep! I stood there, with his blood splashing round me, and I waited for a bit; but all was quiet, so I took heart once more. I looked round, and there was the tin box on a shelf. I had as much right to it as Peter Carey, anyhow, so I took it with me and left the hut. Like a fool I left my baccy-pouch upon the table.

'Now I'll tell you the queerest part of the whole story. I had hardly got outside the hut when I heard someone coming, and I hid among the bushes. A man came slinking along, went into the hut, gave a cry as if he had seen a ghost, and legged it as hard as he could run until he was out of sight. Who he was or what he wanted is more than I can tell. For my part, I walked ten miles, got a train at Tunbridge Wells, and so reached London, and no one the wiser.

'Well, when I came to examine the box I found there was no money in it, and nothing but papers that I would not dare to sell. I had lost my hold on Black Peter, and was stranded in London without a shilling. There was only my trade left. I saw these advertisements about harpooners and high wages, so I went to the shipping agents, and they sent me here. That's all I know, and I say again that if I killed Black Peter, the law should give me thanks, for I saved them the price of a hempen rope.'

'A very clear statement,' said Holmes, rising and lighting his pipe. 'I think, Hopkins, that you should lose no time in conveying your prisoner to a place of safety. This room is not well adapted for a cell, and Mr Patrick Cairns occupies too large a portion of our carpet.'

'Mr Holmes,' said Hopkins, 'I do not know how to express my gratitude. Even now I do not understand how you attained this result.'

'Simply by having the good fortune to get the right clue from the beginning. It is very possible that if I had known about this notebook it might have led away my thoughts, as it did yours. But all I heard pointed in the one direction. The amazing strength, the skill in the use of the harpoon, the rum and water, the sealskin tobacco-pouch, with the coarse tobacco – all these pointed to a seaman, and one who had been a whaler. I was convinced that the initals "P. C." upon the pouch were a coincidence, and not those of Peter Carey, since he seldom smoked, and no pipe was found in his cabin. You remember that I asked whether whisky and brandy were in the cabin. You said they were. How many landsmen are there who would drink rum when they could get these other spirits? Yes, I was certain it was a seaman.'

'And how did you find him?'

'My dear sir, the problem had become a very simple one. If it were a seaman, it could only be a seaman who had been with him on the *Sea Unicorn*. So far as I could learn, he had sailed in no other ship. I spent three days in wiring to Dundee, and at the end of that time I had ascertained the names of the crew of the *Sea Unicorn* in 1883. When I found Patrick Cairns among the harpooners my research was nearing its end. I argued that the man was probably in London, and that he would desire to leave the country for a time. I therefore spent some days in the East End, devised an Arctic expedition, put forward tempting terms for harpooners who would serve under Captain Basil – and behold the result!'

'Wonderful!' cried Hopkins. 'Wonderful!'

'You must obtain the release of young Neligan as soon as possible.' said Holmes. 'I confess that I think you owe him some apology. The tin box must be returned to him, but of course, the securities which Peter Carey has sold are lost for ever. There's the cab, Hopkins, and you can remove your man. If you want me for the trial, my address and that of Watson will be somewhere in Norway – I'll send particulars later.'

CHARLES AUGUSTUS MILVERTON

It is years since the incidents of which I speak took place, and yet it is
with diffidence that I allude to them. For a long time, even with the
utmost discretion and reticence, it would have been impossible to
make the facts public; but now the principal person concerned is
beyond the reach of human law, and with due suppression the story
may be told in such fashion as to injure no one. It records an absolutely
unique experience in the career both of Mr Sherlock Holmes and of
myself. The reader will excuse me if I conceal the date or any other
fact by which he might trace the actual occurrence.

We had been out for one of our evening rambles, Holmes and I,
and had returned about six o'clock on a cold, frosty winter's evening.
As Holmes turned up the lamp the light fell upon a card on the table.
He glanced at it, and then, with an ejaculation of disgust, threw it on
the floor. I picked it up and read:

CHARLES AUGUSTUS MILVERTON[1]

APPLEDORE TOWERS[2]

HAMPSTEAD

Agent

'Who is he?' I asked.

'The worst man in London,' Holmes answered, as he sat down and
stretched his legs before the fire. 'Is anything on the back of the card?'

I turned it over.

'Will call at 6.30. – C.A.M.', I read.

'Hum! He's about due. Do you feel a creeping, shrinking sensation,
Watson, when you stand before the serpents in the Zoo[3] and see

the slithery, gliding, venomous creatures, with their deadly eyes and wicked, flattened faces? Well, that's how Milverton impresses me. I've had to do with fifty murderers in my career, but the worst of them never gave me the repulsion which I have for this fellow. And yet I can't get out of doing business with him – indeed, he is here at my invitation.'

'But who is he?'

'I'll tell you, Watson. He is the king of all the blackmailers. Heaven help the man, and still more the woman, whose secret and reputation come into the power of Milverton. With a smiling face and a heart of marble he will squeeze and squeeze until he has drained them dry. The fellow is a genius in his way, and would have made his mark in some more savoury trade. His method is as follows: he allows it to be known that he is prepared to pay very high sums for letters which compromise people of wealth or position. He receives these wares not only from treacherous valets or maids, but frequently from genteel ruffians who have gained the confidence and affection of trusting women. He deals with no niggard hand. I happen to know that he paid seven hundred pounds to a footman for a note two lines in length, and that the ruin of a noble family was the result. Everything which is in the market goes to Milverton, and there are hundreds in this great city who turn white at his name. No one knows where his grip may fall, for he is far too rich and far too cunning to work from hand to mouth. He will hold a card back for years in order to play it at the moment when the stake is best worth winning. I have said that he is the worst man in London, and I would ask you how could one compare the ruffian who in hot blood bludgeons his mate with this man, who methodically and at his leisure tortures the soul and wrings the nerves in order to add to his already swollen money-bags?'

I had seldom heard my friend speak with such intensity of feeling.

'But surely,' said I, 'the fellow must be within the grasp of the law?'

'Technically, no doubt, but practically not. What would it profit a woman,[4] for example, to get him a few months' imprisonment if her own ruin must immediately follow? His victims dare not hit back. If ever he blackmailed an innocent person, then, indeed, we should have him; but he is as cunning as the Evil One. No, no; we must find other ways to fight him.'

'And why is he here?'

'Because an illustrious client has placed her piteous case in my hands. It is the Lady Eva Brackwell,[5] the most beautiful *débutante* of last season. She is to be married in a fortnight to the Earl of Dovercourt. This fiend has several imprudent letters – imprudent, Watson, nothing worse – which were written to an impecunious young squire in the country. They would suffice to break off the match. Milverton will send the letters to the earl unless a large sum of money is paid him. I have been commissioned to meet him, and – to make the best terms I can.'

At that instant there was a clatter and a rattle in the street below. Looking down I saw a stately carriage and pair, the brilliant lamps gleaming on the glossy haunches of the noble chestnuts. A footman opened the door, and a small, stout man in a shaggy astrakhan overcoat descended. A minute later he was in the room.

Charles Augustus Milverton was a man of fifty, with a large, intellectual head, a round, plump, hairless face, a perpetual frozen smile, and two keen grey eyes, which gleamed brightly from behind broad, golden-rimmed glasses. There was something of Mr Pickwick's benevolence[6] in his appearance, marred only by the insincerity of the fixed smile and by the hard glitter of those restless and penetrating eyes. His voice was as smooth and suave as his countenance, as he advanced with a plump little hand extended, murmuring his regret for having missed us at his first visit.

Holmes disregarded the outstretched hand and looked at him with a face of granite. Milverton's smile broadened; he shrugged his shoulders, removed his overcoat, folded it with great deliberation over the back of a chair, and then took a seat.

'This gentleman,' said he, with a wave in my direction. 'Is it discreet? Is it right?'

'Dr Watson is my friend and partner.'

'Very good, Mr Holmes. It is only in your client's interests that I protested. The matter is so very delicate – '

'Dr Watson has already heard of it.'

'Then we can proceed to business. You say that you are acting for Lady Eva. Has she empowered you to accept my terms?'

'What are your terms?'

'Seven thousand pounds.'

'And the alternative?'

'My dear sir, it is painful to me to discuss it; but if the money is not paid on the 14th there certainly will be no marriage on the 18th.' His insufferable smile was more complacent than ever. Holmes thought for a little.

'You appear to me,' he said at last, 'to be taking matters too much for granted. I am, of course, familiar with the contents of these letters. My client will certainly do what I may advise. I shall counsel her to tell her future husband the whole story and to trust to his generosity.'

Milverton chuckled.

'You evidently do not know the earl,' said he.

From the baffled look upon Holmes's face I could clearly see that he did.

'What harm is there in the letters?' he asked.

'They are sprightly – very sprightly,' Milverton answered. 'The lady was a charming correspondent. But I can assure you that the Earl of Dovercourt would fail to appreciate them. However, since you think otherwise, we will let it rest at that. It is purely a matter of business. If you think that it is in the best interests of your client that these letters should be placed in the hands of the earl, then you would indeed be foolish to pay so large a sum of money to regain them.' He rose and seized his astrakhan coat.

Holmes was grey with anger and mortification.

'Wait a little,' he said. 'You go too fast. We would certainly make every effort to avoid scandal in so delicate a matter.'

Milverton relapsed into his chair.

'I was sure that you would see it in that light,' he purred.

'At the same time,' Holmes continued, 'Lady Eva is not a wealthy woman. I assure you that two thousand pounds would be a drain upon her resources, and that the sum you name is utterly beyond her power. I beg, therefore, that you will moderate your demands, and that you will return the letters at the price I indicate, which is, I assure you, the highest that you can get.'

Milverton's smile broadened and his eyes twinkled humorously.

'I am aware that what you say is true about the lady's resources,' said he. 'At the same time, you must admit that the occasion of a lady's marriage is a very suitable time for her friends and relatives to make some little effort upon her behalf. They may hesitate as to an acceptable wedding present. Let me assure them that this little bundle of letters would give more joy than all the candelabra and butter-dishes in London.'

'It is impossible,' said Holmes.

'Dear me, dear me, how unfortunate!' cried Milverton, taking out a bulky pocket-book. 'I cannot help thinking that ladies are ill-advised in not making an effort. Look at this!' He held up a little note with a coat-of-arms upon the envelope. 'That belongs to – well, perhaps it is hardly fair to tell the name until tomorrow morning. But at that time it will be in the hands of the lady's husband. And all because she will not find a beggarly sum which she could get in an hour by turning her diamonds into paste. It *is* such a pity. Now, you remember the sudden end of the engagement between the Honourable Miss Miles and Colonel Dorking? Only two days before the wedding there was a paragraph in the *Morning Post* to say that it was all off. And why? It is almost incredible, but the absurd sum of twelve hundred pounds would have settled the whole question. Is it not pitiful? And there I find you, a man of sense, boggling about terms when your client's future and honour are at stake. You surprise me, Mr Holmes.'

'What I say is true,' Mr Holmes answered. 'The money cannot be found. Surely it is better for you to take the substantial sum which I offer than to ruin this woman's career, which can profit you in no way?'

'There you make a mistake, Mr Holmes. An exposure would profit me indirectly to a considerable extent. I have eight or ten similar cases maturing. If it was circulated among them that I had made a severe example of the Lady Eva I should find all of them much more open to reason. You see my point?'

Holmes sprang from his chair.

'Get behind him, Watson. Don't let him out! Now, sir, let us see the contents of that notebook.'

Milverton had glided as quick as a rat to the side of the room, and stood with his back against the wall.

'Mr Holmes, Mr Holmes!' he said, turning the front of his coat and exhibiting the butt of a large revolver, which projected from the inside pocket. 'I have been expecting you to do something original. This has been done so often, and what good has ever come from it? I assure you that I am armed to the teeth, and I am perfectly prepared to use my weapon, knowing that the law will support me. Besides, your supposition that I would bring the letters here in a notebook is entirely mistaken. I would do nothing so foolish. And now, gentlemen, I have one or two little interviews this evening, and it is a long drive to Hampstead.' He stepped forward, took up his coat, laid his hand on his revolver, and turned to the door. I picked up a chair, but Holmes shook his head, and I laid it down again. With a bow, a smile, and a twinkle Milverton was out of the room, and a few moments after we heard the slam of the carriage door and the rattle of the wheels as he drove away.

Holmes sat motionless by the fire, his hands buried deep in his trouser pockets, his chin sunk upon his breast, his eyes fixed upon the glowing embers. For half an hour he was silent and still. Then, with the gesture of a man who has taken his decision, he sprang to his feet and passed into his bedroom. A little later a rakish young workman with a goatee beard and a swagger lit his clay pipe at the lamp before descending into the street. 'I'll be back some time, Watson,' said he, and vanished into the night. I understood that he had opened his campaign against Charles Augustus Milverton; but I little dreamed the strange shape which that campaign was destined to take.

For some days Holmes came and went at all hours in this attire, but beyond a remark that his time was spent at Hampstead, and that it was not wasted, I knew nothing of what he was doing. At last, however, on a wild, tempestuous evening, when the wind screamed and rattled against the windows, he returned from his last expedition, and, having removed his disguise, he sat before the fire and laughed heartily in his silent, inward fashion.

'You would not call me a marrying man, Watson?'

'No, indeed!'

'You will be interested to hear that I am engaged.'

'My dear fellow! I congrat – '

'To Milverton's housemaid.'

'Good heavens, Holmes!'

'I wanted information, Watson.'

'Surely you have gone too far?'

'It was a most necessary step. I am a plumber with a rising business, Escott by name. I have walked out with her each evening, and I have talked with her. Good heavens, those talks! However, I have got all I wanted. I know Milverton's house as I know the palm of my hand.'

'But the girl, Holmes?'

He shrugged his shoulders.

'You can't help it, my dear Watson. You must play your cards as best you can when such a stake is on the table. However, I rejoice to say that I have a hated rival who will certainly cut me out the instant that my back is turned. What a splendid night it is!'

'You like this weather?'

'It suits my purpose. Watson, I mean to burgle Milverton's house tonight.'

I had a catching of the breath, and my skin went cold at the words, which were slowly uttered in a tone of concentrated resolution. As a flash of lightning in the night shows up in an instant every detail of a wide landscape, so at one glance I seemed to see every possible result of such an action – the detection, the capture, the honoured career ending in irreparable failure and disgrace, my friend himself lying at the mercy of the odious Milverton.

'For Heaven's sake, Holmes, think what you are doing!' I cried.

'My dear fellow, I have given it every consideration. I am never precipitate in my actions, nor would I adopt so energetic and indeed so dangerous a course if any other were possible. Let us look at the matter clearly and fairly. I suppose that you will admit that the action is morally justifiable, though technically criminal. To burgle his house is no more than to forcibly take his pocket-book – an action in which you were prepared to aid me.'

I turned it over in my mind.

'Yes,' I said; 'it is morally justifiable so long as our object is to take no articles save those which are used for an illegal purpose.'

'Exactly. Since it is morally justifiable, I have only to consider the question of personal risk. Surely a gentleman should not lay much stress upon this when a lady is in most desperate need of his help?'

'You will be in such a false position.'

'Well, that is part of the risk. There is no other possible way of regaining these letters. The unfortunate lady has not the money, and there are none of her people in whom she could confide. Tomorrow is the last day of grace, and unless we can get the letters tonight this villain will be as good as his word, and will bring about her ruin. I must, therefore, abandon my client to her fate, or I must play this last card. Between ourselves, Watson, it's a sporting duel between this fellow Milverton and me. He had, as you saw, the best of the first exchanges; but my self-respect and my reputation are concerned to fight it to a finish.'

'Well, I don't like it; but I suppose it must be,' said I. 'When do we start?'

'You are not coming.'

'Then you are not going,' said I. 'I give you my word of honour – and I never broke it in my life – that I will take a cab straight to the police-station and give you away unless you let me share this adventure with you.'

'You can't help me.'

'How do you know that? You can't tell what may happen. Anyway, my resolution is taken. Other people besides you have self-respect and even reputations.'

Holmes had looked annoyed, but his brow cleared, and he clapped me on the shoulder.

'Well, well, my dear fellow, be it so. We have shared the same room for some years, and it would be amusing if we ended by sharing the same cell. You know, Watson, I don't mind confessing to you that I have always had an idea that I would have made a highly efficient criminal. This is the chance of my lifetime in that direction. See here!' He took a neat little leather case out of a drawer, and opening it he exhibited a number of shining instruments. 'This is a first-class, up-to-date burgling kit, with nickel-plated jemmy, diamond-tipped glass cutter, adaptable keys, and every modern improvement which the march of civilization demands. Here, too, is my dark lantern. Everything is in order. Have you a pair of silent shoes?'

'I have rubber-soled tennis shoes.'

'Excellent. And a mask?'

'I can make a couple out of black silk.'

'I can see that you have a strong natural turn for this sort of thing. Very good; do you make the masks. We shall have some cold supper before we start. It is now nine-thirty. At eleven we shall drive as far as Church Row.[7] It is a quarter of an hour's walk from there to Appledore Towers. We shall be at work before midnight. Milverton is a heavy sleeper, and retires punctually at ten-thirty. With any luck we should be back here by two, with the Lady Eva's letters in my pocket.'

Holmes and I put on our dress-clothes, so that we might appear to be two theatre-goers homeward bound. In Oxford Street[8] we picked up a hansom and drove to an address in Hampstead. Here we paid off our cab, and with our greatcoats buttoned up – for it was bitterly cold, and the wind seemed to blow through us – we walked along the edge of the Heath.

'It's a business that needs delicate treatment,' said Holmes. 'These documents are contained in a safe in the fellow's study, and the study is the ante-room of his bedchamber. On the other hand, like all these stout, little men who do themselves well, he is a plethoric sleeper. Agatha – that's my fiancée – says it is a joke in the servants' hall that it's impossible to wake the master. He has a secretary who is devoted to his interests and never budges from the study all day. That's why we are going at night. Then he has a beast of a dog which roams the garden. I met Agatha late the last two evenings, and she locks the brute up so as to give me a clear run. This is the house, this big one in its own grounds. Through the gate – now to the right among the laurels. We might put on our masks here, I think. You see, there is not a glimmer of light in any of the windows, and everything is working splendidly.'

With our black silk face-coverings, which turned us into two of the most truculent figures in London, we stole up to the silent, gloomy house. A sort of tiled veranda extended along one side of it, lined by several windows and two doors.

'That's his bedroom,' Holmes whispered. 'This door opens straight into the study. It would suit us best, but it is bolted as well as locked, and we should make too much noise getting in. Come round here. There's a greenhouse which opens into the drawing-room.'

The place was locked, but Holmes removed a circle of glass and turned the key from the inside.[9] An instant afterwards he had closed the door behind us, and we had become felons in the eyes of the law. The thick warm air of the conservatory and the rich, choking fragrance of exotic plants took us by the throat. He seized my hand in the darkness and led me swiftly past banks of shrubs which brushed against our faces. Holmes had remarkable powers, carefully cultivated, of seeing in the dark. Still holding my hand in one of his, he opened a door, and I was vaguely conscious that we had entered a large room in which a cigar had been smoked not long before. He felt his way among the furniture, opened another door, and closed it behind us. Putting out my hand I felt several coats hanging from the wall, and I understood that I was in a passage. We passed along it, and Holmes very gently opened a door upon the right-hand side. Something rushed out at us, and my heart sprang into my mouth, but I could have laughed when I realized that it was the cat. A fire was burning in this new room, and again the air was heavy with tobacco smoke. Holmes entered on tiptoe, waited for me to follow, and then very gently closed the door. We were in Milverton's study, and a *portière*[10] at the farther side showed the entrance to his bedroom.

It was a good fire, and the room was illuminated by it. Near the door I saw the gleam of an electric switch, but it was unnecessary, even if it had been safe, to turn it on. At one side of the fireplace was a heavy curtain, which covered the bay window we had seen from outside. On the other side was the door which communicated with the veranda. A desk stood in the centre, with a turning chair of shining red leather. Opposite was a large bookcase, with a marble bust of Athene[11] on the top. In the corner between the bookcase and the wall there stood a tall green safe, the firelight flashing back from the polished brass knobs upon its face. Holmes stole across and looked at it. Then he crept to the door of the bedroom, and stood with slanting head listening intently. No sound came from within. Meanwhile it had struck me that it would be wise to secure our retreat through the outer door, so I examined it. To my amazement it was neither locked nor bolted! I touched Holmes on the arm, and he turned his masked face in that direction. I saw him start, and he was evidently as surprised as I.

'I don't like it,' he whispered, putting his lips to my very ear. 'I can't quite make it out. Anyhow, we have no time to lose.'

'Can I do anything?'

'Yes; stand by the door. If you hear anyone come, bolt it on the inside, and we can get away as we came. If they come the other way, we can get through the door if our job is done, or hide behind these window curtains if it is not. Do you understand?'

I nodded and stood by the door. My first feeling of fear had passed away, and I thrilled now with a keener zest than I had ever enjoyed when we were the defenders of the law instead of its defiers. The high object of our mission, the consciousness that it was unselfish and chivalrous, the villainous character of our opponent, all added to the sporting interest of the adventure. Far from feeling guilty, I rejoiced and exulted in our dangers. With a glow of admiration I watched Holmes unrolling his case of instruments and choosing his tool with the calm, scientific accuracy of a surgeon who performs a delicate operation. I knew that the opening of safes was a particular hobby with him, and I understood the joy which it gave him to be confronted with this green and gold monster, the dragon which held in its maw the reputations of many fair ladies. Turning up the cuffs of his dress-coat – he had placed his overcoat on a chair – Holmes laid out two drills, a jemmy, and several skeleton keys. I stood at the centre door with my eyes glancing at each of the others, ready for any emergency; though, indeed, my plans were somewhat vague as to what I should do if we were interrupted. For half an hour Holmes worked with concentrated energy, laying down one tool, picking up another, handling each with the strength and delicacy of the trained mechanic. Finally I heard a click, the broad green door swung open, and inside I had a glimpse of a number of paper packets, each tied, sealed, and inscribed. Holmes picked one out, but it was hard to read by the flickering fire, and he drew out his little dark lantern, for it was too dangerous, with Milverton in the next room, to switch on the electric light. Suddenly I saw him halt, listen intently, and then in an instant he had swung the door of the safe to, picked up his coat, stuffed his tools into the pockets, and darted behind the window curtain, motioning me to do the same.

It was only when I had joined him there that I heard what had alarmed his quicker senses. There was a noise somewhere within the house. A door slammed in the distance. Then a confused, dull murmur broke itself into the measured thud of heavy footsteps rapidly approaching. They were in the passage outside the room. They paused at the door. The door opened. There was a sharp snick as the electric light was turned on. The door closed once more, and the pungent reek of a strong cigar was borne to our nostrils. Then the footsteps continued backwards and forwards, backwards and forwards, within a few yards of us. Finally, there was a creak from a chair, and the footsteps ceased. Then a key clicked in a lock, and I heard the rustle of papers. So far I had not dared to look out, but now I gently parted the division of the curtains in front of me and peeped through. From the pressure of Holmes's shoulder against mine I knew that he was sharing my observations. Right in front of us, and almost within our reach, was the broad, rounded back of Milverton. It was evident that we had entirely miscalculated his movements, that he had never been to his bedroom, but that he had been sitting up in some smoking- or billiard-room in the farther wing of the house, the windows of which we had not seen. His broad, grizzled head, with its shining patch of baldness, was in the immediate foreground of our vision. He was leaning far back in the red leather chair, his legs outstretched, a long black cigar projecting at an angle from his mouth. He wore a semi-military smoking-jacket, claret-coloured, with a black velvet collar. In his hand he held a long legal document, which he was reading in an indolent fashion, blowing rings of tobacco smoke from his lips as he did so. There was no promise of a speedy departure in his composed bearing and his comfortable attitude.

I felt Holmes's hand steal into mine and give me a reassuring shake, as if to say that the situation was within his powers, and that he was easy in his mind. I was not sure whether he had seen what was only too obvious from my position – that the door of the safe was imperfectly closed, and that Milverton might at any moment observe it. In my own mind I had determined that if I were sure, from the rigidity of his gaze, that it had caught his eye, I would at once spring out, throw my greatcoat over his head, pinion him, and leave the rest to Holmes. But Milverton never looked up. He was languidly interested by the papers in his hand, and page after page was turned as he followed the argument of the lawyer. At least, I thought, when he has finished the document and the cigar he will go to his room; but before he had reached the end of either there came a remarkable development which turned our thoughts into quite another channel.

Several times I had observed that Milverton looked at his watch, and once he had risen and sat down again, with a gesture of impatience. The idea, however, that he might have an appointment at so strange an hour never occurred to me until a faint sound reached my ears from the veranda outside. Milverton dropped his papers and sat rigid in his chair. The sound was repeated, and then there came a gentle tap at the door. Milverton rose and opened it.

'Well,' said he curtly, 'you are nearly half an hour late.'

So this was the explanation of the unlocked door and of the nocturnal vigil of Milverton. There was the gentle rustle of a woman's dress. I had closed the slit between the curtains as Milverton's face turned in our direction, but now I ventured very carefully to open it once more. He had resumed his seat, the cigar still projecting at an insolent angle from the corner of his mouth. In front of him, in the full glare of the electric light, there stood a tall, slim, dark woman, a veil over her face, a mantle drawn round her chin. Her breath came quick and fast and every inch of the lithe figure was quivering with strong emotion.

'Well,' said Milverton, 'you've made me lose a good night's rest, my dear. I hope you'll prove worth it. You couldn't come any other time – eh?'

The woman shook her head.

'Well, if you couldn't you couldn't. If the countess is a hard mistress you have your chance to get level with her now. Bless the girl, what are you shivering about? That's right! Pull yourself together! Now, let us get down to business.' He took a note from the drawer of his desk. 'You say that you have five letters which compromise the Countess d'Albert. You want to sell them. I want to buy them. So far so good. It only remains to fix a price. I should want to inspect the letters, of course. If they are really good specimens – Great heavens, is it you?'

The woman without a word had raised her veil and dropped the mantle from her chin. It was a dark, handsome, clear-cut face which confronted Milverton, a face with a curved nose, strong, dark eyebrows, shading hard, glittering eyes, and a straight, thin-lipped mouth set in a dangerous smile.

'It is I,' she said – 'the woman whose life you have ruined.'

Milverton laughed, but fear vibrated in his voice. 'You were so very obstinate,' said he. 'Why did you drive me to such extremities? I assure you I wouldn't hurt a fly of my own accord, but every man has his business, and what was I to do? I put the price well within your means. You would not pay.'

'So you sent the letters to my husband, and he – the noblest gentleman that ever lived, a man whose boots I was never worthy to lace – he broke his gallant heart and died. You remember that last night when I came through that door I begged and prayed you for mercy, and you laughed in my face as you are trying to laugh now, only your coward heart cannot keep your lips from twitching? Yes; you never thought to see me here again, but it was that night which taught me how I could meet you face to face, and alone. Well, Charles Milverton, what have you to say?'

'Don't imagine that you can bully me,' said he, rising to his feet. 'I have only to raise my voice, and I could call my servants and have you arrested. But I will make allowance for your natural anger. Leave the room at once as you came, and I will say no more.'

The woman stood with her hand buried in her bosom, and the same deadly smile on her thin lips.

'You will ruin no more lives as you ruined mine. You will wring no more hearts as you wrung mine. I will free the world of a poisonous thing. Take that, you hound, and that! – and that! – and that! – and that!'

She had drawn a little gleaming revolver, and emptied barrel after barrel into Milverton's body, the muzzle within two feet of his shirt-front. He shrank away, and then fell forward upon the table, coughing furiously and clawing among the papers. Then he staggered to his feet, received another shot, and rolled upon the floor. 'You've done me,' he cried, and lay still. The woman looked at him intently and ground her heel into his upturned face. She looked again, but there was no sound or movement. I heard a sharp rustle, the night air blew into the heated room, and the avenger was gone.

No interference upon our part could have saved the man from his fate; but as the woman poured bullet after bullet into Milverton's shrinking body, I was about to spring out, when I felt Holmes's cold, strong grasp upon my wrist. I understood the whole argument of that firm, restraining grip – that it was no affair of ours; that justice had overtaken a villain; that we had our own duties and our own objects which were not to be lost sight of. But hardly had the woman rushed from the room when Holmes, with swift, silent steps, was over at the other door. He turned the key in the lock. At the same instant we heard voices in the house and the sound of hurrying feet. The revolver shots had roused the household. With perfect coolness Holmes slipped across to the safe, filled his two arms with bundles of letters, and poured them all into the fire. Again and again he did it, until the safe was empty. Someone turned the handle and beat upon the outside of the door. Holmes looked swiftly round. The letter which had been the messenger of death for Milverton lay, all mottled with his blood, upon the table. Holmes tossed it in among the blazing papers. Then he drew the key from the outer door, passed through after me, and locked it on the outside. 'This way, Watson,' said he; 'we can scale the garden wall in this direction.'

I could not have believed that an alarm could have spread so swiftly. Looking back, the huge house was one blaze of light. The front door was open, and figures were rushing down the drive. The whole garden was alive with people, and one fellow raised a view-halloa as we emerged from the veranda and followed hard at our heels. Holmes seemed to know the ground perfectly, and he threaded his way swiftly among a plantation of small trees, I close at his heels, and our foremost pursuer panting behind us. It was a six-foot wall which barred our path, but he sprang to the top and over. As I did the same I felt the hand of the man behind me grab my ankle; but I kicked myself free, and scrambled over a glass-strewn coping. I fell upon my face among some bushes; but Holmes had me on my feet in an instant, and together we dashed away across the huge expanse of Hampstead Heath. We had run two miles, I suppose, before Holmes at last halted and listened intently. All was absolutely silence behind us. We had shaken off our pursuers, and were safe.

We had breakfasted and were smoking our morning pipe, on the day after the remarkable experience which I have recorded, when Mr Lestrade, of Scotland Yard, very solemn and impressive, was ushered into our modest sitting-room.

'Good morning, Mr Holmes,' said he – 'good morning. May I ask if you are very busy just now?'

'Not too busy to listen to you.'

'I thought that, perhaps, if you had nothing particular on hand, you might care to assist us in a most remarkable case which occurred only last night at Hampstead.'

'Dear me!' said Holmes. 'What was that?'

'A murder – a most dramatic and remarkable murder. I know how keen you are upon these things, and I would take it as a great favour if you would step down to Appledore Towers and give us the benefit of your advice. It is no ordinary crime. We have had our eyes upon this Mr Milverton for some time, and, between ourselves, he was a bit of a villain. He is known to have held papers which he used for blackmailing purposes. These papers have all been burned by the murderers. No article of value was taken, as it is probable that the criminals were men of good position, whose sole object was to prevent social exposure.'

'Criminals!' exclaimed Holmes. 'Plural!'

'Yes, there were two of them. They were, as nearly as possible, captured red-handed. We have their foot-marks, we have their description; it's ten to one that we trace them. The first fellow was a bit too active, but the second was caught by the under-gardener, and only got away after a struggle. He was a middle-sized, strongly built man – square jaw, thick neck, moustache,[12] a mask over his eyes.'

'That's rather vague,' said Sherlock Holmes. 'Why, it might be a description of Watson!'

'It's true,' said the inspector, with much amusement. 'It might be a description of Watson.'

'Well, I am afraid I can't help you, Lestrade,' said Holmes. 'The fact is that I knew this fellow Milverton, that I considered him one of the most dangerous men in London, and that I think there are certain crimes which the law cannot touch, and which therefore, to some extent, justify private revenge. No, it's no use arguing. I have made up my mind. My sympathies are with the criminals rather than with the victim, and I will not handle this case.'

Holmes had not said one word to me about the tragedy which we had witnessed, but I observed all the morning that he was in the most thoughtful mood, and he gave me the impression, from his vacant eyes and his abstracted manner, of a man who is striving to recall something to his memory. We were in the middle of our lunch, when he suddenly sprang to his feet. 'By Jove, Watson! I've got it!' he cried. 'Take your hat! Come with me!' He hurried at his top speed down Baker Street and along Oxford Street, until we had almost reached Regent Circus.[13] Here on the left hand there stands a shop window filled with photographs of the celebrities and beauties of the day. Holmes's eyes fixed themselves upon one of them, and following his gaze I saw the picture of a regal and stately lady in Court dress, with a high diamond tiara upon her noble head. I looked at that delicately curved nose, at the marked eyebrows, at the straight mouth, and the strong little chin beneath it. Then I caught my breath as I read the time-honoured title of the great nobleman and statesman whose wife she had been. My eyes met those of Holmes, and he put his finger to his lips as we turned away from the window.

THE SIX NAPOLEONS

It was no very unusual thing for Mr Lestrade, of Scotland Yard, to look in upon us of an evening, and his visits were welcome to Sherlock Holmes, for they enabled him to keep in touch with all that was going on at the police headquarters. In return for the news which Lestrade would bring, Holmes was always ready to listen with attention to the details of any case upon which the detective was engaged, and was able occasionally, without any active interference, to give some hint or suggestion drawn from his own vast knowledge and experience.

On this particular evening Lestrade had spoken of the weather and the newspapers. Then he had fallen silent, puffing thoughtfully at his cigar. Holmes looked keenly at him.

'Anything remarkable on hand?'[1] he asked.

'Oh, no, Mr Holmes, nothing very particular.'

'Then tell me all about it.'

Lestrade laughed.

'Well, Mr Holmes, there is no use denying that there *is* something on my mind. And yet it is such an absurd business that I hesitated to bother you about it. On the other hand, although it is trivial, it is undoubtedly queer, and I know that you have a taste for all that is out of the common. But in my opinion it comes more in Dr Watson's line than ours.'

'Disease?' said I.

'Madness, anyhow. And a queer madness too! You wouldn't think there was anyone living at this time of day who had such a hatred of Napoleon the First[2] that he would break any image of him that he could see.'

Holmes sank back in his chair.

'That's no business of mine,' said he.

'Exactly. That's what I said. But then, when the man commits burglary in order to break images which are not his own, that brings it away from the doctor and on to the policeman.'

Holmes sat up again.

'Burglary! This is more interesting. Let me hear the details.' Lestrade took out his official notebook and refreshed his memory from its pages.

'The first case reported was four days ago,' said he. 'It was at the shop of Morse Hudson, who has a place for the sale of pictures and statues in the Kennington Road.³ The assistant had left the front shop for an instant, when he heard a crash, and, hurrying in, found a plaster bust of Napoleon, which stood with several other works of art upon the counter, lying shivered into fragments. He rushed out into the road, but, although several passers-by declared that they had noticed a man run out of the shop, he could neither see anyone nor could he find any means of identifying the rascal. It seemed to be one of those senseless acts of hooliganism which occur from time to time, and it was reported to the constable on the beat as such. The plaster cast was not worth more than a few shillings, and the whole affair appeared to be too childish for any particular investigation.

'The second case, however, was more serious and also more singular. It occurred only last night.

'In Kennington Road, and within a few hundred yards of Morse Hudson's shop, there lives a well-known medical practitioner, named Dr Barnicot, who has one of the largest practices upon the south side of the Thames. His residence and principal consulting-room is at Kennington Road, but he has a branch surgery and dispensary at Lower Brixton Road,⁴ two miles away. This Dr Barnicot is an enthusiastic admirer of Napoleon, and his house is full of books, pictures, and relics of the French Emperor. Some little time ago he purchased from Morse Hudson two duplicate plaster casts of the famous head of Napoleon by the French sculptor Devine. One of these he placed in his hall in the house at Kennington Road, and the other on the mantelpiece of the surgery at Lower Brixton. Well, when Dr Barnicot came down this morning he was astonished to find that his house had been burgled during the night, but that nothing had been taken save the plaster head from the hall. It had been carried out, and had been dashed savagely against the garden wall, under which its splintered fragments were discovered.'

Holmes rubbed his hands.

'This is certainly very novel,' said he.

'I thought it would please you. But I have not got to the end yet. Dr Barnicot was due at his surgery at twelve o'clock, and you can imagine his amazement when, on arriving there, he found that the window had been opened in the night, and that the broken pieces of his second bust were strewn all over the room. It had been smashed to atoms where it stood. In neither case were there any signs which could give us a clue as to the criminal or lunatic who had done the mischief. Now, Mr Holmes, you have got the facts.'

'They are singular, not to say grotesque,' said Holmes. 'May I ask whether the two busts smashed in Dr Barnicot's rooms were the exact duplicates of the one which was destroyed in Morse Hudson's shop?'

'They were taken from the same mould.'

'Such a fact must tell against the theory that the man who breaks them is influenced by any general hatred of Napoleon. Considering how many hundreds of statues of the great Emperor must exist in London, it is too much to suppose such a coincidence as that a promiscuous iconoclast should chance to begin upon three specimens of the same bust.'

'Well, I thought as you do,' said Lestrade. 'On the other hand, this Morse Hudson is the purveyor of busts in that part of London, and these three were the only ones which had been in his shop for years. So although, as you say, there are many hundreds of statues in London, it is very probable that these three were the only ones in that district. Therefore a local fanatic would begin with them. What do you think, Dr Watson?'

'There are no limits to the possibilities of monomania,'[5] I answered. 'There is the condition which the modern French psychologists have called the "*idée fixe*",[6] which may be trifling in character, and accompanied by complete sanity in every other way. A man who had read deeply about Napoleon, or who had possibly received some hereditary family injury through the great war, might conceivably form such an "*idée fixe*", and under its influence be capable of any fantastic outrage.'

'That won't do, my dear Watson,' said Holmes, shaking his head; 'for no amount of "*idée fixe*" would enable your interesting mono-maniac to find out where these busts were situated.'

'Well, how you do *you* explain it?'

'I don't attempt to do so. I would only observe that there is a certain method in the gentleman's eccentric proceedings. For example, in Dr Barnicot's hall, where a sound might arouse the family, the bust was taken outside before being broken, whereas in the surgery, where there was less danger of an alarm, it was smashed where it stood. The affair seems absurdly trifling, and yet I dare call nothing trivial when I reflect that some of my most classic cases have had the least promising commencement. You will remember, Watson, how the dreadful business of the Abernetty[7] family was first brought to my notice by the depth which the parsley had sunk into the butter upon a hot day.[8] I can't afford, therefore, to smile at your three broken busts, Lestrade, and I shall be very much obliged to you if you will let me hear of any fresh developments of so singular a chain of events.'

The development for which my friend had asked came in a quicker and an infinitely more tragic form than he could have imagined. I was still dressing in my bedroom next morning, when there was a tap at the door, and Holmes entered, a telegram in his hand. He read it aloud:

Come instantly, 131 Pitt Street, Kensington.[9] LESTRADE

'What is it, then?' I asked.

'Don't know – may be anything. But I suspect it is the sequel of the story of the statues. In that case our friend the image-breaker has begun operations in another quarter of London. There's coffee on the table, Watson, and I have a cab at the door.'

In half an hour we had reached Pitt Street, a quiet little backwater just beside one of the briskest currents of London life. No. 131 was one of a row, all flat-chested,[10] respectable, and most unromantic dwellings.

As we drove up we found the railings in front of the house lined by a curious crowd. Holmes whistled.

'By George! it's attempted murder at the least. Nothing less will hold the London message boy. There's a deed of violence indicated in that fellow's round shoulders and outstretched neck. What's this, Watson? The top step swilled down and the other ones dry. Footsteps enough, anyhow! Well, well, there's Lestrade at the front window, and we shall soon know all about it.'

The official received us with a very grave face and showed us into a sitting-room, where an exceedingly unkempt and agitated elderly man, clad in a flannel dressing-gown, was pacing up and down. He was introduced to us as the owner of the house – Mr Horace Harker, of the Central Press Syndicate.[11]

'It's the Napoleon bust business again,' said Lestrade. 'You seemed interested last night, Mr Holmes, so I thought perhaps you would be glad to be present now that the affair has taken a very much graver turn.'

'What has it turned to, then?'

'To murder. Mr Harker, will you tell these gentlemen exactly what has occurred?'

The man in the dressing-gown turned upon us with a most melancholy face.

'It's an extraordinary thing,' said he, 'that all my life I have been collecting other people's news, and now that a real piece of news has come my own way I am so confused and bothered that I can't put two words together. If I had come in here as a journalist I should have interviewed myself and had two columns in every evening paper. As it is, I am giving away valuable copy by telling my story over and over to a string of different people, and I can make no use of it myself. However, I've heard your name, Mr Sherlock Holmes, and if you'll only explain this queer business I shall be paid for my trouble in telling you the story.'

Holmes sat down and listened.

'It all seems to centre round that bust of Napoleon which I bought for this very room about four months ago. I picked it up cheap from Harding Brothers,[12] two doors from the High Street Station. A great deal of my journalistic work is done at night, and I often write until the early morning. So it was today. I was sitting in my den, which is at the back of the top of the house, about three o'clock, when I was convinced that I heard some sounds downstairs. I listened, but they were not repeated, and I concluded that they came from outside. Then suddenly, about five minutes later, there came a most horrible yell – the most dreadful sound, Mr Holmes, that ever I heard. It will ring in my ears as long as I live. I sat frozen with horror for a minute or two. Then I seized the poker and went downstairs. When I entered this room I found the window wide open, and I at once observed that the bust was gone from the mantelpiece. Why any burglar should take such a thing passes my understanding, for it was only a plaster cast, and of no real value whatever.

'You can see for yourself that anyone going out through that open window could reach the front doorstep by taking a long stride. This was clearly what the burglar had done, so I went round and opened the door. Stepping out into the dark I nearly fell over a dead man who was lying there. I ran back for a light, and there was the poor fellow, a great gash in his throat and the whole place swimming in blood. He lay on his back, his knees drawn up, and his mouth horribly open. I shall see him in my dreams. I had just time to blow on my police whistle, and then I must have fainted, for I knew nothing more until I found the policeman standing over me in the hall.'

'Well, who was the murdered man?' asked Holmes.

'There's nothing to show who he was,' said Lestrade. 'You shall see the body at the mortuary, but we have made nothing of it up to now. He is a tall man, sunburnt, very powerful, not more than thirty. He is poorly dressed, and yet does not appear to be a labourer. A horn-handled clasp-knife was lying in a pool of blood beside him. Whether it was the weapon which did the deed, or whether it belonged to the dead man, I do not know. There was no name on his clothing, and nothing in his pockets save an apple, some string, a shilling map of London, and a photograph. Here it is.'

It was evidently taken by a snap-shot from a small camera. It represented an alert, sharp-featured simian man with thick eyebrows, and a very peculiar projection of the lower part of the face like the muzzle of a baboon.

'And what became of the bust?' asked Holmes, after a careful study of this picture.

'We had news of it just before you came. It has been found in the front garden of an empty house in Campden House Road.[13] It was broken into fragments. I am going round now to see it. Will you come?'

'Certainly. I must just take one look round.' He examined the carpet and the window. 'The fellow had either very long legs or was a most active man,' said he. 'With an area beneath it was no mean feat to reach that window-ledge and open that window. Getting back was comparatively simple. Are you coming with us to see the remains of your bust, Mr Harker?'

The disconsolate journalist had seated himself at a writing-table.

'I must try and make something of it,' said he, 'though I have no doubt that the first editions of the evening papers are out already with full details. It's like my luck! You remember when the stand fell at Doncaster? Well, I was the only journalist in the stand, and my journal the only one that had no account of it, for I was too shaken to write it. And now I'll be too late with a murder done on my own doorstep.'

As we left the room we heard his pen travelling shrilly over the foolscap.

The spot where the fragments of the bust had been found was only a few hundred yards away. For the first time our eyes rested upon this presentment of the great Emperor, which seemed to raise such frantic and destructive hatred in the mind of the unknown. It lay scattered in splintered shards upon the grass. Holmes picked up several of them and examined them carefully. I was convinced from his intent face and purposeful manner that at last he was upon a clue.

'Well?' asked Lestrade.

Holmes shrugged his shoulders.

'We have a long way to go yet,' said he. 'And yet – and yet – well, we have some suggestive facts to act upon. The possession of this trifling bust was worth more in the eyes of this strange criminal than a human life. That is one point. Then there is the singular fact that he did not break it in the house, or immediately outside the house, if to break it was his sole object.'

'He was rattled and bustled by meeting this other fellow. He hardly knew what he was doing.'

'Well, that's likely enough. But I wish to call your attention very particularly to the position of this house in the garden of which the bust was destroyed.'

Lestrade looked about him.

'It was an empty house, and so he knew that he would not be disturbed in the garden.'

'Yes, but there is another empty house farther up the street which he must have passed before he came to this one. Why did he not break it there, since it is evident that every yard that he carried it increased the risk of someone meeting him?'

'I give it up,' said Lestrade.

Holmes pointed to the street lamp above our heads.

'He could see what he was doing here, and he could not there. That was the reason.'

'By Jove! that's true,' said the detective. 'Now that I come to think of it, Dr Barnicot's bust was broken not far from his red lamp. Well, Mr Holmes, what are we to do with that fact?'

'To remember it – to docket it. We may come on something later which will bear upon it. What steps do you propose to take now, Lestrade?'

'The most practical way of getting at it, in my opinion, is to identify the dead man. There should be no difficulty about that. When we have found who he is and who his associates are, we should have a good start in learning what he was doing in Pitt Street last night, and who it was who met him and killed him on the doorstep of Mr Horace Harker. Don't you think so?'

'No doubt; and yet it is not quite the way in which I should approach the case.'

'What would you do then?'

'Oh, you must not let me influence you in any way. I suggest that you go on your line and I on mine. We can compare notes afterwards, and each will supplement the other.'

'Very good,' said Lestrade.

'If you are going back to Pitt Street you might see Mr Horace

Harker. Tell him from me that I have quite made up my mind, and that it is certain that a dangerous homicidal lunatic with Napoleonic delusions was in his house last night. It will be useful for his article.'

Lestrade stared.

'You don't seriously believe that?'

Holmes smiled.

'Don't I? Well, perhaps I don't. But I am sure that it will interest Mr Horace Harker and the subscribers of the Central Press Syndicate. Now, Watson, I think that we shall find that we have a long and rather complex day's work before us. I should be glad, Lestrade, if you could make it convenient to meet us at Baker Street at six o'clock this evening. Until then I should like to keep this photograph[14] found in the dead man's pocket. It is possible that I may have to ask your company and assistance upon a small expedition which will have to be undertaken tonight, if my chain of reasoning should prove to be correct. Until then, goodbye, and good luck.'

Sherlock Holmes and I walked together to the High Street, where he stopped at the shop of Harding Brothers, whence the bust had been purchased. A young assistant informed us that Mr Harding would be absent until afternoon, and that he was himself a newcomer, who could give us no information. Holmes's face showed his disappointment and annoyance.

'Well, well, we can't expect to have it all our own way, Watson,' he said at last. 'We must come back in the afternoon, if Mr Harding will not be here until then. I am, as you have no doubt surmised, endeavouring to trace these busts to their source, in order to find if there is not something peculiar which may account for their remarkable fate. Let us make for Mr Morse Hudson, of the Kennington Road, and see if he can throw any light upon the problem.'

A drive of an hour brought us to the picture-dealer's establishment. He was a small, stout man with a red face and a peppery manner.

'Yes, sir. On my very counter, sir,' said he. 'What we pay rates and taxes for I don't know, when any ruffian can come in and break one's goods. Yes, sir, it was I who sold Dr Barnicot his two statues. Disgraceful, sir! A Nihilist[15] plot, that's what I make it. No one but an Anarchist[16] would go about breaking statues. Red republicans,[17] that's what I call 'em. Who did I get the statues from? I don't see what that has to do with it. Well, if you really want to know, I got them from Gelder & Co., in Church Street, Stepney.[18] They are a well-known house in the trade, and have been this twenty years. How many had I? Three – two and one are three – two of Dr Barnicot's and one smashed in broad daylight on my own counter. Do I know that photograph? No, I don't. Yes, I do though. Why, it's Beppo! He was a kind of Italian piecework man, who made himself useful in the shop. He could carve a bit, and gild a frame, and do odd jobs. The fellow left me last week, and I've heard nothing of him since. No, I don't know where he came from nor where he went to. I had nothing against him while he was here. He was gone two days before the bust was smashed.'

'Well, that's all we could reasonably expect to get from Morse Hudson,' said Holmes, as we emerged from the shop. 'We have this Beppo as a common factor, both in Kennington and in Kensington, so that is worth a ten-mile drive. Now, Watson, let us make for Gelder & Co., of Stepney, the source and origin of busts. I shall be surprised if we don't get some help down there.'

In rapid succession we passed through the fringe of fashionable London, hotel London, theatrical London, literary London, commercial London, and, finally, maritime London,[19] till we came to a riverside city of a hundred thousand souls, where the tenement houses swelter and reek with the outcasts of Europe. Here, in a broad thoroughfare, once the abode of wealthy city merchants, we found the sculpture works for which we searched. Outside was a considerable yard full of monumental masonry. Inside was a large room in which fifty workers were carving or moulding. The manager, a big blond German, received us civilly, and gave a clear answer to all Holmes's questions. A reference to his books showed that hundreds of casts had been taken from a marble copy of Devine's head of Napoleon, but that the three which had been sent to Morse Hudson a year or so before had been half of a batch of six, the other three being sent to Harding Brothers, of Kensington. There was no reason why those six should be different to any of the other casts. He could suggest no possible cause why anyone should wish to destroy them – in fact, he laughed at the idea.

Their wholesale price was six shillings, but the retailer would get twelve or more. The cast was taken in two moulds from each side of the face, and then these two profiles of plaster of Paris were joined together to make the complete bust. The work was usually done by Italians in the room we were in. When finished the busts were put on a table in the passage to dry, and afterwards stored. That was all he could tell us.

But the production of the photograph had a remarkable effect upon the manager. His face flushed with anger, and his brows knotted over his blue Teutonic eyes.

'Ah, the rascal!' he cried. 'Yes, indeed, I know him very well. This has always been a respectable establishment, and the only time that we have ever had the police in it was over this very fellow. It was more than a year ago now. He knifed another Italian in the street, and then he came to the works with the police on his heels, and he was taken here. Beppo was his name – his second name I never knew. Serve me right for engaging a man with such a face. But he was a good workman – one of the best.'

'What did he get?'

'The man lived, and he got off with a year. I have no doubt he is out now; but he has not dared to show his nose here. We have a cousin of his here, and I dare say he could tell you where he is.'

'No, no,' cried Holmes, 'not a word to the cousin – not a word, I beg you. The matter is very important, and the farther I go with it the more important it seems to grow. When you referred in your ledger to the sale of those casts I observed that the date was 3rd June of last year. Could you give me the date when Beppo was arrested?'

'I could tell you roughly by the pay-list,' the manager answered. 'Yes,' he continued, after some turning over of pages, 'he was paid last on May 20th.'

'Thank you,' said Holmes. 'I don't think that I need intrude upon your time and patience any more.' With a last word of caution that he should say nothing as to our researches we turned our faces westward once more.

The afternoon was far advanced before we were able to snatch a hasty luncheon at a restaurant. A news-bill at the entrance announced

'Kensington Outrage. Murder by a Madman', and the contents of the paper showed that Mr Horace Harker had got his account into print after all. Two columns were occupied with a highly sensational and flowery rendering of the whole incident. Holmes propped it against the cruet stand and read it while he ate. Once or twice he chuckled.

'This is all right, Watson,' said he. 'Listen to this: "It is satisfactory to know that there can be no difference of opinion upon this case, since Mr Lestrade, one of the most experienced members of the official force, and Mr Sherlock Holmes, the well-known consulting expert, have each come to the conclusion that the grotesque series of incidents, which have ended in so tragic a fashion, arise from lunacy rather than from deliberate crime. No explanation save mental aberration can cover the facts." The Press, Watson, is a most valuable institution, if you only know how to use it. And now, if you have quite finished, we will hark back to Kensington, and see what the manager of Harding Brothers has to say to the matter.'

The founder of the great emporium proved to be a brisk, crisp little person, very dapper and quick, with a clear head and a ready tongue.

'Yes, sir, I have already read the account in the evening papers. Mr Horace Harker is a customer of ours. We supplied him with the bust some months ago. We ordered three busts of that sort from Gelder & Co., of Stepney. They are all sold now. To whom? Oh, I dare say by consulting our sales book we could very easily tell you. Yes, we have the entries here. One to Mr Harker, you see, and one to Mr Josiah Brown, of Laburnum Lodge, Laburnum Vale,[20] Chiswick, and one to Mr Sandeford, of Lower Grove Road, Reading. No, I have never seen this face which you show me in the photograph. You would hardly forget it – would you, sir? – for I've seldom seen an uglier. Have we any Italians on the staff? Yes, sir, we have several among our workpeople and cleaners. I dare say they might get a peep at that sales book if they wanted to. There is no particular reason for keeping a watch upon that book. Well, well, it's a very strange business, and I hope that you'll let me know if anything comes of your inquiries.'

Holmes had taken several notes during Mr Harding's evidence, and I could see that he was thoroughly satisfied by the turn which affairs were taking. He made no remark, however, save that, unless we hurried, we should be late for our appointment with Lestrade. Sure enough, when we reached Baker Street the detective was already there, and we found him pacing up and down in a fever of impatience. His look of importance showed that his day's work had not been in vain.

'Well?' he asked. 'What luck, Mr Holmes?'

'We have had a very busy day, and not entirely a wasted one,' my friend explained. 'We have seen both the retailers and also the whole-sale manufacturers. I can trace each of the busts now from the beginning.'

'The busts!' cried Lestrade. 'Well, well, you have your own methods, Mr Sherlock Holmes, and it is not for me to say a word against them, but I think I have done a better day's work than you. I have identified the dead man.'

'You don't say so!'

'And found a cause for the crime.'

'Splendid!'

'We have an inspector who makes a speciality of Saffron Hill[21] and the Italian quarter. Well, this dead man had some Catholic emblem round his neck, and that, along with his colour, made me think he was from the South. Inspector Hill knew him the moment he caught sight of him. His name is Pietro Venucci, from Naples, and he is one of the greatest cut-throats in London. He is connected with the Mafia, which, as you know, is a secret political society,[22] enforcing its decrees by murder. Now you see how the affair begins to clear up. The other fellow is probably an Italian also, and a member of the Mafia. He has broken the rules in some fashion. Pietro is set upon his track. Probably the photograph we found in his pocket is the man himself, so that he may not knife the wrong person. He dogs the fellow, he sees him enter a house, he waits outside for him, and in the scuffle receives his own death-wound. How is that, Mr Sherlock Holmes?'

Holmes clapped his hands approvingly.

'Excellent, Lestrade, excellent!' he cried. 'But I didn't quite follow your explanation of the destruction of the busts.'

'The busts! You never can get those busts out of your head. After all, that is nothing; petty larceny, six months at the most. It is the murder that we are really investigating, and I tell you that I am gathering all the threads into my hands.'

'And the next stage?'

'Is a very simple one. I shall go down with Hill to the Italian quarter, find the man whose photograph we have got, and arrest him on the charge of murder. Will you come with us?'

'I think not. I fancy we can attain our end in a simpler way. I can't say for certain, because it all depends – well, it all depends upon a factor which is completely outside our control. But I have great hopes – in fact, the betting is exactly two to one – that if you will come with us tonight I shall be able to help you to lay him by the heels.'

'In the Italian quarter?'

'No; I fancy Chiswick is an address which is more likely to find him. If you will come with me to Chiswick tonight, Lestrade, I'll promise to go to the Italian quarter with you tomorrow, and no harm will be done by the delay. And now I think that a few hours' sleep would do us all good, for I do not propose to leave before eleven o'clock, and it is unlikely that we shall be back before morning. You'll dine with us, Lestrade, and then you are welcome to the sofa until it is time for us to start. In the meantime, Watson, I should be glad if you would ring for an express messenger, for I have a letter to send, and it is important that it should go at once.'

Holmes spent the evening in rummaging among the files of the old daily papers with which one of our lumber-rooms was packed. When at last he descended it was with triumph in his eyes, but he said nothing to either of us as to the result of his researches. For my own part, I had followed step by step the methods by which he had traced the various windings of this complex case, and, though I could not yet perceive the goal which we would reach, I understood clearly that Holmes expected this grotesque criminal to make an attempt upon the two remaining busts, one of which, I remembered, was at Chiswick. No doubt the object of our journey was to catch him in the very act, and I could not but admire the cunning with which my friend had inserted the wrong clue in the evening paper so as to give the fellow the idea that he could continue his scheme with impunity. I was not surprised when Holmes suggested that I should take my revolver with me. He had himself picked up the loaded hunting-crop[23] which was his favourite weapon.

A four-wheeler was at the door at eleven, and in it we drove to a spot at the other side of Hammersmith Bridge. Here the cabman was directed to wait. A short walk brought us to a secluded road fringed with pleasant houses, each standing in its own grounds. In the light of a street lamp we read 'Laburnum Villa' upon the gate-post of one of them. The occupants had evidently retired to rest, for all was dark save for a fanlight over the hall door, which shed a single blurred circle on to the garden path. The wooden fence which separated the grounds from the road threw a dense black shadow upon the inner side, and here it was that we crouched.

'I fear that you'll have a long time to wait,' Holmes whispered. 'We may thank our stars that it is not raining. I don't think we can even venture to smoke to pass the time. However, it's a two to one chance that we get something to pay us for our trouble.'

It proved, however, that our vigil was not to be so long as Holmes had led us to fear, and it ended in a very sudden and singular fashion. In an instant, without the least sound to warn us of his coming, the garden gate swung open, and a lithe, dark figure, as swift and active as an ape, rushed up the garden path. We saw it whisk past the light thrown from over the door and disappear against the black shadow of the house. There was a long pause, during which we held our breath, and then a very gentle creaking sound came to our ears. The window was being opened. The noise ceased, and again there was a long silence. The fellow was making his way into the house. We saw the sudden flash of a dark lantern inside the room. What he sought was evidently not there, for again we saw the flash through another blind, and then through another.

'Let us get to the open window. We will nab him as he climbs out,' Lestrade whispered.

But before we could move the man had emerged again. As he came out into the glimmering patch of light we saw that he carried something white under his arm. He looked stealthily all round him. The silence of the deserted street reassured him. Turning his back upon us, he laid down his burden, and the next instant there was the sound of a sharp tap, followed by a clatter and rattle. The man was so intent upon what he was doing that he never heard our steps as we stole across the grass plot. With the bound of a tiger Holmes was on his back, and an instant later Lestrade and I had him by either wrist, and the handcuffs had been fastened. As we turned him over I saw his hideous, sallow face, with writhing, furious features glaring up at us, and I knew that it was indeed the man of the photograph whom we had secured.

But it was not our prisoner to whom Holmes was giving his attention. Squatted on the doorstep, he was engaged in most carefully examining that which the man had brought from the house. It was a bust of Napoleon like the one which we had seen that morning, and it had been broken into similar fragments. Carefully Holmes held each separate shard to the light, but in no way did it differ from any other shattered piece of plaster. He had just completed his examination, when the hall lights flew up, the door opened and the owner of the house, a jovial, rotund figure in shirt and trousers, presented himself.

'Mr Josiah Brown, I suppose?' said Holmes.

'Yes, sir; and you no doubt are Mr Sherlock Holmes? I had the note which you sent by the express messenger, and I did exactly what you told me. We locked every door in the inside and awaited developments. Well, I'm very glad to see that you have got the rascal. I hope, gentlemen, that you will come in and have some refreshment.'

However, Lestrade was anxious to get his man into safe quarters, so within a few minutes our cab had been summoned and we were all four upon our way to London. Not a word would our captive say; but he glared at us from the shadow of his matted hair, and once, when my hand seemed within his reach, he snapped at it like a hungry wolf. We stayed long enough at the police station to learn that a search of his clothing revealed nothing save shillings and a long sheath knife, the handle of which bore copious traces of recent blood.

'That's all right,' said Lestrade, as we parted. 'Hill knows all these gentry, and he will give a name to him. You'll find that my theory of the Mafia will work out all right. But I'm sure I am exceedingly obliged to you, Mr Holmes, for the workman-like way in which you laid hands upon him. I don't quite understand it all yet.'

'I fear it is rather too late an hour for explanations,' said Holmes. 'Besides, there are one or two details which are not finished off, and it is one of those cases which are worth working out to the very end. If you will come round once more to my rooms at six o'clock tomorrow I think I shall be able to show you that even now you have not grasped the entire meaning of this business, which presents some features which make it absolutely original in the history of crime. If ever I permit you to chronicle any more of my little problems, Watson, I foresee that you will enliven your pages by an account of the singular adventure of the Napoleonic busts.'

When we met again next evening, Lestrade was furnished with much information concerning our prisoner. His name, it appeared, was Beppo, second name unknown. He was a well-known ne'er-do-well among the Italian colony. He had once been a skilful sculptor and had earned an honest living, but he had taken to evil courses, and had twice already been in gaol – once for a petty theft and once, as we had already heard, for stabbing a fellow-countryman. He could talk English perfectly well. His reasons for destroying the busts were still unknown, and he refused to answer any questions upon the subject; but the police had discovered that these same busts might very well have been made by his own hands, since he was engaged in this class of work at the establishment of Gelder & Co. To all this information, much of which we already knew, Holmes listened with polite attention; but I, who knew him so well, could clearly see that his thoughts were elsewhere, and I detected a mixture of mingled uneasiness and expectation beneath that mask which he was wont to assume. At last he started in his chair and his eyes brightened. There had been a ring at the bell. A minute later we heard steps upon the stairs, and an elderly, red-faced man with grizzled side-whiskers was ushered in. In his right hand he carried an old-fashioned carpet-bag, which he placed upon the table.

'Is Mr Sherlock Holmes here?'

My friend bowed and smiled. 'Mr Sandeford, of Reading, I suppose?' said he.

'Yes, sir. I fear that I am a little late; but the trains were awkward. You wrote to me about a bust that is in my possession.'

'Exactly.'

'I have your letter here. You said, "I desire to possess a copy of Devine's Napoleon and am prepared to pay you ten pounds for the one which is in your possession." Is that right?'

'Certainly.'

'I was very much surprised at your letter, for I could not imagine how you knew that I owned such a thing.'

'Of course you must have been surprised, but the explanation is very simple. Mr Harding, of Harding Brothers, said that they had sold you their last copy, and he gave me your address.'

'Oh, that was it, was it? Did he tell you what I paid for it?'

'No, he did not.'

'Well, I am an honest man, though not a very rich one. I only gave fifteen shillings for the bust, and I think you ought to know that before I take ten pounds from you.'

'I am sure the scruple does you honour, Mr Sandeford. But I have named that price, so I intend to stick to it.'

'Well, it is very handsome of you, Mr Holmes. I brought the bust up with me, as you asked me to do. Here it is!'

He opened his bag, and at last we saw placed upon our table a complete specimen of that bust which we had already seen more than once in fragments.

Holmes took a paper from his pocket and laid a ten-pound note upon the table.

'You will kindly sign that paper, Mr Sandeford, in the presence of these witnesses. It is simply to say that you transfer every possible right that you ever had in the bust to me. I am a methodical man, you see, and you never know what turn events might take afterwards. Thank you, Mr Sandeford; here is your money, and I wish you a very good evening.'

When our visitor had disappeared Sherlock Holmes's movements were such as to rivet our attention. He began by taking a clean white cloth from a drawer and laying it over the table. Then he placed his newly acquired bust in the centre of the cloth. Finally he picked up his hunting-crop and struck Napoleon a sharp blow on the top of the head. The figure broke into fragments, and Holmes bent eagerly over the shattered remains. Next instant, with a loud shout of triumph, he held up one splinter, in which a round, dark object was fixed like a plum in a pudding.

'Gentlemen,' he cried, 'let me introduce you to the famous black pearl of the Borgias!'[24]

Lestrade and I sat silent for a moment, and then, with a spontaneous impulse, we both broke out clapping as at the well-wrought crisis of a play. A flush of colour sprang to Holmes's pale cheeks, and he bowed to us like the master dramatist who receives the homage of his audience. It was at such moments that for an instant he ceased to be a reasoning machine and betrayed his human love for admiration and applause. The same singularly proud and reserved nature which turned away with disdain from popular notoriety was capable of being moved to its depth by spontaneous wonder and praise from a friend.

'Yes, gentlemen,' said he, 'it is the most famous pearl now existing in the world, and it has been my good fortune, by a connected chain of inductive reasoning, to trace it from the Prince of Calonna's[25] bedroom at the Dacre Hotel,[26] where it was lost, to the interior of this, the last of the six busts of Napoleon which were manufactured by Gelder & Co., of Stepney. You will remember, Lestrade, the sensation caused by the disappearance of this valuable jewel, and the vain efforts of the London police to recover it. I was myself consulted upon the case; but I was unable to throw any light upon it. Suspicion fell upon the maid of the Princess, who was an Italian, and it was proved that she had a brother in London, but we failed to trace any connection between them. The maid's name was Lucretia Venucci, and there is no doubt in my mind that this Pietro who was murdered two nights ago was the brother. I have been looking up the dates in the old files of the paper, and I find that the disappearance of the pearl was exactly two days before the arrest of Beppo for some crime of violence – an event which took place in the factory of Gelder & Co., at the very moment when these busts were being made. Now you clearly see the sequence of events, though you see them, of course, in the inverse order to the way in which they presented themselves to me. Beppo had the pearl in his possession. He may have stolen it from Pietro, he may have been Pietro's confederate, he may have been the go-between of Pietro and his sister. It is of no consequence to us which is the correct solution.

'The main fact is that he *had* the pearl, and at that moment, when it was on his person, he was pursued by the police. He made for the factory in which he worked, and he knew that he had only a few minutes in which to conceal this enormously valuable prize, which would otherwise be found on him when he was searched. Six plaster casts of Napoleon were drying in the passage. One of them was still soft. In an instant Beppo, a skilful workman, made a small hole in the wet plaster, dropped in the pearl, and with a few touches covered over the aperture once more. It was an admirable hiding-place. No one could possibly find it. But Beppo was condemned to a year's imprisonment, and in the meanwhile his six busts were scattered over London. He could not tell which contained his treasure. Only by breaking them could he see. Even shaking would tell him nothing for as the plaster was wet it was probable that the pearl would adhere to it – as, in fact, it has done. Beppo did not despair, and he conducted his search with considerable ingenuity and perseverance. Through a cousin who works with Gelder he found out the retail firms who had bought the busts. He managed to find employment with Morse Hudson, and in that way tracked down three of them. The pearl was not there. Then with the help of some Italian employee, he succeeded in finding out where the other three busts had gone. The first was at Harker's. There he was dogged by his confederate, who held Beppo responsible for the loss of the pearl, and he stabbed him in the scuffle which followed.'

'If he was his confederate, why should he carry his photograph?' I asked.

'As a means of tracing him if he wished to inquire about him from any third person. That was the obvious reason. Well, after the murder I calculated that Beppo would probably hurry rather than delay his movements. He would fear that the police would read his secret, and so hastened on before they should get ahead of him. Of course, I could not say that he had not found the pearl in Harker's bust. I had not even concluded for certain that it was the pearl; but it was evident to me that he was looking for something, since he carried the bust past the other houses in order to break it in the garden which had a lamp overlooking it. Since Harker's bust was one in three, the chances were exactly as I told you – two to one against the pearl being inside it. There remained two busts, and it was obvious that he would go for the London one first. I warned the inmates of the house, so as to avoid a second tragedy, and we went down, with the happiest results. By that time, of course, I knew for certain that it was the Borgia pearl that we were after. The name of the murdered man linked the one event with the ofter. There only remained a single bust – the Reading one – and the pearl must be there. I bought it in your presence from the owner – and there it lies.'

We sat in silence for a moment.

'Well,' said Lestrade, 'I've seen you handle a good many cases, Mr Holmes, but I don't know that I ever knew a more workmanlike one than that. We're not jealous of you at Scotland Yard. No, sir, we are very proud of you, and if you come down tomorrow there's not a man, from the oldest inspector to the youngest constable, who wouldn't be glad to shake you by the hand.'

'Thank you!' said Holmes. 'Thank you!' and as he turned away it seemed to me that he was more nearly moved by the softer human emotions than I had ever seen him. A moment later he was the cold and practical thinker once more. 'Put the pearl in the safe, Watson,' said he, 'and get out the papers of the Conk-Singleton forgery case.[27] Goodbye, Lestrade. If any little problem comes your way I shall be happy, if I can, to give you a hint or two as to its solution.'

THE ABBEY GRANGE

It was on a bitterly cold and frosty morning during the winter of '97 that I was wakened by a tugging at my shoulder. It was Holmes. The candle in his hand shone upon his eager, stooping face, and told me at a glance that something was amiss.

'Come, Watson, come!' he cried. 'The game is afoot.[1] Not a word! Into your clothes and come!'

Ten minutes later we were both in a cab and rattling through the silent streets on our way to Charing Cross Station. The first faint winter's dawn was beginning to appear, and we could dimly see the occasional figure of an early workman as he passed us, blurred and indistinct in the opalescent London reek. Holmes nestled in silence into his heavy coat, and I was glad to do the same, for the air was most bitter, and neither of us had broken our fast. It was not until we had consumed some hot tea at the station, and taken our places in the Kentish train, that we were sufficiently thawed, he to speak and I to listen. Holmes drew a note from his pocket and read it aloud:

> Abbey Grange, Marsham,[2] Kent, 3.30 am
>
> My dear Mr Holmes – I should be very glad of your immediate assistance in what promises to be a most remarkable case. It is something quite in your line. Except for releasing the lady I will see that everything is kept exactly as I have found it, but I beg you not to lose an instant, as it is difficult to leave Sir Eustace there.
>
> Yours faithfully,
>
> STANLEY HOPKINS

'Hopkins has called me in seven times,[3] and on each occasion his summons has been entirely justified,' said Holmes. 'I fancy that every one of his cases has found its way into your collection, and I must admit, Watson, that you have some power of selection which atones for much which I deplore in your narratives. Your fatal habit of looking at everything from the point of view of a story instead of as a scientific exercise has ruined what might have been an instructive and even classical series of demonstrations. You slur over work of the utmost finesse and delicacy in order to dwell upon sensational details which may excite but cannot possibly instruct the reader.'

'Why do you not write them yourself?' I said, with some bitterness.

'I will, my dear Watson,[4] I will. At present I am, as you know, fairly busy, but I propose to devote my declining years to the composition of a textbook which shall focus the whole art of detection into one volume.[5] Our present research appears to be a case of murder.'

'You think this Sir Eustace is dead, then?'

'I should say so. Hopkins's writing shows considerable agitation, and he is not an emotional man. Yes, I gather there has been violence, and that the body is left for our inspection. A mere suicide would not have caused him to send for me. As to the release of the lady, it would appear that she has been locked in her room during the tragedy. We are moving in high life, Watson – crackling paper, "E. B." monogram, coat-of-arms, picturesque address. I think that friend Hopkins will live up to his reputation, and that we shall have an interesting morning. The crime was committed before twelve last night.'

'How can you possibly tell?'

'By an inspection of the trains and by reckoning the time. The local police had to be called in, they had to communicate with Scotland Yard, Hopkins had to go out, and he in turn had to send for me. All that makes a fair night's work. Well, here we are at Chislehurst Station, and we shall soon set our doubts at rest.'

A drive of a couple of miles through narrow country lanes brought us to a park gate, which was opened for us by an old lodge-keeper, whose haggard face bore the reflection of some great disaster. The avenue ran through a noble park, between lines of ancient elms, and ended in a low, widespread house, pillared in front after the fashion of Palladio.[6] The central part was evidently of a great age and shrouded in ivy, but the large windows showed that modern changes had been carried out, and one wing of the house appeared to be entirely new. The youthful figure and alert, eager face of Inspector Stanley Hopkins confronted us in the open doorway.

'I'm very glad you have come, Mr Holmes. And you, too, Dr Watson! But, indeed, if I had my time over again I should not have troubled you, for since the lady has come to herself she has given so clear an account of the affair that there is not much left for us to do. You remember that Lewisham gang of burglars?'

'What, the three Randalls?'

'Exactly; the father and two sons. It's their work. I have not a doubt of it. They did a job at Sydenham a fortnight ago, and were seen and described. Rather cool to do another so soon and so near; but it is they, beyond all doubt. It's a hanging matter this time.'

'Sir Eustace is dead, then?'

'Yes; his head was knocked in with his own poker.'

'Sir Eustace Brackenstall,[7] the driver tells me.'

'Exactly – one of the richest men in Kent. Lady Brackenstall is in the morning-room. Poor lady, she has had a most dreadful experience. She seemed half dead when I saw her first. I think you had best see her and hear her account of the facts. Then we will examine the dining-room together.'

Lady Brackenstall was no ordinary person. Seldom have I seen so graceful a figure, so womanly a presence, and so beautiful a face. She was a blonde, golden-haired, blue-eyed, and would, no doubt, have had the perfect complexion which goes with such colouring had not her recent experience left her drawn and haggard. Her sufferings were physical as well as mental, for over one eye rose a hideous, plum-coloured swelling, which her maid, a tall, austere woman, was bathing assiduously with vinegar and water. The lady lay back exhausted upon a couch, but her quick, observant gaze as we entered the room, and the alert expression of her beautiful features, showed that neither her wits nor her courage had been shaken by her terrible experience. She was enveloped in a loose dressing-gown of blue and silver, but a black sequin-covered dinner-dress was hung upon the couch beside her.

'I have told you all that happened, Mr Hopkins,' she said wearily; 'could you not repeat it for me? Well, if you think it necessary, I will tell these gentlemen what occurred. Have they been in the dining-room yet?'

'I thought they had better hear your ladyship's story first.'

'I shall be glad when you can arrange matters. It is horrible to me to think of him still lying there.' She shuddered and buried her face for a moment in her hands. As she did so the loose gown fell back from her forearm. Holmes uttered an exclamation.

'You have other injuries, madam! What is this?' Two vivid red spots stood out in one of the white, round limbs. She hastily covered it.

'It is nothing. It has no connection with the hideous business of last night. If you and your friend will sit down I will tell you all I can.

'I am the wife of Sir Eustace Brackenstall. I have been married about a year. I suppose that it is no use my attempting to conceal that our marriage has not been a happy one. I fear that all our neighbours would tell you that, even if I were to attempt to deny it. Perhaps the fault may be partly mine. I was brought up in the freer, less conventional atmosphere of South Australia, and this English life, with its proprieties and its primness, is not congenial to me. But the main reason lies in the one fact which is notorious to everyone, and that is that Sir Eustace was a confirmed drunkard. To be with such a man for an hour is unpleasant. Can you imagine what it means for a sensitive and high-spirited woman to be tied to him for day and night? It is a sacrilege, a crime, a villainy to hold that such a marriage is binding. I say that these monstrous laws of yours will bring a curse upon the land – Heaven will not let such wickedness endure.' For an instant she sat up, her cheeks flushed, and her eyes blazing from under the terrible mark upon her brow. Then the strong, soothing hand of the austere maid drew her head down on to the cushion, and the wild anger died away into passionate sobbing. At last she continued:

'I will tell you about last night. You are aware, perhaps, that in this house all servants sleep in the modern wing. This central block is made up of the dwelling-rooms, with the kitchen behind and our bedroom above. My maid Theresa sleeps above my room. There is no one else, and no sound could alarm those who are in the farther wing. This must have been well known to the robbers, or they would not have acted as they did.

'Sir Eustace retired about half-past ten. The servants had already gone to their quarters. Only my maid was up, and she had remained in her room at the top of the house until I needed her services. I sat until after eleven in this room, absorbed in a book. Then I walked round to see that all was right before I went upstairs. It was my custom to do this myself, for, as I have explained, Sir Eustace was not always to be trusted. I went into the kitchen, the butler's pantry, the gun-room, the billiard-room, the drawing-room, and finally the dining-room. As I approached the window, which is covered with thick curtains, I suddenly felt the wind blown upon my face, and realized that it was open. I flung the curtain aside, and found myself face to face with a broad-shouldered, elderly man who had just stepped into the room. The window is a long french one, which really forms a door leading to the lawn. I held my bedroom candle lit in my hand, and, by its light, behind the first man I saw two others, who were in the act of entering. I stepped back, but the fellow was on me in an instant. He caught me first by the wrist and then by the throat. I opened my mouth to scream, but he struck me a savage blow with his fist over the eye, and felled me to the ground. I must have been unconscious for a few minutes, for when I came to myself I found that they had torn down the bell-rope and had secured me tightly to the oaken chair which stands at the head of the dining-room table. I was so firmly bound that I could not move, and a handkerchief round my mouth prevented me from uttering any sound. It was at this instant that my unfortunate husband entered the room. He had evidently heard some suspicious sounds, and he came prepared for such a scene as he found. He was dressed in his shirt and trousers, with his favourite blackthorn cudgel in his hand. He rushed at one of the burglars, but another – it was the elderly man – stooped, picked the poker out of the grate, and struck him a terrible blow as he passed. He fell without a groan, and never moved again. I fainted once more, but again it could only have been a very few minutes during which I was insensible. When I opened my eyes I found that they had collected the silver from the sideboard, and they had drawn a bottle of wine which stood there. Each of them had a glass in his hand. I have already told you, have I not, that one was elderly, with a beard, and the others young, hairless lads. They might have been a father with his two sons. They talked together in whispers. Then they came over and made sure that I was still securely bound. Finally they withdrew, closing the window after them. It was quite a quarter of an hour before I got my mouth free. When I did so my screams brought the maid to my assistance. The other servants were soon alarmed, and we sent for the local police, who instantly communicated with London. That is really all I can tell you, gentlemen, and I trust that it will not be necessary for me to go over so painful a story again.'

'Any questions, Mr Holmes?' said Hopkins.

'I will not impose any further tax upon Lady Brackenstall's patience and time,' said Holmes. 'Before I go into the dining-room I should be glad to hear your experience.' He looked at the maid.

'I saw the men before ever they came into the house,' said she. 'As I sat by my bedroom window I saw three men in the moonlight down by the lodge gate yonder, but I thought nothing of it at the time. It was more than an hour after that I heard my mistress scream, and down I ran, to find her, poor lamb, just as she says, and him on the floor with his blood and brains over the room. It was enough to drive a woman out of her wits, tied there, and her very dress spotted with him; but she never wanted courage, did Miss Mary Fraser of Adelaide, and Lady Brackenstall of Abbey Grange hasn't learned new ways. You've questioned her long enough, you gentlemen, and now she is coming to her own room, just with her old Theresa, to get the rest that she badly needs.'

With a motherly tenderness the gaunt woman put her arm round her mistress and led her from the room.

'She has been with her all her life,' said Hopkins. 'Nursed her as a baby, and came with her to England when they first left Australia eighteen months ago. Theresa Wright is her name, and the kind of maid you don't pick up nowadays. This way, Mr Holmes, if you please!'

The keen interest had passed out of Holmes's expressive face, and

I knew that with the mystery all the charm of the case had departed. There still remained an arrest to be effected, but what were these commonplace rogues that he should soil his hands with them? An abstruse and learned specialist who finds that he has been called in for a case of measles would experience something of the annoyance which I read in my friend's eyes. Yet the scene in the dining-room of the Abbey Grange was sufficiently strange to arrest his attention and to recall his waning interest.

It was a very large and high chamber, with carved oak ceiling, oaken panelling, and a fine array of deers' heads and ancient weapons around the walls. At the farther end from the door was the high French window of which we had heard. Three smaller windows on the right-hand side filled the apartment with cold winter sunshine. On the left was a large, deep fireplace, with a massive over-hanging oak mantelpiece. Beside the fireplace was a heavy oaken chair with arms and cross-bars at the bottom. In and out through the open woodwork was woven a crimson cord, which was secured at each side to the crosspiece below. In releasing the lady the cord had been slipped off her, but the knots with which it had been secured still remained. These details only struck our attention afterwards, for our thoughts were entirely absorbed by the terrible object which lay spread upon the tiger-skin hearthrug in front of the fire.

It was the body of a tall, well-made man, about forty years of age. He lay upon his back, his face upturned, with his white teeth grinning through his short, black beard. His two clenched hands were raised above his head, and a heavy blackthorn stick lay across them. His dark, handsome, aquiline features were convulsed into a spasm of vindictive hatred, which had set his dead face in a terribly fiendish expression. He had evidently been in his bed when the alarm had broken out, for he wore a foppish, embroidered night-shirt, and his bare feet projected from his trousers. His head was horribly injured, and the whole room bore witness to the savage ferocity of the blow which had struck him down. Beside him lay the heavy poker, bent into a curve by the concussion. Holmes examined both it and the indescribable wreck which it had wrought.

'He must be a powerful man, this elder Randall,' he remarked.

'Yes,' said Hopkins. 'I have some record of the fellow, and he is a rough customer.'

'You should have no difficulty in getting him.'

'Not the slightest. We have been on the lookout for him, and there was some idea that he had got away to America. Now we know that the gang are here I don't see how they can escape. We have the news at every seaport already, and a reward will be offered before evening. What beats me is how they could have done so mad a thing, knowing that the lady would describe them, and that we could not fail to recognize the description.'

'Exactly. One would have expected that they would have silenced Lady Brackenstall as well.'

'They may not have realized,' I suggested, 'that she had recovered from her faint.'

'That is likely enough. If she seemed to be senseless they would not take her life. What about this poor fellow, Hopkins? I seem to have heard some queer stories about him.'

'He was a good-hearted man when he was sober, but a perfect fiend when he was drunk, or rather when he was half drunk, for he seldom really went the whole way. The devil seemed to be in him at such times, and he was capable of anything. From what I hear, in spite of all his wealth and his title, he very nearly came our way once or twice. There was a scandal about his drenching a dog with petroleum and setting it on fire – her ladyship's dog, to make the matter worse – and that was only hushed up with difficulty. Then he threw a decanter at that maid Theresa Wright; there was trouble about that. On the whole, and between ourselves, it will be a brighter house without him. What are you looking at now?'

Holmes was down on his knees examining with great attention the knots upon the red cord with which the lady had been secured. Then he carefully scrutinized the broken and frayed end where it had snapped off when the burglar had dragged it down.

'When this was pulled down the bell in the kitchen must have rung loudly,' he remarked.

'No one could hear it. The kitchen stands right at the back of the house.'

'How did the burglar know no one would hear it? How dare he pull at a bell-rope in that reckless fashion?'

'Exactly, Mr Holmes, exactly. You put the very question which I have asked myself again and again. There can be no doubt that this fellow must have known the house and its habits. He must have perfectly understood that the servants would all be in bed at that comparatively early hour, and that no one could possibly hear a bell ring in the kitchen. Therefore he must have been in close league with one of the servants. Surely that is evident. But there are eight servants, and all of good character.'

'Other things being equal,' said Holmes, 'one would suspect the one at whose head the master threw a decanter. And yet that would involve treachery towards the mistress to whom this woman seems devoted. Well, well, the point is a minor one, and when you have Randall you will probably find no difficulty in securing his accomplices. The lady's story certainly seems to be corroborated, if it needed corroboration, by every detail which we see before us.' He walked to the french window and threw it open. 'There are no signs here, but the ground is iron hard, and one would not expect them. I see that these candles on the mantelpiece have been lighted.'

'Yes, it was by their light and that of the lady's bedroom candle that the burglars saw their way about.'

'And what did they take?'

'Well, they did not take much – only half a dozen articles of plate off the sideboard. Lady Brackenstall thinks that they were themselves so disturbed by the death of Sir Eustace that they did not ransack the house as they would otherwise have done.'

'No doubt that is true. And yet they drank some wine, I understand.'

'To steady their own nerves.'

'Exactly. These three glasses upon the sideboard have been untouched, I suppose?'

'Yes; and the bottle stands as they left it.'

'Let us look at it. Halloa, halloa! what is this?'

The three glasses were grouped together, all of them tinged with wine, and one of them containing some dregs of beeswing.[8] The bottle stood near them, two-thirds full, and beside it lay a long, deeply stained cork. Its appearance and the dust upon the bottle showed that it was no common vintage which the murderers had enjoyed.

A change had come over Holmes's manner. He had lost his listless expression, and again I saw an alert light of interest in his keen deep-set eyes. He raised the cork and examined it minutely.

'How did they draw it?' he asked.

Hopkins pointed to a half-opened drawer. In it lay some table linen and a corkscrew.

'Did Lady Brackenstall say that screw was used?'

'No; you remember that she was senseless at the moment when the bottle was opened.'

'Quite so. As a matter of fact, that screw was *not* used. This bottle was opened by a pocket-screw, probably contained in a knife, and not more than an inch and a half long. If you examine the top of the cork you will observe that the screw was driven in three times before the cork was extracted. It has never been transfixed. This long screw would have transfixed it and drawn it with a single pull. When you catch this fellow you will find that he has one of these multiplex knives in his possession.'

'Excellent!' said Hopkins.

'But these glasses do puzzle me, I confess. Lady Brackenstall actually *saw* the three men drinking, did she not?'

'Yes; she was clear about that.'

'Then there is an end of it. What more is to be said? And yet you must admit that the three glasses are very remarkable, Hopkins. What, you see nothing remarkable? Well, well, let it pass. Perhaps when a man has special knowledge and special powers like my own it rather encourages him to seek a complex explanation when a simpler one is at hand. Of course, it must be a mere chance about the glasses. Well, good morning, Hopkins, I don't see that I can be of any use to you, and you appear to have your case very clear. You will let me know when Randall is arrested, and any further developments which may occur. I trust that I shall soon have to congratulate you upon a successful conclusion. Come, Watson, I fancy that we may employ ourselves more profitably at home.'

During our return journey I could see by Holmes's face that he was much puzzled by something which he had observed. Every now and then, by an effort, he would throw off the impression and talk as if the matter were clear, but then his doubts would settle down upon him again, and his knitted brows and abstracted eyes would show that his thoughts had gone back once more to the great dining-room of the Abbey Grange in which this midnight tragedy had been enacted. At last, by a sudden impulse, just as our train was crawling out of a suburban station, he sprang on to the platform and pulled me out after him.

'Excuse me, my dear fellow,' said he, as we watched the rear carriages of our train disappearing round a curve; 'I am sorry to make you the victim of what may seem a mere whim, but on my life, Watson, I simply *can't* leave that case in this condition. Every instinct that I possess cries out against it. It's wrong – it's all wrong – I'll swear that it's wrong. And yet the lady's story was complete, the maid's corroboration was sufficient, the detail was fairly exact. What have I to put against that? Three wine-glasses, that is all. But if I had not taken things for granted, if I had examined everything with the care which I would have shown had we approached the case *de novo*[9] and had no cut-and-dried story to warp my mind, would I not then have found something more definite to go upon? Of course I should. Sit down on this bench, Watson, until a train for Chislehurst arrives, and allow me to lay the evidence before you, imploring you in the first instance to dismiss from your mind the idea that anything which the maid or mistress may have said must necessarily be true. The lady's charming personality must not be permitted to warp our judgment.

'Surely there are details in her story which, if we look at it in cold blood, would excite our suspicion. These burglars made a considerable haul at Sydenham a fortnight ago. Some account of them and their appearance was in the papers, and would naturally occur to anyone who wished to invent a story in which imaginary robbers should play a part. As a matter of fact, burglars who have done a good stroke of business are, as a rule, only too glad to enjoy the proceeds in peace and quiet without embarking on another perilous undertaking. Again, it is unusual for burglars to strike a lady to prevent her screaming, since one would imagine that was the sure way to make her scream;

it is unusual for them to commit murder when their numbers are sufficient to overpower one man; it is unusual for them to be content with a limited plunder when there is much more within their reach; and, finally, I should say that it was very unusual for such men to leave a bottle half empty. How do all these unusuals strike you, Watson?'

'Their cumulative effect is certainly considerable, and yet each of them is quite possible in itself. The most unusual thing of all, as it seems to me, is that the lady should be tied to the chair.'

'Well, I am not so sure about that, Watson, for it is evident that they must either kill her or else secure her in such a way that she could not give immediate notice of their escape. But at any rate I have shown, have I not, that there is a certain element of improbability about the lady's story? And now on the top of this comes the incident of the wine-glasses.'

'What about the wine-glasses?'

'Can you see them in your mind's eye?'

'I see them clearly.'

'We are told that three men drank from them. Does that strike you as likely?'

'Why not? There was wine in each glass.'

'Exactly; but there was beeswing only in one glass. You must have noticed that fact. What does that suggest to your mind?'

'The last glass filled would be most likely to contain beeswing.'

'Not at all. The bottle was full of it, and it is inconceivable that the first two glasses were clear and the third heavily charged with it. There are two possible explanations, and only two. One is that after the second glass was filled the bottle was violently agitated, and so the third glass received the beeswing. That does not appear probable. No, no; I am sure that I am right.'

'What, then, do you suppose?'

'That only two glasses were used, and that the dregs of both were poured into a third glass, so as to give the false impression that three people had been there. In that way all the beeswing would be in the last glass, would it not? Yes, I am convinced that this is so. But if I have hit upon the true explanation of this one small phenomenon, then in an instant the case rises from the commonplace to the exceedingly remarkable, for it can only mean that Lady Brackenstall and her maid have deliberately lied to us, that not one word of their story is to be believed, that they have some very strong reason for covering the real criminal, and that we must construct our case for ourselves without any help from them. That is the mission which now lies before us, and here, Watson, is the Chislehurst train.'

The household of the Abbey Grange were much surprised at our return, but Sherlock Holmes, finding that Stanley Hopkins had gone off to report to headquarters, took possession of the dining-room, locked the door upon the inside and devoted himself for two hours to one of those minute and laborious investigations which formed the solid basis on which his brilliant edifices of deduction were reared. Seated in a corner like an interested student who observes the demonstration of his professor, I followed every step of that remarkable research. The window, the curtains, the carpet, the chair, the rope – each in turn was minutely examined and duly pondered. The body of the unfortunate baronet had been removed, but all else remained as we had seen it in the morning. Then, to my astonishment, Holmes climbed up on to the massive mantelpiece. Far above his head hung the few inches of red cord which were still attached to the wire. For a long time he gazed upwards at it, and then in an attempt to get nearer to it he rested his knee upon a wooden bracket on the wall. This brought his hand within a few inches of the broken end of the rope; but it was not this so much as the bracket itself which seemed to engage his attention. Finally he sprang down with an ejaculation of satisfaction.

'It's all right, Watson,' said he. 'We have got our case – one of the most remarkable in our collection. But, dear me, how slow-witted I have been, and how nearly I have committed the blunder of my lifetime! Now, I think that with a few missing links my chain is almost complete.'

'You have got your men?'

'Man, Watson, man. Only one, but a very formidable person. Strong as a lion – witness the blow which bent that poker. Six foot three in height, active as a squirrel, dexterous with his fingers; finally, remarkably quick-witted, for this whole ingenious story is of his concoction. Yes, Watson, we have come upon the handiwork of a very remarkable individual. And yet in that bell-rope he has given us a clue which should not have left us a doubt.'

'Where was the clue?'

'Well, if you were to pull down a bell-rope, Watson, where would you expect it to break? Surely at the spot where it is attached to the wire. Why should it break three inches from the top as this one has done?'

'Because it is frayed there?'

'Exactly. This end, which we can examine, is frayed. He was cunning enough to do that with his knife. But the other end is not frayed. You could not observe that from here, but if you were on the mantelpiece you would see that it is cut clean off without any mark of fraying whatever. You can reconstruct what occurred. The man needed the rope. He would not tear it down for fear of giving the alarm by ringing the bell. What did he do? He sprang up on the mantelpiece, could not quite reach it, put his knee on the bracket – you will see the impression in the dust – and got his knife to bear upon the cord. I could not reach the place by at least three inches, from which I infer that he is at least three inches a bigger man than I. Look at that mark upon the seat of the oaken chair! What is it?'

'Blood.'

'Undoubtedly it is blood. This alone puts the lady's story out of court. If she were seated on the chair when the crime was done, how comes that mark? No, no; she was placed in the chair *after* the death of her husband. I'll wager that the black dress shows a corresponding mark to this. We have not yet met our Waterloo, Watson, but this is our Marengo,[10] for it begins in defeat and ends in victory. I should like now to have a few words with the nurse Theresa. We must be wary for a while, if we are to get the information which we want.'

She was an interesting person, this stern Australian nurse. Taciturn, suspicious, ungracious, it took some time before Holmes's pleasant manner and frank acceptance of all that she said thawed her into a corresponding amiability. She did not attempt to conceal her hatred for her late employer.

'Yes, sir, it is true that he threw the decanter at me. I heard him call my mistress a name, and I told him that he would not dare to speak so if her brother had been there. Then it was that he threw it at me. He might have thrown a dozen if he had but left my bonny bird alone. He was for ever ill-treating her, and she was too proud to complain. She will not even tell me all that he has done to her. She never told me of those marks on her arm that you saw this morning, but I know very well that they come from a stab with a hat-pin. The sly fiend – Heaven forgive me that I should speak of him so, now that he is dead, but a fiend he was if ever one walked the earth. He was all honey when we first met him, only eighteen months ago, and we both feel as if it were eighteen years. She had only just arrived in London. Yes, it was her first voyage – she had never been from home before. He won her with his title and his money and his false London ways. If she made a mistake she has paid for it, if ever a woman did. What month did we meet him? Well, I tell you it was just after we arrived. We arrived in June, and it was July. They were married in January of last year. Yes, she is down in the morning-room again, and I have no doubt she will see you, but you must not ask too much of her, for she has gone through all that flesh and blood will stand.'

Lady Brackenstall was reclining on the same couch, but looked brighter than before. The maid had entered with us, and began once more to foment the bruise upon her mistress's brow.

'I hope,' said the lady, 'that you have not come to cross-examine me again?'

'No,' Holmes answered, in his gentlest voice, 'I will not cause you any unnecessary trouble, Lady Brackenstall, and my whole desire is to make things easy for you, for I am convinced that you are a much-tried woman. If you will treat me as a friend and trust me, you may find that I will justify your trust.'

'What do you want me to do?'

'To tell me the truth.'

'Mr Holmes!'

'No, no, Lady Brackenstall, it is no use. You may have heard of any little reputation which I possess. I will stake it all on the fact that your story is an absolute fabrication.'

Mistress and maid were both staring at Holmes with pale faces and frightened eyes.

'You are an impudent fellow!' cried Theresa. 'Do you mean to say that my mistress has told a lie?'

Holmes rose from his chair.

'Have you nothing to tell me?'

'I have told you everything.'

'Think once more, Lady Brackenstall. Would it not be better to be frank?'

For an instant there was hesitation in her beautiful face. Then some new strong thought caused it to set like a mask.

'I have told you all I know.'

Holmes took his hat and shrugged his shoulders. 'I am sorry,' he said, and without another word we left the room and the house. There was a pond in the park, and to this my friend led the way. It was frozen over, but a single hole was left for the convenience of a solitary swan. Holmes gazed at it, and then passed on to the lodge gate. There he scribbled a short note for Stanley Hopkins, and left it with the lodgekeeper.

'It may be a hit, or it may be a miss, but we are bound to do something for friend Hopkins, just to justify this second visit,' said he. 'I will not quite take him into my confidence yet. I think our next scene of operations must be the shipping office of the Adelaide–Southampton line, which stands at the end of Pall Mall,[11] if I remember right. There is a second line of steamers which connect South Australia with England, but we will draw the larger cover first.'

Holmes's card sent in to the manager ensured instant attention, and he was not long in acquiring all the information which he needed. In June of '95 only one of their line had reached a home port. It was the *Rock of Gibraltar*, their largest and best boat. A reference to the passenger list showed that Miss Fraser of Adelaide, with her maid, had made the voyage in her. The boat was now on her way to Australia, somewhere to the south of the Suez Canal. Her officers were the same as in '95, with one exception. The first officer, Mr Jack Croker, had been made a captain, and was to take charge of their new ship, the *Bass Rock*, sailing in two days' time from Southampton. He lived at Sydenham, but he was likely to be in that morning for instructions, if we cared to wait for him.

No; Mr Holmes had no desire to see him, but would be glad to know more about his record and character.

His record was magnificent. There was not an officer in the fleet to touch him. As to his character, he was reliable on duty, but a wild, desperate fellow off the deck of his ship, hot-headed, excitable, but loyal, honest, and kind-hearted. That was the pith of the information with which Holmes left the office of the Adelaide–Southampton Company. Thence he drove to Scotland Yard,[12] but instead of entering he sat in his cab, with his brows drawn down, lost in profound thought. Finally he drove round to the Charing Cross telegraph office, sent off a message, and then, at last, we made for Baker Street once more.

'No, I couldn't do it, Watson,' said he, as we re-entered our room. 'Once that warrant was made out nothing on earth would save him. Once or twice in my career I feel that I have done more real harm by my discovery of the criminal than ever he had done by his crime. I have learned caution now, and I had rather play tricks with the law of England than with my own conscience. Let us know a little more before we act.'

Before evening we had a visit from Inspector Stanley Hopkins. Things were not going very well with him.

'I believe that you are a wizard, Mr Holmes. I really do sometimes think that you have powers that are not human. Now, how on earth could you know that the stolen silver was at the bottom of that pond?'

'I didn't know it.'

'But you told me to examine it.'

'You got it then?'

'Yes, I got it.'

'I am very glad if I have helped you.'

'But you haven't helped me. You have made the affair far more difficult. What sort of burglars are they who steal silver and then throw it into the nearest pond?'

'It was certainly rather eccentric behaviour. I was merely going on the idea that if the silver had been taken by persons who did not want it, who merely took it for a blind, as it were, then they would naturally be anxious to get rid of it.'

'But why should such an idea cross your mind?'

'Well, I thought it was possible. When they came out through the french window there was the pond, with one tempting little hole in the ice right in front of their noses. Could there be a better hiding-place?'

'Ah, a hiding-place – that is better!' cried Stanley Hopkins. 'Yes, yes, I see it all now! It was early, there were folk upon the roads, they were afraid of being seen with the silver, so they sank it in the pond, intending to return for it when the coast was clear. Excellent, Mr Holmes – that is better than your idea of a blind.'

'Quite so; you have an admirable theory. I have no doubt that my own ideas were quite wild, but you must admit that they have ended in discovering the silver.'

'Yes, sir; yes. It was all your doing. But I have had a bad set-back.'

'A set-back?'

'Yes, Mr Holmes. The Randall gang were arrested in New York this morning.'

'Dear me, Hopkins. That is certainly rather against your theory that they committed a murder in Kent last night.'

'It is fatal, Mr Holmes, absolutely fatal. Still, there are other gangs of three besides the Randalls, or it may be some new gang of which the police have never heard.'

'Quite so; it is perfectly possible. What, are you off?'

'Yes, Mr Holmes; there is no rest for me until I have got to the bottom of the business. I suppose you have no hint to give me?'

'I have given you one.'

'Which?'

'Well, I suggested a blind.'

'But why, Mr Holmes, why?'

'Ah, that's the question, of course. But I commend the idea to your mind. You might possibly find that there was something in it. You won't stop for dinner? Well, goodbye, and let us know how you get on.'

Dinner was over and the table cleared before Holmes alluded to

THE RETURN OF SHERLOCK HOLMES

the matter again. He had lit his pipe, and held his slippered feet to the cheerful blaze of the fire. Suddenly he looked at his watch.

'I expect developments, Watson.'

'When?'

'Now – within a few minutes. I dare say you thought I acted rather badly to Stanley Hopkins just now?'

'I trust your judgement.'

'A very sensible reply, Watson. You must look at it this way; what I know is unofficial; what he knows is official. I have the right to private judgement, but he has none. He must disclose all, or he is a traitor to his service. In a doubtful case I would not put him in so painful a position, and so I reserve my information until my own mind is clear upon the matter.'

'But when will that be?'

'The time has come. You will now be present at the last scene of a remarkable little drama.'

There was a sound upon the stairs, and our door was opened to admit as fine a specimen of manhood as ever passed through it. He was a very tall young man, golden-moustached, blue-eyed, with a skin which had been burned by tropical suns, and a springy step which showed that the huge frame was as active as it was strong. He closed the door behind him, and then he stood with clenched hands and heaving breast choking down some overmastering emotion.

'Sit down, Captain Croker. You got my telegram?'

Our visitor sank into an armchair and looked from one to the other of us with questioning eyes.

'I got your telegram, and I came at the hour you said. I heard that you had been down to the office. There was no getting away from you. Let's hear the worst. What are you going to do with me? Arrest me? Speak out, man! You can't sit there and play with me like a cat with a mouse.'

'Give him a cigar,' said Holmes. 'Bite on that, Captain Croker, and don't let your nerves run away with you. I should not sit here smoking with you if I thought that you were a common criminal, you may be sure of that. Be frank with me, and we may do some good. Play tricks with me, and I'll crush you.'

'What do you wish me to do?'

'To give me a true account of all that happened at the Abbey Grange last night – a *true* account, mind you, with nothing added and nothing taken off. I know so much already that if you go one inch off the straight I'll blow this police whistle from my window and the affair goes out of my hands for ever.'

The sailor thought for a little. Then he struck his leg with his great sunburnt hand.

'I'll chance it,' he cried. 'I believe you are a man of your word, and a white man,[13] and I'll tell you the whole story. But one thing I will say first. So far as I am concerned, I regret nothing and I fear nothing, and I would do it all again and be proud of the job. Curse the beast – if he had as many lives as a cat he would owe them all to me! But it's the lady, Mary – Mary Fraser – for never will I call her by that accursed name. When I think of getting her into trouble, I who would give my life just to bring one smile to her dear face, it's that that turns my soul into water. And yet – and yet – what less could I do? I'll tell you my story, gentlemen, and then I'll ask you as man to man what less could I do.

'I must go back a bit. You seem to know everything, so I expect that you know that I met her when she was a passenger and I was the first officer of the *Rock of Gibraltar*. From the first day I met her she was the only woman to me. Every day of that voyage I loved her more, and many a time since have I kneeled down in the darkness of the night watch and kissed the deck of that ship because I knew her dear feet had trod it. She was never engaged to me. She treated me as fairly as ever a woman treated a man. I have no complaint to make. It was all love on my side, and all good comradeship and friendship on hers. When we parted she was a free woman, but I could never again be a free man.

'Next time I came back from sea I heard of her marriage. Well, why shouldn't she marry whom she liked? Title and money – who could carry them better than she? She was born for all that is beautiful and dainty. I didn't grieve over her marriage. I was not such a selfish hound as that. I just rejoiced that good luck had come her way, and that she had not thrown herself away on a penniless sailor. That's how I loved Mary Fraser.

'Well, I never thought to see her again; but last voyage I was promoted, and the new boat was not yet launched, so I had to wait for a couple of months with my people at Sydenham. One day out in a country lane I met Theresa Wright, her old maid. She told me about her, about him, about everything. I tell you, gentlemen, it nearly drove me mad. This drunken hound, that he should dare to raise his hand to her whose boots he was not worthy to lick! I met Theresa again. Then I met Mary herself – and met her again. Then she would meet me no more. But the other day I had a notice that I was to start on my voyage within a week, and I determined that I would see her once before I left. Theresa was always my friend, for she loved Mary and hated this villain almost as much as I did. From her I learned the ways of the house. Mary used to sit up reading in her own little room downstairs. I crept round there last night and scratched at the window. At first she would not open to me, but in her heart I know that now she loves me, and she could not leave me in the frosty night. She whispered to me to come round to the big front window, and I found it open before me so as to let me into the dining-room. Again I heard from her own lips things that made my blood boil, and again I cursed this brute who mishandled the woman that I loved. Well, gentlemen, I was standing with her just inside the window, in all innocence, as Heaven is my judge, when he rushed like a madman into the room, called her the vilest name that a man could use to a woman, and welted her across the face with the stick he had in his hand. I had sprung for the poker, and it was a fair fight between us. See here on my arm where his first blow fell. Then it was my turn, and I went through him as if he had been a rotten pumpkin. Do you think I was sorry? Not I! It was his life or mine; but far more than that – it was his life or hers, for how could I leave her in the power of this madman? That was how I killed him. Was I wrong? Well, then, what would either of you gentlemen have done if you had been in my position?

'She had screamed when he struck her, and that brought old Theresa down from the room above. There was a bottle of wine on the sideboard, and I opened it and poured a little between Mary's lips, for she was half dead with the shock. Then I took a drop myself. Theresa was as cool as ice, and it was her plot as much as mine. We must make it appear that burglars had done the thing. Theresa kept on repeating our story to her mistress, while I swarmed up and cut the rope of the bell. Then I lashed her in her chair, and frayed out the end of the rope to make it look natural, else they would wonder how in the world a burglar could have got up there to cut it. Then I gathered up a few plates and pots of silver, to carry out the idea of a robbery, and there I left them, with orders to give the alarm when I had a quarter of an hour's start. I dropped the silver into the pond and made off for Sydenham, feeling that for once in my life I had done a real good night's work. And that's the truth and the whole truth, Mr Holmes, if it costs me my neck.'

Holmes smoked for some time in silence. Then he crossed the room and shook our visitor by the hand.

'That's what I think,' said he. 'I know that every word is true, for you have hardly said a word which I did not know. No one but an acrobat or a sailor could have got up to the bell-rope from the bracket, and no one but a sailor could have made the knots[14] with which the cord was fastened to the chair. Only once had this lady been brought into contact with sailors, and that was on her voyage, and it was someone of her own class of life, since she was trying hard to shield him and so showing that she loved him. You see how easy it was for me to lay my hands upon you when once I had started upon the right trail.'

'I thought the police never could have seen through our dodge.'

'And the police haven't; nor will they, to the best of my belief. Now, look here, Captain Croker, this is a very serious matter, though I am willing to admit that you acted under the most extreme provocation to which any man could be subjected. I am not sure that in defence of your own life your action will not be pronounced legitimate. However, that is for a British jury to decide. Meanwhile I have so much sympathy for you that if you choose to disappear in the next twenty-four hours I will promise you that no one will hinder you.'

'And then it will all come out?'

'Certainly it will come out.'

The sailor flushed with anger.

'What sort of proposal is that to make to a man? I know enough of law to understand that Mary would be had as accomplice. Do you think I would leave her alone to face the music while I slunk away? No, sir; let them do their worst upon me, but for Heaven's sake, Mr Holmes, find some way of keeping my poor Mary out of the courts.'

Holmes for the second time held out his hand to the sailor.

'I was only testing you, and you ring true every time. Well, it is a great responsibility that I take upon myself, but I have given Hopkins an excellent hint, and if he can't avail himself of it I can do no more. See here, Captain Croker, we'll do this in due form of law. You are the prisoner. Watson, you are a British jury, and I never met a man who was more eminently fitted to represent one. I am the judge. Now, gentlemen of the jury, you have heard the evidence. Do you find the prisoner guilty or not guilty?'

'Not guilty, my lord,' said I.

'*Vox populi, vox Dei.*[15] You are acquitted, Captain Croker. So long as the law does not find some other victim, you are safe from me. Come back to this lady in a year, and may her future and yours justify us in the judgment which we have pronounced this night.'

His Last Bow

CONTENTS

THE ADVENTURE OF THE
BRUCE-PARTINGTON PLANS

In the third week of November, in the year 1895, a dense yellow fog settled down upon London. From the Monday to the Thursday I doubt whether it was ever possible from our windows in Baker Street to see the loom of the opposite houses. The first day Holmes had spent in cross-indexing his huge book of references. The second and third had been patiently occupied upon a subject which he had recently made his hobby – the music of the Middle Ages. But when, for the fourth time, after pushing back our chairs from breakfast we saw the greasy, heavy brown swirl still drifting past us and condensing in oily drops upon the window-panes, my comrade's impatient and active nature could endure this drab existence no longer. He paced restlessly about our sitting-room in a fever of suppressed energy, biting his nails, tapping the furniture, and chafing against inaction.

'Nothing of interest in the paper, Watson?' he said.

I was aware that by anything of interest, Holmes meant anything of criminal interest. There was the news of a revolution,[1] of a possible war,[2] and of an impending change of Government,[3] but these did not come within the horizon of my companion. I could see nothing recorded in the shape of crime which was not commonplace and futile. Holmes groaned and resumed his restless meanderings.

'The London criminal is certainly a dull fellow,' said he, in the querulous voice of the sportsman whose game has failed him. 'Look out of this window, Watson. See how the figures loom up, are dimly seen, and then blend once more into the cloud-bank. The thief or the murderer could roam London on such a day as the tiger does the jungle, unseen until he pounces, and then evident only to his victim.'

'There have,' said I, 'been numerous petty thefts.'

Holmes snorted his contempt.

'This great and sombre stage is set for something more worthy than that,' said he. 'It is fortunate for this community that I am not a criminal.'

'It is, indeed!' said I, heartily.

'Suppose that I were Brooks or Woodhouse, or any of the fifty men who have good reason for taking my life, how long could I survive against my own pursuit? A summons, a bogus appointment, and all would be over. It is well they don't have days of fog in the Latin countries – the countries of assassination. By Jove! here comes something at last to break our dead monotony.'

It was the maid with a telegram. Holmes tore it open and burst out laughing.

'Well, well! What next?' said he. 'Brother Mycroft is coming round.'

'Why not?' I asked.

'Why not? It is as if you met a tram-car coming down a country lane. Mycroft has his rails and he runs on them. His Pall Mall lodgings, the Diogenes Club,[4] Whitehall – that is his cycle. Once, and only once, he has been here.[5] What upheaval can possibly have derailed him?'

'Does he not explain?'

Holmes handed me his brother's telegram.

'Must see you over Cadogan West. Coming at once, MYCROFT.'

'Cadogan West? I have heard the name.'

'It recalls nothing to my mind. But that Mycroft should break out in this erratic fashion! A planet might as well leave its orbit. By the way, do you know what Mycroft is?'

I had some vague recollection of an explanation at the time of the Adventure of the Greek Interpreter.

'You told me that he had some small office under the British Government.'

Holmes chuckled.

'I did not know you quite so well in those days. One has to be discreet when one talks of high matters of state. You are right in thinking that he is under the British Government. You would also be right in a sense if you said that occasionally he *is* the British Government.'

'My dear Holmes!'

'I thought I might surprise you. Mycroft draws four hundred and fifty pounds a year, remains a subordinate, has no ambitions of any kind, will receive neither honour nor title, but remains the most indispensable man in the country.'

'But how?'

'Well, his position is unique. He has made it for himself. There has never been anything like it before, nor will be again. He has the tidiest and most orderly brain, with the greatest capacity for storing facts, of any man living. The same great powers which I have turned to the detection of crime he has used for this particular business. The conclusions of every department are passed to him, and he is the central exchange, the clearing-house, which makes out the balance. All other men are specialists, but his specialism is omniscience. We will suppose that a Minister needs information as to a point which involves the Navy, India, Canada and the bimetallic question[6]; he could get his separate advices from various departments upon each, but only Mycroft can focus them all, and say off-hand how each factor would affect the other. They began by using him as a short-cut, a convenience; now he has made himself an essential. In that great brain of his everything is pigeon-holed, and can be handed out in an instant. Again and again his word has decided the national policy. He lives in it. He thinks of nothing else save when, as an intellectual exercise, he unbends if I call upon him and ask him to advise me on one of my little problems. But Jupiter is descending today. What on earth can it mean? Who is Cadogan West, and what is he to Mycroft?'[7]

'I have it,' I cried, and plunged among the litter of papers upon the sofa. 'Yes, yes, here he is, sure enough! Cadogan West was the young man who was found dead on the Underground on Tuesday morning.'

Holmes sat up at attention, his pipe half-way to his lips.

'This must be serious, Watson. A death which has caused my brother to alter his habits can be no ordinary one. What in the world can he have to do with it? The case was featureless as I remember it. The young man had apparently fallen out of the train and killed himself. He had not been robbed, and there was no particular reason to suspect violence. Is that not so?'

'There has been an inquest,' said I, 'and a good many fresh facts have come out. Looked at more closely, I should certainly say that it was a curious case.'

'Judging by its effect upon my brother, I should think it must be a most extraordinary one.' He snuggled down in his armchair. 'Now, Watson, let us have the facts.'

'The man's name was Arthur Cadogan West. He was twenty-seven years of age, unmarried, and a clerk at Woolwich Arsenal.'[8]

'Government employ. Behold the link with brother Mycroft!'

'He left Woolwich suddenly on Monday night. Was last seen by his fiancée, Miss Violet Westbury, whom he left abruptly in the fog about 7.30 that evening. There was no quarrel between them and she can give no motive for his action. The next thing heard of him was when his dead body was discovered by a plate-layer named Mason, just outside Aldgate Station[9] on the Underground system in London.'

'When?'

'The body was found at six on the Tuesday morning. It was lying wide of the metals upon the left hand of the track as one goes eastward, at a point close to the station, where the line emerges from the tunnel in which it runs. The head was badly crushed – an injury which might well have been caused by a fall from the train. The body could only have come on the line in that way. Had it been carried down from any neighbouring street, it must have passed the station barriers, where a collector is always standing. This point seems absolutely certain.'

'Very good. The case was definite enough. The man, dead or alive, either fell or was precipitated from a train. So much is clear to me. Continue.'

'The trains which traverse the lines of rail beside which the body was found are those which run from west to east, some being purely Metropolitan, and some from Willesden and out-lying junctions.[10] It can be stated for certain that this young man, when he met his death, was travelling in this direction at some late hour of the night, but at what point he entered the train it is impossible to state.'

'His ticket, of course, would show that.'

'There was no ticket in his pockets.'

'No ticket! Dear me, Watson, this is really very singular. According to my experience it is not possible to reach the platform of a Metropolitan train without exhibiting one's ticket. Presumably, then, the young man had one. Was it taken from him in order to conceal the station from which he came? It is possible. Or did he drop it in the carriage? That also is possible. But the point is of curious interest. I understand that there was no sign of robbery?'

'Apparently not. There is a list here of his possessions. His purse contained two pounds fifteen. He had also a chequebook on the Woolwich branch of the Capital and Counties Bank.[11] Through this his identity was established. There were also two dress-circle tickets for the Woolwich Theatre, dated for that very evening. Also a small packet of technical papers.'

Holmes gave an exclamation of satisfaction.

'There we have it at last, Watson! British Government – Woolwich Arsenal – Technical papers – Brother Mycroft, the chain is complete. But here he comes, if I am not mistaken, to speak for himself.'

A moment later the tall and portly form of Mycroft Holmes was ushered into the room. Heavily built and massive, there was a suggestion of uncouth physical inertia in the figure, but above this unwieldy frame there was perched a head so masterful in its brow, so alert in its steel-grey, deep-set eyes, so firm in its lips, and so subtle in its play of expression, that after the first glance one forgot the gross body and remembered only the dominant mind.

At his heels came our old friend Lestrade, of Scotland Yard – thin and austere. The gravity of both their faces foretold some weighty quest. The detective shook hands without a word. Mycroft Holmes struggled out of his overcoat and subsided into an armchair.

'A most annoying business, Sherlock,' said he. 'I extremely dislike altering my habits, but the powers that be would take no denial. In the present state of Siam[12] it is most awkward that I should be away from the office. But it is a real crisis. I have never seen the Prime Minister[13] so upset. As to the Admiralty – it is buzzing like an overturned bee-hive. Have you read up the case?'

'We have just done so. What were the technical papers?'

'Ah, there's the point! Fortunately, it has not come out. The Press would be furious if it did. The papers which this wretched youth had in his pocket were the plans of the Bruce-Partington submarine.'[14]

Mycroft Holmes spoke with a solemnity which showed his sense of the importance of the subject. His brother and I sat expectant.

'Surely you have heard of it? I thought everyone had heard of it.'

'Only as a name.'

'Its importance can hardly be exaggerated. It has been the most jealously guarded of all Government secrets.[15] You may take it from me that naval warfare becomes impossible within the radius of a Bruce-Partington's operation.[16] Two years ago a very large sum was smuggled through the Estimates[17] and was expended in acquiring a monopoly of the invention. Every effort has been made to keep the secret. The plans, which are exceedingly intricate, comprising some thirty separate patents, each essential to the working of the whole, are kept in an elaborate safe in a confidential office adjoining the Arsenal, with burglar-proof doors and windows. Under no conceivable circumstances were the plans to be taken from the office. If the Chief Constructor of the Navy desired to consult them, even he was forced to go to the Woolwich office for the purpose. And yet here we find them in the pockets of a dead junior clerk in the heart of London. From an official point of view it's simply awful.'

'But you have recovered them?'

'No, Sherlock, no! That's the pinch. We have not. Ten papers were taken from Woolwich. There were seven in the pockets of Cadogan West. The three most essential are gone – stolen, vanished. You must drop everything, Sherlock. Never mind your usual petty puzzles of the police-court. It's a vital international problem that you have to solve. Why did Cadogan West take the papers, where are the missing ones, how did he die, how came his body where it was found, how can the evil be set right? Find an answer to all these questions, and you will have done good service for your country.'

'Why do you not solve it yourself, Mycroft? You can see as far as I.'

'Possibly, Sherlock. But it is a question of getting details. Give me your details, and from an armchair I will return you an excellent expert opinion. But to run here and run there, to cross-question railway guards, and lie on my face with a lens to my eye – it is not my métier. No, you are the one man who can clear the matter up. If you have a fancy to see your name in the next honours list –'

My friend smiled and shook his head.

'I play the game for the game's own sake,' said he. 'But the problem certainly presents some points of interest, and I shall be very pleased to look into it. Some more facts, please.'

'I have jotted down the more essential ones upon this sheet of paper, together with a few addresses which you will find of service. The actual official guardian of the papers is the famous Government expert, Sir James Walter, whose decorations and sub-titles fill two lines of a book of reference. He has grown grey in the service, is a gentleman, a favoured guest in the most exalted houses, and above all a man whose patriotism is beyond suspicion. He is one of two who have a key of the safe. I may add that the papers were undoubtedly in the office during working hours on Monday, and that Sir James left for London about three o'clock taking his key with him. He was at the house of Admiral Sinclair at Barclay Square[18] during the whole of the evening when this incident occurred.'

'Has the fact been verified?'

'Yes; his brother, Colonel Valentine Walter, has testified to his departure from Woolwich, and Admiral Sinclair to his arrival in London; so Sir James is no longer a direct factor in the problem.'

'Who was the other man with a key?'

'The senior clerk and draughtsman, Mr Sidney Johnson. He is a man of forty, married, with five children. He is a silent, morose man, but he has, on the whole, an excellent record in the public service. He is unpopular with his colleagues, but a hard worker. According to his own account, corroborated only by the word of his wife, he was at home the whole of Monday evening after office hours, and his key has never left the watch-chain upon which it hangs.'

'Tell us about Cadogan West.'

'He has been ten years in the Service, and has done good work. He has the reputation of being hot-headed and impetuous, but a straight, honest man. We have nothing against him. He was next Sidney Johnson in the office. His duties brought him into daily, personal contact with the plans. No one else had the handling of them.'

'Who locked the plans up that night?'

'Mr Sidney Johnson, the senior clerk.'

'Well, it is surely perfectly clear who took them away.[19] They are actually found upon the person of this junior clerk, Cadogan West. That seems final, does it not?'

'It does, Sherlock, and yet it leaves so much unexplained. In the first place, why did he take them?'

'I presume they were of value?'

'He could have got several thousands for them very easily.'

'Can you suggest any possible motive for taking the papers to London except to sell them?'

'No, I cannot.'

'Then we must take that as our working hypothesis. Young West took the papers. Now this could only be done by having a false key –'

'Several false keys. He had to open the building and the room.'

'He had, then, several false keys. He took the papers to London to sell the secret, intending, no doubt, to have the plans themselves back in the safe next morning before they were missed. While in London on this treasonable mission he met his end.'

'How?'

'We will suppose that he was travelling back to Woolwich when he was killed and thrown out of the compartment.'

'Aldgate, where the body was found, is considerably past the station for London Bridge,[20] which would be his route to Woolwich.'

'Many circumstances could be imagined under which he would pass London Bridge.[21] There was someone in the carriage, for example, with whom he was having an absorbing interview. This interview led to a violent scene, in which he lost his life. Possibly he tried to leave the carriage, fell out on the line, and so met his end. The other closed the door. There was a thick fog, and nothing could be seen.'

'No better explanation can be given with our present knowledge;

and yet consider, Sherlock, how much you leave untouched. We will suppose, for argument's sake, that young Cadogan West *had* determined to convey these papers to London. He would naturally have made an appointment with the foreign agent and kept his evening clear. Instead of that, he took two tickets for the theatre, escorted his fiancée half way there, and then suddenly disappeared.'

'A blind,' said Lestrade, who had sat listening with some impatience to the conversation.

'A very singular one. That is objection No. 1. Objection No. 2: we will suppose that he reaches London and sees the foreign agent. He must bring back the papers before morning or the loss will be discovered. He took away ten. Only seven were in his pocket. What had become of the other three? He certainly would not leave them of his own free will. Then, again, where is the price of his treason? One would have expected to find a large sum of money in his pocket.'

'It seems to me perfectly clear,' said Lestrade. 'I have no doubt at all as to what occurred. He took the papers to sell them. He saw the agent. They could not agree as to price. He started home again, but the agent went with him. In the train the agent murdered him, took the more essential papers, and threw his body from the carriage. That would account for everything, would it not?'

'Why had he no ticket?'

'The ticket would have shown which station was nearest the agent's house. Therefore he took it from the murdered man's pocket.'

'Good, Lestrade, very good,' said Holmes. 'Your theory holds together. But if this is true, then the case is at an end. On the one hand the traitor is dead. On the other the plans of the Bruce-Partington submarine are presumably already on the Continent. What is there for us to do?'

'To act, Sherlock – to act!' cried Mycroft, springing to his feet. 'All my instincts are against this explanation. Use your powers! Go to the scene of the crime! See the people concerned! Leave no stone unturned! In all your career you have never had so great a chance of serving your country.'

'Well, well!' said Holmes, shrugging his shoulders. 'Come, Watson! And you, Lestrade, could you favour us with your company for an hour or two? We will begin our investigation by a visit to Aldgate Station. Goodbye, Mycroft. I shall let you have a report before evening, but I warn you in advance that you have little to expect.'

An hour later, Holmes, Lestrade and I, stood upon the Underground railroad at the point where it emerges from the tunnel immediately before Aldgate Station. A courteous red-faced old gentleman represented the railway company.

'This is where the young man's body lay,' said he, indicating a spot about three feet from the metals. 'It could not have fallen from above, for these, as you see, are all blank walls. Therefore, it could only have come from a train, and that train, so far as we can trace it, must have passed about midnight on Monday.'

'Have the carriages been examined for any sign of violence?'

'There are no such signs, and no ticket has been found.'

'No record of a door being found open?'

'None.'

'We have had some fresh evidence this morning,' said Lestrade. 'A passenger who passed Aldgate in an ordinary Metropolitan train about 11.40 on Monday night declares that he heard a heavy thud, as of a body striking the line, just before the train reached the station. There was dense fog, however, and nothing could be seen. He made no report of it at the time. Why, whatever is the matter with Mr Holmes?'

My friend was standing with an expression of strained intensity upon his face, staring at the railway metals where they curved out of the tunnel. Aldgate is a junction, and there was a network of points.[22] On these his eager, questioning eyes were fixed, and I saw on his keen, alert face that tightening of the lips, that quiver of the nostrils, and concentration of the heavy tufted brows which I knew so well.

'Points,' he muttered; 'the points.'

'What of it? What do you mean?'

'I suppose there are no great number of points on a system such as this?'

'No; there are very few.'

'And a curve, too. Points, and a curve. By Jove! if it were only so.'

'What is it, Mr Holmes? Have you a clue?'

'An idea – an indication, no more. But the case certainly grows in interest. Unique, perfectly unique, and yet why not? I do not see any indications of bleeding on the line.'

'There were hardly any.'

'But I understand that there was a considerable wound.'

'The bone was crushed, but there was no great external injury.'

'And yet one would have expected some bleeding. Would it be possible for me to inspect the train which contained the passenger who heard the thud of a fall in the fog?'

'I fear not, Mr Holmes. The train has been broken up before now, and the carriages redistributed.'

'I can assure you, Mr Holmes,' said Lestrade, 'that every carriage has been carefully examined. I saw to it myself.'

It was one of my friend's most obvious weaknesses that he was impatient with less alert intelligences than his own.

'Very likely,' said he, turning away. 'As it happens, it was not the carriages which I desired to examine. Watson, we have done all we can here. We need not trouble you any further, Mr Lestrade. I think our investigations must now carry us to Woolwich.'

At London Bridge Holmes wrote a telegram to his brother, which he handed to me before dispatching it. It ran thus:

See some light in the darkness, but it may possibly flicker out. Meanwhile, please send by messenger, to await return at Baker Street, a complete list of all foreign spies or international agents known to be in England, with full address.   SHERLOCK

'That should be helpful, Watson,' he remarked, as we took our seats in the Woolwich train. 'We certainly owe brother Mycroft a debt for having introduced us to what promises to be a really very remarkable case.'

His eager face still wore that expression of intense and high-strung energy, which showed me that some novel and suggestive circumstance had opened up a stimulating line of thought. See the foxhound with hanging ears and drooping tail as it lolls about the kennels, and compare it with the same hound as, with gleaming eyes and straining muscles, it runs upon a breast-high scent – such was the change in Holmes since the morning. He was a different man to the limp and lounging figure in the mouse-coloured dressing-gown who had prowled so restlessly only a few hours before round the fog-girt room.

'There is material here. There is scope,' said he. 'I am dull indeed not to have understood its possibilities.'

'Even now they are dark to me.'

'The end is dark to me also, but I have hold of one idea which may lead us far. The man met his death elsewhere, and his body was on the *roof* of a carriage.'

'On the roof!'

'Remarkable, is it not? But consider the facts. Is it a coincidence that it is found at the very point where the train pitches and sways as it comes round on the points? Is not that the place where an object upon the roof might be expected to fall off? The points would affect no object inside the train. Either the body fell from the roof, or a very curious coincidence has occurred. But now consider the question of the blood. Of course, there was no bleeding on the line if the body had bled elsewhere. Each fact is suggestive in itself. Together they have a cumulative force.'

'And the ticket, too!' I cried.

'Exactly. We could not explain the absence of a ticket. This would explain it. Everything fits together.'

'But suppose it were so, we are still as far as ever from unravelling the mystery of his death. Indeed, it becomes not simpler, but stranger.'

'Perhaps,' said Holmes, thoughtfully; 'perhaps.' He relapsed into a silent reverie, which lasted until the slow train drew up at last in Woolwich Station. There he called a cab and drew Mycroft's paper from his pocket.

'We have quite a little round of afternoon calls to make,' said he. 'I think that Sir James Walter claims our first attention.'

The house of the famous official was a fine villa with green lawns stretching down to the Thames. As we reached it the fog was lifting, and a thin, watery sunshine was breaking through. A butler answered our ring.

'Sir James, sir!' said he, with solemn face. 'Sir James died this morning.'

'Good heavens!' cried Holmes, in amazement. 'How did he die?'

'Perhaps you would care to step in, sir, and see his brother, Colonel Valentine?'

'Yes, we had best do so.'

We were ushered into a dim-lit drawing-room, where an instant later we were joined by a very tall, handsome, light-bearded man of fifty, the younger brother of the dead scientist. His wild eyes, stained cheeks, and unkempt hair all spoke of the sudden blow which had fallen upon the household. He was hardly articulate as he spoke of it.

'It was this horrible scandal,' said he. 'My brother, Sir James, was a man of very sensitive honour, and he could not survive such an affair. It broke his heart. He was always so proud of the efficiency of his department, and this was a crushing blow.'

'We had hoped that he might have given us some indications which would have helped us to clear the matter up.'

'I assure you that it was all a mystery to him as it is to you and to all of us. He had already put all his knowledge at the disposal of the police. Naturally, he had no doubt that Cadogan West was guilty. But all the rest was inconceivable.'

'You cannot throw any new light upon the affair?'

'I know nothing myself save what I have read or heard. I have no desire to be discourteous, but you can understand, Mr Holmes, that we are much disturbed at present, and I must ask you to hasten this interview to an end.'

'This is indeed an unexpected development,' said my friend when we had regained the cab. 'I wonder if the death was natural, or whether the poor old fellow killed himself! If the latter, may it be taken as some sign of self-reproach for duty neglected? We must leave that question to the future. Now we shall turn to the Cadogan Wests.'

A small but well-kept house in the outskirts of the town sheltered the bereaved mother. The old lady was too dazed with grief to be of any use to us, but at her side was a white-faced young lady, who introduced herself as Miss Violet Westbury, the fiancée of the dead man, and the last to see him upon that fatal night.

'I cannot explain it, Mr Holmes,' she said. 'I have not shut an eye since the tragedy, thinking, thinking, thinking, night and day, what the true meaning of it can be. Arthur was the most single-minded, chivalrous, patriotic man upon earth. He would have cut his right hand off before he would sell a State secret confided to his keeping. It is absurd, impossible, preposterous to anyone who knew him.'

'But the facts, Miss Westbury?'

'Yes, yes; I admit I cannot explain them.'

'Was he in any want of money?'

'No; his needs were very simple and his salary ample. He had saved a few hundreds, and we were to marry at the New Year.'

'No signs of any mental excitement? Come, Miss Westbury, be absolutely frank with us.'

The quick eye of my companion had noted some change in her manner. She coloured and hesitated.

'Yes,' she said, at last. 'I had a feeling that there was something on his mind.'

'For long?'

'Only for the last week or so. He was thoughtful and worried. Once I pressed him about it. He admitted that there was something, and that it was concerned with his official life. "It is too serious for me to speak about, even to you," said he. I could get nothing more.'

Holmes looked grave.

'Go on, Miss Westbury. Even if it seems to tell against him, go on. We cannot say what it may lead to.'

'Indeed, I have nothing more to tell. Once or twice it seemed to me that he was on the point of telling me something. He spoke one evening of the importance of the secret, and I have some recollection that he said that no doubt foreign spies would pay a great deal to have it.'

My friend's face grew graver still.

'Anything else?'

'He said that we were slack about such matters – that it would be easy for a traitor to get the plans.'

'Was it only recently that he made such remarks?'

'Yes, quite recently.'

'Now tell us of that last evening.'

'We were to go to the theatre. The fog was so thick that a cab was useless. We walked, and our way took us close to the office. Suddenly he darted away into the fog.'

'Without a word?'

'He gave an exclamation; that was all. I waited but he never returned. Then I walked home. Next morning, after the office opened, they came to inquire. About twelve o'clock we heard the terrible news. Oh, Mr Holmes, if you could only, only save his honour! It was so much to him.'

Holmes shook his head sadly.

'Come, Watson,' said he, 'our ways lie elsewhere. Our next station must be the office from which the papers were taken.

'It was black enough before against this young man, but our inquiries make it blacker,' he remarked, as the cab lumbered off. 'His coming marriage gives a motive for the crime. He naturally wanted money. The idea was in his head, since he spoke about it. He nearly made the girl an accomplice in the treason by telling her his plans. It is all very bad.'

'But surely, Holmes, character goes for something? Then, again, why should he leave the girl in the street and dart away to commit a felony?'

'Exactly! There are certainly objections. But it is a formidable case which they have to meet.'

Mr Sidney Johnson, the senior clerk, met us at the office, and received us with that respect which my companion's card always commanded. He was a thin, gruff, bespectacled man of middle age, his cheeks haggard, and his hands twitching from the nervous strain to which he had been subjected.

'It is bad, Mr Holmes, very bad! Have you heard of the death of the chief?'

'We have just come from his house.'

'The place is disorganized. The chief dead, Cadogan West dead, our papers stolen. And yet, when we closed our door on Monday evening we were as efficient an office as any in the Government service. Good God, it's dreadful to think of! That West, of all men, should have done such a thing!'

'You are sure of his guilt, then?'

'I can see no other way out of it. And yet I would have trusted him as I trust myself.'

'At what hour was the office closed on Monday?'

'At five.'

'Did you close it?'

'I am always the last man out.'

'Where were the plans?'

'In that safe. I put them there myself.'

'Is there no watchman to the building?'

'There is, but he has other departments to look after as well. He is an old soldier and a most trustworthy man. He saw nothing that evening. Of course, the fog was very thick.'

'Suppose that Cadogan West wished to make his way into the building after hours; he would need three keys, would he not, before he could reach the papers?'

'Yes, he would. The key of the outer door, the key of the office, and the key of the safe.'

'Only Sir James Walter and you had those keys?'

'I had no keys of the doors – only of the safe.'

'Was Sir James a man who was orderly in his habits?'

'Yes, I think he was. I know that so far as those three keys are concerned he kept them on the same ring. I have often seen them there.'

'And that ring went with him to London?'

'He said so.'

'And your key never left your possession?'

'Never.'

'Then West, if he is the culprit, must have had a duplicate. And yet none was found upon his body. One other point: if a clerk in this office desired to sell the plans, would it not be simpler to copy the plans for himself than to take the originals, as was actually done?'

'It would take considerable technical knowledge to copy the plans in an effective way.'

'But I suppose either Sir James, or you, or West had that technical knowledge?'

'No doubt we had, but I beg you won't try to drag me into the matter, Mr Holmes. What is the use of our speculating in this way when the original plans were actually found on West?'

'Well, it is certainly singular that he should run the risk of taking originals if he could safely have taken copies, which would have equally served his turn.'

'Singular, no doubt – and yet he did so.'

'Every inquiry in this case reveals something inexplicable. Now there are three papers still missing. They are, as I understand, the vital ones.'

'Yes, that is so.'

'Do you mean to say that anyone holding these three papers, and without the seven others, could construct a Bruce-Partington submarine?'

'I reported to that effect to the Admiralty. But today I have been over the drawings again, and I am not so sure of it. The double valves with the automatic self-adjusting slots are drawn in one of the papers which have been returned. Until the foreigners had invented that for themselves they could not make the boat. Of course, they might soon get over the difficulty.'

'But the three missing drawings are the most important?'

'Undoubtedly.'

'I think, with your permission, I will now take a stroll round the premises. I do not recall any other question which I desired to ask.'

He examined the lock of the safe, the door of the room, and finally the iron shutters of the window. It was only when we were on the lawn outside that his interest was strongly excited. There was a laurel bush outside the window, and several of the branches bore signs of having been twisted or snapped. He examined them carefully with his lens, and then some dim and vague marks upon the earth beneath. Finally he asked the chief clerk to close the iron shutters, and he pointed out to me that they hardly met in the centre, and that it would be possible for anyone outside to see what was going on within the room.

'The indications are ruined by three days' delay. They may mean something or nothing. Well, Watson, I do not think that Woolwich can help us further. It is a small crop which we have gathered. Let us see if we can do better in London.'

Yet we added one more sheaf to our harvest before we left Woolwich Station. The clerk in the ticket office was able to say with confidence that he saw Cadogan West – whom he knew well by sight – upon the Monday night. He was alone, and took a single third-class ticket. The clerk was struck at the time by his excited and nervous manner. So shaky was he that he could hardly pick up his change, and the clerk had helped him with it. A reference to the timetable showed that the 8.15 was the first train which it was possible for West to take after he had left the lady about 7.30.

'Let us reconstruct, Watson,' said Holmes, after half an hour of silence. 'I am not aware that in all our joint researches we have ever had a case which was more difficult to get at. Every fresh advance which we make only reveals a fresh ridge beyond. And yet we have surely made some appreciable progress.

'The effect of our inquiries at Woolwich has in the main been against young Cadogan West; but the indications at the window would lend themselves to a more favourable hypothesis. Let us suppose, for example, that he had been approached by some foreign agent. It might have been done under such pledges as would have prevented him from speaking of it, and yet would have affected his thoughts in the direction indicated by his remarks to his fiancée. Very good. We will now suppose that as he went to the theatre with the young lady he suddenly, in the fog, caught a glimpse of this same agent going in the direction of the office. He was an impetuous man, quick in his decisions. Everything gave way to his duty. He followed the man, reached the window, saw the abstraction of the documents, and pursued the thief. In this way we get over the objection that no one would take originals when he could make copies. This outsider had to take originals. So far it holds together.'

'What is the next step?'

'Then we come into difficulties. One would imagine that under such circumstances the first act of young Cadogan West would be to seize the villain and raise the alarm. Why did he not do so? Could it have been an official superior who took the papers? That would explain West's conduct. Or could the thief have given West the slip in the fog, and West started at once to London to head him off from his own rooms, presuming that he knew where the rooms were? The call must have been very pressing, since he left his girl standing in the fog, and made no effort to communicate with her. Our scent runs cold here, and there is a vast gap between either hypothesis and the laying of West's body, with seven papers in his pocket, on the roof of a Metropolitan train. My instinct now is to work from the other end. If Mycroft has given us the list of addresses we may be able to pick our man, and follow two tracks instead of one.'

Surely enough, a note awaited us at Baker Street. A Government messenger had brought it post-haste. Holmes glanced at it and threw it over to me.

There are numerous small fry, but few who would handle so big an affair. The only men worth considering are Adolph Meyer, of 13, Great George Street, Westminster,[23] Louis La Rothière, of Campden Mansions,[24] Notting Hill; and Hugo Oberstein, 13, Caulfield Gardens,[25] Kensington. The latter was known to be in town in Monday, and is now reported as having left. Glad to hear you have seen some light. The Cabinet awaits your final report with the utmost anxiety. Urgent representations have arrived from the very highest quarter. The whole force of the State is at your back if you should need it.

MYCROFT

'I'm afraid,' said Holmes, smiling, 'that all the Queen's horses and all the Queen's men cannot avail in this matter.' He had spread out his big map of London, and leaned eagerly over it. 'Well, well,' said he presently, with an exclamation of satisfaction, 'things are turning a little in our direction at last. Why, Watson, I do honestly believe that we are going to pull it off after all.' He slapped me on the shoulder with a sudden burst of hilarity. 'I am going out now. It is only a reconnaissance. I will do nothing serious without my trusted comrade and biographer at my elbow. Do you stay here, and the odds are that you will see me again in an hour or two. If time hangs heavy get foolscap and a pen, and begin your narrative of how we saved the State.'

I felt some reflection of his elation in my own mind, for I knew well that he would not depart so far from his usual austerity of demeanour unless there was good cause for exultation. All the long November evening I waited, filled with impatience for his return. At last, shortly after nine o'clock there arrived a messenger with a note:

Am dining at Goldini's Restaurant, Gloucester Road, Kensington. Please come at once and join me there. Bring with you a jemmy, a dark lantern, a chisel, and a revolver.   s. h.

It was a nice equipment for a respectable citizen to carry through the dim, fog-draped streets. I stowed them all discreetly away in my overcoat, and drove straight to the address given. There sat my friend at a little round table near the door of the garish Italian restaurant.

'Have you had something to eat? Then join me in a coffee and curaçao.[26] Try one of the proprietor's cigars. They are less poisonous than one would expect. Have you the tools?'

'They are here, in my overcoat.'

'Excellent. Let me give you a short sketch of what I have done, with some indication of what we are about to do. Now it must be evident to you, Watson, that this young man's body was *placed* on the roof of the train. That was clear from the instant that I determined the fact that it was from the roof, and not from a carriage, that he had fallen.'

'Could it not have been dropped from a bridge?'

'I should say it was impossible. If you examine the roofs you will find that they are slightly rounded, and there is no railing round them. Therefore, we can say for certain that young Cadogan West was placed on it.'

'How could he be placed there?'

'That was the question which we had to answer. There is only one possible way. You are aware that the Underground runs clear of tunnels at some points in the West End. I had a vague memory that as I have travelled by it I have occasionally seen windows just above my head. Now, suppose that a train halted under such a window, would there be any difficulty in laying a body upon the roof?'

'It seems most improbable.'

'We must fall back upon the old axiom that when all other contingencies fail, whatever remains, however improbable, must be the truth. Here all other contingencies *have* failed. When I found that the leading international agent, who had just left London, lived in a row of houses which abutted upon the Underground,[27] I was so pleased that you were a little astonished at my sudden frivolity.'

'Oh, that was it, was it?'

'Yes, that was it. Mr Hugo Oberstein, of 13, Caulfield Gardens, had become my objective. I began my operations at Gloucester Road Station, where a very helpful official walked with me along the track, and allowed me to satisfy myself, not only that the back-stair windows of Caulfield Gardens open on the line, but the even more essential fact that, owing to the intersection of one of the larger railways, the Underground trains are frequently held motionless for some minutes at that very spot.[28]

'Splendid, Holmes! You have got it!'

'So far – so far, Watson. We advance, but the goal is afar. Well, having seen the back of Caulfield Gardens, I visited the front and satisfied myself that the bird was indeed flown. It is a considerable house, unfurnished, so far as I could judge, in the upper rooms. Oberstein lived there with a single valet, who was probably a confederate entirely in his confidence. We must bear in mind that Oberstein has gone to the Continent to dispose of his booty, but not with any idea of flight; for he had no reason to fear a warrant, and the idea of an amateur domiciliary visit would certainly never occur to him. Yet this is precisely what we are about to make.'

'Could we not get a warrant and legalize it?'

'Hardly on the evidence.'

'What can we hope to do?'

'We cannot tell what correspondence may be there.'

'I don't like it, Holmes.'

'My dear fellow, you shall keep watch in the street. I'll do the criminal part. It's not a time to stick at trifles. Think of Mycroft's note, of the Admiralty, the Cabinet, the exalted person who waits for news. We are bound to go.'

My answer was to rise from the table.

'You are right, Holmes. We are bound to go.'

He sprang up and shook me by the hand.

'I knew you would not shrink at the last,' said he, and for a moment I saw something in his eyes which was nearer to tenderness than I had ever seen. The next instant he was his masterful, practical self once more.

'It is nearly half a mile, but there is no hurry. Let us walk,' said he. 'Don't drop the instruments, I beg. Your arrest as a suspicious character would be a most unfortunate complication.'

Caulfield Gardens was one of those lines of flat-faced, pillared, and porticoed houses which are so prominent a product of the middle Victorian epoch in the West End of London. Next door there appeared to be a children's party, for the merry buzz of young voices and the clatter of a piano resounded through the night. The fog still hung about and screened us with its friendly shade. Holmes had lit his lantern and flashed it upon the massive door.

'This is a serious proposition,' said he. 'It is certainly bolted as well as locked. We would do better in the area.[29] There is an excellent archway down yonder in case a too zealous policeman should intrude. Give me a hand, Watson, and I'll do the same for you.'

A minute later we were both in the area. Hardly had we reached the dark shadows before the step of the policeman was heard in the fog above. As its soft rhythm died away, Holmes set to work upon the lower door. I saw him stoop and strain until with a sharp crash it flew open. We sprang through into the dark passage, closing the area door behind us. Holmes led the way up the curving, uncarpeted stair. His little fan of yellow light shone upon a low window.

'Here we are, Watson – this must be the one.' He threw it open, and as he did so there was a low, harsh murmur, growing steadily into a loud roar as a train dashed past us in the darkness. Holmes swept his light along the window-sill. It was thickly coated with soot from the passing engines, but the black surface was blurred and rubbed in places.

'You can see where they rested the body. Halloa, Watson! what is this? There can be no doubt that it is a blood mark.' He was pointing to faint discolorations along the woodwork of the window. 'Here it is on the stone of the stair also. The demonstration is complete. Let us stay here until a train stops.'

We had not long to wait. The very next train roared from the tunnel as before, but slowed in the open, and then, with a creaking of brakes, pulled up immediately beneath us. It was not four feet from the window-ledge to the roof of the carriages. Holmes softly closed the window.

'So far we are justified,' said he. 'What do you think of it, Watson?'

'A masterpiece. You have never risen to a greater height.'

'I cannot agree with you there. From the moment that I conceived the idea of the body being upon the roof, which surely was not a very abstruse one, all the rest was inevitable.[30] If it were not for the grave interests involved, the affair up to this point would be insignificant. Our difficulties are still before us. But perhaps we may find something here which may help us.'

We had ascended the kitchen stair and entered the suite of rooms upon the first floor. One was a dining-room, severely furnished and containing nothing of interest. A second was a bedroom, which also drew blank. The remaining room appeared more promising, and my companion settled down to a systematic examination. It was littered with books and papers, and was evidently used as a study. Swiftly and methodically Holmes turned over the contents of drawer after drawer and cupboard after cupboard, but no gleam of success came to brighten his austere face. At the end of an hour he was no further than when he started.

'The cunning dog has covered his tracks,' said he. 'He has left nothing to incriminate him. His dangerous correspondence has been destroyed or removed. This is our last chance.'

It was a small tin cash-box which stood upon the writing-desk. Holmes prised it open with his chisel. Several rolls of paper were within, covered with figures and calculations, without any note to show to what they referred. The recurring words, 'Water pressure' and 'Pressure to the square inch' suggested some possible relation to a submarine. Holmes tossed them all impatiently aside. There only remained an envelope with some small newspaper slips inside it. He shook them out on the table, and at once I saw by his eager face that his hopes had been raised.

'What's this, Watson? Eh? What's this? Record of a series of messages in the advertisements of a paper. *Daily Telegraph* agony column by the print and paper. Right-hand top corner of a page. No date – but messages arrange themselves. This must be the first:

' "Hoped to hear sooner. Terms agreed to. Write fully to address given on card. – Pierrot."

'Next comes: "Too complex for description. Must have full report. Stuff awaits you when goods delivered. – Pierrot."

'Then comes: "Matter presses. Must withdraw offer unless contract completed. Make appointment by letter. Will confirm by advertisement. – Pierrot."

'Finally: "Monday night after nine. Two taps. Only ourselves. Do not be so suspicious. Payment in hard cash when goods delivered. – Pierrot."

'A fairly complete record, Watson! If we could only get at the man at the other end!' He sat lost in thought, tapping his fingers on the table. Finally he sprang to his feet.

'Well, perhaps it won't be so difficult after all. There is nothing more to be done here, Watson. I think we might drive round to the offices of the *Daily Telegraph*, and so bring a good day's work to a conclusion.'

Mycroft Holmes and Lestrade had come round by appointment after breakfast next day, and Sherlock Holmes had recounted to them our proceedings of the day before. The professional shook his head over our confessed burglary.

'We can't do these things in the force, Mr Holmes,' said he. 'No wonder you get results that are beyond us. But some of these days you'll go too far, and you'll find yourself and your friend in trouble.'

'For England, home and beauty[31] – eh, Watson? Martyrs on the altar of our country. But what do you think of it, Mycroft?'

'Excellent, Sherlock! Admirable! But what use will you make of it?'

Holmes picked up the *Daily Telegraph* which lay upon the table.

'Have you seen Pierrot's advertisement today?'

'What! Another one?'

'Yes, here it is: "Tonight. Same hour. Same place. Two taps. Most vitally important. Your own safety at stake. – Pierrot."'

'By George!' cried Lestrade. 'If he answers that we've got him!'

'That was my idea when I put it in. I think if you could both make it convenient to come with us about eight o'clock to Caulfield Gardens we might possibly get a little nearer to a solution.'

One of the most remarkable characteristics of Sherlock Holmes was his power of throwing his brain out of action and switching all his thoughts on to lighter things whenever he had convinced himself that he could no longer work to advantage. I remember that during the whole of that memorable day he lost himself in a monograph which he had undertaken upon the Polyphonic Motets of Lassus.[32] For my own part I had none of this power of detachment, and the day, in consequence, appeared to be interminable. The great national importance of the issue, the suspense in high quarters, the direct nature of the experiment which we were trying, all combined to work upon my nerves. It was a relief to me when at last, after a light dinner, we set out upon our expedition. Lestrade and Mycroft met us by appointment at the outside of Gloucester Road Station. The area door of Oberstein's house had been left open the night before, and it was necessary for me, as Mycroft Holmes absolutely and indignantly declined to climb the railings, to pass in and open the hall door. By nine o'clock we were all seated in the study, waiting patiently for our man.

An hour passed and yet another. When eleven struck the measured beat of the great church clock[33] seemed to sound the dirge of our hopes. Lestrade and Mycroft were fidgeting in their seats and looking twice a minute at their watches. Holmes sat silent and composed, his eyelids half shut, but every sense on the alert. He raised his head with a sudden jerk.

'He is coming,' said he.

There had been a furtive step past the door. Now it returned. We heard a shuffling sound outside, and then two sharp taps with the knocker. Holmes rose, motioning to us to remain seated. The gas in the hall was a mere point of light. He opened the outer door, and then as a dark figure slipped past him he closed and fastened it. 'This way!' we heard him say, and a moment later our man stood before us. Holmes had followed him closely, and as the man turned with a cry of surprise and alarm he caught him by the collar and threw him back into the room. Before our prisoner had recovered his balance the door was shut and Holmes standing with his back against it. The man glared round him, staggered, and fell senseless upon the floor. With the shock, his broad-brimmed hat flew from his head, his cravat slipped down from his lips, and there was the long light beard and the soft, handsome delicate features of Colonel Valentine Walter.

Holmes gave a whistle of surprise.

'You can write me down an ass this time, Watson,' said he. 'This was not the bird that I was looking for.'[34]

'Who is he?' asked Mycroft eagerly.

The younger brother of the late Sir James Walter, the head of the Submarine Department. Yes, yes; I see the fall of the cards. He is coming to. I think that you had best leave his examination to me.'

We had carried the prostrate body to the sofa. Now our prisoner sat up, looked round him with a horror-stricken face, and passed his hand over his forehead, like one who cannot believe his own senses.

'What is this?' he asked. 'I came here to visit Mr Oberstein.'

'Everything is known, Colonel Walter,' said Holmes. 'How an English gentleman could behave in such a manner is beyond my comprehension. But your whole correspondence and relations with Oberstein are within our knowledge. So also are the circumstances connected with the death of young Cadogan West. Let me advise you to gain at least the small credit for repentance and confession, since there are still some details which we can only learn from your lips.'

The man groaned and sank his face in his hands. We waited, but he was silent.

'I can assure you,' said Holmes, 'that every essential is already known. We know that you were pressed for money; that you took an impress of the keys which your brother held; and that you entered into a correspondence with Oberstein, who answered your letters through the advertisement columns of the *Daily Telegraph*. We are aware that you went down to the office in the fog of Monday night, but that you were seen and followed by young Cadogan West, who had probably some previous reason to suspect you. He saw your theft, but could not give the alarm, as it was just possible that you were taking the papers to your brother in London. Leaving all his private concerns, like the good citizen that he was, he followed you closely in the fog, and kept at your heels until you reached this very house. There he intervened, and then it was, Colonel Walter, that to treason you added the more terrible crime of murder.'

'I did not! I did not! Before God I swear that I did not!' cried our wretched prisoner.

'Tell us, then, how Cadogan West met his end before you laid him upon the roof of a railway carriage.'

'I will. I swear to you that I will. I did the rest. I confess it. It was just as you say. A Stock Exchange debt had to be paid. I needed the money badly. Oberstein offered me five thousand. It was to save myself from ruin. But as to murder, I am as innocent as you.'

'What happened then?'

'He had his suspicions before, and he followed me as you describe. I never knew it until I was at the very door. It was thick fog, and one could not see three yards. I had given two taps and Oberstein had come to the door. The young man rushed up and demanded to know what we were about to do with the papers. Oberstein had a short life-preserver. He always carried it with him. As West forced his way after us into the house Oberstein struck him on the head. The blow was a fatal one. He was dead within five minutes. There he lay in the hall, and we were at our wits' end what to do. Then Oberstein had this idea about the trains which halted under his back window. But first he examined the papers which I had brought. He said that three of them were essential, and that he must keep them. "You cannot keep them," said I. "There will be a dreadful row at Woolwich if they are not returned." "I must keep them," said he, "for they are so technical that it is impossible in the time to make copies." "Then they must all go back together tonight," said I. He thought for a little, and then he cried out that he had it. "Three I will keep," said he. "The others we will stuff into the pocket of this young man. When he is found the whole business will assuredly be put to his account." I could see no other way out of it, so we did as he suggested. We waited half an hour at the window before a train stopped. It was so thick that nothing could be seen, and we had no difficulty in lowering West's body on to the train. That was the end of the matter so far as I was concerned.'

'And your brother?'

'He said nothing, but he had caught me once with his keys, and I think that he suspected. I read in his eyes that he suspected. As you know, he never held up his head again.'

There was silence in the room. It was broken by Mycroft Holmes.

'Can you not make reparation? It would ease your conscience, and possibly your punishment.'

'What reparation can I make?'

'Where is Oberstein with the papers?'

'I do not know.'

'Did he give you no address?'

'He said that letters to the Hôtel du Louvre, Paris, would eventually reach him.'

'Then reparation is still within your power,' said Sherlock Holmes.

'I will do anything I can. I owe this fellow no particular good-will. He has been my ruin and my downfall.'

'Here are paper and pen. Sit at this desk and write to my dictation. Direct the envelope to the address given. That is right. Now the letter: "Dear Sir, – With regard to our transaction, you will no doubt have observed by now that one essential detail is missing. I have a tracing which will make it complete. This has involved me in extra trouble, however, and I must ask you for a further advance of five hundred pounds. I will not trust it to the post, nor will I take anything but gold or notes. I would come to you abroad, but it would excite remark if I left the country at present. Therefore I shall expect to meet you in the smoking-room of the Charing Cross Hotel[35] at noon on Saturday. Remember that only English notes, or gold, will be taken." That will do very well. I shall be very much surprised if it does not fetch our man.'

*

And it did! It is a matter of history – that secret history of a nation which is often so much more intimate and interesting than its public chronicles – that Oberstein, eager to complete the coup of his lifetime, came to the lure and was safely engulfed for fifteen years in a British prison.[36] In his trunk were found the invaluable Bruce-Partington plans, which he had put up for auction in all the naval centres of Europe.[37]

Colonel Walter died in prison towards the end of the second year of his sentence. As to Holmes, he returned refreshed to his monograph upon the Polyphonic Motets of Lassus, which has since been printed for private circulation, and is said by experts to be the last word upon the subject. Some weeks afterwards I learned incidentally that my friend spent a day at Windsor, whence he returned with a remarkably fine emerald tie-pin. When I asked him if he had bought it, he answered that it was a present from a certain gracious lady[38] in whose interests he had once been fortunate enough to carry out a small commission. He said no more; but I fancy that I could guess at the Lady's august name, and I have little doubt that the emerald pin will for ever recall to my friend's memory the adventure of the Bruce-Partington plans.

THE ADVENTURE OF THE
DYING DETECTIVE

Mrs Hudson, the landlady of Sherlock Holmes, was a long-suffering woman. Not only was her first-floor flat invaded at all hours by throngs of singular and often undesirable characters, but her remarkable lodger showed an eccentricity and irregularity in his life which must have sorely tried her patience. His incredible untidiness, his addiction to music at strange hours, his occasional revolver practice within doors, his weird and often malodorous scientific experiments, and the atmosphere of violence and danger which hung around him made him the very worst tenant in London. On the other hand, his payments were princely. I have no doubt that the house might have been purchased at the price which Holmes paid for his rooms during the years that I was with him.

The landlady stood in the deepest awe of him, and never dared to interfere with him, however outrageous his proceedings might seem. She was fond of him, too, for he had a remarkable gentleness and courtesy in his dealings with women. He disliked and distrusted the sex, but he was always a chivalrous opponent. Knowing how genuine was her regard for him, I listened earnestly to her story when she came to my rooms in the second year of my married life[1] and told me of the sad condition to which my poor friend was reduced.

'He's dying, Dr Watson,' said she. 'For three days he has been sinking, and I doubt if he will last the day. He would not let me get a doctor. This morning when I saw his bones sticking out of his face and his great bright eyes looking at me I could stand no more of it. "With your leave or without it, Mr Holmes, I am going for a doctor this very hour," said I. "Let it be Watson, then," said he. I wouldn't waste an hour in coming to him, sir, or you may not see him alive.'

I was horrified, for I had heard nothing of his illness. I need not say that I rushed for my coat and my hat. As we drove back I asked for the details.

'There is little I can tell you, sir. He has been working at a case down at Rotherhithe,[2] in an alley near the river, and he has brought this illness back with him. He took to his bed on Wednesday afternoon and has never moved since. For these three days neither food nor drink has passed his lips.'

'Good God! Why did you not call in a doctor?'

'He wouldn't have it, sir. You know how masterful he is. I didn't dare to disobey him. But he's not long for this world, as you'll see for yourself the moment that you set eyes on him.'

He was indeed a deplorable spectacle. In the dim light of a foggy November day the sick-room was a gloomy spot, but it was that gaunt, wasted face staring at me from the bed which sent a chill to my heart. His eyes had the brightness of fever, there was a hectic flush upon either cheek, and dark crusts clung to his lips; the thin hands upon the coverlet twitched incessantly, his voice was croaking and spasmodic. He lay listlessly as I entered the room, but the sight of me brought a gleam of recognition to his eyes.

'Well, Watson, we seem to have fallen upon evil days,' said he, in a feeble voice, but with something of his old carelessness of manner.

'My dear fellow!' I cried, approaching him.

'Stand back! Stand right back!' said he, with the sharp imperiousness which I had associated only with moments of crisis. 'If you approach me, Watson, I shall order you out of the house.'

'But why?'

'Because it is my desire. Is that not enough?'

Yes, Mrs Hudson was right. He was more masterful than ever. It was pitiful, however, to see his exhaustion.

'I only wished to help,' I explained.

'Exactly! You will help best by doing what you are told.'

'Certainly, Holmes.'

He relaxed the austerity of his manner.

'You are not angry?' he asked, gasping for breath.

Poor devil, how could I be angry when I saw him lying in such a plight before me?

'It's for your own sake, Watson,' he croaked.

'For *my* sake?'

'I know what is the matter with me. It is a coolie[3] disease from Sumatra[4] – a thing that the Dutch know more about than we, though they have made little of it up to date. One thing only is certain. It is infallibly deadly, and it is horribly contagious.'

He spoke now with a feverish energy, the long hands twitching and jerking as he motioned me away.

'Contagious by touch, Watson – that's it, by touch. Keep your distance and all is well.'

'Good heavens, Holmes! Do you suppose that such a consideration weighs with me for an instant? It would not affect me in the case of a stranger. Do you imagine it would prevent me from doing my duty to so old a friend?'

Again I advanced, but he repulsed me with a look of furious anger.

'If you will stand there I will talk. If you do not you must leave the room.'

I have so deep a respect for the extraordinary qualities of Holmes that I have always deferred to his wishes, even when I least understood them. But now all my professional instincts were aroused. Let him be my master elsewhere, I at least was his in a sick-room.

'Holmes,' said I, 'you are not yourself. A sick man is but a child, and so I will treat you. Whether you like it or not, I will examine your symptoms and treat you for them.'

He looked at me with venomous eyes.

'If I am to have a doctor whether I will or not, let me at least have someone in whom I have confidence,' said he.

'Then you have none in me?'

'In your friendship, certainly. But facts are facts, Watson, and after all you are only a general practitioner with very limited experience and mediocre qualifications. It is painful to have to say these things, but you leave me no choice.'

I was bitterly hurt.

'Such a remark is unworthy of you, Holmes. It shows me very clearly the state of your own nerves. But if you have no confidence in me I would not intrude my services. Let me bring Sir Jasper Meek or Penrose Fisher, or any of the best men in London. But someone you *must* have, and that is final. If you think that I am going to stand here and see you die without either helping you myself or bringing anyone else to help you, then you have mistaken your man.'

'You mean well, Watson,' said the sick man, with something between a sob and a groan. 'Shall I demonstrate your own ignorance? What do you know, pray, of Tapanuli fever?[5] What do you know of the black Formosa corruption?[6]

'I have never heard of either.'

'There are many problems of disease, many strange pathological possibilities, in the East, Watson.' He paused after each sentence to collect his failing strength. 'I have learned so much during some recent researches which have a medico-criminal aspect. It was in the course of them that I contracted this complaint. You can do nothing.'

'Possibly not. But I happen to know that Dr Ainstree, the greatest living authority upon tropical disease, is now in London. All remonstrance is useless, Holmes. I am going this instant to fetch him.' I turned resolutely to the door.

Never have I had such a shock! In an instant, with a tiger-spring, the dying man had intercepted me. I heard the sharp snap of a twisted key. The next moment he had staggered back to his bed, exhausted and panting after his one tremendous outflame of energy.

'You won't take the key from me by force, Watson. I've got you, my friend. Here you are, and here you will stay until I will otherwise. But I'll humour you.' (All this in little gasps, with terrible struggles for breath between.) 'You've only my own good at heart. Of course I know that very well. You shall have your way, but give me time to get my strength. Not now, Watson, not now. It's four o'clock. At six you can go.'

'This is insanity, Holmes.'

'Only two hours, Watson, I promise you will go at six. Are you content to wait?'

'I seem to have no choice.'

'None in the world, Watson. Thank you, I need no help in arranging the clothes. You will please keep your distance. Now, Watson, there is one other condition that I would make. You will seek help, not from the man you mention, but from the one that I choose.'

'By all means.'

'The first three sensible words that you have uttered since you entered this room, Watson. You will find some books over there. I am somewhat exhausted; I wonder how a battery feels when it pours electricity into a non-conductor? At six, Watson, we resume our conversation.'

But it was destined to be resumed long before that hour, and in circumstances which gave me a shock hardly second to that caused by his spring to the door. I had stood for some minutes looking at the silent figure in the bed. His face was almost covered by the clothes and he appeared to be asleep. Then, unable to settle down to reading, I walked slowly round the room, examining the pictures of celebrated criminals with which every wall was adorned. Finally, in my aimless perambulation, I came to the mantelpiece. A litter of pipes, tobacco-pouches, syringes, penknives, revolver cartridges, and other debris was scattered over it. In the midst of these was a small black and white ivory box with a sliding lid. It was a neat little thing, and I had stretched out my hand to examine it more closely, when –

It was a dreadful cry that he gave – a yell which might have been heard down the street. My skin went cold and my hair bristled at that horrible scream. As I turned I caught a glimpse of a convulsed face and frantic eyes. I stood paralysed, with the little box in my hand.

'Put it down! Down, this instant, Watson – this instant, I say!' His head sank back upon the pillow and he gave a deep sigh of relief as I replaced the box upon the mantelpiece. 'I hate to have my things touched, Watson. You know that I hate it. You fidget me beyond endurance. You, a doctor – you are enough to drive a patient into an asylum. Sit down, man, and let me have my rest!'

The incident left a most unpleasant impression upon my mind. The violent and causeless excitement, followed by this brutality of speech, so far removed from his usual suavity, showed me how deep was the disorganization of his mind. Of all ruins, that of a noble mind is the most deplorable. I sat in silent dejection until the stipulated time had passed. He seemed to have been watching the clock as well as I, for it was hardly six before he began to talk with the same feverish animation as before.

'Now, Watson,' said he. 'Have you any change in your pocket?'

'Yes.'

'Any silver?'

'A good deal.'

'How many half-crowns?'

'I have five.'

'Ah, too few! Too few! How very unfortunate, Watson! However, such as they are you can put them in your watch-pocket. And all the rest of your money in your left trouser-pocket. Thank you. It will balance you so much better like that.'

This was raving insanity. He shuddered, and again made a sound between a cough and a sob.

'You will now light the gas, Watson, but you will be very careful that not for one instant shall it be more than half on. I implore you to be careful, Watson. Thank you, that is excellent. No, you need not draw the blind. Now you will have the kindness to place some letters and papers upon this table within my reach. Thank you. Now some of that litter from the mantelpiece. Excellent, Watson! There is a sugar-tongs there. Kindly raise that small ivory box with its assistance. Place it here among the papers. Good! You can now go and fetch Mr Culverton Smith, of 13, Lower Burke Street.'[7]

To tell the truth, my desire to fetch a doctor had somewhat weakened, for poor Holmes was so obviously delirious that it seemed dangerous to leave him. However, he was as eager now to consult the person named as he had been obstinate in refusing.

'I never heard the name,' said I.

'Possibly not, my good Watson. It may surprise you to know that the man upon earth who is best versed in this disease is not a medical man, but a planter. Mr Culverton Smith is a well-known resident of Sumatra, now visiting London. An outbreak of the disease upon his plantation, which was distant from medical aid, caused him to study it himself, with some rather far-reaching consequences. He is a very methodical person, and I did not desire you to start before six because I was well aware that you would not find him in his study. If you could persuade him to come here and give us the benefit of his unique experience of this disease, the investigation of which has been his dearest hobby, I cannot doubt that he could help me.'

I give Holmes's remarks as a consecutive whole, and will not attempt to indicate how they were interrupted by gaspings for breath and those clutchings of his hands which indicated the pain from which he was suffering. His appearance had changed for the worse during the few hours that I had been with him. Those hectic spots were more pronounced, the eyes shone more brightly out of darker hollows, and a cold sweat glimmered upon his brow. He still retained, however, the jaunty gallantry of his speech. To the last gasp he would always be the master.

'You will tell him exactly how you have left me,' said he. 'You will convey the very impression which is in your own mind – a dying man – a dying and delirious man. Indeed, I cannot think why the whole bed of the ocean is not one solid mass of oysters, so prolific the creatures seem. Ah, I am wandering! Strange how the brain controls the brain! What was I saying, Watson?'

'My directions for Mr Culverton Smith.'

'Ah, yes, I remember. My life depends upon it. Plead with him, Watson. There is no good feeling between us. His nephew, Watson – I had suspicions of foul play and I allowed him to see it. The boy died horribly. He has a grudge against me. You will soften him, Watson. Beg him, pray him, get him here by any means. He can save me – only he!'

'I will bring him in a cab, if I have to carry him down to it.'

'You will do nothing of the sort. You will persuade him to come. And then you will return in front of him. Make any excuse so as not to come with him. Don't forget, Watson. You won't fail me. You never did fail me. No doubt there are natural enemies which limit the increase of the creatures. You and I, Watson, we have done our part. Shall the world, then, be overrun by oysters? No, no; horrible! You'll convey all that is in your mind.'

I left him full of the image of this magnificent intellect babbling like a foolish child. He had handed me the key, and with a happy thought I took it with me lest he should lock himself in. Mrs Hudson was waiting, trembling and weeping, in the passage. Behind me as I passed from the flat I heard Holmes's high, thin voice in some delirious chant. Below, as I stood whistling for a cab, a man came on me through the fog.

'How is Mr Holmes, sir?' he asked.

It was an old acquaintance, Inspector Morton, of Scotland Yard, dressed in unofficial tweeds.

'He is very ill,' I answered.

He looked at me in a most singular fashion. Had it not been too fiendish, I could have imagined that the gleam of the fanlight showed exultation in his face.

'I heard some rumour of it,' said he.

The cab had driven up, and I left him.

Lower Burke Street proved to be a line of fine houses lying in the vague borderland between Notting Hill and Kensington. The particular one at which my cabman pulled up had an air of smug and demure respectability in its old-fashioned iron railings, its massive folding-door, and its shining brasswork. All was in keeping with a solemn butler who appeared framed in the pink radiance of a tinted electric light behind him.

'Yes, Mr Culverton Smith is in. Dr Watson! Very good, sir, I will take up your card.'

My humble name and title did not appear to impress Mr Culverton Smith. Through the half-open door I heard a high, petulant, penetrating voice.

'Who is this person? What does he want? Dear me, Staples, how often have I said that I am not to be disturbed in my hours of study?'

There came a gentle flow of soothing explanation from the butler.

'Well, I won't see him, Staples. I can't have my work interrupted like this. I am not at home. Say so. Tell him to come in the morning if he really must see me.'

Again the gentle murmur.

'Well, well, give him that message. He can come in the morning, or he can stay away. My work must not be hindered.'

I thought of Holmes tossing upon his bed of sickness, and counting the minutes, perhaps, until I could bring help to him. It was not a time to stand upon ceremony. His life depended upon my promptness. Before the apologetic butler had delivered his message I had pushed past him and was in the room.

With a shrill cry of anger a man rose from a reclining chair beside the fire. I saw a great yellow face, coarse-grained and greasy, with heavy, double-chin, and two sullen, menacing grey eyes which glared at me from under tufted and sandy brows. A high bald head had a small velvet smoking-cap poised coquettishly upon one side of its pink curve. The skull was of enormous capacity, and yet, as I looked down, I saw to my amazement that the figure of the man was small and frail, twisted in the shoulders and back like one who has suffered from rickets in his childhood.

'What's this?' he cried, in a high, screaming voice. 'What is the meaning of this intrusion? Didn't I send you word that I would see you tomorrow morning?'

'I am sorry,' said I, 'but the matter cannot be delayed. Mr Sherlock Holmes –'

The mention of my friend's name had an extraordinary effect upon the little man. The look of anger passed in an instant from his face. His features became tense and alert.

'Have you come from Holmes?' he asked.

'I have just left him.'

'What about Holmes? How is he?'

'He is desperately ill. That is why I have come.'

The man motioned me to a chair, and turned to resume his own. As he did so I caught a glimpse of his face in the mirror over the mantelpiece. I could have sworn that it was set in a malicious and abominable smile. Yet I persuaded myself that it must have been some nervous contraction which I had surprised, for he turned to me an instant later with genuine concern upon his features.

'I am sorry to hear this,' said he. 'I only know Mr Holmes through some business dealings which we have had, but I have every respect for his talents and his character. He is an amateur of crime, as I am of disease. For him the villain, for me the microbe. There are my prisons,' he continued, pointing to a row of bottles and jars which stood upon a side table. 'Among these gelatine cultivations some of the very worst offenders in the world are now doing time.'

'It was on account of your special knowledge that Mr Holmes desired to see you. He has a high opinion of you, and thought that you were the one man in London who could help him.'

The little man started, and the jaunty smoking-cap slid to the floor.

'Why?' he asked. 'Why should Mr Holmes think that I could help him in his trouble?'

'Because of your knowledge of Eastern diseases.'

'But why should he think that this disease which he has contracted is Eastern?'

'Because, in some professional inquiry, he has been working among Chinese sailors down in the docks.'

Mr Culverton Smith smiled pleasantly and picked up his smoking-cap.

'Oh, that's it – is it?' said he. 'I trust the matter is not so grave as you suppose. How long has he been ill?'

'About three days.'

'Is he delirious?'

'Occasionally.'

'Tut, tut! This sounds serious. It would be inhuman not to answer his call. I very much resent any interruption to my work, Dr Watson, but this case is certainly exceptional. I will come with you at once.'

I remembered Holmes's injunction.

'I have another appointment,' said I.

'Very good. I will go alone. I have a note of Mr Holmes's address. You can rely upon my being there within half an hour at most.'

It was with a sinking heart that I re-entered Holmes's bedroom. For all that I knew the worst might have happened in my absence. To my enormous relief, he had improved greatly in the interval. His appearance was as ghastly as ever, but all trace of delirium had left him and he spoke in a feeble voice, it is true, but with even more than his usual crispness and lucidity.

'Well, did you see him, Watson?'

'Yes, he is coming.'

'Admirable, Watson! Admirable! You are the best of messengers.'

'He wished to return with me.'

'That would never do, Watson. That would be obviously imposs-ible. Did he ask what ailed me?'

'I told him about the Chinese in the East End.[8]

'Exactly! Well, Watson, you have done all that a good friend could. You can now disappear from the scene.'

'I must wait and hear his opinion, Holmes.'

'Of course you must. But I have reasons to suppose that this opinion would be very much more frank and valuable if he imagines that we are alone. There is just room behind the head of my bed, Watson.'

'My dear Holmes!'

'I fear there is no alternative, Watson. The room does not lend itself to concealment, which is as well, as it is the less likely to arouse suspicion. But just there, Watson, I fancy that it could be done.' Suddenly he sat up with a rigid intentness upon his haggard face. 'There are the wheels, Watson. Quick, man, if you love me! And don't budge, whatever happens – whatever happens, do you hear? Don't speak! Don't move! Just listen with all your ears.' Then in an instant his sudden access of strength departed, and his masterful, purposeful talk droned away into the low, vague murmurings of a semi-delirious man.

From the hiding-place into which I had been so swiftly hustled I heard the footfalls upon the stair, with the opening and the closing of the bedroom door. Then, to my surprise, there came a long silence, broken only by the heavy breathings and gaspings of the sick man. I could imagine that our visitor was standing by the bedside and looking down at the sufferer. At last that strange hush was broken.

'Holmes!' he cried. 'Holmes!' in the insistent tone of one who awakens a sleeper. 'Can't you hear me, Holmes?' There was a rustling, as if he had shaken the sick man roughly by the shoulder.

'Is that you, Mr Smith?' Holmes whispered. 'I hardly dared hope that you would come.'

The other laughed.

'I should imagine not,' he said. 'And yet, you see, I am here. Coals of fire,[9] Holmes – coals of fire!'

'It is very good of you – very noble of you. I appreciate your special knowledge.'

Our visitor sniggered.

'You do. You are, fortunately, the only man in London who does. Do you know what is the matter with you?'

'The same,' said Holmes.

'Ah! You recognize the symptoms?'

'Only too well.'

'Well, I shouldn't be surprised, Holmes. I shouldn't be surprised if it *were* the same. A bad look-out for you if it is. Poor Victor was a dead man on the fourth day – a strong, hearty young fellow. It was certainly, as you said, very surprising that he should have contracted an out-of-the-way Asiatic disease in the heart of London – a disease, too, of which I had made such a very special study. Singular coincidence, Holmes. Very smart of you to notice it, but rather uncharitable to suggest that it was cause and effect.'

'I knew that you did it.'

'Oh, you did, did you? Well, you couldn't prove it, anyhow. But what do you think of yourself spreading reports about me like that, and then crawling to me for help the moment you are in trouble? What sort of a game is that – eh?'

I heard the rasping, laboured breathing of the sick man. 'Give me the water!' he gasped.

'You're precious near your end, my friend, but I don't want you to go till I have had a word with you. That's why I give you water. There, don't slop it about! That's right. Can you understand what I say?'

Holmes groaned.

'Do what you can for me. Let bygones be bygones,' he whispered. 'I'll put the words out of my head – I swear I will. Only cure me, and I'll forget it.'

'Forget what?'

'Well, about Victor Savage's death. You as good as admitted just now that you had done it. I'll forget it.'

'You can forget it or remember it, just as you like. I don't see you in the witness-box. Quite another shaped box, my good Holmes, I assure you. It matters nothing to me that you should know how my nephew died. It's not him we are talking about. It's you.'

'Yes, yes.'

'The fellow who came for me – I've forgotten his name – said that you contracted it down in the East End among the sailors.'

'I could only account for it so.'

'You are proud of your brains, Holmes, are you not? Think yourself smart, don't you? You came across someone who was smarter this time. Now cast your mind back, Holmes. Can you think of no other way you could have got this thing?'

'I can't think. My mind is gone. For Heaven's sake help me!'

'Yes, I will help you. I'll help you to understand just where you are and how you got there. I'd like you to know before you die.'

'Give me something to ease my pain.'

'Painful, is it? Yes, the coolies used to do some squealing towards the end. Takes you as cramp, I fancy.'

'Yes, yes; it is cramp.'

'Well, you can hear what I say, anyhow. Listen now! Can you remember any unusual incident in your life just about the time your symptoms began?'

'No, no; nothing.'

'Think again.'

'I'm too ill to think.'

'Well, then, I'll help you. Did anything come by post?'

'By post?'

'A box of chance?'

'I'm fainting – I'm gone!'

'Listen, Holmes!' There was a sound as if he was shaking the dying man, and it was all that I could do to hold myself quiet in my hiding-place. 'You must hear me. You *shall* hear me. Do you remember a box – an ivory box? It came on Wednesday. You opened it – do you remember?'

'Yes, yes, I opened it. There was a sharp spring inside it. Some joke –'

'It was no joke, as you will find to your cost. You fool, you would have it and you have got it. Who asked you to cross my path? If you had left me alone I would not have hurt you.'

'I remember,' Holmes gasped. 'The spring! It drew blood.[10] This box – this on the table.'

'The very one, by George! And it may as well leave the room in my pocket. There goes your last shred of evidence. But you have the truth now, Holmes, and you can die with the knowledge that I killed you. You knew too much of the fate of Victor Savage, so I have sent you to share it. You are very near your end, Holmes. I will sit here and I will watch you die.'

Holmes's voice had sunk to an almost inaudible whisper.

'What is that?' said Smith. 'Turn up the gas? Ah, the shadows begin to fall, do they? Yes, I will turn it up, that I may see you the better.' He crossed the room and the light suddenly brightened. 'Is there any other little service that I can do you, my friend?'

'A match and a cigarette.'

I nearly called out in my joy and my amazement. He was speaking in his natural voice – a little weak, perhaps, but the very voice I knew. There was a long pause, and I felt that Culverton Smith was standing in silent amazement looking down at his companion.

'What's the meaning of this?' I heard him say at last, in a dry, rasping tone.

'The best way of successfully acting a part is to be it,' said Holmes. 'I give you my word that for three days I have tasted neither food nor drink until you were good enough to pour me out that glass of water. But it is the tobacco which I find most irksome. Ah, here *are* some cigarettes.' I heard the striking of a match. 'That is very much better. Halloa! halloa! Do I hear the step of a friend?'

There were footfalls outside, the door opened, and Inspector Morton appeared.

'All is in order and this is your man,' said Holmes.

The officer gave the usual cautions.

'I arrest you on the charge of the murder of one Victor Savage,' he concluded.

'And you might add of the attempted murder of one Sherlock Holmes,' remarked my friend with a chuckle. 'To save an invalid trouble, inspector, Mr Culverton Smith was good enough to give our signal by turning up the gas. By the way, the prisoner has a small box in the right-hand pocket of his coat which it would be as well to remove. Thank you. I would handle it gingerly if I were you. Put it down here. It may play its part in the trial.'

There was a sudden rush and a scuffle, followed by the clash of iron and a cry of pain.

'You'll only get yourself hurt,' said the inspector. 'Stand still, will you?' There was the click of the closing handcuffs.

'A nice trap!' cried the high, snarling voice. 'It will bring *you* into the dock, Holmes, not me. He asked me to come here to cure him. I was sorry for him and I came. Now he will pretend, no doubt, that I have said anything which he may invent which will corroborate his insane suspicions. You can lie as you like, Holmes. My word is always as good as yours.'

'Good heavens!' cried Holmes. 'I had totally forgotten him. My dear Watson, I owe you a thousand apologies. To think that I should have overlooked you! I need not introduce you to Mr Culverton Smith, since I understand that you met somewhat earlier in the evening. Have you the cab below? I will follow you when I am dressed, for I may be of some use at the station.

'I never needed it more,' said Holmes, as he refreshed himself with a glass of claret and some biscuits in the intervals of his toilet. 'However, as you know, my habits are irregular, and such a feat means less to me than to most men. It was very essential that I should impress Mrs Hudson with the reality of my condition, since she was to convey it to you, and you in turn to him. You won't be offended, Watson? You will realize that among your many talents dissimulation finds no place, and that if you had shared my secret you would never have been able to impress Smith with the urgent necessity of his presence, which was the vital point of the whole scheme. Knowing his vindictive nature, I was perfectly certain that he would come to look upon his handiwork.'

'But your appearance, Holmes – your ghastly face?'

'Three days of absolute fast does not improve one's beauty, Watson. For the rest, there is nothing which a sponge may not cure. With vaseline upon one's forehead, belladonna in one's eyes, rouge over the cheek-bones, and crusts of beeswax round one's lips, a very satisfying effect can be produced. Malingering is a subject upon which

I have sometimes thought of writing a monograph. A little occasional talk about half-crowns, oysters, or any other extraneous subject produces a pleasing effect of delirium.'

'But why would you not let me near you, since there was in truth no infection?'

'Can you ask, my dear Watson? Do you imagine that I have no respect for your medical talents? Could I fancy that your astute judgment would pass a dying man who, however weak, had no rise of pulse or temperature? At four yards, I could deceive you. If I failed to do so, who would bring my Smith within my grasp? No, Watson, I would not touch that box. You can just see if you look at it sideways where the sharp spring like a viper's tooth emerges as you open it. I dare say it was by some such device that poor Savage, who stood between this monster and a reversion,[11] was done to death. My correspondence, however, is, as you know, a varied one, and I am somewhat upon my guard against any packages which reach me. It was clear to me, however, that by pretending that he had really succeeded in his design I might surprise a confession. That pretence I have carried out with the thoroughness of the true artist. Thank you, Watson, you must help me on with my coat. When we have finished at the police-station I think that something nutritious at Simpson's[12] would not be out of place.'

THE DISAPPEARANCE OF
LADY FRANCES CARFAX

'But why Turkish?' asked Mr Sherlock Holmes, gazing fixedly at my boots. I was reclining in a cane-backed chair at the moment, and my protruded feet had attracted his ever-active attention.

'English,' I answered, in some surprise. 'I got them at Latimer's,[1] in Oxford Street.'

Holmes smiled with an expression of weary patience.

'The bath!' he said; 'the bath! Why the relaxing and expensive Turkish rather than the invigorating home-made article?'

'Because for the last few days I have been feeling rheumatic and old. A Turkish bath is what we call an alterative in medicine – a fresh starting-point, a cleanser of the system.

'By the way, Holmes,' I added, 'I have no doubt the connection between my boots and a Turkish bath is a perfectly self-evident one to a logical mind, and yet I should be obliged to you if you would indicate it.'

'The train of reasoning is not very obscure, Watson,' said Holmes, with a mischievous twinkle. 'It belongs to the same elementary class of deduction which I should illustrate if I were to ask you who shared your cab in your drive this morning.'

'I don't admit that a fresh illustration is an explanation,' said I, with some asperity.

'Bravo, Watson! A very dignified and logical remonstrance. Let me see, what were the points? Take the last one first – the cab. You observe that you have some splashes on the left sleeve and shoulder of your coat. Had you sat in the centre of a hansom you would probably have had no splashes, and if you had they would certainly have been symmetrical. Therefore it is clear that you sat at the side. Therefore it is equally clear that you had a companion.'

'That is very evident.'

'Absurdly commonplace, is it not?'

'But the boots and the bath?'

'Equally childish. You are in the habit of doing up your boots in a certain way. I see them on this occasion fastened with an elaborate double bow, which is not your usual method of tying them. You have, therefore, had them off. Who has tied them? A bootmaker – or the boy at the bath. It is unlikely that it is the bootmaker, since your boots are nearly new. Well, what remains? The bath. Absurd, is it not? But, for all that, the Turkish bath has served a purpose.'

'What is that?'

'You say that you have had it because you need a change. Let me suggest that you take one. How would Lausanne do, my dear Watson – first-class tickets and all expenses paid on a princely scale?'

'Splendid! But why?'

Holmes leaned back in his armchair and took his notebook from his pocket.

'One of the most dangerous classes in the world,' said he, 'is the drifting and friendless woman. She is the most harmless, and often the most useful of mortals, but she is the inevitable inciter of crime in others. She is helpless. She is migratory. She has sufficient means to take her from country to country and from hotel to hotel. She is lost, as often as not, in a maze of obscure *pensions* and boarding-houses. She is a stray chicken in a world of foxes. When she is gobbled up she is hardly missed. I much fear that some evil has come to the Lady Frances Carfax.'

I was relieved at this sudden descent from the general to the particular. Holmes consulted his notes.

'Lady Frances,' he continued, 'is the sole survivor of the direct family of the late Earl of Rufton. The estates went, as you may remember, in the male line. She was left with limited means, but with some very remarkable old Spanish jewellery of silver and curiously-cut diamonds to which she was fondly attached – too attached, for she refused to leave them with her banker and always carried them about with her. A rather pathetic figure, the Lady Frances, a beautiful woman, still in fresh middle age, and yet, by a strange chance, the last derelict of what only twenty years ago was a goodly fleet.'

'What has happened to her, then?'

'Ah, what has happened to the Lady Frances? Is she alive or dead? There is our problem. She is a lady of precise habits, and for four years it has been her invariable custom to write every second week to Miss Dobney, her old governess, who has long retired, and lives in Camberwell. It is this Miss Dobney who consulted me. Nearly five weeks have passed without a word. The last letter was from the Hôtel National at Lausanne.[2] Lady Frances seems to have left there and given no address. The family are anxious, and, as they are exceedingly wealthy, no sum will be spared if we can clear the matter up.'

'Is Miss Dobney the only source of information? Surely she had other correspondents?'

'There is one correspondent who is a sure draw, Watson. That is the bank. Single ladies must live, and their pass-books are compressed diaries. She banks at Silvester's. I have glanced over her account. The last cheque but one paid her bill at Lausanne, but it was a large one and probably left her with cash in hand. Only one cheque has been drawn since.'

'To whom, and where?'

'To Miss Marie Devine. There is nothing to show where the cheque was drawn. It was cashed at the Crédit Lyonnais at Montpelier less than three weeks ago. The sum was fifty pounds.'

'And who is Miss Marie Devine?'

'That also I have been able to discover. Miss Marie Devine was the maid of Lady Frances Carfax. Why she should have paid her this cheque we have not yet determined. I have no doubt, however, that your researches will soon clear the matter up.'

'*My* researches!'

'Hence the health-giving expedition to Lausanne. You know that I cannot possibly leave London while old Abrahams is in such mortal terror of his life. Besides, on general principles it is best that I should not leave the country. Scotland Yard feels lonely without me, and it causes an unhealthy excitement among the criminal classes. Go, then, my dear Watson, and if my humble counsel can ever be valued at so extravagant a rate as twopence a word, it waits your disposal night and day at the end of the Continental wire.'ᐟ

Two days later found me at the National Hotel at Lausanne, where I received every courtesy at the hands of M. Moser, the well-known manager. Lady Frances, as he informed me, had stayed there for several weeks. She had been much liked by all who met her. Her age was not more than forty. She was still handsome, and bore every sign of having in her youth been a very lovely woman. M. Moser knew nothing of any valuable jewellery, but it had been remarked by the servants that the heavy trunk in the lady's bedroom was always scrupulously locked. Marie Devine, the maid, was as popular as her mistress. She was actually engaged to one of the head waiters in the hotel, and there was no difficulty in getting her address. It was 11, Rue de Trajan, Montpelier.³ All this I jotted down, and felt that Holmes himself could not have been more adroit in collecting his facts.

Only one corner still remained in the shadow. No light which I possessed could clear up the cause for the lady's sudden departure. She was very happy at Lausanne. There was every reason to believe that she intended to remain for the season in her luxurious rooms overlooking the lake. And yet she had left at a single day's notice, which involved her in the useless payment of a week's rent. Only Jules Vibart, the lover of the maid, had any suggestion to offer. He connected the sudden departure with the visit to the hotel a day or two before of a tall, dark, bearded man. '*Un sauvage – un véritable sauvage!*'⁴ cried Jules Vibart. The man had rooms somewhere in the town. He had been seen talking earnestly to madame on the promenade by the lake. Then he had called. She had refused to see him. He was English, but of his name there was no record. Madame had left the place immediately afterwards. Jules Vibart, and, what was of more importance, Jules Vibart's sweetheart, thought that this call and this departure were cause and effect. Only one thing Jules could not discuss. That was the reason why Marie had left her mistress. Of that he could or would say nothing. If I wished to know, I must go to Montpelier and ask her.

So ended the first chapter of my inquiry. The second was devoted to the place which Lady Frances Carfax had sought when she left Lausanne. Concerning this there had been some secrecy, which confirmed the idea that she had gone with the intention of throwing someone off her track. Otherwise why should not her luggage have been openly labelled for Baden?[5] Both she and it reached the Rhenish spa by some circuitous route. Thus much I gathered from the manager of Cook's local office.[6] So to Baden I went, after dispatching to Holmes an account of all my proceedings, and receiving in reply a telegram of half-humorous commendation.

At Baden the track was not difficult to follow. Lady Frances had stayed at the Englischer Hof[7] for a fortnight. Whilst there she had made the acquaintance of a Dr Shlessinger and his wife, a missionary from South America. Like most lonely ladies. Lady Frances found her comfort and occupation in religion. Dr Shlessinger's remarkable personality, his wholehearted devotion, and the fact that he was recovering from a disease contracted in the exercise of his apostolic duties, affected her deeply. She had helped Mrs Shlessinger in the nursing of the convalescent saint. He spent his day, as the manager described it to me, upon a lounge-chair on the veranda, with an attendant lady upon either side of him. He was preparing a map of the Holy Land, with special reference to the kingdom of the Midianites,[8] upon which he was writing a monograph. Finally, having improved much in health, he and his wife had returned to London, and Lady Frances had started thither in their company. This was just three weeks before, and the manager had heard nothing since. As to the maid, Marie, she had gone off some days beforehand in floods of tears, after informing the other maids that she was leaving service for ever. Dr Shlessinger had paid the bill of the whole party before his departure.

'By the way,' said the landlord, in conclusion, 'you are not the only friend of Lady Frances Carfax who is inquiring after her just now. Only a week or so ago we had a man here upon the same errand.'

'Did he give a name?' I asked.

'None; but he was an Englishman, though of an unusual type.'

'A savage?' said I, linking my facts after the fashion of my illustrious friend.

'Exactly. That describes him very well. He is a bulky, bearded, sunburned fellow, who looks as if he would be more at home in a farmers' inn than in a fashionable hotel. A hard, fierce man, I should think, and one whom I should be sorry to offend.'

Already the mystery began to define itself, as figures grow clearer with the lifting of a fog. Here was this good and pious lady pursued from place to place by a sinister and unrelenting figure. She feared him, or she would not have fled from Lausanne. He had still followed. Sooner or later he would overtake her. Had he already overtaken her? Was *that* the secret of her continued silence? Could the good people who were her companions not screen her from his violence or his blackmail? What horrible purpose, what deep design, lay behind this long pursuit? There was the problem which I had to solve.

To Holmes I wrote showing how rapidly and surely I had got down to the roots of the matter. In reply I had a telegram asking for a description of Dr Shlessinger's left ear. Holmes's ideas of humour are strange and occasionally offensive, so I took no notice of his ill-timed jest – indeed, I had already reached Montpelier in my pursuit of the maid, Marie, before his message came.

I had no difficulty in finding the ex-servant and in learning all that she could tell me. She was a devoted creature, who had only left her mistress because she was sure that she was in good hands, and because her own approaching marriage made a separation inevitable in any case. Her mistress had, as she confessed with distress, shown some irritability of temper towards her during their stay in Baden, and had even questioned her once as if she had suspicions of her honesty, and this had made the parting easier than it would otherwise have been. Lady Frances had given her fifty pounds as a wedding-present. Like me, Marie viewed with deep distrust the stranger who had driven her mistress from Lausanne. With her own eyes she had seen him seize the lady's wrist with great violence on the public promenade by the lake. He was a fierce and terrible man. She believed that it was out of dread of him that Lady Frances had accepted the escort of the Shlessingers to London. She had never spoken to Marie about it, but many little signs had convinced the maid that her mistress lived in a state of continual nervous apprehension. So far she had got in her narrative, when suddenly she sprang from her chair and her face was convulsed with surprise and fear. 'See!' she cried. 'The miscreant follows still! There is the very man of whom I speak.'

Through the open sitting-room window I saw a huge, swarthy man with a bristling black beard walking slowly down the centre of the street and staring eagerly at the numbers of the houses. It was clear that, like myself, he was on the track of the maid. Acting upon the impulse of the moment, I rushed out and accosted him.

'You are an Englishman,' I said.

'What if I am?' he asked, with a most villainous scowl.

'May I ask what your name is?'

'No, you may not,' said he, with decision.

The situation was awkward, but the most direct way is often the best.

'Where is the Lady Frances Carfax?' I asked.

He stared at me in amazement.

'What have you done with her? Why have you pursued her? I insist upon an answer!' said I.

The fellow gave a bellow of anger and sprang upon me like a tiger. I have held my own in many a struggle, but the man had a grip of iron and the fury of a fiend. His hand was on my throat and my senses were nearly gone before an unshaven French *ouvrier*,[9] in a blue blouse, darted out from a *cabaret*[10] opposite, with a cudgel in his hand, and struck my assailant a sharp crack over the forearm, which made him leave go his hold. He stood for an instant fuming with rage and uncertain whether he should not renew his attack. Then, with a snarl of anger, he left me and entered the cottage from which I had just come. I turned to thank my preserver, who stood beside me in the roadway.

'Well, Watson,' said he, 'a very pretty hash you have made of it! I rather think you had better come back with me to London by the night express.'

An hour afterwards Sherlock Holmes, in his usual garb and style, was seated in my private room at the hotel. His explanation of his sudden and opportune appearance was simplicity itself, for, finding that he could get away from London, he determined to head me off at the next obvious point of my travels. In the disguise of a working-man he had sat in the *cabaret* waiting for my appearance.

'And a singularly consistent investigation you have made, my dear Watson,' said he. 'I cannot at the moment recall any possible blunder which you have omitted. The total effect of your proceedings has been to give the alarm everywhere and yet to discover nothing.'

'Perhaps you would have done no better,' I answered, bitterly.

'There is no "perhaps" about it. I *have* done better.[11] Here is the Hon. Philip Green, who is a fellow-lodger with you in this hotel, and we may find in him the starting-point for a more successful investigation.'

A card had come up on a salver, and it was followed by the same bearded ruffian who had attacked me in the street. He started when he saw me.

'What is this, Mr Holmes?' he asked. 'I had your note and I have come. But what has this man to do with the matter?'

'This is my old friend and associate, Dr Watson, who is helping us in this affair.'

The stranger held out a huge, sunburned hand, with a few words of apology.

'I hope I didn't harm you. When you accused me of hurting her I lost my grip of myself. Indeed, I'm not responsible in these days. My nerves are like live wires. But this situation is beyond me. What I want to know, in the first place, Mr Holmes, is, how in the world you came to hear of my existence at all.'

'I am in touch with Miss Dobney, Lady Frances's governess.'

'Old Susan Dobney with the mob cap![12] I remember her well.'

'And she remembers you. It was in the days before – before you found it better to go to South Africa.'

'Ah, I see you know my whole story. I need hide nothing from you. I swear to you, Mr Holmes, that there never was in this world a man who loved a woman with a more wholehearted love than I had for Frances. I was a wild youngster, I know – not worse than others of my class. But her mind was pure as snow. She could not bear a shadow of coarseness. So, when she came to hear of things that I had done, she would have no more to say to me. And yet she loved me – that is the wonder of it! – loved me well enough to remain single all her sainted days just for my sake alone. When the years had passed and I had made my money at Barberton[13] I thought perhaps I could seek her out and soften her. I had heard that she was still unmarried. I found her at Lausanne, and tried all I knew. She weakened, I think, but her will was strong, and when next I called she had left the town. I traced her to Baden, and then after a time heard that her maid was here. I'm a rough fellow, fresh from a rough life, and when Dr Watson spoke to me as he did I lost hold of myself for a moment. But for God's sake tell me what has become of the Lady Frances.'

'That is for us to find out,' said Sherlock Holmes, with peculiar gravity. 'What is your London address, Mr Green?'

'The Langham Hotel[14] will find me.'

'Then may I recommend that you return there and be on hand in case I should want you? I have no desire to encourage false hopes, but you may rest assured that all that can be done will be done for the safety of Lady Frances. I can say no more for the instant. I will leave you this card so that you may be able to keep in touch with us. Now, Watson, if you will pack your bag I will cable to Mrs Hudson to make one of her best efforts for two hungry travellers at seven-thirty tomorrow.'

A telegram was awaiting us when we reached our Baker Street rooms, which Holmes read with an exclamation of interest and threw across to me. 'Jagged or torn,' was the message, and the place of origin Baden.

'What is this?' I asked.

'It is everything,' Holmes answered. 'You may remember my seemingly irrelevant question as to this clerical gentleman's left ear. You did not answer it.'

'I had left Baden, and could not inquire.'

'Exactly. For this reason I sent a duplicate to the manager of the Englischer Hof, whose answer lies here.'

'What does it show?'

'It shows, my dear Watson, that we are dealing with an exception-ally astute and dangerous man. The Rev. Dr Shlessinger, missionary from South America, is none other than Holy Peters, one of the most unscrupulous rascals that Australia has ever evolved – and for a young country it has turned out some very finished types. His particular speciality is the beguiling of lonely ladies by playing upon their religious feelings, and his so-called wife, an Englishwoman named Fraser, is a worthy helpmate. The nature of his tactics suggested his identity to me, and this physical peculiarity – he was badly bitten in a saloon-fight at Adelaide in '89 – confirmed my suspicion. This poor lady is in the hands of a most infernal couple, who will stick at nothing, Watson. That she is already dead is a very likely supposition. If not, she is undoubtedly in some sort of confinement, and unable to write to Miss Dobney or her other friends. It is always possible that she never reached London, or that she has passed through it, but the former is improbable, as, with their system of registration, it is not easy for foreigners to play tricks with the Continental police; and the latter is also unlikely, as these rogues could not hope to find any other place where it would be as easy to keep a person under restraint. All my instincts tell me that she is in London, but, as we have at present no possible means of telling where, we can only take the obvious steps, eat our dinner, and possess our souls in patience.[15] Later in the evening I will stroll down and have a word with friend Lestrade at Scotland Yard.'

But neither the official police nor Holmes's own small, but very efficient, organization[16] sufficed to clear away the mystery. Amid the crowded millions of London the three persons we sought were as completely obliterated as if they had never lived. Advertisements were tried, and failed. Clues were followed, and led to nothing. Every criminal resort which Shlessinger might frequent was drawn in vain. His old associates were watched, but they kept clear of him. And then suddenly, after a week of helpless suspense, there came a flash of light. A silver-and-brilliant[17] pendant of old Spanish design had been pawned at Bevington's[18] in Westminster Road. The pawner was a large, clean-shaven man of clerical appearance. His name and address were demonstrably false. The ear had escaped notice, but the description was surely that of Shlessinger.

Three times had our bearded friend from the Langham called for news – the third time within an hour of this fresh development. His clothes were getting looser on his great body. He seemed to be wilting away in his anxiety. 'If you will only give me something to do!' was his constant wail. At last Holmes could oblige him.

'He has begun to pawn the jewels. We should get him now.'

'But does this mean that any harm has befallen the Lady Frances?'

Holmes shook his head very gravely.

'Supposing that they have held her prisoner up to now, it is clear that they cannot let her loose without their own destruction. We must prepare for the worst.'

'What can I do?'

'These people do not know you by sight?'

'No.'

'It is possible that he will go to some other pawnbroker in the future. In that case, we must begin again. On the other hand, he has had a fair price and no questions asked, so if he is in need of ready money he will probably come back to Bevington's. I will give you a note to them, and they will let you wait in the shop. If the fellow comes you will follow him home. But no indiscretion, and, above all, no violence. I put you on your honour that you will take no step without my knowledge and consent.'

For two days the Hon. Philip Green (he was, I may mention, the son of the famous admiral of that name who commanded the Sea of Azof[19] fleet in the Crimean War) brought us no news. On the evening of the third he rushed into our sitting-room, pale, trembling, with every muscle of his powerful frame quivering with excitement.

'We have him! We have him!' he cried.

He was incoherent in his agitation. Holmes soothed him with a few words, and thrust him into an armchair.

'Come, now, give us the order of events,' said he.

'She came only an hour ago. It was the wife, this time, but the pendant she brought was the fellow of the other. She is a tall, pale woman, with ferret eyes.'

'That is the lady,' said Holmes.

'She left the office and I followed her. She walked up the Kennington Road, and I kept behind her. Presently she went into a shop. Mr Holmes, it was an undertaker's.'

My companion started. 'Well?' he asked, in that vibrant voice which told of the fiery soul behind the cold, grey face.

'She was talking to the woman behind the counter. I entered as well. "It is late," I heard her say, or words to that effect. The woman was excusing herself. "It should be there before now," she answered. "It took longer, being out of the ordinary." They both stopped and looked at me, so I asked some question and then left the shop.'

'You did excellently well. What happened next?'

'The woman came out, but I had hid myself in a doorway. Her suspicions had been aroused, I think, for she looked round her. Then she called a cab and got in. I was lucky enough to get another and so to follow her. She got down at last at No. 36, Poultney Square,[20] Brixton. I drove past, left my cab at the corner of the square, and watched the house.'

'Did you see anyone?'

'The windows were all in darkness save one on the lower floor. The blind was down, and I could not see in. I was standing there, wondering what I should do next, when a covered van drove up with two men in it. They descended, took something out of the van, and carried it up the steps to the hall door. Mr Holmes, it was a coffin.'

'Ah!'

'For an instant I was on the point of rushing in. The door had been opened to admit the men and their burden. It was the woman who had opened it. But as I stood there she caught a glimpse of me, and I think that she recognized me. I saw her start, and she hastily closed the door. I remembered my promise to you, and here I am.'

'You have done excellent work,' said Holmes scribbling a few words upon a half-sheet of paper. 'We can do nothing legal without a warrant, and you can serve the cause best by taking this note down to the authorities and getting one. There may be some difficulty, but I should think that the sale of the jewellery should be sufficient. Lestrade will see to all details.'

'But they may murder her in the meanwhile. What could the coffin mean, and for whom could it be but for her?'

'We will do all that can be done, Mr Green. Not a moment will be lost. Leave it in our hands. Now, Watson,' he added, as our client hurried away, 'he will set the regular forces on the move. We are, as usual, the irregulars, and we must take our own line of action. The situation strikes me as so desperate that the most extreme measures are justified. Not a moment is to be lost in getting to Poultney Square.

'Let us try to reconstruct the situation,' said he, as we drove swiftly past the Houses of Parliament and over Westminster Bridge. 'These villains have coaxed this unhappy lady to London, after first alienating her from her faithful maid. If she has written any letters they have been intercepted. Through some confederate they have engaged a furnished house. Once inside it, they have made her a prisoner, and they have become possessed of the valuable jewellery which has been their object from the first. Already they have begun to sell part of it, which seems safe enough to them, since they have no reason to think that anyone is interested in the lady's fate. When she is released she will, of course, denounce them. Therefore, she must not be released. But they cannot keep her under lock and key for ever. So murder is their only solution.'

'That seems very clear.'

'Now we will take another line of reasoning. When you follow two separate chains of thought, Watson, you will find some point of intersection which should approximate to the truth. We will start now, not from the lady, but from the coffin, and argue backwards. That incident proves, I fear, beyond all doubt that the lady is dead. It points also to an orthodox burial with proper accompaniment of medical certificate and official sanction. Had the lady been obviously murdered, they would have buried her in a hole in the back garden. But here all is open and regular. What does that mean? Surely that they have done her to death in some way which has deceived the doctor, and simulated a natural end – poisoning, perhaps. And yet how strange that they should ever let a doctor approach her unless he were a confederate, which is hardly a credible proposition.'

'Could they have forged a medical certificate?'

'Dangerous, Watson, very dangerous. No, I hardly see them doing that. Pull up, cabby! This is evidently the undertaker's, for we have just passed the pawnbroker's. Would you go in, Watson? Your appearance inspires confidence. Ask what hour the Poultney Square funeral takes place tomorrow.'

The woman in the shop answered me without hesitation that it was to be at eight o'clock in the morning.

'You see, Watson, no mystery; everything above board! In some way the legal forms have undoubtedly been complied with, and they think that they have little to fear. Well, there's nothing for it now but a direct frontal attack. Are you armed?'

'My stick!'

'Well, well, we shall be strong enough. "Thrice is he armed who hath his quarrel just."[21] We simply can't afford to wait for the police, or to keep within the four corners of the law. You can drive off, cabby. Now, Watson, we'll just take our luck together, as we have occasionally done in the past.'

He had rung loudly at the door of a great dark house in the centre of Poultney Square. It was opened immediately, and the figure of a tall woman was outlined against the dim-lit hall.

'Well, what do you want?' she asked, sharply, peering at us through the darkness.

'I want to speak to Dr Shlessinger,' said Holmes.

'There is no such person here,' she answered, and tried to close the door, but Holmes had jammed it with his foot.

'Well, I want to see the man who lives here, whatever he may call himself,' said Holmes firmly.

She hesitated. Then she threw open the door. 'Well, come in!' said she. 'My husband is not afraid to face any man in the world.' She closed the door behind us, and showed us into a sitting-room on the right side of the hall, turning up the gas as she left us. 'Mr Peters will be with you in an instant,' she said.

Her words were literally true, for we had hardly time to look round the dusty and moth-eaten apartment in which we found ourselves before the door opened and a big, clean-shaven, bald-headed man stepped lightly into the room. He had a large red face, with pendulous cheeks, and a general air of superficial benevolence which was marred by a cruel, vicious mouth.

'There is surely some mistake here, gentlemen,' he said, in an unctuous, make-everything-easy voice. 'I fancy that you have been misdirected. Possibly if you tried farther down the street –'

'That will do; we have no time to waste,' said my companion, firmly. 'You are Henry Peters, of Adelaide, late the Rev. Dr Shlessinger, of Baden and South America. I am as sure of that as that my own name is Sherlock Holmes.'

Peters, as I will now call him, started and stared hard at his formidable pursuer. 'I guess your name does not frighten me, Mr Holmes,' said he, coolly. 'When a man's conscience is easy, you can't rattle him. What is your business in my house?'

'I want to know what you have done with the Lady Frances Carfax, whom you brought away with you from Baden.'

'I'd be very glad if you could tell me where that lady may be,' Peters answered, coolly. 'I've a bill against her for nearly a hundred pounds, and nothing to show for it but a couple of trumpery pendants that the dealer would hardly look at. She attached herself to Mrs Peters and me at Baden (it is a fact that I was using another name at the time), and she stuck on to us until we came to London. I paid her bill and her ticket. Once in London, she gave us the slip, and, as I say, left these out-of-date jewels to pay her bills. You find her, Mr Holmes, and I'm your debtor.'

'I *mean* to find her,' said Sherlock Holmes. 'I'm going through this house till I do find her.'

'Where is your warrant?'

Holmes half drew a revolver from his pocket. 'This will have to serve till a better one comes.'

'Why, you are a common burglar.'

'So you might describe me,' said Holmes cheerfully. 'My companion is also a dangerous ruffian. And together we are going through your house.'

Our opponent opened the door.

'Fetch a policeman, Annie!' said he. There was a whisk of feminine skirts down the passage, and the hall door was opened and shut.

'Our time is limited, Watson,' said Holmes. 'If you try to stop us, Peters, you will most certainly get hurt. Where is that coffin which was brought into your house?'

'What do you want with the coffin? It is in use. There is a body in it.'

'I must see that body.'

'Never with my consent.'

'Then without it.' With a quick movement Holmes pushed the fellow to one side and passed into the hall. A door half open stood immediately before us. We entered. It was the dining-room. On the table, under a half-lit chandelier, the coffin was lying. Holmes turned up the gas and raised the lid. Deep down in the recesses of the coffin lay an emaciated figure. The glare from the lights above beat down upon an aged and withered face. By no possible process of cruelty, starvation, or disease could this worn-out wreck be the still beautiful Lady Frances. Holmes's face showed his amazement, and also his relief.

'Thank God!' he muttered. 'It's someone else.'

'Ah, you've blundered badly for once, Mr Sherlock Holmes,' said Peters, who had followed us into the room.

'Who is this dead woman?'

'Well, if you really must know, she is an old nurse of my wife's, Rose Spender her name, whom we found in the Brixton Workhouse Infirmary. We brought her round here, called in Dr Horsom, of 13, Firbank Villas – mind you take the address, Mr Holmes – and had her carefully tended, as Christian folk should. On the third day she died – certificate says senile decay – but that's only the doctor's opinion, and, of course, you know better. We ordered her funeral to be carried out by Stimson and Co., of the Kennington Road, who will bury her at eight o'clock tomorrow morning. Can you pick any hole in that, Mr Holmes? You've made a silly blunder, and you may as well own up to it. I'd give something for a photograph of your gaping, staring face when you pulled aside that lid expecting to see the Lady Frances Carfax, and only found a poor old woman of ninety.'

Holmes's expression was as impassive as ever under the jeers of his antagonist, but his clenched hands betrayed his acute annoyance.

'I am going through your house,' said he.

'Are you, though!' cried Peters, as a woman's voice and heavy steps sounded in the passage. 'We'll soon see about that. This way, officers, if you please. These men have forced their way into my house, and I cannot get rid of them. Help me to put them out.'

A sergeant and a constable stood in the doorway. Holmes drew his card from his case.

'This is my name and address. This is my friend, Dr Watson.'

'Bless you, sir, we know you very well,' said the sergeant, 'but you can't stay here without a warrant.'

'Of course not. I quite understand that.'

'Arrest him!' cried Peters.

'We know where to lay our hands on this gentleman if he is wanted,' said the sergeant, majestically, 'but you'll have to go, Mr Holmes.'

'Yes, Watson, we shall have to go.'

A minute later we were in the street once more. Holmes was as cool as ever, but I was hot with anger and humiliation. The sergeant had followed us.

'Sorry, Mr Holmes, but that's the law.'

'Exactly, sergeant; you could not do otherwise.'

'I expect there was good reason for your presence there. If there is anything I can do –'

'It's a missing lady, sergeant, and we think she is in that house. I expect a warrant presently.'

'Then I'll keep my eye on the parties, Mr Holmes. If anything comes along, I will surely let you know.'

It was only nine o'clock, and we were off full cry upon the trail at once. First we drove to Brixton Workhouse Infirmary, where we found that it was indeed the truth that a charitable couple had called some days before, that they had claimed an imbecile old woman as a former servant, and that they had obtained permission to take her away with them. No surprise was expressed at the news that she had since died.

The doctor was our next goal. He had been called in, had found the woman dying of pure senility, had actually seen her pass away, and had signed the certificate in due form. 'I assure you that everything was perfectly normal and there was no room for foul play in the matter,' said he. Nothing in the house had struck him as suspicious, save that for people of their class it was remarkable that they should have no servant. So far and no farther went the doctor.

Finally, we found our way to Scotland Yard. There had been difficulties of procedure in regard to the warrant. Some delay was inevitable. The magistrate's signature might not be obtained until next morning. If Holmes would call about nine he could go down with Lestrade and see it acted upon. So ended the day, save that near midnight our friend, the sergeant, called to say that he had seen flickering lights here and there in the windows of the great dark house, but that no one had left it and none had entered. We could but pray for patience, and wait for the morrow.

Sherlock Holmes was too irritable for conversation and too restless for sleep. I left him smoking hard, with his heavy, dark brows knotted together, and his long, nervous fingers tapping upon the arms of his chair, as he turned over in his mind every possible solution of the mystery. Several times in the course of the night I heard him prowling about the house. Finally, just after I had been called in the morning, he rushed into my room. He was in his dressing-gown, but his pale, hollow-eyed face told me that his night had been a sleepless one.

'What time was the funeral? Eight, was it not?' he asked, eagerly. 'Well, it is seven-twenty now. Good heavens, Watson, what has become of any brains that God has given me? Quick, man, quick! It's life or death – a hundred chances on death to one on life. I'll never forgive myself, never, if we are too late!'

Five minutes had not passed before we were flying in a hansom down Baker Street. But even so it was twenty-five to eight as we passed Big Ben, and eight struck as we tore down the Brixton Road. But others were late as well as we. Ten minutes after the hour the hearse was still standing at the door of the house, and even as our foaming horse came to a halt the coffin, supported by three men, appeared on the threshold. Holmes darted forward and barred their way.

'Take it back!' he cried, laying his hand on the breast of the foremost. 'Take it back this instant!'

'What the devil do you mean? Once again I ask you, where is your warrant?' shouted the furious Peters, his big red face glaring over the farther end of the coffin.

'The warrant is on its way. This coffin shall remain in the house until it comes.'

The authority in Holmes's voice had its effect upon the bearers. Peters had suddenly vanished into the house, and they obeyed these new orders. 'Quick, Watson, quick! Here is a screw-driver!' he shouted as the coffin was replaced upon the table. 'Here's one for you, my man! A sovereign if the lid comes off in a minute! Ask no questions – work away! That's good! Another! And another! Now pull all together! It's giving! It's giving! Ah, that does it at last!'

With a united effort we tore off the coffin-lid. As we did so there came from the inside a stupefying and overpowering smell of chloroform. A body lay within, its head all wreathed in cotton-wool, which had been soaked in the narcotic. Holmes plucked it off and disclosed the statuesque face of a handsome and spiritual woman of middle age. In an instant he had passed his arm round the figure and raised her to a sitting position.

'Is she gone, Watson? Is there a spark left? Surely we are not too late!'

For half an hour it seemed that we were. What with actual suffocation, and what with the poisonous fumes of the chloroform, the Lady Frances seemed to have passed the last point of recall. And then, at last, with artificial respiration, with injected ether,[22] with every device that science could suggest, some flutter of life, some quiver of the eyelids, some dimming of a mirror, spoke of the slowly returning life. A cab had driven up, and Holmes, parting the blind, looked out at it. 'Here is Lestrade with his warrant,' said he. 'He will find that his birds have flown. And here,' he added, as a heavy step hurried along the passage, 'is someone who has a better right to nurse this lady than we have. Good morning, Mr Green; I think that the sooner we can move the Lady Frances the better. Meanwhile, the funeral may proceed, and the poor old woman who still lies in that coffin may go to her last resting-place alone.'

'Should you care to add the case to your annals, my dear Watson,' said Holmes that evening, 'it can only be as an example of that temporary eclipse to which even the best-balanced mind may be exposed. Such slips are common to all mortals, and the greatest is he who can recognize and repair them. To this modified credit I may, perhaps, make some claim. My night was haunted by the thought that somewhere a clue, a strange sentence, a curious observation, had come under my notice and had been too easily dismissed. Then, suddenly, in the grey of the morning, the words came back to me. It was the remark of the undertaker's wife, as reported by Philip Green. She had said, "It should be there before now. It took longer, being out of the ordinary." It was the coffin of which she spoke. It had been out of the ordinary. That could only mean that it had been made to some special measurement. But why? Why? Then in an instant I remembered the deep sides, and the little wasted figure at the bottom. Why so large a coffin for so small a body? To leave room for another body. Both would be buried under the one certificate. It had all been so clear, if only my own sight had not been dimmed. At eight the Lady Frances would be buried. Our one chance was to stop the coffin before it left the house.

'It was a desperate chance that we might find her alive, but it *was* a chance, as the result showed. These people had never, to my knowledge, done a murder. They might shrink from actual violence at the last. They could bury her with no sign of how she met her end, and even if she were exhumed there was a chance for them. I hoped that such considerations might prevail with them. You can reconstruct the scene well enough. You saw the horrible den upstairs, where the poor lady had been kept so long. They rushed in and overpowered her with their chloroform, carried her down, poured more into the coffin to insure against her waking, and then screwed down the lid. A clever device, Watson. It is new to me in the annals of crime. If our ex-missionary friends escape the clutches of Lestrade, I shall expect to hear of some brilliant incidents in their future career.'

HIS LAST BOW

An Epilogue of Sherlock Holmes[1]

It was nine o'clock at night upon the second of August – the most terrible August in the history of the world.[2] One might have thought already that God's curse hung heavy over a degenerate world, for there was an awesome hush and a feeling of vague expectancy in the sultry and stagnant air. The sun had long set, but one blood-red gash like an open wound lay low in the distant west. Above, the stars were shining brightly; and below, the lights of the shipping glimmered in the bay.[3] The two famous Germans stood beside the stone parapet of the garden walk, with the long, low, heavily gabled house behind them, and they looked down upon the broad sweep of the beach at the foot of the great chalk cliff[4] on which Von Bork, like some wandering eagle, had perched himself four years before. They stood with their heads close together, talking in low, confidential tones. From below, the two glowing ends of their cigars might have been the smouldering eyes of some malignant fiend looking down in the darkness.

A remarkable man this Von Bork – a man who could hardly be matched among all the devoted agents of the Kaiser.[5] It was his talents which had first recommended him for the English mission, the most important mission of all, but since he had taken it over, those talents had become more and more manifest to the half-dozen people in the world who were really in touch with the truth. One of these was his present companion, Baron Von Herling,[6] the chief secretary of the legation, whose huge 100-horse-power Benz[7] car was blocking the country lane as it waited to waft its owner back to London.

'So far as I can judge the trend of events, you will probably be back in Berlin within the week,' the secretary was saying. 'When you get there, my dear Von Bork, I think you will be surprised at the welcome you will receive. I happen to know what is thought in the highest quarters of your work in this country.' He was a huge man, the secretary, deep, broad, and tall, with a slow, heavy fashion of speech which had been his main asset in his political career.

Von Bork laughed.

'They are not very hard to deceive,' he remarked. 'A more docile, simple folk could not be imagined.'

'I don't know about that,' said the other thoughtfully. 'They have strange limits and one must learn to observe them. It is that surface simplicity of theirs which makes a trap for the stranger. One's first impression is that they are entirely soft. Then one comes suddenly upon something very hard, and you know that you have reached the limit, and must adapt yourself to the fact. They have, for example, their insular conventions which simply *must* be observed.'

'Meaning "good form" and that sort of thing?' Von Bork sighed, as one who had suffered much.

'Meaning British prejudice in all its queer manifestations. As an example I may quote one of my own worst blunders – I can afford to talk of my blunders, for you know my work well enough to be aware of my successes. It was on my first arrival. I was invited to a weekend gathering at the country house of a cabinet minister. The conversation was amazingly indiscreet.'

Von Bork nodded. 'I've been there,' said he dryly.

'Exactly. Well, I naturally sent a résumé of the information to Berlin. Unfortunately our good Chancellor is a little heavy-handed in these matters, and he transmitted a remark which showed that he was aware of what had been said. This, of course, took the trail straight up to me. You've no idea the harm that it did me. There was nothing soft about our British hosts on that occasion, I can assure you. I was two years living it down. Now you, with this sporting pose of yours.'

'No, no, don't call it a pose. A pose is an artificial thing. This is quite natural. I am a born sportsman. I enjoy it.'

'Well, that makes it the more effective. You yacht against them, you hunt with them, you play polo, you match them in every game, your four-in-hand[8] takes the prize at Olympia.[9] I have even heard that you go to the length of boxing with the young officers. What is the result? Nobody takes you seriously. You are a "good old sport", "quite a decent fellow for a German", hard-drinking, night-club, knock-about-town, devil-may-care young fellow. And all the time this quiet country house of yours is the centre of half the mischief in England, and the sporting squire the most astute secret-service man in Europe. Genius, my dear Von Bork – genius!'

'You flatter me, Baron. But certainly I may claim that my four years in this country have not been unproductive. I've never shown you my little store. Would you mind stepping in for a moment.'

The door of the study opened straight on to the terrace. Von Bork pushed it back, and, leading the way, he clicked the switch of the electric light. He then closed the door behind the bulky form which followed him, and carefully adjusted the heavy curtain over the latticed window. Only when all these precautions had been taken and tested did he turn his sunburned aquiline face to his guest.

'Some of my papers have gone,' said he; 'when my wife and the household left yesterday for Flushing[10] they took the less important with them. I must, of course, claim the protection of the Embassy for the others.'

'Your name has already been filed as one of the personal suite. There will be no difficulties for you or your baggage. Of course, it is just possible that we may not have to go. England may leave France to her fate. We are sure that there is no binding treaty between them.'

'And Belgium?'

'Yes, and Belgium, too.'

Von Bork shook his head. 'I don't see how that could be. There is a definite treaty there. She could never recover from such a humiliation.'

'She would at least have peace for the moment.'

'But her honour?'

'Tut, my dear sir, we live in a utilitarian age. Honour is a mediaeval conception. Besides England is not ready. It is an inconceivable thing, but even our special war tax of fifty million, which one would think made our purpose as clear as if we had advertised it on the front page of *The Times*, has not roused these people from their slumbers. Here and there one hears a question. It is my business to find an answer. Here and there also there is an irritation. It is my business to soothe it. But I can assure you that so far as the essentials go – the storage of munitions, the preparation for submarine attack, the arrangements for making high explosives – nothing is prepared. How then can England come in, especially when we have stirred her up such a devil's brew of Irish civil war,[11] window-breaking Furies,[12] and God knows what to keep her thoughts at home?'

'She must think of her future.'

'Ah, that is another matter. I fancy that in the future, we have our own very definite plans about England, and that your information will be very vital to us. It is today or tomorrow with Mr John Bull.[13] If he prefers today we are perfectly ready. If it is tomorrow we shall be more ready still. I should think they would be wiser to fight with allies than without them, but that is their own affair. This week is their week of destiny. But you were speaking of your papers.' He sat in the armchair with the light shining upon his broad bald head, while he puffed sedately at his cigar.

The large oak-panelled, book-lined room had a curtain hung in the further corner. When this was drawn it disclosed a large brass-bound safe. Von Bork detached a small key from his watch-chain, and after some considerable manipulation of the lock he swung open the heavy door.

'Look!' said he, standing clear, with a wave of his hand.

The light shone vividly into the opened safe, and the secretary of the Embassy gazed with an absorbed interest at the rows of stuffed pigeon-holes with which it was furnished. Each pigeon-hole had its label, and his eyes as he glanced along them read a long series of such titles as 'Fords',[14] 'Harbour-defences', 'Aeroplanes', 'Ireland', 'Egypt',[15] 'Portsmouth forts',[16] 'The Channel', 'Rosyth',[17] and a score of others. Each compartment was bristling with papers and plans.

'Colossal!' said the secretary. Putting down his cigar he softly clapped his fat hands.

'And all in four years, Baron. Not such a bad show for the hard-drinking, hard-riding country squire. But the gem of my collection is coming and there is the setting all ready for it.' He pointed to a space over which 'Naval Signals' was printed.

'But you have a good dossier there already.'

'Out of date and waste paper. The Admiralty in some way got the alarm and every code has been changed. It was a blow, Baron – the worst set-back in my whole campaign. But thanks to my cheque-book and the good Altamont all will be well tonight.'

The Baron looked at his watch, and gave a guttural exclamation of disappointment.

'Well, I really can wait no longer. You can imagine that things are moving at present in Carlton House Terrace[18] and that we have all to be at our posts. I had hoped to be able to bring news of your great coup. Did Altamont name no hour?'

Von Bork pushed over a telegram.

'Will come without fail tonight and bring new sparking plugs. Altamont.'

'Sparking plugs, eh?'

'You see he poses as a motor expert and I keep a full garage. In our code everything likely to come up is named after some spare part. If he talks of a radiator it is a battleship, of an oil pump a cruiser, and so on. Sparking plugs are naval signals.'

'From Portsmouth at midday,' said the secretary, examining the superscription. 'By the way, what do you give him?'

'Five hundred pounds for this particular job. Of course he has a salary as well.'

'The greedy rogue. They are useful, these traitors, but I grudge them their blood money.'

'I grudge Altamont nothing. He is a wonderful worker. If I pay him well, at least he delivers the goods, to use his own phrase. Besides he is not a traitor. I assure you that our most pan-Germanic Junker[19] is a sucking dove in his feelings towards England as compared with a real bitter Irish-American.'

'Oh, an Irish-American?'

'If you heard him talk you would not doubt it. Sometimes I assure you I can hardly understand him. He seems to have declared war on the King's English as well as on the English King. Must you really go? He may be here any moment.'

'No. I'm sorry but I have already over-stayed my time. We shall expect you early tomorrow, and when you get that signal book through the little door on the Duke of York's steps[20] you can put a triumphant Finis to your record in England. What! Tokay![21] He indicated a heavily sealed dust-covered bottle which stood with two high glasses upon a salver.

'May I offer you a glass before your journey?'

'No, thanks. But it looks like revelry.'

'Altamont has a nice taste in wines, and he took a fancy to my Tokay. He is a touchy fellow and needs humouring in small things. I have to study him, I assure you.' They had strolled out on to the terrace again, and along it to the further end where at a touch from the Baron's chauffeur the great car shivered and chuckled. 'Those are the lights of Harwich, I suppose,' said the secretary, pulling on his dust coat. 'How still and peaceful it all seems. There may be other lights within the week, and the English coast a less tranquil place! The heavens, too, may not be quite so peaceful if all that the good Zeppelin[22] promises us comes true. By the way, who is that?'

Only one window showed a light behind them; in it there stood a lamp, and beside it, seated at a table, was a dear old ruddy-faced woman in a country cap. She was bending over her knitting and stopping occasionally to stroke a large black cat upon a stool beside her.

'That is Martha,[23] the only servant I have left.'

The secretary chuckled.

'She might almost personify Britannia,' said he, 'with her complete self-absorption and general air of comfortable somnolence. Well, au revoir, Von Bork!' – with a final wave of his hand he sprang into the car, and a moment later the two golden cones from the headlights shot forward through the darkness. The secretary lay back in the cushions of the luxurious limousine, with his thoughts so full of the impending European tragedy that he hardly observed that as his car swung round the village street it nearly passed over a little Ford coming in the opposite direction.

Von Bork walked slowly back to the study when the last gleams of the motor lamps had faded into the distance. As he passed he observed that his old housekeeper had put out her lamp and retired. It was a new experience for him, the silence and darkness of his widespread house, for his family and household had been a large one. It was a relief to him, however, to think that they were all in safety and that, but for that one old woman who had lingered in the kitchen, he had the whole place to himself. There was a good deal of tidying up to do inside his study and he set himself to do it, until his keen, handsome face was flushed with the heat of the burning papers. A leather valise stood beside his table, and into this he began to pack very neatly and systematically the precious contents of his safe. He had hardly got started with the work, however, when his quick ears caught the sound of a distant car. Instantly he gave an exclamation of satisfaction, strapped up the valise, shut the safe, locked it, and hurried out on to the terrace. He was just in time to see the lights of a small car come to a halt at the gate. A passenger sprang out of it and advanced swiftly towards him, while the chauffeur, a heavily built, elderly man, with a grey moustache, settled down, like one who resigns himself to a long vigil.

'Well?' asked Von Bork eagerly, running forward to meet his visitor.

For answer the man waved a small brown-paper parcel triumphantly above his head.

'You can give me the glad hand tonight, Mister,' he cried. 'I'm bringing home the bacon at last.'

'The signals?'

'Same as I said in my cable. Every last one of them, semaphore, lamp code, Marconi – a copy, mind you, not the original. That was too dangerous. But it's the real goods, and you can lay to that.' He slapped the German upon the shoulder with a rough familiarity from which the other winced.

'Come in,' he said. 'I'm all alone in the house. I was only waiting for this. Of course a copy is better than the original. If an original were missing they would change the whole thing. You think it's all safe about the copy?'

The Irish-American had entered the study and stretched his long limbs from the armchair. He was a tall, gaunt man of sixty, with clear-cut features and a small goatee beard which gave him a general resemblance to the caricatures of Uncle Sam.[24] A half-smoked, sodden cigar hung from the corner of his mouth, and as he sat down he struck a match and relit it. 'Making ready for a move?' he remarked as he looked round him. 'Say, Mister,' he added, as his eyes fell upon the safe from which the curtain was now removed, 'you don't tell me you keep your papers in that?'

'Why not?'

'Gosh, in a wide-open contraption like that! And they reckon you to be some spy. Why, a Yankee crook would be into that with a can-opener. If I'd known that any letter of mine was goin' to lie loose in a thing like that I'd have been a mug to write to you at all.'

'It would puzzle any crook to force that safe,' Von Bork answered. 'You won't cut that metal with any tool.'

'But the lock?'

'No, it's a double combination lock. You know what that is?'

'Search me,' said the American.

'Well, you need a word as well as a set of figures before you can get the lock to work.' He rose and showed a double-radiating disc round the keyhole. 'This outer one is for the letters, the inner one for the figures.'

'Well, well, that's fine.'

'So it's not quite as simple as you thought. It was four years ago that I had it made, and what do you think I chose for the word and figures?'

'It's beyond me.'

'Well, I chose August for the word, and 1914 for the figures, and here we are.'

The American's face showed his surprise and admiration.

'My, but that was smart! You had it down to a fine thing.'

'Yes, a few of us even then could have guessed the date. Here it is, and I'm shutting down tomorrow morning.'

'Well, I guess you'll have to fix me up also. I'm not staying in this goldarned country all on my lonesome. In a week or less, from what I see, John Bull will be on his hind legs and fair ramping. I'd rather watch him from over the water.'

'But you're an American citizen?'

'Well, so was Jack James an American citizen, but he's doing time in Portland[25] all the same. It cuts no ice with a British copper to tell him you're an American citizen. "It's British law and order over here," says he. By the way, Mister, talking of Jack James it seems to me you don't do much to cover your men.'

'What do you mean?' Von Bork asked sharply.

'Well, you are their employer, ain't you? It's up to you to see that they don't fall down. But they do fall down and when did you ever pick them up? There's James –'

'It was James's own fault. You know that yourself. He was too self-willed for the job.'

'James was a bonehead – I give you that. Then there was Hollis.'

'The man was mad.'

'Well, he went a bit woozy towards the end. It's enough to make a man bughouse when he has to play a part from morning to night with a hundred guys all ready to set the coppers wise to him. But now there is Steiner –'

Von Bork started violently, and his ruddy face turned a shade paler.

'What about Steiner?'

'Well, they've got him, that's all. They raided his store last night, and he and his papers are all in Portsmouth gaol. You'll go off and he, poor devil, will have to stand the racket, and lucky if he gets off with his life. That's why I want to get over the water as soon as you do.'

Von Bork was a strong, self-contained man, but it was easy to see that the news had shaken him.

'How could they have got on to Steiner?' he muttered. 'That's the worst blow yet.'

'Well, you nearly had a worse one, for I believe they are not far off me.'

'You don't mean that!'

'Sure thing. My landlady down Fratton[26] way had some inquiries, and when I heard of it I guessed it was time for me to hustle. But what

I want to know, Mister, is how the coppers know these things? Steiner is the fifth man you've lost since I signed on with you, and I know the name of the sixth if I don't get a move on. How do you explain it, and ain't you ashamed to see your men go down like this?'

Von Bork flushed crimson.

'How dare you speak in such a way!'

'If I didn't dare things, Mister, I wouldn't be in your service. But I'll tell you straight what is in my mind. I've heard that with you German politicians, when an agent has done his work you are not sorry to see him put away.'

Von Bork sprang to his feet.

'Do you dare to suggest that I have given away my own agents!'

'I don't stand for that, Mister, but there's a stool pigeon or a cross somewhere, and it's up to you to find out where it is. Anyhow I am taking no more chances. It's me for little Holland, and the sooner the better.'

Von Bork had mastered his anger.

'We have been allies too long to quarrel now at the very hour of victory,' he said. 'You've done splendid work, and taken risks and I can't forget it. By all means go to Holland, and you can get a boat from Rotterdam to New York. No other line will be safe a week from now. I'll take that book and pack it with the rest.'

The American held the small parcel in his hand, but made no motion to give it up.

'What about the dough?' he asked.

'The what?'

'The boodle. The reward. The £500. The gunner turned damned nasty at the last, and I had to square him with an extra hundred dollars or it would have been nitsky[27] for you and me. "Nothin' doin'!" says he, and he meant it too, but the last hundred did it. It's cost me two hundred pound from first to last, so it isn't likely I'd give it up without gettin' my wad.'

Von Bork smiled with some bitterness. 'You don't seem to have a very high opinion of my honour,' said he, 'you want the money before you give up the book.'

'Well, Mister, it is a business proposition.'

'All right. Have your way.' He sat down at the table and scribbled a cheque, which he tore from the book, but he refrained from handing it to his companion. 'After all, since we are to be on such terms, Mr Altamont,' said he, 'I don't see why I should trust you any more than you trust me. Do you understand?' he added, looking back over his shoulder at the American. 'There's the cheque upon the table. I claim the right to examine that parcel before you pick the money up.'

The American passed it over without a word. Von Bork undid a winding of string and two wrappers of paper. Then he sat gazing for a moment in silent amazement at a small blue book which lay before him. Across the cover was printed in golden letters *Practical Handbook of Bee Culture*. Only for one instant did the master spy glare at this strangely irrelevant inscription. The next he was gripped at the back of his neck by a grasp of iron, and a chloroformed sponge was held in front of his writhing face.

'Another glass, Watson!' said Mr Sherlock Holmes, as he extended the bottle of Imperial Tokay.

The thickset chauffeur, who had seated himself by the table, pushed forward his glass with some eagerness.

'It is a good wine, Holmes.'

'A remarkable wine, Watson. Our friend upon the sofa has assured me that it is from Franz Joseph's special cellar at the Schoenbrunn Palace.[28] Might I trouble you to open the window, for chloroform vapour does not help the palate.'

The safe was ajar, and Holmes standing in front of it was removing dossier after dossier, swiftly examining each, and then packing it neatly in Von Bork's valise. The German lay upon the sofa sleeping stertorously with a strap round his upper arms and another round his legs.

'We need not hurry ourselves, Watson. We are safe from interruption. Would you mind touching the bell. There is no one in the house except old Martha, who has played her part to admiration. I got her the situation when first I took the matter up. Ah, Martha, you will be glad to hear that all is well.'

The pleasant old lady had appeared in the doorway. She curtseyed with a smile to Mr Holmes, but glanced with some apprehension at the figure upon the sofa.

'It is all right, Martha. He has not been hurt at all.'

'I am glad of that, Mr Holmes. According to his lights he has been a kind master. He wanted me to go with his wife to Germany yesterday, but that would hardly have suited your plans, would it, sir?'

'No, indeed, Martha. So long as you were here I was easy in my mind. We waited some time for your signal tonight.'

'It was the secretary, sir.'

'I know. His car passed ours.'

'I thought he would never go. I knew that it would not suit your plans, sir, to find him here.'

'No, indeed. Well, it only meant that we waited half an hour or so until I saw your lamp go out and knew that the coast was clear. You can report to me tomorrow in London, Martha, at Claridge's Hotel.'[29]

'Very good, sir.'

'I suppose you have everything ready to leave.'

'Yes, sir. He posted seven letters today. I have the addresses as usual.'

'Very good, Martha. I will look into them tomorrow. Goodnight. These papers,' he continued, as the old lady vanished, 'are not of very great importance for, of course, the information which they represent has been sent off long ago to the German Government. These are the originals which could not safely be got out of the country.'

'Then they are of no use.'

'I should not go so far as to say that, Watson. They will at least show our people what is known and what is not. I may say that a good many of these papers have come through me, and I need not add are thoroughly untrustworthy. It would brighten my declining years to see a German cruiser navigating the Solent[30] according to the minefield plans which I have furnished. But you, Watson,' he stopped his work and took his old friend by the shoulders, 'I've hardly seen you in the light yet. How have the years used you? You look the same blithe boy as ever.'

'I feel twenty years younger, Holmes. I have seldom felt so happy as when I got your wire asking me to meet you at Harwich with the car. But you, Holmes – you have changed very little – save for that horrible goatee.'

'These are the sacrifices one makes for one's country, Watson,' said Holmes, pulling at his little tuft. 'Tomorrow it will be but a dreadful memory. With my hair cut and a few other superficial changes I shall no doubt reappear at Claridge's tomorrow as I was before this American stunt – I beg your pardon, Watson, my well of English seems to be permanently defiled – before this American job came my way.'

'But you had retired, Holmes. We heard of you as living the life of a hermit among your bees and your books in a small farm upon the South Downs.'

'Exactly, Watson. Here is the fruit of my leisured ease, the magnum opus of my latter years!' He picked up the volume from the table and read out the whole title, *Practical Handbook of Bee Culture, with some Observations upon the Segregation of the Queen.* 'Alone I did it.[31] Behold the fruit of pensive nights and laborious days, when I watched the little working gangs as once I watched the criminal world of London.'

'But how did you get to work again?'

'Ah, I have often marvelled at it myself. The Foreign Minister[32] alone I could have withstood, but when the Premier[33] also deigned to visit my humble roof – ! The fact is, Watson, that this gentleman upon the sofa was a bit too good for our people. He was in a class by himself. Things were going wrong, and no one could understand why they were going wrong. Agents were suspected or even caught, but there was evidence of some strong and secret central force. It was absolutely necessary to expose it. Strong pressure was brought upon me to look into the matter. It has cost me two years, Watson, but they have not been devoid of excitement. When I say that I started my pilgrimage at Chicago,[34] graduated in an Irish secret society[35] at Buffalo, gave serious trouble to the constabulary at Skibbereen[36] and so eventually caught the eye of a subordinate agent of Von Bork, who recommended me as a likely man,[37] you will realize that the matter was complex. Since then I have been honoured by his confidence, which has not prevented most of his plans going subtly wrong and five of his best agents being in prison. I watched them, Watson, and I picked them as they ripened. Well sir, I hope that you are none the worse!'

The last remark was addressed to Von Bork himself, who after much gasping and blinking had lain quietly listening to Holmes's statement. He broke out now into a furious stream of German invective, his face convulsed with passion. Holmes continued his swift investigation of documents while his prisoner cursed and swore.

'Though unmusical, German is the most expressive of all languages,' he observed, when Von Bork had stopped from pure exhaustion. 'Hullo! Hullo!' he added, as he looked hard at the corner of a tracing before putting it in the box. 'This should put another bird in the cage. I had no idea that the paymaster was such a rascal, though I have long had an eye upon him. Mister Von Bork, you have a great deal to answer for.'

The prisoner had raised himself with some difficulty upon the sofa and was staring with a strange mixture of amazement and hatred at his captor.

'I shall get level with you, Altamont,' he said, speaking with slow deliberation, 'if it takes me all my life I shall get level with you!'

'The old sweet song,' said Holmes. 'How often have I heard it in days gone by. It was a favourite ditty of the late lamented Professor Moriarty. Colonel Sebastian Moran has also been known to warble it. And yet I live and keep bees upon the South Downs.'

'Curse you, you double traitor!' cried the German, straining against his bonds and glaring murder from his furious eyes.

'No, no, it is not so bad as that,' said Holmes, smiling. 'As my speech surely shows you, Mr Altamont of Chicago had no existence in fact. I used him and he is gone.'

'Then who are you?'

'It is really immaterial who I am, but since the matter seems to interest you, Mr Von Bork, I may say that this is not my first acquaintance with the members of your family. I have done a good deal of business in Germany in the past and my name is probably familiar to you.'

'I would wish to know it,' said the Prussian grimly.

'It was I who brought about the separation[38] between Irene Adler and the late King of Bohemia when your cousin Heinrich was the Imperial Envoy. It was I also who saved from murder, by the Nihilist

Klopman, Count Von and Zu Grafenstein,[39] who was your mother's elder brother. It was I –'

Von Bork sat up in amazement.

'There is only one man,' he cried.

'Exactly,' said Holmes.

Von Bork groaned and sank back on the sofa. 'And most of that information came through you,' he cried. 'What is it worth? What have I done? It is my ruin for ever!'

'It is certainly a little untrustworthy,' said Holmes. 'It will require some checking and you have little time to check it. Your admiral may find the new guns rather larger than he expects, and the cruisers perhaps a trifle faster.'

Von Bork clutched at his own throat in despair.

'There are a good many other points of detail which will, no doubt, come to light in good time. But you have one quality which is very rare in a German, Mr Von Bork; you are a sportsman and you will bear me no ill-will when you realize that you, who have outwitted so many other people, have at last been outwitted yourself. After all, you have done your best for your country, and I have done my best for mine, and what could be more natural? Besides,' he added, not unkindly, as he laid his hand upon the shoulder of the prostrate man, 'it is better than to fall before some more ignoble foe. These papers are now ready, Watson. If you will help me with our prisoner, I think that we may get started for London at once.'

It was no easy task to move Von Bork, for he was a strong and a desperate man. Finally, holding either arm, the two friends walked him very slowly down the garden walk which he had trod with such proud confidence when he received the congratulations of the famous diplomatist only a few hours before. After a short, final struggle he was hoisted, still bound hand and foot, into the spare seat of the little car. His precious valise was wedged in beside him.

'I trust that you are as comfortable as circumstances permit,' said Holmes, when the final arrangements were made. 'Should I be guilty of a liberty if I lit a cigar and placed it between your lips?'

But all amenities were wasted upon the angry German.

'I suppose you realize, Mr Sherlock Holmes,' said he, 'that if your

Government bears you out in this treatment it becomes an act of war.'

'What about your Government and all this treatment?' said Holmes, tapping the valise.

'You are a private individual. You have no warrant for my arrest. The whole proceeding is absolutely illegal and outrageous.'

'Absolutely,' said Holmes.

'Kidnapping a German subject.'

'And stealing his private papers.'

'Well, you realize your position, you and your accomplice here. If I were to shout for help as we pass through the village –'

'My dear sir, if you did anything foolish you would probably enlarge the too limited titles of our village inns by giving us "The Dangling Prussian" as a sign-post. The Englishman is a patient creature, but at present his temper is a little inflamed and it would be as well not to try him too far. No, Mr Von Bork, you will go with us in a quiet, sensible fashion to Scotland Yard, whence you can send for your friend Baron Von Herling and see if even now you may not fill that place which he has reserved for you in the ambassadorial suite. As to you, Watson, you are joining up with your old service,[40] as I understand, so London won't be out of your way. Stand with me here upon the terrace for it may be the last quiet talk that we shall ever have.'

The two friends chatted in intimate converse for a few minutes, recalling once again the days of the past whilst their prisoner vainly wriggled to undo the bonds that held him. As they turned to the car, Holmes pointed back to the moonlit sea, and shook a thoughtful head.

'There's an east wind coming, Watson.'

'I think not, Holmes. It is very warm.'

'Good old Watson! You are the one fixed point in a changing age. There's an east wind coming all the same, such a wind as never blew on England yet. It will be cold and bitter, Watson, and a good many of us may wither before its blast. But it's God's own wind none the less, and a cleaner, better, stronger land will lie in the sunshine when the storm has cleared. Start her up, Watson, for it's time that we were on our way. I have a cheque for five hundred pounds which should be cashed early, for the drawer is quite capable of stopping it, if he can.'

NOTES

The Valley of Fear

First published in the *Strand* magazine, September 1914–May 1915. The opening section at Birlstone is set in 1888.

PART ONE

CHAPTER I
The Warning

1. *said I*: Conan Doyle did not originally intend to use Watson as narrator. The original manuscript includes expressions such as 'said Dr Watson'.

2. *Porlock's writing*: Samuel Taylor Coleridge claimed that the arrival of a man from Porlock (a town in Somerset) woke him out of the drug-induced reverie in which he produced *Kubla Khan* (1816). Conan Doyle's use of the name suggests that the letter from Porlock jolts Holmes out of a drug-induced torpor, and indeed we learn later that 'a long series of sterile weeks lay behind us', a sign that Holmes has been indulging his habit of taking cocaine.

3. *nom de plume*: French – pen name.

4. *You have heard me speak of Professor Moriarty*: This poses a chronological problem. In 'The Final Problem', from *The Memoirs of Sherlock Holmes*, set later in 1891, in which Moriarty dies, Watson claims not to know of his existence.

5. *A touch – a distinct touch*: A turn of phrase that Holmes used in *The Hound of the Baskervilles* when it was revealed to him that a pursuer had given his name to the cabman as Sherlock Holmes.

6. *libel*: A libel has to be written. Watson is uttering a slander.

7. *solatium*: Compensation awarded for injury to feelings.

8. *The Dynamics of an Asteroid*: Conan Doyle's usual source of inspiration for astronomical references was Major-General Alfred Wicks Drayson, who lectured on 'Thirty Thousand Years of the Earth's History read by the aid of Astronomy' in Conan Doyle's presence in Southsea.

9. *Birlstone*: To birl, according to the Oxford English Dictionary, is to move with rotary motion, as a rifle bullet does.

10. *apocrypha*: Greek – hidden things; also the name given to the fourteen books of the Bible included as an appendix to certain versions only.

11. *Machiavellian*: Cunning and opportunist statesmanship in the style of Niccolò Machiavelli (1469–1527), Italian politician and author.

12. *Bradshaw*: The national rail timetable, named after Manchester printer George Bradshaw (1801–53), who drew up the first railway timetable in 1839.

13. *inadmissible*: On the contrary, any dictionary would be ideal as it would contain almost every word needed: but the many different editions pose the same difficulty as the Bible.

14. *Whitaker's Almanack*: Originally compiled by Joseph Whitaker in 1868.

15. *Mahratta*: A group of Indian chieftains broken up by the British in 1818.

16. *We are undone*: 'Woe is me! for I am undone' Isaiah 6: 5.

17. *seventh of January*: The previous night, 6 January, being twelfth night. Some commentators have claimed that 6 January is Holmes's birthday and that he can't eat breakfast as he has been celebrating the night before.

CHAPTER 2
Mr Sherlock Holmes Discourses

1. *Camberwell*: Working-class suburb of south-east London, three miles from the centre.

2. *C.I.D.*: Criminal Investigation Department of Scotland Yard, the Metropolitan Police headquarters, which was then based on Derby Gate, to the north-west of Westminster Bridge.

3. *Jean Baptiste Greuze*: Jean Baptiste Greuze (1725–1805), French artist whose vanity so upset his fellow artists he failed to be elected to the Academy in 1769.

4. *All knowledge comes useful to the detective*: Contrast with the passage in *A Study in Scarlet* (Chapter 2) in which Holmes, rebuffing Watson's astonishment that he didn't realize that the earth travelled round the sun, replies that now he knows he will do his best to forget it so that he doesn't lumber his 'brain-attic' with unnecessary information.

5. *Portalis sale*: Benjamin Disraeli bought a Greuze in the Portale (not Portalis) Gallery of Art sale in Paris in 1865 for £1,800. When it turned out to be a forgery the gallery agreed to buy it back and later sold it as 'after Greuze' for £45.

6. *Jonathan Wild*: Well-known English criminal (1682–1725) who led a scam involving selling back stolen property to its owner. He was hanged at Tyburn, in central London, on 24 May 1725.

7. *he wasn't in a novel*: He was: Henry Fielding's *The Life of Jonathan Wild the Great* (1743).

8. *Colonel Sebastian Moran*: He attempted to assassinate Holmes in 'The Empty House' from *The Return of Sherlock Holmes*.

9. *the Prime Minister*: The Conservative Lord Salisbury (Robert Arthur Talbot Gascoyne Cecil, 1830–1903) was prime minister from 1886 to 1892, a period which covers the possible dates for the setting of this episode.

CHAPTER 3
The Tragedy of Birlstone

1. *I will ask leave to remove my own insignificant personality*: The only instance in the canon of Watson beginning as narrator and then introducing a purely descriptive piece. Although most of the second section of the first Holmes story, the novella *A Study in Scarlet*, is in the third person it is not introduced by Watson.

2. *the great Weald forest*: It covers parts of Sussex, Kent and Surrey.

3. *Tunbridge Wells*: A popular town in Kent which attained importance after the discovery of chalybeate springs in 1606.

4. *ten or twelve miles*: Conan Doyle once revealed that the model for Birlstone Manor was Groombridge House, *three* miles from Tunbridge Wells.

5. *time of the first Crusade*: The first Crusade took place between 1095 and 1099 and led to the capture of Jerusalem by the Seljuk Turks.

6. *Hugo de Capus*: Capus is a portmanteau Latin concoction of capus (head) and corpus (body), and the name echoes that of Hugh Capet, king of France 987–96.

7. *fortalice in the centre of the estate, which had been granted to him by the Red King*: A cleverly worded Carrollian joke. A fortalice is a small fort; and the Red King is William Rufus, England's King William II (1056–1100), but the name also conjures up the twisted logic of Lewis Carroll's *Through the Looking Glass* (1871).

8. *Jacobean times*: Referring to the period when James I was on the throne (1603–25).

CHAPTER 5
The People of the Drama

1. *I have been in the Valley of Fear. I am not out of it yet*: 'Yea, though I walk through the valley of the shadow of death, I will fear no evil' – Psalm 23: 4.

2. *Bodymaster*: The head of a quasi-masonic lodge.

CHAPTER 6
A Dawning Light

1. *genius loci*: Latin – the atmosphere, or guardian spirit, of a place.

CHAPTER 7
The Solution

1. *East Ham*: District now in Greater London, then in Essex, a mile north of the Thames.

2. *fifth year of James I*: 1608.

3. *the second George*: George II reigned 1727–60 and was the last British king to lead his troops in battle (at the War of the Austrian Succession).

4. *Possess our souls in patience and make as little noise as possible*: 'In your patience possess ye your souls.' Luke 21: 19. In 'The Adventure of Wisteria Lodge', from *His Last Bow*, Holmes says, 'We can only possess our souls in patience.'

5. *dénouement*: French – an untying, i.e. the resolution of a plot.

6. *Vermissa*: Pottsville in the Schuylkill Valley, Pennsylvania.

7. *peine forte et dure*: French – heavy and harsh punishment.

8. *twenty years in time*: Not quite that long, for the story that follows begins in 1875 whereas the preceding section obviously takes place some time before the death of Moriarty, which according to 'The Final Problem', from *The Memoirs of Sherlock Holmes*, happened in 1891.

PART TWO

The second section of *The Valley of Fear* was based on Allan J. Pinkerton's book *The Mollie Maguires and the Detectives* (1877) and to a lesser extent F. P. Dewees's *The Molly Maguires: The Origin, Growth, and Character of the Organisation* (also 1877), and the Scowrers are evidently the Molly Maguires, a secret society founded in Ireland in the 1840s. Some see them as socialist martyrs and victims of ethnic prejudice but the majority view is that they were unprincipled megalomanic terrorists who, as James Mackay in *Allan Pinkerton: The Eye Who Never Slept* (Mainstream, Edinburgh, 1996) explained, 'terrorised and intimidated the English, Welsh and German miners in Pennsylvania and reacted ferociously against fellow Irishmen who crossed them'. They attained their unusual name from their habit of dressing in women's clothes and were also known as the White Boys, owing to their habit of dressing in white sheets, and the Buckshots, as they would often let fly at the intended victim with buckshot. As Owen Dudley Edwards noted, Conan Doyle probably took the name Scowrers from a line in Macaulay's *History of England* about gangs of late seventeenth-century London youths called the Scourers.

CHAPTER I
The Man

1. *Gilmerton Mountains*: Gilmerton is a district in Edinburgh, and there is a Gilberton near Shenandoah.

2. *Vermissa*: Based on Pottsville in the Schuylkill Valley (Vermissa Valley), Pennsylvania.

3. *the Ancient Order of Freemen*: Based on the Ancient Order of Hibernians, a fraternal society of Catholics promoting unity, friendship and Christian charity. It dates back to 1565 in Ireland and 1836 in America.

4. *He raised his right hand to his right eyebrow*: When two members of the Order of Hibernians met one would raise the top of the little finger of the right hand to the outer corner of the right eye while the other would catch the right lapel of the first member's coat with the little finger and the thumb of the right hand. This ritual and others were regularly changed by the head lodges in Ireland.

5. *Dark nights are unpleasant*: The Order used 'The nights are very dark'; 'I hope they will soon mend'.

6. *Sheridan Street*: There was a Sheridan House, Centre Street, Pottsville, mentioned in *The Mollie Maguires and the Detectives*.

7. *Black Jack McGinty*: The name is based on Black Jack Kehoe, Bodymaster of Girardville, but his characteristics are attributable to Bodymaster Big Pat Dormer, proprietor of Sheridan House, Pottsville.

8. *By gosh*: Some texts use the more aggressive 'By gar', which was possibly a corruption of 'By Gard', a phonetic representation of how an American might say 'By God'. George Newnes, proprietor of the *Strand*, frowned upon blasphemous oaths and even bowdlerizations such as By Gar.

9. *Swedish*: In Conan Doyle's original text the Shafters were German, but when the Great War broke in 1914 Greenhough Smith, editor of the *Strand*, urged Conan Doyle prior to publication to change their ethnicity.

CHAPTER 2
The Bodymaster

1. *County Monaghan*: Irish county belonging to the old province of Ulster, now in the Republic of Ireland.

2. *Buffalo*: City on the western edge of New York State by Lake Erie.

3. *acushla*: Cod Irish, translatable as 'O darling'.

4. *You've sowed – and, by the Lord, I'll see that you reap*: 'For whatsoever a man soweth, that shall he also reap' – Galatians 6: 7.

5. *elevated his little finger as he drank it*: Evidently another secret sign rather than the much-clichéd upper-middle-class English mannerism it is now.

CHAPTER 3
Lodge 341, Vermissa

1. *paid tool of the men of capital*: As Mackay notes, 'the Molly Maguires are often held up as martyrs of the labour movement . . . the plain fact is that the Molly Maguires were gangsters and hoodlums without any redeeming features.'

2. *greatness thrust upon him*: 'Some men are born great, some achieve greatness, and some have greatness thrust upon them' – Malvolio in Shakespeare's *Twelfth Night*, II.v.144.

3. *there were particular rites in Vermissa*: To be initiated into the Molly Maguires, applicants went through a ceremony which began: 'The neophyte will kneel. Now get down on your prayer-boxes. We're joined together to promote friendship, unity and true Christian charity among our members . . .' Drinking toasts usually began, 'The emperor of France and Don Carlos of Spain may unite together and the people's rights maintain.'

4. *D.M.A.O.F.*: Division Master Ancient Order of Freemen.

5. *James Stanger, of the Herald*: The name comes from Thomas Sanger, a colliery boss whom the Molly Maguires murdered, but the character is based on Thomas Foster of the *Shenandoah Herald*.

CHAPTER 5
The Darkest Hour

1. *Evans Pott*: There was a Welsh gang in the Schuylkill region, the Modocs, who clashed with the Molly Maguires in the 1870s.

2. *the huge Danton may have felt for the puny but dangerous Robespierre*: Georges Jacques Danton (1759–94), French revolutionary, lawyer and a powerful speaker, who led the 1792 uprising which overthrew the French monarchy. He was arrested for conspiracy in 1794 and guillotined on Robespierre's orders. Maximilien François Marie Isidore de Robespierre (1758–94) was a more extreme French revolutionary who as leader of the Jacobins supported the execution of Louis XVI. He was also guillotined in 1794.

3. *Lawler and Andrews*: There were two Molly Maguires called Muff Lawler and Frank McAndrew but their characteristics do not coincide with *The Valley of Fear*'s Lawler and Andrews.

4. *Josiah H. Dunne*: A Henry H. Dunne, superintendent of one of the largest coal-mining corporations in the county, who lived in Pottsville, was killed by the Mollies in January 1866. However the nature of the murder of Dunne and Menzies here is reminiscent of the Mollies' murder of Thomas Sanger, a colliery superintendent, and William Uren.

5. *the shooting of Policemen Hunt and Evans*: Two policemen, Benjamin Yost and Barney McCarron, were murdered by the Molly Maguires in July 1875.

6. *Mrs Larbey*: Based on Mrs Ellen McAllister, who was killed by the Molly Maguires on 10 December 1875.

CHAPTER 6
Danger

1. *Pinkerton's*: The Pinkerton National Detective Agency, founded by Alan Pinkerton in 1850, which helped break the Molly Maguires.

2. *There's business here that wants a Solomon in judgement*: As in the biblical Solomon, king of Israel, whose wisdom permeates the First Book of Kings.

CHAPTER 7
The Trapping of Birdy Edwards

1. *I am Birdy Edwards!*: This is the 'surprise' which Conan Doyle hoped would be a 'real staggerer', as he outlined to Herbert Greenhough Smith, editor of the *Strand* magazine. When T. S. Eliot was asked at a meeting of the Wednesday Club in the 1950s to name his favourite piece of prose, he recited McMurdo's 'confession', to the amazement of his fellow guests of the literary club, none of whom recognized the piece.

2. *of Pinkerton's*: Allan Pinkerton, asked by Franklin Benjamin Gowen of the Philadelphia and Reading Coal and Iron Company to help break the Molly Maguires, sent a detective called James McParland, who went under the alias James McKenna and arrived in Pennsylvania in October 1873 disguised as a tramp and supposedly a fugitive from a murder charge in Buffalo. He soon won the trust of the Mollies in Pottsville, Girardville, Mahanoy City and Shenandoah, but was so cavalier in his dealings that by February 1876 one bodymaster was laying bets that McParland was the informer they had been looking for. He managed to placate critics but faced considerable psychological discomfort when the police began hauling in members of the gang, and only blew his cover when he began testifying in court against the organization.

3. *three months of it*: McParland/McKenna was in the coalfield region for two-and-a-half years.

4. *The trial of the Scowrers*: The real trial in fact began in Pottsville on 4 May 1876 with McParland alias McKenna appearing as chief witness against, at first, eleven leading Mollies. A year later nineteen of the Mollies were hanged and it is now generally accepted that almost all of those hanged did commit the crimes for which they were convicted. One bodymaster, Black Jack Kehoe, suffered an agonizingly slow death when the hangman failed to tie the knot correctly. Ironically, he was later posthumously pardoned for the murder for which he was indicted.

5. *cringing and whining*: On the contrary, those hanged failed to cringe and whine, leading the *New York Times* to declare that no good had come of the trials, which the authorities had hoped would break the spirit of the remaining Mollies.

Epilogue

1. *He was murdered?*: The Philadelphia and Reading Coal and Iron Company executive Franklin Benjamin Gowen, who enlisted Pinkerton's aid to help break the Molly Maguires, was found dead in his hotel room in Washington DC on 13 December 1889. He had supposedly shot himself but there was much speculation that the Mollies had taken revenge.

Selected Cases
from *The Return of Sherlock Holmes*

THE EMPTY HOUSE

First published in the *Strand* magazine, October 1903. Conan Doyle rated 'The Empty House' the sixth best Holmes short story (excluding those that appeared in *The Case-Book of Sherlock Holmes*), as revealed in the *Strand*, June 1927. The story is set in 1894, when Holmes has been missing, presumed dead, for three years, since supposedly falling into the Reichenbach Falls, Switzerland, after a battle with his long-time adversary, Professor Moriarty, in 1891, at the end of 'The Final Problem'.

1. *the Honourable*: The title denotes that Adair is the son of a peer.
2. *ten years*: The events take place in 1894; the story was first published in October 1903.
3. *Earl of Maynooth*: Maynooth is a town in Ireland fifteen miles west of Dublin.
4. *427 Park Lane*: Park Lane, which lies between Hyde Park to the west and Mayfair to the east, forms part of the western border of London's West End. The eastern side of the street is now lined with expensive hotels but in the 1890s there were fewer hotels and more private apartment blocks as well as a few houses. The numbers have never reached as high as 427.
5. *the Baldwin*: A card club that stood at 79a Pall Mall.
6. *the Cavendish*: A club that was then based at 307 Regent Street.
7. *Bagatelle*: Fictitious, although the word is used in gambling circles as a euphemism for a big financial loss.

NOTES

8. *crocuses in full bloom*: The end of March is rather late for crocuses, especially in London.

9. *The Origin of Tree Worship*: Part-title of an essay by Conan Doyle's friend, the minor novelist Grant Allen.

10. *Church Street*: Kensington Church Street, which connects Notting Hill and Kensington.

11. *British Birds*: Possibly the six-volume *A History of British Birds* by the Revd F. O. Morris (1857).

12. *Catullus*: Gaius Valerius Catullus (*c.* 84–54BC), Roman lyric poet.

13. *The Holy War*: Perhaps a 1639 first edition of Thomas Fuller's *History of the Holy Warre* or John Bunyan's *The Holy War* (1682).

14. *baritsu*: Conan Doyle probably meant bartitsu, a new method of unarmed self-defence devised by E. W. Barton-Wright and outlined in 'The New Art of Self-Defence' in *Pearson's Magazine*, spring 1899.

15. *land of the living*: 'Man knoweth not the price therefore neither is it found in the land of the living' – Job 28: 13.

16. *visiting Lhasa*: No European was allowed into the Tibetan city of Lhasa at the time. In 1903 Lieutenant-Colonel Younghusband's troops forced their way in.

17. *head Lama*: The Dalai Lama, originally the abbot of the Bras-spuns monastery outside Lhasa, Tibet. In Buddhist tradition his successors are seen as reincarnations of an indefinite series. Had anyone such as Holmes been able to enter Lhasa they would have probably met the reclusive Dalai Lama, the Teshai Lama Pan-chen Rim-Poche, or the Regent, the abbot of the Ten-gye-ling monastery in Lhasa. Over the years some texts have used the word 'Llama' (a South American animal) rather than 'Lama', which prompted Ogden Nash (1902–71) to quip: 'The one-l lama, He's a priest. The two-l llama, He's a beast.'

18. *Sigerson*: Based on the Swede Sven Hedin (1865–1952).

19. *Mecca*: Holy city in what is now Saudi Arabia and birthplace of Muhammad. In summer 1893 trouble had broken out between the Ottoman rulers and community leaders.

20. *the Khalifa at Kartoum*: The Khalifa (then Said Abdullah ibn-Said Muhammad) was the Muslim ruler of the Sudan. He moved his seat to nearby Omdurman after the sacking of Khartoum, the Sudanese capital, in 1885. Omdurman itself was overthrown by General Kitchener in 1898, and he returned the Sudanese government to Khartoum.

21. *my own sad bereavement*: presumed to be the death of Watson's wife.

22. *hansom*: A two-wheeled covered carriage drawn by one horse and named after its designer, J. A. Hansom (1803–82).

23. *Cavendish Square*: Square lying north-west of Oxford Circus laid out in 1717.

24. *Our route was certainly a singular one*: Holmesian scholars have expended much energy trying to trace an appropriate route from Cavendish Square to the Empty House, and Holmes-flavoured literary tours of the area follow any number of supposed routes. However it is worth remembering that no route is given in the text or described anywhere else by the author.

25. *small road, lined with old, gloomy houses*: This is likely to be Dorset Street.

26. *Here he turned swiftly down a narrow passage, passed through a wooden gate into a deserted yard, and then opened with a key the back door of a house*: The piece is based on an episode in Edgar Allan Poe's 'The Murders in the Rue Morgue' in which Dupin and the narrator first visit the scene of the murders: 'Before going in we walked up the street, turned down an alley, and then, again turning, passed in the rear of the building.'

Conan Doyle scholars have seized on the phrase 'down a narrow passage [from Blandford Street]' as proof that the empty house must lie on either Broadstone Place (then Blandford Mews), which runs north from Blandford Street to Dorset Street, or Kendall Place (then Kendall's Mews), which runs south from Blandford Street to George Street. This would locate the Empty House somewhere in the modern-day numbers 20–70 Baker Street, with number 221B opposite in a stretch which has since been completely redeveloped.

27. *Camden House*: There was a Camden House Preparatory School at 13 York Place (now 118 Baker Street), a few hundred yards to the north rather than the south of Dorset Street. It is now occupied by chartered accountants.

28. *opposite*: Given the address of the real-life Camden House, in 1894 the properties opposite were 30 York Place (now 111 Baker Street), home of the Portman Estate Office in 1894 and now a post office, or 29 York Place (now 109 Baker Street), a boys' school in 1894 and now offices for several companies.

29. *I trust that age doth not wither nor custom stale my infinite variety*: 'Age cannot wither her, nor custom stale/Her infinite variety.' Enobarbus in Shakespeare's *Antony and Cleopatra* II.ii.241.

30. *jew's-harp*: A small lyre-shaped musical instrument with a metal frame which is held between the teeth while a steel tongue is plucked by the fingers.

31. *as the old play says*: Shakespeare's *Twelfth Night*; the phrase can be found in Act II, Scene iii, line 42.

32. *shikari*: Hindi – sportsman.

33. *air-gun*: First developed by Güter of Nuremberg in 1530.

34. *Von Herder, the blind German mechanic*: Fictitious.

35. *1st Bengalore Pioneers*: Named after Bangalore, the fifth most populous city in India.

36. *Jowaki*: A Pathan tribe in Afghanistan who were subdued in 1878–9.

37. *Afghan Campaign*: The second Afghan War (1878–80), which began out of Britain's concern with Russian influence in the mountainous country.

38. *Charasiab*: Two and a half thousand soldiers, including 800 Europeans, beat off 10,000 Afghans at a battle in this village five miles south of the capital, Kabul, on 6 October 1879.

39. *Sherpur*: A district near Kabul where a battle botched by the British took place on 23 December 1879.

40. *Cabul*: Or Kabul, the capital of Afghanistan, which Lieutenant-General Frederick Roberts occupied in 1879.

41. *Conduit Street*: It runs west off Regent Street towards Berkeley Square.

42. *Anglo-Indian*: Fictitious.

43. *Tankerville*: Fictitious.

44. *Bagatelle Card Club*: Fictitious, as in Note 7.

45. *crawled down a drain after a wounded man-eating tiger*: T. S. Eliot adapted this line in 'Gus, The Theatre Cat', from *Old Possum's Book of Practical Cats* (1939); Gus had played a tiger chased down a drain by an Indian Colonel.

46. *Lauder*: Berwickshire town thirty miles south-east of Edinburgh.

47. *Colonel Moran will trouble us no more*: Moran would surely have been hanged, yet Holmes refers to him as still being alive in 'The Adventure of the Illustrious Client' from *The Case-Book of Sherlock Holmes*, which is set in 1902.

THE DANCING MEN

First published in the *Strand* magazine, December 1903. Hilton Cubitt explains that the previous year he 'came up to London for the Jubilee'; therefore the story is set either in 1888, the year after Queen Victoria's Golden Jubilee, or 1898, after her Diamond Jubilee. The idea of the dancing men came courtesy of G. J. Cubitt, the seven-year-old son of the proprietor of the Hill House Hotel, Happisburgh, Norfolk, where Conan Doyle stayed in May 1903 while visiting his brother-in-law, E. W. Hornung. Asked to sign an autograph book, Conan Doyle saw a group of dancing matchstick-like characters which the seven-year-old had drawn on the page. The boy may have got the idea from an article called 'The Language of the Restless Imps', which had appeared in the *St Nicholas Magazine* in May 1874, while a cipher similar to the one used in this story appeared in the *Boy's Own Paper* in January 1881. Other suggested sources are the writings of the Italian secret political society the Carbonari, the 'Alphabet of Hermes' in Albert Mackey's *Encyclopaedia of Freemasonry* (1874), and the second edition of 'A Manual of Signals' (1866) in which Major Alfred J. Meyer of the Signal Corps of the Union Army (USA) explained how one could turn letters of the alphabet into signals that could be sent by flags and sketched out 'little figures of men' to show the form that ciphers could take. (Semaphore, developed by a French engineer, Claude Chappe, in 1794 and used mainly by the military is a similar system.)

The plot also borrows from Edgar Allan Poe's 'The Gold-Bug', which Conan Doyle called the prototype of all 'treasure-hunting, cryptogram-solving yarns' and which centres around Legrand's deciphering of a code on a piece of paper left by the pirate Captain Kidd by reasoning that the most common letter in the English language is 'E'. Conan Doyle rated 'The Dancing Men' as the third best Holmes story (excluding those that appeared in *The Case-Book of Sherlock Holmes*), as revealed in the *Strand* magazine in June 1927.

1. *Dancing*: Poe's 'The Gold-Bug', partly responsible for 'The Dancing Men', is headed with an epigraph from Charles Dibdin's *All in the Wrong*: 'What ho! what ho! this fellow is dancing mad!/He hath been bitten by the Tarantula.'

2. *South African securities*: A few months before writing the story Conan Doyle had invested in a South African mine.

3. *this sudden intrusion into my most intimate thoughts*: Holmes's opening gambit of breaking in on Watson's thoughts come from Poe's 'The Murders in the Rue Morgue' in which Dupin breaks in on the narrator's thoughts after fifteen minutes of silence while the two walk through Paris. Ironically Holmes in *A Study In Scarlet* had denigrated Dupin's habit of doing this as 'really very showy and superficial'.

4. *You never play billiards except with Thurston*: The name of Watson's billiards partner is an obvious reference to the firm of John Thurston and Co., perhaps the best-known billiard-table manufacturer in the nineteenth century, based on Catherine Street, off the Strand.

5. *Hilton Cubitt, of Ridling Thorpe Manor, Norfolk*: Cubitt was the name of the proprietor of the Hill House Hotel in Happisburgh, Norfolk, where Conan Doyle first came upon the idea of the dancing men (see above). Ridling Thorpe is a combination of the Norfolk villages Ridlington and Edingthorpe.

6. *Jubilee*: Queen Victoria celebrated her Golden Jubilee, marking her 50th year on the throne, in 1887 and her Diamond Jubilee, the 60th anniversary, in 1897.

7. *Russell Square*: Large square in Bloomsbury, laid out in 1800.

8. *North Walsham*: A Norfolk village fifteen miles north of Norwich.

9. *enormous square-towered churches*: Norfolk is renowned for its old churches: according to Pevsner there are 659 pre-1700 churches in the county.

10. *German Ocean*: Until the First World War this was a common name for the North Sea.

11. *The bullet had passed through the front of her brain*: surely she would be dead, rather than merely unconscious, after this.

12. *East Ruston*: Village five miles south of North Walsham where E. W. Horning, Conan Doyle's brother-in-law and creator of the Raffles books, lived.

13. *secret writings*: Fletcher Pratt in 'The Secret Message of the Dancing Men' explains how there are 784 possible permutations of combining the legs, arms and various postures in positions similar to those used in the story. Turning each character on its head as with D, G and T allows 1,568 combinations.

14. *As you are aware, E is the most common letter in the English alphabet*: Based on the speech by Legrand in Poe's 'The Gold-Bug': 'Now in English, the letter which most frequently occurs is *e* . . .'

15. *Speaking roughly, T, A, O, I, N, S, H, R, D and L are the numerical order in which letters occur*: This is the frequency that compositors cite. In 'The Gold-Bug' the order given is E, A, O, I, D, H, N, R, S, T, U, Y, C, F, G, L, M, W, B, K, P, Q, X, Z, with J and V ignored. William Baring-Gould noted that Laurence Dwight Smith in *Cryptography: The Science of Secret Writing* gave the order of frequency as E, T, O, A, N, I, R, S, H, D, L, C, W, U, M, F, Y, G, P. B, V, K, X, Q, J, Z.

16. *What one man can invent another can discover*: Holmes's claim echoes Legrand's statement in Poe's 'The Gold-Bug' – 'It may well be doubted whether human ingenuity can construct an enigma of the kind which human ingenuity may not, by proper application, resolve.'

BLACK PETER

First published in the *Strand* magazine, March 1904 (and set in 1895). Inspiration came from Conan Doyle's experiences as ship's doctor on an Arctic whaler, the *Hope*, in 1880.

1. *the Duke of Holdernesse*: The story is recounted in 'The Priory School', included in the full collection of *The Return of Sherlock Holmes*.

2. *his Holiness the Pope*: In 1895 this would have been Leo XIII.

3. *whale fisher*: Conan Doyle served on an Arctic whaler, the *Hope*, in 1880 and wrote about his experiences in the article 'Life on a Greenland Whaler' in the *Strand* of January 1897. Black Peter may have been based on an unnamed member of the crew who was believed to be on the run from the law.

4. *Woodman's Lee, near Forest Row, in Sussex*: There is a Compton's Lea in Horsham, ten miles west of Forest Row.

5. *tantalus*: A locked case in which bottles are kept, their contents tantalizingly displayed; named after Tantalus, a Greek mythological king and son of Pelops, who was punished by having to stand in water which receded as he tried to drink it.

6. *Ratcliff Highway*: The main road leading east from the Tower of London towards Limehouse (now simply The Highway), named after the red cliff ('ratcliff') at its eastern end by the Thames. It was the first road of importance that sailors disembarking from ships in the port of London would come across. Ratcliff Highway became infamous in 1811 following the so-called Ratcliff Highway murders in which members of the Marr household at number twenty-nine were butchered by an unknown assailant believed to be a sailor, John Williams.

7. *Lord Street*: Fictitious.

8. *ribston-pippin*: A type of apple. 'A little hard-headed, Ripstone-pippin-faced man' – Charles Dickens, *The Pickwick Papers*, Chapter 6.

9. *Patrick Cairns*: Probably based on another of Conan Doyle's whaler ship-mates, Colin Maclean, a hot-tempered harpooner.

10. *Shetland lights*: Lighthouses off the Shetland Islands, north of Scotland.

CHARLES AUGUSTUS MILVERTON

First published in the *Strand* magazine, April 1904. Original title: 'The Worst Man in London'. Holmes scholars are torn over when this story is set, with various years between 1882 and 1899 cited.

1. *Charles Augustus Milverton*: The subject of the story was probably based on a mixture of Charles Augustus Howell, secretary to John Ruskin and a black-mailer, and Charles Augustus Bynoe, a contemporary forger.

2. *Appledore Towers*: Humphrey Morton, in 'A Milvertonian Identification' in the *Sherlock Holmes Journal* (Winter 1962), claimed that the house is The Logs, a riot of eccentric Gothic embellishments, which is situated in Hampstead at the corner of Well Road and East Heath Road and was built in 1868 to the designs of J. S. Nightingale. In the 1960s it was the home of the comedian Marty Feldman.

3. *Zoo*: Given that the first letter of the word is capitalized, Conan Doyle must be referring to the Zoological Gardens in Regent's Park, north-west London, founded in 1826.

4. *What would it profit a woman*: 'For what shall it profit a man, if he shall gain the whole world, and lose his own soul.' – Mark 8: 36.

5. *Lady Eva Brackwell*: The name is perhaps reminiscent of Oscar Wilde's Lady Bracknell from *The Importance of Being Earnest* (1895). Also see Note 7 for 'The Abbey Grange'.

6. *Mr Pickwick's benevolence*: Mr Pickwick, hero of Charles Dickens's first novel, *The Pickwick Papers*, was renowned for his benevolence and all-round geniality.

7. *Church Row*: A small Georgian terrace leading from the main road through Hampstead village to the church of St John. H. G. Wells lived at number 17 from 1909 to 1912.

8. *Oxford Street*: Presumably Conan Doyle wanted to convey the idea that Holmes and Watson to deflect suspicion travelled a short distance south from Baker Street, i.e. in the opposite direction to Hampstead, rather than hailed a cab outside 221B.

9. *Holmes removed a circle of glass and turned the key from the inside*: At this point Holmes and Watson are burglars. In *The Sign of Four* Watson, seeing Holmes on the scent, remarked: 'I cannot but think what a terrible criminal he would have made.'

10. *portière*: A curtain hung in a doorway.

11. *Athene*: In Greek mythology the daughter of Zeus and the virgin goddess of wisdom.

12. *a middle-sized, strongly built man – square jaw, thick neck, moustache*: This is the only time in the canon that Watson describes his own appearance and it is a very fair description of Conan Doyle himself.

13. *Regent Circus*: There is no Regent Circus as such but from the description Conan Doyle is referring to Oxford Circus, the junction of Oxford Street and Regent Street.

THE SIX NAPOLEONS

First published in the *Strand* magazine, May 1904. A possible source for the plot was 'The Gift of the Emperor' (1899) by Conan Doyle's brother-in-law, E. W. Hornung, in which Raffles hides a pearl in a bullet. William S. Baring-Gould cites 1900 as a probable year for the setting of the story.

1. *Anything remarkable on hand?*: The banter between Lestrade and Holmes recalls the conversation between Monsieur G——, Prefect of the Parisian Police, Dupin, the detective, and the narrator in Edgar Allan Poe's 'The Purloined Letter'.

2. *Napoleon the First*: Napoleon Bonaparte (1769–1821), emperor of the French (1804–15) and conqueror of much of Europe in the early nineteenth century.

3. *Kennington Road*: Drab main road in south London leading from a junction just south of Waterloo station towards the Kennington Oval cricket ground.

4. *Lower Brixton Road*: There is no *Lower* Brixton Road but there is a Brixton Road, home of Mrs Oakshott and her geese in 'The Blue Carbuncle' from *The Adventures of Sherlock Holmes*, which connects Kennington with Brixton.

5. *monomania*: Preoccupation with one idea.

6. *ideé fixe*: French for obsession.

7. *Abernetty*: The name is taken from Abernethy, a doctor in Poe's 'The Purloined Letter'.

8. *by the depth which the parsley had sunk into the butter upon a hot day*: There is a pastiche of this idea in 'The Dreadful Business of the Abernetty Family' by Richard W. Clarke in the *Baker Street Journal* Vol. XI, No 1, Jan 1961.

9. *131 Pitt Street, Kensington*: Pitt Street is a small turning in Kensington just south of the Campden Hill estate and too small to run to a number 131. E. W. Hornung, author of the Raffles stories and Conan Doyle's brother-in-law, lived at number 9.

10. *No. 131 was one of a row, all flat-chested*: Numbers 10–18 Pitt Street correspond to this description.

11. *Central Press Syndicate*: Probably based on the Central News Ltd, 5 New Bridge Street, just off Fleet Street in the City of London. Conan Doyle offered to be a correspondent for the agency in 1898 when it looked as if Britain and France were about to go to war.

12. *Harding Brothers, two doors from the High Street Station*: Based on Ponting Brothers, 123 Kensington High Street, now Marks & Spencer's.

13. *Campden House Road*: This road, which ran from Holland Street to Sheffield Terrace, has since been renamed Hornton Street.

14. *I should like to keep this photograph*: Surely no Scotland Yard detective would allow an amateur to keep hold of so crucial a lead?

15. *Nihilist*: The Nihilists were nineteenth-century Russian revolutionaries whose aims were to destroy morality, God and justice. They murdered Tsar Alexander II in 1881.

16. *Anarchist*: One who believes in no organized government.

17. *Red republicans*: In the 1890s Italian Socialists began to take advantage of national banking scandals and corruption involving Italian politicians by organizing *fasci dei lavoratori*, worker's groups, intent on insurrection. In May 1898, following an increase in the price of bread, rioting broke out across Italy and martial law was briefly declared in Milan, Florence and Naples.

18. *Church Street, Stepney*: Church Street is a common street name in London but there are none in Stepney, east London.

19. *fashionable London . . . maritime London*: Morse Hudson's shop is in Kennington, some distance from the 'fringe of fashionable London', i.e. the West End and districts to the immediate west of Hyde Park. A journey from Kennington to Stepney would *not* pass through 'hotel London' (around Charing Cross), 'theatrical London' (the Strand), 'literary London' (then around St Paul's) or 'commercial London' (the City), although Stepney was then 'maritime London', being near the port and docks. Conan Doyle has evidently misplaced Morse Hudson's shop in his mind as being in Kensington rather than Kennington, in which case such a journey would be possible.

20. *Laburnum Vale*: Fictitious.

21. *Saffron Hill*: A shabby market street in Clerkenwell which in those days was the centre of London's Italian Quarter. Saffron Hill features in Charles Dickens's *Oliver Twist* (1839), Fagin having his den nearby.

22. *the Mafia, which, as you know, is a secret political society*: The mafia was then still relatively obscure, but then as now was more concerned with settling familial rather than political scores.

23. *loaded hunting crop*: It is filled with lead.

24. *black pearl of the Borgias*: The Borgias were an infamous fifteenth-century Italian family, best known for Rodrigo Borgia (1431–1503) who became Pope Alexander VI in 1492, and his daughter Lucrezia Borgia (1480–1523).

25. *Prince of Calonna*: Adapted from the name of a mediaeval Roman family, the Colonnas. Oddone Colonna (1368–1431) became Pope Martin V in 1417.

26. *Dacre Hotel*: Fictitious.

27. *Conk-Singleton forgery case*: The Mystery Writers of America acted out a playlet based on this fictitious case in 1948. It was published in the *Unicorn Mystery Book Club News* Vol. I No. 9.

THE ABBEY GRANGE

First published in the *Strand* magazine, September 1904. The plot may have been based on the murder of a Thomas Bonar and his wife who lived in Chislehurst, Kent, near the site of the fictional Abbey Grange, in 1810. Bonar died in a manner reminiscent of the story's Sir Eustace, his head crushed by a poker.

1. *Come, Watson, come! . . . The game is afoot*: 'The game's afoot', King Henry in Shakespeare's *Henry V*, III.i.32; 'The game is a-foot!', the Earl of Northumberland in Shakespeare's *Henry IV, Part 1* I.iii.276.

2. *Marsham*: Holmes scholar Michael Harrison claimed that Marsham is based on St Mary Cray, a small community two miles east of Chislehurst.

3. *Hopkins has called me in seven times*: Hopkins appears in 'Black Peter', 'The Golden Pince-Nez' and 'The Missing Three-Quarter', all in the full edition of *The Return of Sherlock Holmes*.

4. *I will, my dear Watson*: Holmes takes the narrative in 'The Adventure of the Blanched Soldier' and 'The Adventure of The Lion's Mane' from *The Case-Book of Sherlock Holmes*.

5. *focus the whole art of detection into one volume*: A reference to Hans Gross's *System der Kriminalistick* (1893).

6. *Palladio*: Andrea Palladio (1518–80), probably the best known Italian architect as far as the English are concerned, was a leading figure during the Renaissance, creating harmonious structures based on classical Roman forms. Inigo Jones (1573–1652) introduced Palladianism to Britain.

7. *Sir Eustace Brackenstall*: A name reminiscent of Oscar Wilde's Lady Bracknell in *The Importance of Being Earnest* (1895). Also see Note 5 for 'Charles Augustus Milverton'.

8. *beeswing*: Filmy crust that forms in some wines if they are kept too long in the bottle.

9. *de novo*: Latin – afresh.

10. *Marengo*: A battle during the Napoleonic Wars between the French and the Austrians which took place in the village of Marengo near Piedmont, Italy, on 14 June 1800. It began as an apparent defeat for the French, caused by Napoleon's errors of judgement. Then, when the Austrians became too casual, the French hit back and routed them, and as a result Austria ceded what is now Northern Italy to France.

11. *Adelaide–Southampton line, which stands at the end of Pall Mall*: The main Australian shipping line in those days was the Orient, which was based at 16 Cockspur Street near the eastern end of Pall Mall.

12. *Scotland Yard*: The headquarters of the Metropolitan Police, then based on Derby Gate just west of Westminster Bridge.

13. *a white man*: 'White' here means 'pure' or 'moral'.

14. *no one but a sailor could have made the knots*: In Edgar Allan Poe's 'The Murders in the Rue Morgue' (1841) Dupin realizes that the owner of the Ourang-Outang must be a sailor on account of the nature of a ribbon knot he finds at the scene of the crime. In the follow-up story, 'The Mystery of Marie Rogêt' (1843), Dupin realizes that the murderer is a sailor by the knots which tie the bonnet-ribbon.

15. *Vox populi, vox Dei*: 'The voice of the people is the voice of God', as first used by the English church reformer Albinus or Alcuin (735–804) in a letter to Charlemagne.

Selected Cases
from *His Last Bow*

THE ADVENTURE OF THE
BRUCE-PARTINGTON PLANS

First published in the *Strand* magazine, December 1908. A year before its publication the Irish Crown jewels were stolen and Conan Doyle was consulted by Sir Arthur Vicars, a distant relation who was in charge of the gems at Dublin Castle. Conan Doyle wouldn't have been able to present this episode fictionally so soon after the events (not that this has stopped some commentators suggesting that several characters in 'The Bruce-Partington Plans' are modelled on those involved in the Irish jewels story), but he evidently adapted its basic plot, the theft of something dear to the state, for the story. The story is set in 1895.

1. *news of a revolution*: Probably the Cuban War of Independence against the Spanish.

2. *of a possible war*: Britain, Russia and Austria had mobilized forces following the slaughter of Armenians in Turkey. The crisis petered out when France refused to get involved.

3. *impending change of government*: Owen Dudley Edwards noted that at the end of October 1895 the French government of Alexandre Ribot was defeated and the socialist Leon Bourgeois formed a cabinet.

4. *Diogenes Club*: Mycroft, Holmes's brother, was first introduced in 'The Greek Interpreter', from *The Memoirs of Sherlock Holmes*, as was the fictitious Diogenes Club (named after Diogenes of Sinope, 412–322 BC, a leading Cynic), which was based on the Athenaeum club on Pall Mall.

5. *Once, and only once, he has been here*: Yet in 'The Empty House', from *The Return of Sherlock Holmes*, we learned that during Holmes's absence 'Mycroft had preserved [Holmes's] rooms . . . exactly as they had always been'.

6. *the bi-metallic question*: The ratio between gold and silver in the coinage, which became an issue in North America in 1896 when the US Democratic presidential candidate, William Bryan, supported a 16:1 ratio of silver over gold in the currency, whereas his opponents proposed a lower proportion of gold. Bryan lost to William McKinley in 1896 and 1900, and to William Howard Taft in 1908, the year in which 'The Bruce-Partington Plans' was published.

7. *Who is Cadogan West, and what is he to Mycroft?*: Inspired by Hamlet's 'What's Hecuba to him or he to Hecuba?' in Shakespeare's *Hamlet* II.ii.560, as Professor Clarke Olney pointed out in the *Sherlock Holmes Journal* Winter 1955.

8. *Woolwich Arsenal*: Arms manufacturing centre in Woolwich, then a town on the outskirts of London, in Kent. It was founded in 1717, but is now being redeveloped. Arsenal Football Club was founded by Woolwich Arsenal workmen in 1886 but later moved to north London.

9. *Aldgate station*: A station on the Metropolitan and Circle lines, situated on the eastern edge of the City of London.

10. *some being purely Metropolitan, and some from Willesden and out-lying junctions*: Conan Doyle neglects to add that the Circle Line runs through Aldgate.

11. *Capital and Counties Bank*: Conan Doyle's bank and Holmes's, as revealed in 'The Priory School', from *The Return of Sherlock Holmes*.

12. *In the present state of Siam*: There was a dispute between Britain and France over Siam (now Thailand) in the 1890s. In 1896 the two powers guaranteed independence to part of the south-east Asian territory.

13. *Prime Minister*: The Conservative Lord Salisbury (Robert Arthur Talbot Gascoyne Cecil, 1830–1903) was prime minister in November 1895.

14. *the Bruce-Partington submarine*: Britain built no submarines of its own until 1903.

15. *the most jealously guarded of all Government secrets*: How could 'everyone' have 'heard of it', as Mycroft had exclaimed two sentences earlier, if it was 'the most jealously guarded of secrets'?

16. *naval warfare becomes impossible within the radius of a Bruce-Partington's operation*: It took another decade before a submarine was built that could endanger ships. In 1913 Conan Doyle wrote a short story, 'Danger!', which explained how a submarine blockade could prevent food reaching the British Isles. The story's concerns were dismissed by the Admiralty.

17. *smuggled through the Estimates*: The Estimates are the planned budgetary figures presented to Parliament by different Government departments and are based on work planned for the forthcoming year. It would not be uncommon for ministers and officials to falsify the figures in order to conceal the cost of strategic weaponry and hardware. In 1900 the First Lord of the Admiralty, George Goschen, misled Parliament by stating that the Admiralty was not particularly interested in using submarines as they were the weapons of the weaker nation. A year later it was revealed that five submarines designed by John Holland with torpedo parts manufactured at Woolwich Arsenal had been bought.

18. *Barclay Square*: There is no *Barclay* Square but there is a *Berkeley* Square in Mayfair which in the 18th and 19th centuries was one of the most exclusive residential areas in London.

19. *Well, it is surely perfect clear who took them away*: This sounds like the sort of glib claim Watson usually makes to Holmes.

20. *considerably past the station for London Bridge*: If Cadogan West wanted to get to London Bridge he would have taken a Circle Line train and alighted at Monument, two stations before Aldgate.

21. *under which he would pass London Bridge*: London Bridge and Aldgate stations were not then, and are not now, on the same line; this is shorthand for 'the station for London Bridge'.

22. *Aldgate is a junction, and there was a network of points*: The Circle Line consists almost entirely of other lines (the District Line, the Metropolitan Line and, since the 1980s, the Hammersmith & City Line) except in two places: just to the west of Gloucester Road station in west London and between Tower Hill and Aldgate in east London – hence the points where the Circle meets other lines.

23. *13, Great George Street, Westminster*: Then the address of the London Building Acts Tribunal Office, the building is now part of the Royal Institution of Chartered Surveyors. Great George Street leads west from Parliament Square towards Buckingham Palace.

24. *Campden Mansions*: Fictitious, but possibly based on Campden Hill Court, Campden Hill Road, in the Campden Hill estate between Notting Hill and Kensington.

25. *13, Caulfield Gardens*: Caulfield Gardens is fictitious, but see Note 27 below.

26. *curaçao*: A liqueur flavoured with the peel of bitter oranges, named after an island in the West Indies.

27. *lived in a row of houses which abutted upon the Underground*: There is a row of houses on Courtfield Gardens (phonetically similar to Caulfield Gardens) in the borough of Kensington which stands near the District Line. There is also a row of houses on Cornwall Gardens, a few hundred yards to the north of Courtfield Gardens across the Cromwell Road, where the Circle Line runs in what was then an open cutting visible, and almost accessible, from the back of some of the houses, but not number 13.

28. *owing to the intersection of one of the larger railways, the Underground trains are frequently held motionless for some minutes at that very spot*: The stretch of track that was overlooked by some of the Cornwall Gardens houses is one of only two sections of the Circle Line which belong solely to that line. A little further south the Circle Line is joined by the District Line, which is why Circle Line trains would be held motionless for some minutes, and still are today.

29. *area*: The name given to a recess under the steps which gives access to the cellar, where Holmes and Watson could conceal themselves.

30. *all the rest was inevitable*: If a body was placed on the roof of a train from a house on Cornwall Gardens (not as easy in reality as Conan Doyle makes it in this story) at the spot where the Circle Line meets the District Line then it could well fall off when the train hits the points just outside Aldgate station at the spot where the Circle Line joins the Metropolitan Line.

31. *For England, home and beauty*: A traditional Navy toast.

32. *Polyphonic Motets of Lassus*: A motet is a musical composition similar to an anthem. Orlandus Lassus, also known as Roland de Lattre (1530–94), was a Flemish composer mostly of masses and magnificats.

33. *the great church clock*: The church probably being based on St Jude, Courtfield Gardens.

34. *This was not the bird that I was looking for*: Holmes was presumably expecting to find Sidney Johnson, the senior clerk.

35. *Charing Cross Hotel*: It stands above Charing Cross station.

36. *fifteen years in a British prison*: Surely Oberstein would have been hanged even though his knowledge of European military secrets would have been useful to the British government?

37. *put up for auction in all the naval centres of Europe*: John Philip Holland (1840–1915), an Irish-American submarine designer, approached the US government in 1875 with plans for a submarine. Holland's ideas were rejected but after he had built the experimental *Fenian Ram* submarine in 1881 he auctioned his plans around various governments, this time being taken on by the United States.

38. *emerald tie-pin . . . gracious lady*: One would suppose that Queen Victoria would have honoured a detective who had brought off such a coup rather more handsomely.

THE ADVENTURE OF THE DYING DETECTIVE

First published in the *Strand* magazine, December 1913, and probably set in 1890, the second year of Watson's married life. The idea for Culverton Smith probably came from a recommendation by Joseph Bell, Conan Doyle's university tutor and part model for Sherlock Holmes, who in the early 1890s suggested to Conan Doyle the idea of a short story involving a 'bacteriological criminal'. Conan Doyle rejected the idea at the time as being too complicated but later incorporated the idea into this story.

1. *second year of my married life*: Watson married Mary Morstan at the end of *The Sign of Four*.

2. *Rotherhithe*: Seedy riverside district of south-east London.

3. *coolie*: Unskilled, badly paid Oriental workman. The word originates in the Tamil 'kuli' – 'hire'.

4. *Sumatra*: The second largest Indonesian island, then ruled by the Dutch, now part of Indonesia. For Holmesologists the island conjures up Holmes's reference in 'The Sussex Vampire' (from *The Case-Book of Sherlock Holmes*) to the giant rat of Sumatra, 'a story for which the world is not yet prepared', a parody of which has been written by Gilbert Adair.

5. *Tapanuli fever*: Tapanuli is a mountainous area on the north-west coast of Sumatra.

6. *the black Formosa corruption*: Named after the South China Sea island of Formosa, now Taiwan.

7. *Lower Burke Street*: Fictitious, but almost certainly a reference to William Burke (1792–1829), who with William Hare murdered at least fifteen people in Edinburgh and sold their bodies to doctors. Burke was hanged on the evidence of Hare.

8. *East End*: Rotherhithe is not in the East End.

9. *Coals of fire*: 'For thou shalt heap coals of fire upon his head' – Proverbs 25: 22.

10. *The spring! It drew blood*: Hugh L'Etang in 'Some Observations on the Black Formosa Corruption' (*Sherlock Holmes Journal*, Spring 1959) imagined a box loaded with a fake snake's fang which excreted poisonous venom when opened.

11. *a reversion*: In law the transfer of an estate to one person after the death of another.

12. *Simpson's*: Restaurant at 100 Strand, which opened in 1818 as Simpson's Tavern and Divan, a 'home of chess', in which players lounged on divans while playing. It began catering when a John Simpson took over in 1848, and by the early twentieth century was one of the smartest restaurants in the area. Holmes and Watson dine here twice in 'The Illustrious Client', from *The Case-Book of Sherlock Holmes*.

THE DISAPPEARANCE OF LADY FRANCES CARFAX

First published in the *Strand* magazine, December 1911. Alternative title: 'The Disappearance of Lady Carfax' (*American Magazine* of New York). William S. Baring-Gould claims it is set in 1902.

1. *Latimer's*: Owen Dudley Edwards suggests a subconscious association by Conan Doyle of this fictitious shop name with that of Hugh Latimer (1485–

1555), a Protestant leader burnt as a heretic, the 'boot', a Stuart form of torturing the feet later used against Protestant Dissidents, and the acceptably painful way of treating the body in a Turkish baths.

2. *Hôtel National at Lausanne*: It opened in 1886 and closed in 1951. Watson's description of it as having 'luxurious rooms overlooking the lake [Geneva]' is a fair one.

3. *Rue de Trajan, Montpelier*: A fictitious street in Montpellier (modern spelling), a university town in southern France, thirty miles south-west of Nîmes.

4. *un véritable sauvage*: 'a real savage'.

5. *Baden*: A spa resort in the Black Forest fashionable in the nineteenth century.

6. *Cook's local office*: The pioneering travel agent Thomas Cook had offices throughout Europe by the end of the nineteenth century.

7. *Englischer Hof*: Baden-Baden's Englischer Hof changed its name during the First World War.

8. *Midianites*: A Palestinian tribe that appears in Chapter 6 of the Book of Judges.

9. *ouvrier*: French – workman.

10. *cabaret*: bar.

11. *I have done better*: One is tempted to defend Watson at this point. Contrary to Holmes's claims he hasn't discovered 'nothing' – he has begun the trail in pursuit of Lady Frances and found out with whom she left Baden. Holmes, meanwhile, has appeared in Montpellier, needlessly disguised in French workman's clothes, at the point when he would be better engaged back in London.

12. *mob cap*: By the end of the nineteenth century, only a very old-fashioned woman would have worn a mob cap – it conjures up a picture of an elderly spinster.

13. *Barberton*: South African gold-mining town in Transvaal. Its inclusion, given the hirsute appearance of the Hon. Philip Green, appears to be a trifle Gilbert and Sullivan-ish.

14. *The Langham Hotel*: A luxurious hotel in Langham Place on the eastern edge of Marylebone which appears in 'A Scandal in Bohemia', from *The Adventures of Sherlock Holmes*, and in *The Sign of Four*, the novella that Conan Doyle wrote after receiving a commission from *Lippincott's* magazine at a lunch in the hotel in August 1889.

15. *possess our souls in patience*: 'In your patience possess ye your souls' – Luke 21: 19.

16. *Holmes's own small, but very efficient, organization*: His local force of street urchins also known as the Baker Street Irregulars.

17. *silver-and-brilliant*: A top quality diamond set in silver.

18. *Bevington's*: Fictitious.

19. *Sea of Azof fleet in the Crimean War*: The Sea of Azov is an almost entirely enclosed sea to the immediate north-east of the Crimean peninsula. Once the British had cleared it of Russian shipping the Crimean War (1853–6) began to go in their favour.

20. *Poultney Square*: Fictitious. Conan Doyle often uses Brixton as a location for wrongdoing, for instance the murder of Enoch J. Drebber in *A Study in Scarlet* and James Ryder's insertion of the Countess of Morcar's missing gem into a goose in 'The Blue Carbuncle', from *The Adventures of Sherlock Holmes*.

21. *Thrice is he armed, who hath his quarrel just*: King Henry in Shakespeare's *Henry VI, Part 2*, III.ii.233.

22. *with injected ether*: Did Conan Doyle really mean to say this? It's a very odd way of reviving someone who's unconscious!

HIS LAST BOW

First published in the *Strand* magazine, September 1917. The story germinated after an incident in June 1916 when Conan Doyle, on a visit to the French front, was asked by an army official: 'Sherlock Holmes, *est-ce qu'il est un soldat dans l'armée anglaise?*', to which he replied: *'Mais, mon géneral, il est trop vieux pour service.'* 'His Last Bow' is the last story in the canon in Holmesian time, being set in 1914, around ten years after the detective had retired to keep bees in Sussex. During the 1920s Conan Doyle penned several more Holmes stories (mostly gathered together in *The Casebook of Sherlock Holmes*), but these are set prior to Holmes's retirement.

1. *An Epilogue of Sherlock Holmes*: In the *Strand* the sub-title was 'The War Service of Sherlock Holmes'.

2. *the most terrible August in the history of the world*: The First World War broke out in August 1914, the culmination of events that ensued following the assassination of Archduke Franz Ferdinand, heir to the Austro-Hungarian throne, by Gavrilo Princip in the Bosnian capital Sarajevo on 28 June 1914. The Serbian terrorist society the Black Hand claimed responsibility, but Austria-Hungary blamed the Serbian state and, determined to punish Serbian nationalism, bombarded Belgrade, declaring war on Serbia on 28 July. Meanwhile Russia, traditional supporter of Serbia, mobilized against Austria-Hungary; Germany urged Russia to back down; and Britain asked Germany to pledge that it would respect Belgian neutrality if it wanted to attack France, with whom it was locked in dispute over Alsace-Lorraine.

On 1 August Germany declared war on Russia. The same day Britain told Germany that it could not ignore the threat to Belgian neutrality. On 2 August German troops invaded Luxembourg. That day the British prime minister, Herbert Henry Asquith, ordered the mobilization of British forces. On 3 August Belgium rejected Germany's request to march through that country to counteract a possible threat from the French, and so Germany declared war on France. On 4 August Germany invaded Belgium. Britain demanded that Germany withdraw; Germany refused; and so Britain declared war on Germany.

3. *the bay*: Mill Bay, south of the port of Harwich in Essex, fits the requirements outlined later in the story.

4. *great chalk cliff*: There are cliffs north of Walton-on-the-Naze, five miles south of Harwich, although they are not so 'great' as those on the south-east corner of England by Dover.

5. *Kaiser*: The kaiser was then Wilhelm II (1859–1941), grandson of Queen Victoria, who reigned 1888–1918, abdicating at the end of the First World War.

6. *Von Herling*: Should really be written von Herling ('of the sour grape'). The name is based on Richard von Kühlmann, who worked at the German Embassy up till the start of the war and whom the prime minister Asquith later identified in his memoirs as a spy.

7. *Benz*: German car manufacturers who merged with Mercedes in the mid-1920s.

8. *four-in-hand*: A four-horse carriage driven by one person.

9. *Olympia*: A large exhibition centre in West Kensington, London, built in 1886 as the National Agricultural Hall but known since as Olympia.

10. *Flushing*: A Dutch seaport also known as Vlissingen.

11. *Irish civil war*: There was German funding for the Easter Rising and at the same time supplies of weapons to Unionists.

12. *window-breaking Furies*: A dig by Conan Doyle at the suffragettes, whom he had publicly criticized just before the war.

13. *Mr John Bull*: A metaphor for the robust, roast-beef-eating Englishman. Nowadays one would write of the English 'bulldog'.

14. *Fords*: Conan Doyle must have meant 'fiords' – narrow inlets of the sea between high cliffs – knowledge of which would be helpful for submarines.

15. *Egypt*: Egypt had become a British protectorate in 1882 and threw its support behind the Allied Powers on outbreak of war. Its position by the Suez Canal made it a place of strategic importance in counteracting German influence in the Near East.

16. *Portsmouth Forts*: Conan Doyle had worked as a doctor in Portsmouth in the 1880s.

17. *Rosyth*: Scottish naval base on the Firth of Forth.

18. *Carlton House Terrace*: The original text in the *Strand* read 'Carlton House Terrace', hence our correction. The German Embassy in London was then based at 9 Carlton House Terrace to the west of Trafalgar Square. The book version uses 'Carlton Terrace' – the text contains a number of differences from the *Strand* which suggests that the original book publishers, John Murray of London, may have been using a pre-proof *Strand* magazine version of the text.

19. *Pan-Germanic Junker*: The Junkers were aristocratic Prussian landowners and the term came to be used derogatively to describe arrogant German army officers.

20. *through the little door on the Duke of York's steps*: The Duke of York's Steps, named after Frederick, Duke of York, second son of George III, lead from The Mall to Carlton House Terrace and are dominated by a statue to the Duke on top of a 124-foot column. The 'little door' remains but now leads to a covered car park.

21. *Tokay*: A sweet wine from Tokaj, Hungary. Thaddeus Sholto offers Mary Morstan a glass of Tokay in *The Sign of Four*.

22. *Zeppelin*: Airship invented in 1900 by Count Ferdinand von Zeppelin (1838–1917), used to bomb Britain in the First World War.

23. *Martha*: Some commentators have identified Martha as Mrs Hudson, landlady of 221B Baker Street, but there is no evidence that Conan Doyle meant this to be so.

24. *Uncle Sam*: Personification of the initials U.S. in USA, Uncle Sam is usually used as a metaphor for the United States and is popularly depicted as a tall figure with white hair and moustache dressed in a jacket with stars, striped trousers and a top hat decorated with stars and stripes. The name originated in 1812 when opponents of the Spanish–American War used it as a derogatory term for troops.

25. *Portland*: Prison on Portland Island, Dorset, famous for its stone quarries.

26. *Fratton*: District in Portsmouth.

27. *nitsky*: Yiddish for 'nothing'.

28. *Schoenbrunn Palace*: Viennese summer residence of the Austrian Emperor Franz Joseph I (1830–1916).

29. *Claridge's Hotel*: An exclusive hotel in Brook Street, Mayfair, opened by William Claridge in 1855 and bought by the owners of the Savoy Hotel in 1895.

30. *the Solent*: Wide estuary on the south coast on which Southampton stands.

31. *Alone I did it*: Coriolanus in Shakespeare's *Coriolanus* V.vi.115.

32. *The Foreign Minister*: The foreign secretary, who in 1914 was Edward Grey (1862–1933).

33. *the Premier*: Then the Liberal Herbert Henry Asquith (1852–1928), prime minister 1908–16.

34. *When I say that I started my pilgrimage at Chicago*: William Baring-Gould mused over Holmes's arriving not in New York but in Canada to avoid being spotted, making his way quietly into New York State, and biding his time in the town of Altamont, hence the pseudonym. Alternative theories are that Conan Doyle borrowed the name of Thackeray's villain in *Pendennis*, Walter Scott's villain in *The Pirate*, or the middle name of his father, Charles Altamont Doyle.

35. *graduated in an Irish secret society*: Reminiscent of McMurdo's efforts amongst the Scowrers in *The Valley of Fear*, although Conan Doyle is including Chicago and Buffalo for their role in the history of the secret society Clan-na-Gael, an Irish-American society founded in 1867 to work for Irish independence, and which sought German help during the First World War. Since the formation of the Irish Free State in the 1920s it has been purely a social club.

36. *Skibbereen*: A town in County Cork, Ireland.

37. *who recommended me as a likely man*: Several of the Clan-na-Gael tried to forge links with the Germans in the United States until the latter declared war on Germany.

38. *separation*: This refers to the story of how the King of Bohemia had become entangled with an opera singer, Irene Adler, in 'A Scandal in Bohemia', from *The Adventures of Sherlock Holmes*, but there was no account of Holmes bringing about the separation.

39. *Count Von und Zu Grafstein*: A piece of cod Germanic nonsense translatable as 'Count from and to Countstone'.

40. *your old service*: At the start of the Holmes canon, Watson is a retired Army doctor, having been shot in Afghanistan.